Praise for
Very Sincerely Yours

"*Very Sincerely Yours* is such a special, unique love story that made me laugh and warmed my heart. Kerry Winfrey creates the best casts of family and friends in her books, and the hero of this one, Everett St. James, is truly one of a kind—I've never seen anyone like him in romance. And the emails! *So* romantic. A delightful *You've Got Mail*-esque touch."
—Sarah Hogle, author of *Twice Shy*

"Kerry Winfrey charms again in the delightful romantic comedy *Very Sincerely Yours*. With a slow-burn romance full of pitch-perfect prose and brainy banter, it is impossible not to be swept up in the story of Theodora and Everett as they navigate love and life, desperately seeking the way to their happily ever after." —Jenn McKinlay, author of *Wait For It*

"A sweet and fluffy rom-com. . . . Winfrey lets their love blossom at a believable pace as they overcome emotional and professional obstacles with the help of their convincing sets of friends. With plenty of smile-worthy misadventures along the way, this light, down-to-earth romance is sure to charm." —*Publishers Weekly*

"Fans will be happy to settle into this cozy rom-com and its comfortably unfolding story." —*Kirkus Reviews*

"Readers will find themselves rooting for the pair of quirky lovers through their funny email exchanges to awkward in-person encounters and hoping that their quests to find themselves lead them down a path together." —*USA Today*

"A sweet and lighthearted rom-com that will appeal to readers who prefer stories that focus more on character than conflict. . . . *Very Sincerely Yours* is a reminder of how important it is for you to focus on you—on the things that make you happy, that make you feel good, and on all your goals and hopes and dreams." —*BookPage*

"A sweet romance. . . . This will hit a very sweet spot and encourage those who feel like they are stuck in a rut to bite the bullet and embrace whatever scares them witless, as there is simply more to life than living to work and living to please others." —Harlequin Junkie

"A charming story as much about finding yourself as finding love. Mr. Rogers but for adults." —Under the Covers Book Blog

"*Very Sincerely Yours* is one of the most delightful romantic comedies I've read so far this year. It's a gem of a book that is sure to put a smile on your face." —The Bookish Libra

JOVE TITLES
BY KERRY WINFREY

Waiting for Tom Hanks

Not Like the Movies

Very Sincerely Yours

Just Another Love Song

JUST ANOTHER LOVE SONG

KERRY WINFREY

JOVE
New York

A JOVE BOOK
Published by Berkley
An imprint of Penguin Random House LLC
penguinrandomhouse.com

Library of Congress Cataloging-in-Publication Data

Names: Winfrey, Kerry, author.
Title: Just another love song / Kerry Winfrey.
Description: First Edition. | New York: Jove, 2022.
Identifiers: LCCN 2022011006 (print) | LCCN 2022011007 (ebook) |
ISBN 9780593333433 (trade paperback) | ISBN 9780593333440 (ebook)
Subjects: LCGFT: Novels.
Classification: LCC PS3623.I6444 J87 2022 (print) |
LCC PS3623.I6444 (ebook) | DDC 813/.6—dc23
LC record available at https://lccn.loc.gov/2022011006
LC ebook record available at https://lccn.loc.gov/2022011007

First Edition: August 2022

Printed in the United States of America
1st Printing

BOOK DESIGN BY KATY RIEGEL

For Catherine Stoner,

the Honey

to my Sandy

JUST
ANOTHER
LOVE SONG

CHAPTER ONE

I'VE IMAGINED RUNNING into Hank Tillman roughly one million times since I last saw him years ago. Maybe he'd see me walking my Great Dane, Toby, down Main Street, my hair blowing in the wind in a casual yet gorgeous way, and he'd be rendered speechless by my beauty. Maybe he'd see me at work and be impressed that Sandy Macintosh had grown into a competent, successful, but (most important) extremely sexy business owner. Or maybe he'd see me attempting to play basketball with my best friend Honey's three kids, and he'd be mesmerized by my athletic prowess and ease with children. (Forget the fact that I can't make a basket to save my own damn life and that Honey's six-year-old, Rosie, makes fun of me every time we play because she's a bad sport.)

But never, in any of my wild imaginings, did I picture our reunion happening in the soda aisle of Tillman's Grocery with me covered in dirt, my hair twisted into a messy, lopsided bun, and the Santana / Rob Thomas song "Smooth" playing softly through the grocery store speakers.

"Hey, Sandy," he says casually, as if we see each other every day. In reality, the last time I saw his face in person was a lifetime ago, right after a kiss I wish I could forget.

And what a face it was . . . and *is*. I allow my eyes a moment to roam over him, to take in the lines that weren't there fifteen years ago, the crease of his forehead and the crinkles by his eyes. The way his nose is the slightest bit crooked because he broke it at football practice freshman year. Those eyelashes that made me jealous because they were longer than any boy's really had to be, and mine were always so short and stubby. I have the desire to reach my hand out and touch his face, to run my fingers over the topography there and see what's changed.

His eyes dart over my face like he's doing the same thing, and I look away quickly. I'm covered in dirt because, well, I've been in the dirt all day installing a new garden for a client. I only ran to the store because my employee, Marcia, has a monstrous Diet Coke addiction and gets twitchy if I don't keep the mini fridge at the greenhouse stocked.

I try not to wonder what he thinks of how I've changed. I don't exactly make myself easy to find—I use social media like anyone else, but mostly to keep up with everyone who moved out of Baileyville or to like the constant stream of kid photos that Honey posts. I keep my personal updates minimal and focus on pictures of gardens and flowers. Scrolling through my feeds won't turn up a single selfie.

But I've had plenty of opportunities to see Hank, of course. Album covers. A recording of *Austin City Limits* on PBS. A magazine article here and there. Because Hank Tillman became what he always said he'd be: a musician.

I try not to look at that stuff because I try not to live in the past, try not to think about all the things I said I'd be back then, back when we were seventeen and stupid and so, so in love.

"Hey, Hank," I almost whisper, willing myself to look anywhere but at him. I glance at the root beer and the orange soda, but I look back at him as he sticks his hands in his pockets. My eyes dart to his arms sticking out below the rolled-up sleeves of his faded red flannel shirt. They're tanned and rough, like he's spent the entire summer, his entire life, outside.

I hate this, hate that he's somehow become even more handsome, and that I know all these details about him down in my bones, like they're a part of me, like I'll never be rid of him no matter how hard I try. *He moved on*, I remind myself. *He left town and he left you and you did just fine for yourself, didn't you? You own a business. You have a house. You have employees and a dog and a front porch and a very expensive espresso machine.*

I know I should be an adult here, make polite conversation, ask him why he's back in town . . . but every cell of my body is screaming, *Get out of this store now!* I attempt to walk past him, but my bare arm brushes against his bare forearm, and I gasp. It's been so long since the last time I touched him, and it's pathetic the way that simply grazing his skin brings me right back to being seventeen, the radio playing in his truck, the windows open and the breeze warm as we drove the winding back roads of Baileyville.

The case of Diet Coke slips out of my hand and crashes onto my toes. "Shit," I hiss as I bend down to pick it up.

"Are you okay?" Hank asks, reaching out to help, but I just nod quickly.

"I'm fine!" I say, pretending that it doesn't feel like one of my toes is on fire. "I gotta go!"

I turn around, attempting to make my way to the cash register as quickly as I can. From now on, I will not enable Marcia's addiction; trying to be a good boss only leads to injury and makes me run into my first love.

"Sandy . . ." he says, and I turn around.

Our eyes meet and I see it all for a moment, a flash of everything we went through when we were just kids. Passing notes in class. Promising everything. Kissing in his parents' barn. Never dreaming that things would end up this way.

"It's good to see you," he finishes.

I nod, not trusting myself to speak. Because what could I say? *Well, it's not good to see you, Hank, because I like to pretend you don't exist.*

Instead, I hobble to the register.

MARCIA CLAPS WHEN I walk in the door holding the box of Diet Coke aloft. "Thank you so much, and oh my God, are you *limping*?"

"I think I broke my toe when I dropped this case of poison liquid on my foot," I say, handing it to her. "I'll take over the register if you can go put this in the fridge."

"My hero," she says, hugging the box.

"You need help," I tell her.

"And you need medical attention," she says before heading to the break room.

I roll my eyes, then lean over the counter and take a look around me. The interior of my greenhouse, Country Colors, isn't huge—this room, with the register, is fully enclosed and full of garden tools, indoor plants, and lawn decorations. The front of the store is lined in garage-style doors that we pull open on summer days like today, letting the breeze blow through.

But the double doors open into the greenhouse proper, where we keep the plants. Not that we have any customers right now, because it's late July, and as the saying goes, the corn should've already been knee-high back on the Fourth. There's still plenty of gardening to be done, of course, but people have their eyes on harvest, not putting new plants in the ground, so we're in a bit of a slow period until things pick up for the pumpkins and mums in September.

This is mine, I remind myself. Country Colors was tiny when I started working here in college. I felt like I'd been left behind by the friends who'd gone away to school while I stayed in place, attending Baileyville Community College. I'd dreamed of being an artist, but BCC didn't even have art classes. I majored in marketing, which my mom insisted was very creative and basically the same thing as painting. She's always known how to put a positive spin on things, my mom.

When I hit my situational-depression-induced rock bottom, it was Honey who encouraged me to start working at the greenhouse. Being outside and helping things grow would be good for me, she said. As usual, she was right, and the job grew (pun intended) into something so much more. Unlike marketing, gardening actually *was* creative. Planting things and watching them grow was rewarding in a way that little else in my life was, and more than that, it was surprising. Flowers, as it turned out, had minds of their own.

Soon, I was spending all my free time at the greenhouse, and when my boss retired, she asked me if I wanted to take over. And so Country Colors became mine—my sanctuary, my second home, my new dream. Did I still miss art, the feeling of paint under my fingernails? Sure, but now I had dirt under my fingernails. Maybe the dream hadn't changed so much as the medium did.

And in the off-season, I spend my time designing gardens for the people of Baileyville who don't know where to start. When I'm sketching out garden beds and planning where to put trellises, I feel like I've truly ended up where I'm meant to be.

I'm happy with the way things turned out. Really, I am. If only Hank Tillman hadn't showed up to remind me of how different things could've been.

A bloodcurdling scream jolts me out of my contemplation, and I run into the break room, sure Marcia's been hacked to bits by a serial killer who targets greenhouses (which might seem unlikely, but I've watched a *lot* of true crime documentaries, and at this point, I assume the worst).

"What happened?" I ask as I burst into the room.

Marcia is standing stock-still, Diet Coke dripping off her face. She looks at me, her eyes wide in shock.

"Oh," I say. "I should've warned you not to open it yet. I guess it got kind of shaken up when I dropped it."

She slowly smiles. "This is disgusting."

"You look very sticky," I agree. "Why don't you go home and get cleaned up? I think I can handle it here until close."

"Fantastic," she says. "That shaken up can of Diet Coke was a blessing, not a curse, because tonight's my and Aimee's anniversary."

I swat her on the arm, which was a bad idea because that's also covered in soda. "You should've told me! I would've let you leave early anyway."

She shrugs, and I smile as I think about her wedding to Aimee three years ago. It happened in her backyard under an arbor covered in pink climbing roses, with the reverend from the Baileyville Unitarian Universalist Church marrying them. We all blew bubbles at the end as they got on a tandem bike and rode to their reception in the park.

As I watch Marcia now, humming to herself as she attempts to dry off her shirt with paper towels, a pang of longing hits me. It's not that I want what she has, exactly . . . it's that I want to even know what it's like to have someone waiting at home, someone I can't wait to see. I'm happy with my life—my job, my friends, my home—but it would be nice, wouldn't it, to have another person to share it all with?

It doesn't help my expectations that my family has a history of lifelong, love-filled relationships. My grandparents got married when they were teenagers and stayed married until they died, just days apart. And while my parents waited a little longer before they got married, they've been in love and working together ever since.

Dating isn't exactly easy in a small town, though. Apps have a very different vibe when everyone on them is someone you went to kindergarten with (or, in one case, is your recently divorced kindergarten teacher who wants to "get back out there").

"Okay, I'm headed home," Marcia says, tossing the soda-soaked paper towel in the trash.

"Happy anniversary," I call after her, and she shoots me a quick smile as she hurries out to her car.

I head back up to the register and look out over the shop once more. And although I don't want to, I find myself wondering again what Hank Tillman is doing back in Baileyville.

Chapter Two

"SO WHAT DO you think?" I ask, peering over Honey's shoulder as I sit on the examining table at her veterinary clinic.

"In my professional opinion, your toe isn't broken," she says, standing up. "And you're surprisingly big for a tabby cat."

"Please don't mock me in my time of need," I say. "I didn't want to drive all the way to urgent care to be, like, 'Someone please help me! My toe hurts!'"

She laughs, her curls bouncing. "You know what I always say. People and animals aren't that different on the inside." She pauses for a minute. "Except for cows' stomachs."

It's not that I'm using my veterinarian BFF as my primary care physician, but sometimes in the case of an emergency or a late-night medical question, I *do* take advantage of her expertise. Once, she even gave me stitches when I got overzealous attempting to open a box of new seeds with a knife and sliced my hand open.

"You didn't even tell me," she says, washing her hands. "How did you hurt your toe? Stub it on something?"

I bite my lip. As my designated best friend, Honey Michaels had a front-row seat to the entire Hank Tillman situation. My initial crush. The beginning of our relationship. My intense, earth-shattering feelings. And the way those feelings sort of . . . *took over* when he left.

And that was all years ago—fifteen years ago, to be exact. It sounds like a song Hank might write. (Don't judge me for listening to his music . . . I try my best to avoid it, but when your ex-boyfriend is a celebrated musician who, you suspect, has written at least a few heartbreaking ballads about the demise of your teenage love affair, it's hard not to check out a song or two.) Something with a title like "Fifteen Years Without You."

Part of me doesn't want to put her through it again and make her deal with the Hank obsession I long ago boxed up and shoved into the dustiest corners of my mind. But the other part . . . well, that's what best friends are for, right? For listening to the embarrassing tale of the time you ran into your ex-boyfriend when you were covered in dirt, and then you dropped soda on your foot?

"Hank's back," I say. "And I ran into him at the store."

"Ran into him as in . . . spoke to him?" she asks delicately, drying her hands and giving me a cautious look.

Because of course Hank has been back to Baileyville since we broke up; his family still lives here. His family who, surprisingly, still loves me, and his dad who is still my dad's best friend. I see them all the time, and they're kind enough to avoid mentioning Hank.

So yes, Hank's been back here on occasion, but I pretend he hasn't. No one tells me if they see him around, and I pretend that this is all normal and that the heartbreak of my youth doesn't haunt me on the streets of my town and also occasionally on the extremely limited radio airwaves we get down here in the Baileyville valley.

Not that Hank gets all that much airtime on traditional country stations, but occasionally, I hear a snippet of one of his songs on an NPR station that manages to throw its signal all the way here from Columbus. And yes, I know that the answer is to get Sirius or listen to Spotify, but I'm an elderly woman at heart. I love my radio.

"I spoke to him," I confirm. "And through a series of very Sandy events, I ended up dropping a case of soda on my foot. Hence," I say, gesturing toward my toe.

"How is he?" Honey puts a hand on her hip.

I sigh. "Completely gorgeous."

She shakes her head. "It's unfair. The boy was always too good-looking."

"Feels like a personal affront," I agree. "Like the universe is attacking me. But I'm extremely eager to go back to talking about anything that isn't Hank Tillman, so what's going on with you? Why are you at work so late?"

"Emergency surgery on a pit bull that ate an entire box of condoms," she says. "So I was still here when you called."

"Whoa, back up. Was the pit bull okay?"

She nods, unconcerned. "Oh yeah. Technically, he vomited most of them up. But keep your condoms out of Toby's reach, okay?"

"Strangely enough, he's never shown much interest in them. Anyway, you probably need to get home to relieve Brian," I say, referring to her husband. When they had their first child, Brian quit his job to become a stay-at-home dad, which was kind of a given for them since Honey had way more of an investment in her career, both timewise and moneywise, than he did in his. And now that they have three kids, he's still taking care of them and loving it. There aren't a lot of dads in the pickup line at Baileyville Elementary, but subverting Baileyville's gender norms is no big deal for Honey. As one of the only biracial kids in our class (Honey's dad is Black and her mom is white), she got plenty used to doing things her own way early on in our childhood.

She nods. "Every night, I mix us both up tropical cocktails so we can put our feet up and watch TV made for grown-ups. He says he looks forward to it the entire time he's driving to soccer practice and pretending to be the chicken from *Moana*."

"Sorry I kept you here so late."

She sighs dramatically. "You know the busy life of a veterinarian. Constantly taking care of animals and also the occasional best friend who wanders in. Come on, I'll lock up. Think you can drive home with your bum toe?"

I slide off the table and hobble out of the exam room. "Somehow, I'll manage. You know, it feels a little bit better already. I think you're a miracle worker."

She gives me side-eye as we walk through the reception area. "I think you might be a little bit of a drama queen."

I gasp, letting my hand fly to my heart. *"Moi?"*

She smacks me on the arm with her purse as she holds open the front door. "Go home. I've got places to be and piña coladas to make."

I STEP INTO my foyer and immediately hear the *thumpthump thump* of Toby's feet as he runs across the hardwood floor to greet me. I crouch down to receive his kisses, although I don't need to—he could easily place his paws on my shoulders and lick my face. Not that I would want to encourage that behavior . . . I've learned the hard way that some people in this world actually don't want a 120-pound Great Dane to slobber on them and possibly knock them over. It takes all kinds, I suppose.

I toss my keys into the bowl I picked up at the Baileyville Antique Mart. It's a Billy Joel record that someone melted and repurposed into a bowl that's the perfect size for whatever I remove from my pockets or purse at the end of the day. I call it the Joel Bowl, which so far hasn't made a single person other than me and Honey laugh, but I remain optimistic. Baileyville has a lot of things going for it, but what it doesn't have is enough people who appreciate my puns.

Toby trots along beside me as I kick off my boots, light an Island Vibes candle (because what says "island vibes" more than landlocked Ohio?), and pull my hair out of its now ratty bun. Several clumps of dirt fall onto the floor.

"Gonna need the broom, Tobes," I say. That's a side effect of living by yourself: you spend a lot of time narrating your actions to your pet.

My place is calm. Quiet. Colorful. Exactly the way I like it. Every time I step through the door, I feel a sense of pride wash over me, the same as the day I bought it. Sometimes it still seems unreal—I bought a house by myself. I bought this house and, with the help of my family and friends, painted the rooms all different colors, switched out the drapes from the musty old lace ones the sellers had left behind to a bright floral, repainted the cabinets a dusty blue and swapped out the countertops with butcher block, and replaced the scuffed laminate flooring with a funky geometric tile. Every inch of this house is exactly what I and I alone wanted.

It's enough to make me want to blast the Destiny's Child song "Independent Women," the one that Honey and I used to listen to in my bedroom when we were painting our nails in high school and daydreaming about where we'd be when we grew up. Honey wanted to be a veterinarian, marry Brian Lerner, and have three kids, and even if it took her a while to make it through vet school, that's exactly what she did.

I wanted to be an artist and marry Hank Tillman and travel the world and . . . well, the thing is, some people always know what they want out of life. Like Honey. Every year when she blew out her birthday candles, she wished that she'd save cheetahs from extinction . . . and then when she was in college, she scored an internship where she actually got to work with cheetahs. It was like she manifested the future using some sort of child version of *The Secret*, or more likely, she was freakishly determined.

But it's not like that for all of us. Some of us grow up and realize that our childhood dreams are just that—dreams. And like that dream where I'm performing on *The Voice* in my nightgown, not all dreams should come true. Sometimes you end up making your own life out of what you're given. Sometimes you can build something yourself that won't ever fall apart or leave you. Sometimes you can make your own foundation instead of waiting around for someone else to do it with you. And maybe that's better.

Or maybe not better. *Just different*, I think as I scrub my hands in the kitchen sink, getting all the dirt out from under my fingernails. There's nothing wrong with different, not if you actually can't move away, and your childhood sweetheart gets married and has a kid while you're still back at home.

I stop scrubbing and stare out the window, because there it is. There's the origin of the feeling that's been swirling and coalescing in me ever since I saw Hank at the store. I hadn't felt it in a long time, because I'm happy here. *So* happy. I look out my beautiful kitchen window into my own backyard, the one filled with sunflowers and dahlias and marigolds in the flower bed, green beans and tomatoes and zucchini growing wildly out of control in the vegetable garden. I have my best friend, my business, my house, my parents, and a whole town full of people I more or less love. I have my morning coffee from my trusty espresso machine, pancake breakfasts with Honey at Betty's Diner, long walks on the bike trail, watch Honey's kids perform in holiday concerts at the elementary school, deliver library books to old Mr. Anderson down the street. I have everything—more than I need—and it feels ungrateful to complain.

But Hank reminds me of what I've tried to forget. Both of us said we were getting out of here. Both of us said we'd be different, we'd use our God-given and time-nurtured talents to forge our own paths, ones that would take us far from the lives our parents had planned for us. Ones that didn't involve staying in Baileyville.

And he did it. He started a whole life, a whole family, while I've been letting my roots grow deeper and deeper here in town, so deep that they're now all tangled and gnarled far below the surface. And I know, better than anyone, how hard it is to remove a plant once it's taken root.

I inhale deeply and shake my head. There's no use in regret; I know it won't get me anywhere. But I still can't help but wish that I had someone to share the beauty of this house with, someone to help pull the weeds out of the garden, someone to be here.

CHAPTER THREE

Sixteen years ago

T HE TRUTH IS, I'd been in love with Hank Tillman forever by the time we kissed. In elementary school, when Lewis Coyne peed his pants during silent reading time, everyone else stared or laughed while the teacher ran to the office to get a pair of sweatpants reserved for this purpose. But Hank stood up, took off his own pants, and handed them to Lewis. He stood there in his underwear, right in the middle of the room, and good-naturedly took in our laughter so that everyone, even Lewis, forgot what had just happened. He was always that kind of kid—the one who would literally go without clothing if it meant he could help somebody else.

I came home that day and told my mom I was going to marry Hank Tillman because he could never be mean to anyone. I also thought I was going to grow up to a be a combination ballerina /doctor/astronaut, so not everything I said then made sense, but still. I knew he was special.

And as we got older, that specialness never faded—if anything, it intensified. Hank Tillman *sparkled*. The usual rules didn't apply to him; he was friendly with everyone, involved in everything, and beloved by all the teachers. One time, I saw him running the bake sale table for the choir, and *he wasn't even in the choir*. Opportunities to give your pants to someone who peed in theirs dwindle as you get older, but it was clear that he still would've done it if necessary.

Our high school was small—only sixty-five kids in the graduating class—but even with so few of us, everyone pretty much stuck to their own group. Except for Hank. He stood outside of groups, not popular or unpopular, doing what he wanted. He was the only freshman boy to make the varsity football team, but he also spent his free time working in his dad's store. He hung out with the football kids and the band kids and the stoners, and on one occasion, I even saw him coming out of the teachers' lounge with Mr. Laurence, the tenth-grade history teacher, animatedly talking about something.

And as for me . . . I watched him. Not in a "stalker hiding outside in his bushes" way, but in the way you might follow your favorite actor. I was always aware of him, like my eyes were pulled toward him no matter where we were, even if he didn't know I was there.

He was perfectly nice to me, of course, the same way he was perfectly nice to everyone else. But outside of the occasional group project, we didn't hang out.

Until junior year English.

My favorite thing about English, besides my teacher Mrs. Sales, was getting completely lost in books. It didn't matter what we read, whether it was *Moby-Dick* or *Go Tell It on the Mountain*— I wanted to be somewhere, anywhere other than Baileyville, and I could do that in books. I wanted to meet people I hadn't known since birth, explore the world, expand my mind. I loved so much about Baileyville, about the quiet of the cornfields and the gentle bubbling of the river, but sometimes those same things felt less quiet and more suffocating. Like I could never grow here, like my body and spirit would simply never fit.

My mom had sworn I'd grow into my body, but that hadn't happened—I was still a jumble of too-long limbs, my awkward arms and bony knees forever bruised from clumsily bumping into desks and drawers and chairs. But books, I found, made me feel the same way I did when I was painting. Like my physical body didn't exist, didn't matter. I was merely a floating mind in a jar, nothing but thoughts and needs and imaginings.

And so I basically lived for art and English classes and gritted my teeth to get through the rest of the school day (math and biology, which I did quite well in even though I would rather have been doing anything else, and gym, the bane of my awkward existence), waiting for the time when I could daydream and slip away from my everyday life.

One day after class, Mrs. Sales pulled me aside and told me that Hank was failing several classes. "He has about a month to get his grades up," she said. "If he can't . . . I don't think he'll be moving on to senior year. And since you have some of the best grades in the class, I wondered if maybe you could tutor him."

I've always been vulnerable to flattery, but I'd never tutored anyone before. In fact, I wasn't even sure if I *could* teach anyone else.

"I know it's a lot to ask," Mrs. Sales said, noticing my hesitation.

I thought about Hank helping poor little Lewis that day when he peed. And then I thought about Hank's lopsided smile, the way one side of his mouth tugged up a little higher than the other, as if he were reluctantly laughing.

The afternoon sunlight shone through the streaked windows of Mrs. Sales's classroom. I nodded at her through the dust motes that floated through the air. "Okay," I said.

Hank and I met up every day after school—it was spring, so he didn't have practice, and Hank's dad cared enough about his grades to let him study before he went into work at the store. Sometimes we met up at Betty's (Hank was always hungry and could reliably eat two meat loaf sandwiches before I'd finished one patty melt), sometimes the dining room of my parent's B&B, and sometimes, when the weather was nice, my front porch. Those were my favorite days, the two of us sitting there on the wicker furniture, waving to old Mr. Anderson as he shuffled down the street on his afternoon walk.

Hank tried to make jokes about his poor grades, but he was struggling. The concepts that came so easily to me got tangled up somewhere in his brain, and I was determined to help him. Together, we solved equations, and I made him flash cards with biology terms. But the subject he had the hardest time with was English.

One day after school, Hank and I both sat on the wicker couch on the porch reviewing concepts for our upcoming biology test. I was cross-legged, facing him, and he was spilling off the couch, his body liquid in the way teenage boys often are.

He held up one of the rose-patterned pillows. "This is nice," he said.

"Focus," I said, throwing another pillow at him. My mom had only recently opened the Ohio Inn, her bed-and-breakfast, but her floral and wicker porch furniture was proof that B&Bs had always been in her blood.

He sighed good-naturedly. "Right, right, right."

I held up a flash card. "Nucleus."

He stared at the card for a minute, then reached out and grabbed my hand. I stopped breathing.

"What's this?" he murmured.

The moment of my death? I thought but did not say.

"My . . . my hand?"

He shook his head, studying my hand as intently as a palm reader. The flash card had long since dropped to the ground, and I couldn't have cared less. I had bigger concerns at the moment.

"No. This." He pointed to the ever-present paint on my hands. It never washed off fully, so I'd become used to having a kaleidoscope of colors on my skin at all times.

"Oh, I was working on something earlier," I said. That morning, I'd woken up early before school so I'd have time to focus on my latest painting, an abstract depiction of the spring flowers popping up in our yard.

"For class?" he asked.

I shook my head. "No, um . . . for me, I guess? I want to be an artist."

Hank looked up and blinded me with that lopsided smile. "You don't want to be an artist."

"What?" I asked in a whisper.

"You *are* an artist," he corrected. "If you're painting, you're an artist."

I rolled my eyes. "Yeah, well, you haven't seen my work, so that's easy for you to say."

"I've seen it," he said casually, dropping my hand. "You did that big mural down by the FFA room, right?"

I swallowed, thinking of all the hours I'd spent painting animals in the hallway by the Future Farmers of America classroom. "Yeah. That was me."

"I couldn't paint cows that lifelike." He raised his eyebrows, looking at me as if he'd won an argument. "Kinda seems like something an artist would do."

"Point taken," I said with a laugh. "I am Baileyville's preeminent cow artist. Everyone should bow to my greatness."

And then Hank surprised me by peeling his long body off the couch and getting down on one knee. "I bow to you, Sandy Macintosh, painter of cows and keeper of flash cards."

He picked up the flash card that had fallen underneath the couch. "Not such a great keeper of the flash cards, but that's beside the point."

I grabbed it out of his hand. "We're getting kinda off track," I said, not caring even a little bit. I wanted to find a way for this moment to stretch and comprise the entire rest of my high school career.

He stood up and sat down beside me again, but this time closer. "You want things, don't you?" he asked.

I froze. Was he reading my mind? Because there was one want pulsing through my brain right now, and it was him. "What?" I asked.

"You want things," he repeated, then gestured around us. "You want something different than this."

"Than the shabby chic stylings of my mom's porch?" I joked, holding up the floral pillow.

Hank shook his head, not falling for my attempt to use humor to change the subject. "You don't want to do the same thing everyone else is doing. You want something that's all your own. Don't you?"

I stared back into his eyes. I didn't like to say anything bad about Baileyville out loud . . . it was, after all, my home. The place where I could walk down the street and be confident I'd know every single person I passed. The place where, when I was a kid and my mom broke her ankle (roller-skating, because of *course* my mother had to roller-skate around town like she was the quirky heroine in the movie of her life) and had to be on crutches, everyone organized a meal train and brought us dinner each night for weeks. The place where people shoveled each other's driveways in the winter and raked one another's leaves in the fall. The place where I understood the landscape as instinctively as I understood the beating of my own heart: the river, the rolling hills, the acres and acres of flat fields. *Thump thump thump.*

It was mine and I wasn't eager to disown it. But something about Hank's eyes let me know he understood. Maybe he felt that same itch, that same sense of unease sometimes. His eyes showed me everything I loved about Baileyville and everything I dreamed about in the outside world, all in one person. Those blue-gray irises sparkled with the gently swaying flowers of my present and the skyscrapers of my dreams.

"I want to go to art school," I said quietly, as if I was afraid someone might overhear. "And I want to travel. And I want to see what it's like to be somewhere other than Baileyville."

Hank's smile broke across his face. "Me too," he said.

I frowned. "You? But . . . you *are* Baileyville. You love it here."

He looked toward the street, which was completely quiet, as it so often was. "I do *not* love it here. In fact, I want to leave here."

"But everyone loves you," I said, shaking my head.

"Everyone?" he asked as he turned to look at me again.

I could feel myself starting to blush. "What about your parents, and your sister, and the store? And football?" I stammered.

He raised an eyebrow. "Did you know that high school football doesn't actually last past high school?"

"Don't make me throw another pillow at you. I know that. But there's college, right? A scholarship?"

Sports scholarships were the holy grail in Baileyville, where there was no higher honor than winning any kind of championship. In our cafeteria, there was an entire Athletic Wall of Fame with the pictures of every Baileyville student, back to the dawn of photography, who'd won a championship. There was no Academic Wall of Fame.

"I'm gonna let you in on a little secret, Sandy," he said, and a tingle went through my entire body when he said my name. "You ever hear the term 'big fish in a small pond'? That's me on the football team. I'm not all that great."

"But you *are* great!" I protested.

"You ever been to a game?" he asked, crossing his arms and leaning back. The wicker chair creaked under his weight.

"Sometimes I go to watch Honey in the halftime show!" I said proudly. She played the clarinet in the marching band, and Brian and I liked to cheer her on as they played an inventive version of "Everybody Dance Now."

He gave me a knowing smile. "And do you *watch* any of the game?"

I slumped. "After halftime, I eat nachos by the concession stand. Sorry."

He shook his head. "Sounds like you've got your priorities straight. I don't even like football. I'm not playing next year."

My jaw dropped. "You're not playing your *senior year*?"

"Nope," he said with a pop. "Last year I broke my arm in practice, and I couldn't play guitar for months. Not worth it."

"You play guitar?"

He nodded slowly. "Sure do."

"And is that . . . what you wanna do? With your life?" I asked slowly.

He reached over and picked up my hand. I shivered.

"How do you feel when you do this?" he asked, rubbing a thumb over the paint marks on my palm.

"Like I'm the best version of me," I said, surprising myself. "Like I'm doing what I'm supposed to be doing. Like nothing else even matters, like the rest of the world melts away, and I'm not in Baileyville anymore. I'm not anywhere. I'm just me."

Hank smiled at me, his eyes searching my face. "That's how I feel when I play music. I knew you'd understand."

I didn't stop to think about what made him think I'd understand. Instead, I said, "I've never even heard you play."

He grinned. "Well, maybe someday you will, Sandy Macintosh."

CHAPTER FOUR

Present day

AUGUST IS, IN my mind, the strangest month of the year. It's still blazing hot (at least it is here in Ohio) and everything is greener than it's ever been. Gardens are bursting with vegetables, and everyone has more zucchini than they know what to do with. But if you pause for a moment and look beyond the sweltering heat and the sticky sweat and the ripe tomatoes, you'll see fall nipping at your heels, reminding you that it's ready to take this all away. Of course, as a gardener, I know all too well that it will be back eventually, that spring will always come after winter, but it's still hard for me to look at the bounty of harvest, the tomato vines sagging under the weight of heavy beefsteaks, and not think about what's to come. Earlier sunsets, shriveled plants, and garden beds tucked away under a blanket of snow.

It's enough to make you grab every tomato you can and shove them in your mouth before they rot, enough to make you spend every single second outside under the summer sun.

It's with that cheerful thought in mind that I walk to work on another blue-sky day. Every so often, a breeze comes through and brings some relief, but other than that, it's almost too hot to handle. I'm wearing a light blue sundress to the Ohio Inn, the kind of thing I could never wear at the greenhouse because it would immediately be covered in dirt. But as I walk through town, I feel summery and light, almost like I could start whistling, if that wasn't an extremely annoying thing to do.

I walk past the library, which still holds as much wonder for me as it did when I was a kid. Past Lydia's bakery, past the hardware store in front of the big lawn that, in the winter, becomes an ice-skating rink and in a few weeks will be where we hold our Baileyville Street Fair concerts. Past the huge white gazebo, the one where people take their wedding photos. It's also the place where any outdoor town event is held—the Halloween costume contest, the Arbor Day poetry contest (which, not to brag, I won in the second grade with my ode to pine trees), and the ceremonial lantern lighting at Christmastime, complete with horse-drawn carriage rides.

The streetlights up and down Main Street all have a hanging basket full of brightly colored petunias, each one donated by a local business and purchased from Country Colors. My parents donated the one on the streetlamp directly in front of the Ohio Inn, and as I glance up to make sure it's looking healthy and properly watered, I see something else. Or, rather, someone else.

It's Hank Tillman on a ladder leaning up against the roof. A very shirtless and sweaty Hank Tillman.

He's absorbed in whatever he's doing, so he doesn't notice me here on the sidewalk, blatantly ogling him in a way that should make me embarrassed. But I'm so shocked by the sight of his naked upper half that embarrassment doesn't even register. Shame? I don't know her. All I know is that Hank's build has changed significantly since the last time I saw him shirtless roughly fifteen years ago. His shoulders are broader, his arms thicker—and not in the off-putting way of an actor in a blockbuster movie who has to eat thirty-seven chicken breasts a day and drink protein shakes to achieve a physique worthy of a superhero suit. Hank looks like someone who's earned his muscles through years of working.

I'm mentally composing a soliloquy inspired by the way his back is shimmering in the sun when he turns to look at me.

"Hey, Macintosh. Take a picture. It'll last longer."

I shake my head quickly. The embarrassment I didn't feel earlier rushes in. "I'm sorry. I was startled by someone half naked on the roof."

He manages to look like he's making fun of me even though he's frowning. "You're making me feel like a piece of meat, you know? I simply removed my shirt because it's too damn hot, not because I wanted the women of this town to objectify me."

"I'm not objectifying you—" I start to protest but change my mind and take a different direction. After all, I was kind of objectifying him. "What are you doing up there?"

"My dad told me Papa Macintosh had a fall when he was up here fixing the gutters," Hank says. "So I decided I'd fix them myself. Save him another injury."

Hank taking the time to help out my parents is almost as hot as the sight of him up there shirtless, but I keep that to myself. "That's, uh, nice of you. But you didn't have to do that."

"I don't mind helping out," Hank says.

We look at each other for another moment, me on the sidewalk and him up on the ladder, and then he throws his T-shirt at me.

"Stop staring, you perv," he says. "You're making me feel dirty."

I catch his shirt and throw it back up on the roof. "Okay, I'm going inside. Thanks for helping my parents. Please put some clothes on."

CHAPTER FIVE

EVEN THOUGH I don't have to (and, in fact, my mom often proclaims, "Oh, Sandy, you don't need to spend all your free time hanging around here!"), I help out my parents at the Ohio Inn whenever I can. You might think people wouldn't come to stay in Baileyville all that often, since (a) it's in the middle of nowhere and (b) not a whole hell of a lot is ever going on, aside from the upcoming Baileyville Street Fair. But what Baileyville lacks in activity, it makes up for in remoteness and natural wonder, as well as that quirky small-town feel people can usually only find on television. We're surrounded by hiking and, in the winter, skiing, and we also have the drawback or benefit of being over an hour from any major city. Bad if you want access to a large hospital but great if you want to go off the grid.

And so my parents' inn is usually pretty full of guests who appreciate the, frankly, kind of eccentric atmosphere. Mama Macintosh has always loved a theme, and that extends to the decor and vibe of the Ohio Inn. Everything is Ohio themed, and I mean *everything*. The furniture is all made by local craftspeople. The quilts on the beds were pieced together by the Baileyville Quilting Society. The maple syrup is from a farm in the country, and the wine and beer are from Ohio, too. Almost everything on the menu is from within a few miles of here, and if my mom can't source it in Baileyville, she'll look elsewhere in the state.

But the real excitement comes from the rooms. Each room in the Ohio Inn is decorated to honor a famous Ohioan (hence the name of the B&B . . . clearly my love of wordplay is hereditary). There's the Neil Armstrong room, with constellation wallpaper and a lamp made out of a replica astronaut helmet. The Thomas Edison room, complete with a reproduction crank wall phone, which you can really only use to call the front desk and request room service. The Toni Morrison room, with floor-to-ceiling bookshelves featuring all her books and many from other Ohio authors. It might seem unusual to base decor around these notable Ohioans, but Mama Macintosh also chooses a theme for her daily outfits—this is normal behavior for her.

Before she started the inn, she worked in insurance, a profession she absolutely hated and complained about daily. And then, when I was in high school, our beloved golden retriever, Sophie, passed away. I was devastated, but my mother had a full-on epiphany.

"None of us know how long we have on this earth," she told me through tears as we picked up Sophie's ashes. "And I'm not wasting any more of my time in *insurance*." She always said "insurance" as if it were a particularly vile curse word.

"I need to follow my dreams," she said, hands gripping the steering wheel like she was a captain navigating her ship through tumultuous storms. "It's what Sophie would have wanted."

I didn't point out that Sophie mostly seemed to want treats, naps, belly rubs, and McDonald's cheeseburgers on her birthday. Sophie, at the very least, probably wouldn't have *objected* to my mom opening a bed-and-breakfast, if only because she couldn't talk. If it took our dog's death to awaken my mom to life's possibilities, so be it.

The next week, our town's sole bed-and-breakfast went up for sale after sitting empty for years, which my mom said was Sophie smiling down on her from doggy heaven. My parents didn't really have the money to buy an entire inn, but my grandma, who passed away a few years later, believed in signs, dreams, and dog-death-inspired epiphanies, so she gave my parents a loan.

And so my mom created the Ohio Inn. My dad—who loves nothing more than me, Mom, and the Ohio State Buckeyes—dedicated all of his nonwork hours to turning the building into the bed-and-breakfast of her dreams. In retrospect, maybe this is why I have such a hard time dating—there aren't a lot of guys who will do the manual labor necessary to rehab and reopen a themed B&B, all because their wife wants one. I realize saying, "My dad gave me unrealistic relationship expectations," is basically the same as saying, "Well, here's something I need to unpack in therapy," but it's true.

"Your mother supported me when I was starting my career," he once told me as he sanded a chest of drawers my mom planned to repaint and put in the LeBron James room. "Now it's my turn to support her."

And as I walk into the inn today, leaving Hank and his shirtless chest behind me, I see my mom standing at the hostess stand, her curly hair flowing down her back and her bracelets jangling as she writes something down. The many bangles she wears on her left arm are her trademark . . . well, in addition to her dangly earrings, her themed outfits, and her colorful shoes. She's the sort of woman who has a lot of trademarks.

She looks up. "Were you being chased?" she asks, her pen poised in midair.

I realize I'm embarrassingly out of breath. I need to get ahold of myself—I'm like a tween girl in the mid-2000s who just glimpsed a picture of shirtless Zac Efron. I've seen shirtless men before, often close up and in 3D. Why should my former high school flame on a ladder give me this sort of reaction?

"By memories, yes," I say, fanning myself. "Were you aware that Hank Tillman is currently on a ladder outside your place of business?"

"Oh yes. Very aware. So far, Edith has brought him three glasses of lemonade, and I've seen Shelby Wilson drive by at least twice." Mom stops to think. "You know, I wonder if Hank would consider doing this a few times a week. It would be great for business."

"I doubt Hank is free to stand shirtless on a ladder a few times a week. Presumably, he has other things to do," I say, looking at Hank's (thankfully clothed) legs through the floor-to-ceiling windows that line the front of the inn. Of course, I don't know what those things are—in our limited conversations since he's been back in town, we haven't discussed why he's actually here. It can't be to emotionally torment me and give Edith a show.

Edith herself wanders out of the dining room holding a glass of lemonade and fluffing up her gray hair.

"Oh, Sandy!" she says cheerfully. "Sweetie, did you get a sunburn? Your nose looks a bit pink."

I cover my nose. "Really, Edith? How many glasses of lemonade is this?"

She looks at the glass in her hands sheepishly. "Dehydration is a serious problem, you know! I wouldn't want Hank to fall off the ladder because of a lack of lemonade and have that on my conscience."

"You're a good woman, Edith," my mom says with a smile.

"What would Bill say about this?" I ask her, my eyebrows raised. Bill is Edith's husband, and I've never seen two people—elderly or otherwise—so crazy about each other. Edith has a *Cowboy Butts Drive Me Nuts* bumper sticker on her truck. (Bob's a cattle farmer, which I guess is close enough to a cowboy.) They're always holding hands or touching in some way, and they actually got kicked out of the Baileyville pool last summer for violating the "no PDA" rule, which might've been the first time that rule was ever broken by anyone who wasn't a teenager.

Edith waves me off. "Oh, honey, Bill doesn't care. We have a rule in our marriage—you can look but you can't touch. Lord knows our relationship would never have survived this long if I wasn't allowed to flirt a little bit whenever I see a good-looking man. It's like I always say . . . you can get hungry wherever you want, as long as you come home to dinner."

I wrinkle my nose, turning to my mom as Edith walks out the door. "Why do I get the feeling she actually meant to use a word other than 'hungry'?"

"Not a bad philosophy, you know," my mom says thoughtfully.

"I really don't want to talk about this with you."

Mom steps out from behind the hostess stand and inspects my look—the blue sundress, the basic brown sandals, the tiny gold hoops in my ears, and my hair hanging down straight. "Small-town Hallmark movie heroine who doesn't yet know that she's about to fall in love with the business developer from the city who's threatening to bulldoze her grandfather's apple orchard to build an undefined, but clearly very important, building," she says, holding out her hands as if she's framing me for a shot.

I look down at my dress and frown. "Really? I thought my vibe was more 'Look, I actually got dressed in real clothes today.'"

Mom shakes her head with finality. "Nope. You're giving me full-on 'sitcom actress from twenty years ago who's about to fall in love with a former boy band member who pivoted to acting.'"

I sigh. "Well, what's *your* look today?"

She gestures toward her black capri pants and black-and-white-striped shirt. "Mime."

"Mime?"

"Yes," she says, offering no other explanation as she goes back behind the stand. Leave it to my mom to find fashion inspiration from mimes. "A big shipment of honey came in this morning if you don't mind helping out," she says. It's sweet that she always phrases it this way—"if you don't mind"—as if I didn't come here with the express purpose of helping. After all, I've seen what happens when I don't help. My dad falls off a ladder and breaks his ankle, thus conjuring up Hank Tillman out of thin air.

"I think you mean if I don't *mime*," I say, waggling my eyebrows.

She points at me. "Good one." And then, putting her pen down again, she sighs. "You sure this is okay with you?"

"Unpacking the honey?" I ask. "No problem. I have the time and—"

"No." She gestures toward the window. "Hank being here. He offered to help, and it's been a long time since high school, but if seeing him is too much, I'm happy to tell him to skedaddle. I don't want you to feel—"

"I feel great!" I say brightly, standing up tall and trying to look as unfragile as possible. That's me . . . strong, sturdy, and in no way affected by Hank Tillman's presence, yards from me and separated by mere glass.

"Okay," she says uncertainly, and I spin on my heels and speed-walk toward the kitchen before she can say anything else.

When I walk through the swinging doors, I find my dad in

the corner peeling potatoes with the Ohio Inn's chef, Scott. Potatoes are kind of Scott's specialty—people come in just for the home fries, and everyone's tried to figure out his secret, but no one can. You wouldn't think the humble potato could taste this good, but clearly Scott knows something the rest of us don't about potato preparation.

"Hey, Sweet Baby Girl!" Dad says, using the nickname he's been calling me since I was born. He grunts and reaches for his crutch.

"No! Scott, under no circumstances is that man allowed to stand up!" I bark.

"Sit down," Scott says in a monotone, adjusting his glasses. "That's an order from Sweet Baby Girl."

"Thanks, Scott," I say, crossing my arms as I look down at my dad. "Were you attempting to get up on that ladder and fix the gutters again?"

"Yes, I was," my dad says, giving me a dignified nod.

"Despite the fact that you broke your foot doing that before? And that you're still wearing a boot?"

"I don't need to sit here and be interrogated like this," he says pleasantly, looking at the potato in his hand as if it's his adoring audience.

"Dad! You could hurt yourself! Again!" I cry, throwing my hands in the air.

He remains unmoved. "You know me. I'm a fixer. That's what I do . . . your mother needs something fixed, I make it happen."

"I'm fairly certain Mom didn't want you to climb up on that ladder again."

"Nope!" he says with a smile. "She did threaten to divorce me. But then Hank Tillman showed up and took care of things and, well, long story short, we're still married."

Scott offers him a fist bump and Dad looks at me smugly.

"Don't encourage him." I point at Scott.

"Sandy, you shouldn't worry about me. You can trust that your dad will be okay," Dad says with gentle eyes.

"Once again, you *fell off a ladder*. You could've been hurt way worse than you are."

"Well, life hurts sometimes." Then he stops and stares at me. "Are you doing okay seeing Hank Tillman out there? Mr. Tillman sent him because your mom was down at the market complaining to everyone within earshot about how I was a damn fool and—"

"I'm totally fine!" I say, turning and walking away from them. I call over my shoulder, "See you guys later! Scott, try to make sure he doesn't cut off a finger or whatever!"

"See you, Sweet Baby Girl," Scott says in his deep voice.

I head off to find today's shipment of honey, which will at least take my mind off of this. What I don't need is everyone assuming I'm going to fall apart when I see Hank outside. Just because he's shirtless and fixing things like he stepped out of the pages of a book called *Sexual Fantasies of Apparently Everyone in Baileyville* doesn't mean I'm going to faint or cry or, well, do what I did the last time Hank Tillman broke my heart.

I'm not a teenager anymore—now I'm a grown woman, like Beyoncé. She's an international superstar; I own a greenhouse. We're basically the same person.

Except that Beyoncé, presumably, doesn't still try her best to forget all about the first time she kissed her high school boyfriend.

CHAPTER SIX

Sixteen years ago

AS I KEPT tutoring Hank and got to know him better, I tried to think about him as a boy who only needed me to help him pass junior year . . . not like a boy who'd grabbed my hands and looked into my eyes and, somehow, understood me.

I failed miserably. I caught myself doodling his name in my Trigonometry notes, the bubble letters betraying my descent into Hank Tillman–induced madness.

Hank was kind to *everyone*; that was his thing. He was perfectly nice when he saw me in the hallways at school—saying hi, setting up our next study date—but it wasn't like he was blowing me kisses or telling everyone that I understood the secrets deep inside his soul. Him shining his Hank Tillman spotlight on me for a minute didn't mean I was *special* or anything.

Our study sessions continued like normal. He was doing well—as it turned out, I was a pretty okay tutor.

But then we had to write an essay on *Pride and Prejudice*. I loved *Pride and Prejudice* when we read it in class. *Loved* it. I found myself longing for free moments so that I could read a few more pages, thinking about Elizabeth and Jane and their quirky sisters as I brushed my teeth, dreaming about grumpy Mr. Darcy at night. I had a million essay idea topics locked and loaded.

When it came to Hank, however, the essay was almost secondary. The real challenge was getting him to even read the book. We sat on my parents' porch one spring afternoon, one of those perfect first warm days where, all of a sudden, you remember what birds sound like and see those tiny little buds on the trees and know that winter is finally over. We didn't share the love seat this time; I was afraid such close proximity might cause me to spontaneously combust. I sat in a rocking chair, and he lay sprawled across the porch swing, head propped up on a decorative pillow, steadfastly not answering any of my questions.

"So wait, which one's Elizabeth?" he asked, spinning the book in his hands.

I looked up from my paper printout of reading comprehension questions. "Seriously? She's the main character, Hank."

I won't lie and pretend it didn't give me a tiny jolt of a thrill just to say his name. It was still a novelty for those sounds to come out of my mouth instead of bouncing around in my head.

He sighed. The book stopped spinning. "I don't get what's happening in this story."

"What's your favorite book?" I asked.

He snorted and didn't look at me. "I don't like books."

My pencil dropped on my lap, rolled off the paper and onto the porch. "You don't like *any* book? Not even one?"

Hank sat up and picked up my pencil, then handed it to me. His fingers brushed mine, just for a moment, so lightly.

He leaned back again in the porch swing. "I guess I liked

Goosebumps when I was a kid, but maybe that's because my mom used to read them to me before bed."

I was about to comment on the boldness of reading *Goosebumps* to a small child at bedtime, but I stopped. "Hand me your book."

"Gladly," he said.

I opened the beat-up, creased cover and started reading.

"'It is a truth universally acknowledged, that a single man in possession of a good fortune must be in want of a wife. However little known the feelings or views of such a man may be on his first entering a neighborhood, this truth is so well fixed in the minds of the surrounding families, that he is considered as the rightful property of some one or other of their daughters.'"

Hank pretended to snore, but I ignored him. I read the entire first chapter, getting lost in the words the way I always did when I had a book in front of me, to the point that I forgot Hank was even listening. When I was done, I looked up, dazed, to see him smiling.

His smile could make a girl want things.

"I understand it when you read it to me," he said, looking up at me through those stupidly thick eyelashes.

I smiled back.

And that's how I ended up reading the entirety of *Pride and Prejudice* out loud to Hank Tillman over the course of a few days. It took a while, but it was worth it, because Hank treated it like a basketball game, heckling the text and shouting things like, "Wait, *what* did Darcy say?" and "Man, I hate George Wickham. I hate him so much."

One evening, when we knew he had to finish the book because the essay was due in a few days, he said he had a surprise for me.

"The porch is nice," he said, "but I promise you I've found the ideal reading spot."

"There's an ideal reading spot?" I asked, my heart fluttering—fluttering!—like I myself was in a Jane Austen novel.

"See, there are some things I know that you don't," Hank said, and that crooked, charming smile made me say yes.

"OH." I EXHALED twenty minutes later, when we'd driven to some property the Tillmans owned way out in the country, past Baileyville village limits, and climbed to the highest point on the land that had once belonged to Hank's grandpa. The woods were behind us, an old barn beside us, but in front of us . . . a perfect view of the entire town.

"You can see everything from up here," I said. "There's the library!"

"Only you would pick out the library, Sandy," Hank said, but he said it with a smile in his voice, and I got stuck on how familiarly nice my name sounded coming out of his mouth.

I wrapped my arms around myself. It was warm, but the breeze made it feel cool. A gray cloud passed over the sun, covering us in shadow for a moment. "I really like the Baileyville library," I admitted. And, sure, their collection was fifty percent books about Amish women, but they had the classics and they had romance novels, which were perfect for my daydreaming mind. When I got lost in a love story or something written a hundred years ago, I could pretend I wasn't here—I could daydream about the way life should be, romantic and magical and full of potential.

"I know," Hank said, lying down on the ground and propping himself up on his elbows. He squinted up at me as the sun came out from behind the clouds. "I'm not making fun of you. I like that about you."

I was afraid my grin was going to take over my entire face. If I could paint this picture right now—the sun and the clouds, the bright green spring grass and Hank's blue eyes, him looking up at me like I was somebody special, not just a tutor he was being nice to—it would be my favorite painting. I would hang it in my room and stare at it every day. *Click.* I mentally took the picture to think about it later, to see if I could get it down on canvas.

Hank patted the ground beside him, so I sat down, being sure not to sit too close.

"See? Ideal reading spot." He leaned back so his head rested on his hands. "*Pride and Prejudice.* The end. Let's do this."

I read slowly, savoring each word, because I knew this was it. Once this book was done, I'd look over Hank's paper, but finals were next week. We didn't have a lot of study time, and we certainly didn't have another book to read out loud. This moment— of Hank listening to me, looking at me like I had the answers to everything, cherishing each word I said even if they were really Jane Austen's—would be over. We'd be back to hellos in the hall, maybe the occasional conversation, but that was it.

In my reading trance, I didn't notice the sky growing darker, the clouds looking heavier. When I read the last word and closed the paperback, I moved my eyes to Hank and almost jumped when I saw how he looked at me. It was the way I imagined a boy might look at a girl he really liked, at a girl he really thought was beautiful, eyelids heavy and gaze steady.

"That was a good book," he said softly, and then the first rain-drop fell on his face. Then another, then another, hard and in-sistent.

Soon the sky was pelting us, and I stood up, shrieking.

"Come on," he said, grabbing my hand, and I let him pull me to the barn. It was old and grimy—dirt floor, straw everywhere, nothing inside but some farm equipment—but at least it was dry. I couldn't hear anything but the rain hitting the grass and our own ragged breaths.

"What is this?" Hank asked with a smile in his voice, gesturing at me. I looked down to see that I'd instinctively shoved *Pride and Prejudice* under my shirt.

"Oh," I said, embarrassed, as I pulled it out. "I didn't want it to get wet."

Hank smiled and took a step toward me. "That's sweet."

I shrugged, not knowing what else to do.

"Thanks for helping me," he said. "With the book and with everything else. I know you probably had plenty of other things to do."

"I really didn't," I said quickly, then wished I'd kept my mouth shut.

Hank let out a little snort-laugh. "That's what I like about you. You don't waste any time trying to look cool."

Maybe that last part could've seemed like an insult, but I was still too stuck on the first part. *That's what I like about you.*

Hank took another step toward me, and now we were close, so close, *too* close. This felt like something—nothing I'd experienced in real life, of course, but something from a book. Like swirling colors, red and orange and yellow, pulsing warmth from the canvas.

I stepped back.

"Hey, Sandy?" Hank asked, his voice less sure than I'd ever heard it.

"Yeah?" I asked.

"Can I kiss you?"

I dropped *Pride and Prejudice* onto the dirt barn floor, saying a silent apology to the book gods, and stepped toward him. He put his hands on my face, so gently, and he kissed me. The feeling of his fingertips on my burning cheeks was enough to make me faint, but combined with his lips on mine? Well, I thought I might die. It was my first kiss, so I had nothing to compare it to, but it felt like waking up. Like a beginning.

I stepped back and widened my eyes. What had I done? I'd kissed Hank Tillman, or let him kiss me. And then I'd stopped.

"What's this look for?" Hank asked, brow furrowed.

I shook my head and opened my mouth a few times, searching for words. "I'm . . . I'm just surprised."

"So this whole time, you haven't noticed me flirting with you?" he asked, crooked smile on his face.

I shook my head slowly. This couldn't be real.

He sighed, mock-frustrated. "Then I guess I need to do a better job."

He kissed me again as the rain fell even harder outside, and the sky turned practically black from the weight of the heavy clouds. *This is real, this is happening*, I told myself over and over in my head. I'm kissing a boy in a barn in the rain, and I feel like I'm a million miles away from Baileyville.

HANK DROVE ME home in his rusty truck. The sky had cleared, and now the sun hung low and orange over the horizon, casting everything in a rosy glow that matched my mood. Baileyville, being in a valley, only got a few radio stations, most of them country, so he settled on one of them as Shania Twain's "You're Still the One" started playing.

The song wasn't even remotely new when I was in high school. But hearing it here, with Hank? It felt fresh, like Shania was singing just for me. I bit my lip and looked out the window, trying not to smile as I looked at the leaves on the trees, wet and glittering in the sun.

I was used to hearing love songs at school dances when Honey was dancing with Brian, and I—their third wheel as usual—retreated to the bathroom so I wouldn't look pathetic standing there by myself.

But now I wasn't a bystander or a sidekick. I was the one singing the song, glittering and shimmering like those leaves.

"Can I tell you something?" Hank asked.

I whipped my head around to look at him, certain this was the moment he'd tell me he regretted our kiss. That it was all a big mistake or that it had been quite nice but would not be repeated. Which would be unfortunate, since I was already thinking about how much I'd like to repeat it.

I nodded, watching his hands gripping the steering wheel. Hank had nice hands. Hands that looked like they worked.

"This song is cheesy as hell, but I kinda love it," he said.

I smiled as his eyes met mine before they went back to the road. "Yeah," I said quietly. "Me too."

And from that point on, Hank Tillman and I were a couple.

CHAPTER SEVEN

Present day

AFTER LEAVING MY dad to happily peel potatoes, I unload our new shipment of honey and ask my mom what else needs to be done.

She checks her computer. "The Rutherford B. Hayes room is ready to be cleaned, if you don't mind."

I give her a thumbs-up. "You got it."

If it's been a while since you've brushed up on your U.S. history, allow me to explain: Rutherford B. Hayes was the nineteenth president of the United States, and most importantly for our purposes, he was born in Delaware, Ohio. By all accounts, Rutherford seemed like a pretty okay guy—he was a staunch abolitionist, he fought for the Union, he loved his wife, Lucy (who was the first First Lady to have a college degree, by the way). There's an entire museum dedicated to Rutherford, but if you can't make it all the way up to Fremont, this is the next best thing.

I strip the sheets off the bed and replace them with clean ones, then straighten the quilt with a disturbingly lifelike vision of Rutherford's face pieced together by Baileyville's star quilter, Hotpants Ed (so named because if it's above sixty-five degrees, he wears the shortest shorts you've ever seen everywhere he goes—and he's a six-foot-tall man with a ponytail and a gray beard, so it's a striking look). Then I fluff the decorative pillows, one of which is a shockingly detailed needlepoint of, again, Rutherford's face, this one done by Baileyville's star needlepointer, Edith Paterson—she of the cowboy whose butt drives her nuts. I dust the side table, topped by a lamp that is actually a recreation of his daughter's dollhouse, and straighten the frame of the hand-lettered quote of his last words: *I know that I'm going where Lucy is.*

I guess it's romantic, but it's also kind of a morbid vibe for an inn. But no one could ever question my mom's attention to detail.

"Hey, Sandy."

I turn to see a stocky guy in an Ohio Inn polo shirt leaning against the doorframe.

"Hey, Burger," I say. "What's up?"

Burger is, I should probably note, not his first name. No, his entire God-given name is Chad Hamburger, which our classmates shortened to "Burger" sometime around first grade. The nickname stuck, partly because it was too hard to believe a real live human who wasn't a fast-food-chain mascot had the last name Hamburger, but also because it sounded right in the context that people tended to mention Burger. For example, "Did you catch Burger barfing in the pool at Matt's party this weekend?" It's almost poetry.

Burger sighs heavily. "You see they raised the price of PBR down at the River Horse to frickin' two fifty?"

The River Horse is the literal one bar in Baileyville and, as such, one of the few places adults can hang out after-hours. Not that I spend much time there, given that I'm not looking to hook up with any of my former classmates. Especially not Burger, who I did actually go on one ill-fated date with many years ago. At this point, I've been set up with every eligible man in Baileyville, always with unpleasant results.

I shake my head sympathetically. "I didn't see that. Bummer, though."

"It's some kinda bullshit," he mutters, but then he brightens up. "Hey, you planning on coming to the reunion?"

"What reunion?" I ask, gathering the dirty sheets into the laundry bag.

"Our high school reunion," he says as if I'm being deliberately obtuse. "Fifteen years, dude."

I stop in my tracks. "Are you joking?"

Burger frowns. "No. You want a joke? Because I heard a good one this morning from Brad Emmerhoffer over at Baileyville Bank. What do you call someone who won't fart in public?"

I grimace. "I don't want to hear a joke, Burger. I mean, is it really already time for our fifteenth reunion?"

He nods. "Yeah, dude! We're gonna have it down at Amvets Park, and lemme tell you, I already know it's gonna get crazy. Kenny Crunkleton's gonna make his famous Crunk Drivers. You remember those from high school?"

I shake my head. "I didn't really do parties in high school."

"Ah." Burger gives me a look of understanding. "You were always busy studying."

And not puking up my guts in Matt's pool or drinking anything called a Crunk Driver, I think to myself. "Yeah, well . . . I don't know if I'll be at the reunion. We all kinda see each other pretty often anyway, right?"

Burger looks thoughtful. "True. Those of us who stuck around, anyway."

"Right," I say. "Anyway, gotta get these sheets—"

"Oh, speaking of people who left, I saw Hank outside on the roof!" Burger says. "Don't worry, I didn't go up there."

"Good," I say. Last winter, my mom banned Burger from the roof because he pretended to fall off the ladder while putting up Christmas lights but then actually fell off the ladder, and we had to call the squad. Fortunately, he didn't break anything, which he claimed was because his bones are "strong as hell."

"Maybe we can get him to perform at the reunion. Not any of his songs. They're kinda depressing. He can probably do a cover of something fun, though, right? He's gotta know some Jimmy Buffett."

"I'm not sure his music and Jimmy's are really comparable," I say. "No offense to Jimmy."

"None taken," Burger says. "Well, think about it. We're gonna have cornhole."

"Oh, now, don't let me get too excited," I say, squeezing past him to make my way to the laundry room. "See you later, Burger."

"A private tutor," he calls out.

I turn around. "Pardon me?"

"That's what you call someone who refuses to fart in public. Get it? Tutor? Like toot-er. Like a fart."

"Good one. I'm gonna . . ." I gesture with my head and make my way down the stairs. *This is why I haven't found a life partner here in Baileyville*, I remind myself. Because the thirty-three-year-old men make fart jokes and try to entice me with offers of questionable alcohol. It has nothing to do with the fact that, in the past fifteen years, no one has measured up to Hank Tillman.

CHAPTER EIGHT

Fifteen years ago

AFTER THAT FIRST kiss in his parents' barn, Hank and I were inseparable all through summer and into senior year. On the rare occasion that his hand wasn't in mine, my fingers reached out for him, searching for his warmth. Hank really did quit football, devoting his free time to offering guitar lessons to elementary school kids and working on his own music. We spent our daytime hours (the ones we weren't in school, that is) chasing our dreams in the same room, him playing his guitar as I painted, our bodies together even as our minds drifted to other worlds. But even when we were drifting, it always felt like we were drifting toward the same place, daydreaming about a future together, one where our big dreams were a reality and not something that made the adults in our lives smile condescendingly and say, "Well, that sounds like a good hobby!"

We were in high school in the dark ages, when cell phones were gigantic and text messaging barely existed, so we communicated during the day via notes passed in the hall. Hank wrote me poems and proto-songs, and I drew him pictures of Mr. Waldorf teaching calculus with his famous, ever-present pit stains. Honey was overjoyed that I finally had someone like she had Brian, and she came up with big plans for us to double-date to the homecoming dance. There was a part of me that wanted to do the typical Baileyville routine—drive half an hour to eat at the Olive Garden in Richfield in our formal wear before driving to the high school and slowly swaying back and forth in the gym while some terrible song played and our classmates covertly groped one another. But a much, much larger part of me wanted nothing to do with that, and so we left Honey and Brian to their gropefest (she didn't seem to mind—after all, it is a truth universally acknowledged that a high school girl in possession of a boyfriend wants more time alone with said boyfriend) and instead drove out to the barn, where we ate McDonald's in the bed of Hank's truck while watching the sunset from the highest point in Baileyville.

My parents were on their standing weekly date that night, something I found gross at the time but now think was sort of sweet. They barely even cared that Hank and I were going to be out, alone, while all the rest of the town's teenagers were in the gym with copious adult supervision. This was probably because, up until Hank, I'd spent all of my free time either painting, reading, or choreographing dance routines to Destiny's Child's "Bootylicious" with Honey in her basement. It simply didn't occur to them that I could get into trouble, especially not with Hank Tillman, a boy beloved by every Baileyville parent.

"This is better than homecoming," I said, shoving a fry in my mouth as the sun cast an orange glow over the valley.

"I would've gone, you know," Hank said, watching the sky. "If you wanted me to."

I paused, burger halfway to my mouth. "Did you want to go?"

He laughed. "No. But I don't want you to miss out on, I don't know, a high school tradition."

I smiled at the sky because I was too embarrassed to look at him as I said, "You're better than any high school tradition."

"Well, I'd go anywhere if it meant I could be with you," he said, and I finally met his eyes. He was watching me like I was the sunset, like I was a brief but beautiful natural occurrence that he got lucky enough to look at every day.

"Hank Tillman," I said. "Are you gonna put this moment in a song?"

His crooked smile appeared for a moment. "Maybe."

We ate in silence, watching as the sun sank lower and shadows formed across the valley. The leaves were just starting to change colors, so the trees were a furious swirl of green, orange, red, and yellow. I felt like I was inside a painting or a song.

"Are we stupid for wanting to live anywhere else?" I asked.

"I'm fairly certain the sun sets all over the world, Sandy," he said.

I smacked him on the arm. "You know what I mean. Is it a mistake to leave here?"

Hank stared at the sunset for so long that I thought he wasn't going to answer me. But then he said, "I don't think so. No matter where we go, we'll always have this. No one can take these memories away."

It was the perfect answer. The sun finally disappeared as we finished our food, and we lay down in the truck bed to watch the stars come out. It involved less K-Ci & JoJo than the homecoming dance we could've attended, but it was a lot more comfortable, and there were fewer sequins scratching at my arms.

"C'mere," Hank said, grabbing my hand and helping me jump out of the truck bed. He reached into the cab and turned the radio on. The sound of Willie Nelson's "Always on My Mind" filled the air.

"I know we skipped homecoming," he said, putting his hands around my waist. It still felt thrilling when he touched me. "But may I have this dance?"

My smile took over my entire face. "Yes, you may."

I put my head on his shoulder and closed my eyes, and there in the dark, next to the big old barn where we'd had our first kiss, with the twinkling lights of Baileyville below us and the stars shining above us, we danced to Willie Nelson. If we looked down into the valley, we could see the lights around the high school, where our classmates were currently dancing exactly like this. But we weren't looking down there, and we weren't thinking about them. Or at least, I wasn't.

"I love you so much, Sandy," Hank said into my ear.

I kept my eyes shut, afraid that if I opened them, this moment would be over. Maybe he'd accidentally said he loved me, but as long as I didn't question it, he wouldn't take it back. It was the first time he'd ever said it, but I'd felt it for a long time. I'd had the first stirrings of it way back in elementary school when he offered another kid his pants—it wasn't as deep as what I felt now, of course, but it was the beginning. It was something like love, something that bloomed big and tall and bold like a sunflower.

And so we swayed gently, like one of those big sunflowers in the breeze, until I finally opened my eyes and pulled back to look at his face. Hank hadn't asked me if I heard him, and he hadn't been waiting for a response. Instead, he was letting me take my time, like he always did.

"I love you too, Hank," I said. "I love you more than anything."

He leaned forward and kissed me. It was different than our slow and tentative first kiss in the barn, different than the quick kisses we'd exchanged since then, always afraid our parents would walk in. This time, it was us and the stars and the music, up here with the best view of Baileyville. This time, our kisses were harder, more urgent, and communicating something entirely different.

"Always on My Mind" ended, and the opening notes of "She Thinks My Tractor's Sexy" started playing. I smiled into Hank's mouth, then couldn't stop myself from giggling.

"I know what you're thinking," Hank said, kissing my neck. "Hank, did you plan this romantic moment? Did you set things up so that Kenny Chesney's instant classic would be playing right after the moment that you told the girl of your dreams that you were hopelessly, stupidly in love with her? And the answer is . . . no, this is fate. This is our song now. 'She Thinks My Tractor's Sexy' will play at our wedding."

I threw my head back and laughed, even as a tiny harmonium in my chest played a tune at the word *wedding*. I was seventeen, and I would've married Hank Tillman the next day if he'd asked me. I'd get a tattoo of his name on my neck. Name an ill-advised decision, and I'd say, *Let's go.*

"That's fine," I said. "I love this song. Kenny Chesney is a poet."

"Is this a hint that you'd like me to get a tractor? Because right now, the closest thing I have is a riding mower." He reached into the cab of the truck to turn off the radio.

"Maybe you should write that song. 'She Thinks My Mower's Sexy.' You know, about a woman who finds lawn maintenance incredibly hot."

"It's a good idea," Hank said, leaning down to kiss me again. "But I have a better one."

It sounds a little strange to say that we had sex for the first time in the bed of Hank's truck right after Kenny Chesney took the liberty of setting the mood, but that's what happened. And of course, it was awkward—there's a reason most grown adults don't conduct their sex lives in truck beds. But for me, at seventeen, it was perfect. It was perfect because it was Hank and me, and the stars twinkling and the crickets chirping and the words he whispered in my ear.

"Sandy, I want you to be my girl forever."

SENIOR YEAR FLEW by. Our guidance counselor encouraged us to apply to Baileyville Community College and a religious college two towns over where students weren't allowed to dance or watch R-rated movies. Hank and I spent all year giving each other knowing looks whenever some well-meaning adult doled out advice about being "practical" and having a "backup plan."

Honey did exactly what she'd been planning to do since she was old enough to come up with a plan: she got into the animal sciences undergraduate program at OSU. Brian was going to BCC, so they wouldn't be too far from each other. "Close enough to spend our weekends together," she said, the possibility of breaking up with him never even entering her mind.

Things felt trickier to figure out for Hank and me. Of course I wanted to stay together—the idea of not being with him was like willingly deciding to give up breathing. But I didn't know where we'd end up. Hank had applied to a lot of places, but Berklee College of Music was his top choice. Our guidance counselor had taken one look at the price tag and told him not to bother.

The guidance counselor wasn't wrong that it was expensive, and Hank's family certainly didn't have the money for it—but he got in, with a substantial scholarship. I'd applied all over, but also to schools near Berklee just in case, and when I got into Massachusetts College of Art and Design, it felt like fate, like another Kenny Chesney song from the universe. We'd be right there together.

But only a couple of months before we were supposed to leave, during that last long, hot summer of being children, I got a call from MassArt. There was a problem with my scholarship—namely, that it didn't exist. Well, it sort of existed, but some wires had gotten crossed, and the actual amount of money they could give me was much, much less than what they'd initially said.

I didn't even know this was possible. My mom was unruffled. "We'll figure it out," she said, giving me a pat on the hand. "No one can say no to a Macintosh woman."

But it turned out that the world outside of Baileyville was actually quite adept at saying no to Macintosh women. My mom sent the school angry emails, letters, and in one case, a very profane phone call, but nothing changed. And with my parents' jobs (running a niche B&B and working at a community college), there was no chance they could afford to send me to art school. *I* certainly couldn't afford to send me to art school, either.

Since my dad worked at BCC as the sports facility manager (a fancy way of saying he was in charge of the student gym), I got free tuition there. "It's a good deal!" Mom kept saying, trying to put a positive spin on my disappointment, as if my college experience was a coat she found on discount at the end of the season.

I didn't complain or pout or yell around them. In front of my parents, I cheerfully accepted my fate. I knew my mom was right, anyway—I knew what we could afford, and I knew what made sense. I didn't even tell Honey how upset I was, afraid that my disappointment would cast a pall over her excitement. It felt ungrateful and churlish to complain about a free college education that wasn't quite what I wanted—I knew there were kids who would love to go to any school, even BCC, for free.

But with Hank, I cried.

I wouldn't be going to Massachusetts. I wouldn't be going anywhere. All of those big dreams, of getting out of Baileyville and being able to study the things that made us who we were . . . they weren't going to happen. Instead of studying with real live working artists, I'd be studying marketing with Mr. Watterson, who also owned the feed and supply store. Instead of living in the dorm, I'd be staying in my childhood bedroom.

Instead of being near Hank, I'd be eight hundred miles away.

"This is temporary," he told me every time I cried. "This is one tiny obstacle. All artists have roadblocks, right?"

"Are you even gonna want to stay with me?" I asked through my tears, barely caring about the snot streaming down my face. "Or are you gonna meet some . . . some Massachusetts girl and fall in love with her?"

"There is no woman in the entire Commonwealth of Massachusetts who can hold a candle to you," he said seriously. "You're my girl forever, Sandy."

I nodded. I still felt like I was on fire every time he said those words, but I had a hard time believing them now.

CHAPTER NINE

Present day

THE BIGGEST EVENT of the year in Baileyville is, without a doubt, the Baileyville Street Fair. The entirety of Main Street shuts down for the better part of a week, and it involves months of planning. There's a planning committee which, of course, I'm on—when I finally realized that I was staying in Baileyville for good, I took an "if you can't beat 'em, join 'em" attitude, and I jump on almost every volunteer opportunity I get.

The Street Fair always takes place in the last week of August on Thursday, Friday, and Saturday (with Wednesday afternoon and evening reserved for setup, and Sunday morning reserved for cleanup). Thursday and Friday nights involve concerts and the big Baileyville Street Fair Dance, while Saturday usually has a performance by the high school band. The rest of the fair includes but is not limited to a tractor pull; a kiddie tractor pull; livestock exhibitions; a doll show; a pet show; an art show; a companion children's art show, where every exhibitor wins a ribbon and a dollar; pie, cake, and cookie competitions; a pumpkin-growing contest; a sunflower growing contest; a zucchini-growing contest (after Barb O'Dell, who's also on the planning committee, got upset a few years ago that she'd grown a very big zucchini and had no means with which to be rewarded for it); a cake auction; square dancing; a pop-up arcade in a tent in the empty lot by the bank; several child-sized rides; an exhibition of all kinds of needlework; weekend concerts that, in the past, have included an Elvis impersonator and an ABBA tribute band; about twenty different food vendors; and a dance in the fire station (don't worry, all the fire trucks park elsewhere during the dance) that, last year, ended with Hotpants Ed pulling a muscle while attempting to show us a dance he learned on TikTok.

Needless to say, it all takes a lot of planning and a whole host of volunteers.

After closing down the greenhouse, I head over to the Baileyville Community Center, which also happens to be the basement of the Baileyville Assisted Living Facility. (All buildings here, much like all people, need to have at least two jobs.)

"Sandy!" Honey shrieks to me from across the parking lot, where she's getting out of her minivan.

"Honey!" I yell back, then we pretend to run toward each other in slow motion before meeting in a hug.

"It's been too long," she says, attempting to lift me and failing because she's five foot five and I'm five foot eleven.

"I think we saw each other yesterday," I remind her.

"Too long," she repeats. "Move in with me and Brian. Be our nanny."

"You sure you want to hire a nanny *this* sexy? Might be too much temptation for Brian." I gesture toward my Country Colors T-shirt and cutoff jean shorts, both of which are, as usual, covered in dirt.

"Good point." She sighs. "I wouldn't want a torrid affair between you and my husband to ruin our lifelong friendship."

"Or your marriage."

"Yet *another* good point. You're impossibly sexy and your logic is impeccable! I can't compete."

We open the door and walk down the stairs, the rumble of voices carrying into the stairwell.

"Hello, all!" Honey says, and I wave as we step in.

The group stops their conversation briefly to greet us, then goes back to talking. Honey and I linger a moment by the snack table, which is always provided by Lydia Suzuki, who runs the town's combination bakery / coffee shop / pizza place.

"I know I say this every time, but I am one hundred percent here for the snacks," Honey says, grabbing a muffin.

"And because you care about the community," I remind her.

"Ooooh, Lydia did pumpkin this time!" Honey squeals.

We join everyone else in the circle of folding chairs in between Hotpants Ed and Lydia.

"And all I'm saying is the pet show needs better security," Barb says with a sniff. "Patricia Barker's poodle peed on the prizewinning pumpkin last year. Just lifted his leg and let 'er rip, and the judge didn't even notice."

"Mr. Sprinkles did that?" Ed asks.

Barb nods, her impressively tall blue-gray hair not moving at all. She gets it set once a week down at Hair Affair, and I'm fairly certain it could survive a nuclear attack. "I would like some assurance that the rest of our vegetables won't be covered in dog urine just because Patricia Barker can't control her poodle."

"Barb is *on* tonight," Honey whispers to me.

"Your concerns are noted," Sean Fitzsimmons says, writing something down in his notes with a serious expression on his face.

Sean is objectively handsome, with sand-colored hair and eyes blue like sea glass. Basically, looking at Sean is like taking a mental trip to the beach. He's hardworking and involved in the community . . . he is, to put it mildly, a real catch in Baileyville. He also has absolutely no sense of humor. When I attempted to explain the name of the Joel Bowl to him on the one date we went on years ago, he gave me a blank look before asking, "So . . . it's just a normal bowl?" We ran out of conversation topics about five minutes into the date.

And so, naturally, he wasn't the one for me. Now he's married with twin boys, and I'm happy someone gets to enjoy his beachy good looks and complete lack of knowledge about pop culture.

There's got to be a happy medium between someone who doesn't understand humor as a concept and Burger's fart jokes, I think. Surely that man is out there. Or maybe he is, but he's not in Baileyville. After all, this is a small town, and the good ones got snapped up early—which I know, because I had my chance with most of them. And I turned them all down, like an idiot. Would it have been so bad to accept a life consigned to constantly explaining my attempts at jokes? Maybe not if it meant a warm body next to me in my bed, someone to walk Toby with me in the morning, someone to dance around the kitchen with while cooking.

Scratch that. Sean also told me he didn't really care for music. Well, we could've danced around the kitchen to silence. I could've made it work!

I attempt to pay attention to the conversation going on around me. Shelby Wilson, who owns Hair Affair over by the car wash and is the talent behind Barb's magical never-moving hairdo, is proposing a new fair event.

Once upon a time, Shelby and I were, if not exactly enemies, then at least two people who really, really didn't get along. It wasn't like she dramatically bullied me teen-movie-style, but she did once tell me that my bangs looked like I'd cut them with a hedge trimmer.

But now we're friends. That's kind of how it is with those of us who stuck around—it's too much work to nurture dislike when you have to see someone every day. And anyway, she was right about my bangs—now she cuts my hair and it looks a million times better.

"What is nail art?" Sean asks with a frown as I mentally tune back into the conversation. "Do you mean you hammer a nail into something?"

Shelby sighs, exasperated. "No, Sean. *Finger*nail art." She wiggles her nails in the air. "People can do some amazing things with such a small canvas. And I'm proposing we allow me to judge them."

"I second this motion!" I say, and Shelby smiles at me gratefully.

Sean gives me a patient look. "Once again, Sandy, there's no need to second anything. We'll take a formal vote at the end of the meeting."

"Sorry," I say as Honey stifles a giggle beside me. "I was caught up in the moment. It's a good idea."

"Thank you," Shelby says. "And when you get some time, let's work on *your* nails. Don't think I haven't noticed the situation you've got there."

I fold my hands in my lap. "I work with my hands all day!"

Shelby shakes her head, admiring her own nails. "There's no excuse for those cuticles, so don't bother trying to make one."

I can't even argue with her. Shelby is indisputably the most glamorous person in Baileyville (aside from Hotpants Ed, who has a more eccentric style). Her makeup is always flawless, her hair is divine, and she knows exactly how to dress to show off her hourglass figure. And I know that her heckling me about my nails is all done out of love—she once told me, straight-faced, "Sandy, the only thing bigger than my boobs is my *heart*." And the thing is . . . she's right. I know for a fact that she picks Barb up for her appointment every week, since Barb lives alone and can't drive because of her cataracts.

We discuss a few more items on Sean's list (the logistics of the tractor pull, the ordering of the ribbons, Lydia's updates on the number of entrants for the baked goods contest, the cost involved in bringing in security for the pet show and what said security would entail and whether Ed could simply stand there and yell a warning whenever a dog lifts their leg), and Honey and I volunteer to call all the residents who donated cakes to the cake auction last year to confirm that they're in for this year. We vote on our proposed new fair content (all ayes, all around). The meeting is winding down when the door creaks open, and someone thumps down the stairs.

All of us turn toward the source of the noise, and suddenly, the smile left on my face from the dog-pee discussion falls away. Hank Tillman walks into the room.

"Sorry I'm late," he says, out of breath, raking a hand through his hair. "Kid emergency. I mean, everything's fine, but for a minute there, we couldn't find Purple Kyle."

When all of us stare at him in silence, he clarifies. "Purple Kyle is Henry's stuffed dinosaur. The name separates him from Orange Kyle. I don't know why he named all his dinosaurs Kyle."

"We've been there," Honey says, smiling sympathetically. "Blue Puppy and Pink Puppy are always going missing."

Hank gives her a grateful nod, then his eyes slide over to me. I attempt a smile, but my mouth refuses to open, so I end up stretching my mouth in a way that makes me feel like a depressed jack-o'-lantern.

"Stop making that face," Honey hisses as Hank grabs a chair and drags it into the circle.

"I can't help it," I whisper back.

"Thank you for coming, Hank," Sean says. "As you all know, the Baileyville Street Fair is reliant on the generosity of our community. We don't charge admission, but we do ask for donations to keep the fair running with the quality programming our town is accustomed to."

I manage to keep myself from yelling, "Get to the point, Sean," but seriously . . . what does this have to do with why Hank is here?

"You may remember that we wanted to bring the ABBA tribute band back, but they canceled on us at the last minute, and I was left scrambling for a replacement act."

"I remember," I say. "You put out an SOS."

"'Mamma mia!' you yelled," Honey adds.

Sean frowns at us. "What?"

"They're ABBA songs . . ." I trail off. "You know what? Never mind."

"It's too bad they canceled. They were transcendent," Hotpants Ed says, looking heavenward as if thanking God himself for their performance of "Winner Takes It All" (which, to be fair, made us all cry and was a topic of conversation for weeks afterward).

"You just liked them because they wore those tight little jumpsuits," Barb says.

Hotpants Ed shrugs. "A good look is a good look. If I could pull off a jumpsuit, I would."

Honey and I shoot each other a quizzical glance, then try to pay attention to Sean.

"I was afraid we'd have to rely on Ed for two nights of entertainment," Sean continues, "and while I'm sure everyone in the community would love that, it's a lot to ask of one man. I'm not even sure if Ed knows enough magic tricks for two nights."

Ed smiles. "I do have other talents beside magic, you know. You want a ukulele, accordion, piccolo, *or* tuba performance, you just say the word, Sean. I'm quad instrumental."

Sean holds up a hand. "That won't be necessary. I ran into Hank Tillman down at the store and took the liberty of asking him if he'd be interested in performing."

"And I said yes," Hank says, but gives a nod of apology when Sean shoots him a disappointed look. "Sorry to kill the suspense."

"He did say yes," Sean says, addressing us again. "But, of course, this is subject to board approval. What does everyone think?"

"Oh, I love your music, Hank," Lydia says. "Michael and I picked 'When the World Melts Away' as our first dance at our wedding! So romantic."

"Sounds great to me," says Ed. "Although I'm still willing to play backup piccolo if necessary. Do any of your songs have piccolo solos?"

Hank pauses before responding. "Not *yet*."

"Let's take a vote," Sean says. "All those in favor, say aye."

"Aye," says Hotpants Ed.

"Aye," says Lydia.

"Aye-aye," says Barb.

"You only get one vote, Barb," Sean says.

"I'm aware," she says. "I was just communicating my enthusiasm."

Honey shoots a cautious glance at me, and I give her a tiny nod. I can't stop Hank from being here, after all, and I certainly can't stop the rest of the town from enjoying a performance of his award-winning alt-country jams and/or choosing a song that feels like an arrow through my heart as their wedding song. I'm not a monster.

Honey and I both raise our hands. "Aye," we say in unison.

"It's settled," Sean says with a decisive nod. "Hank Tillman will be the Friday night performer. The other nights will, as usual, showcase performances by the high school band and Ed's magic act."

"I've been practicing a lot over the past year," Ed says, wiggling his eyebrows. "You wouldn't believe the places I can hide a rabbit now."

"Well, don't ruin the surprise," I say.

"Before we adjourn, Sandy, are you still willing to go door to door this weekend to solicit donations?" Sean asks.

"Yes, sir," I say. Even though it sounds like it would be a drag, I actually love asking for fair donations. You'd think knocking on doors and soliciting money would elicit some angry responses, but I know all of these people, and they all love the fair. It's usually an easy morning spent catching up with everyone in town while collecting funds, and nothing is better than feeling useful by basically hanging out with my neighbors all day.

"I can help with that."

It takes me a minute to realize who just spoke. Not Lydia or Barb or even Ed. No, those words came from the mouth of Hank Tillman, the very one who's looking at Sean right now and resolutely avoiding my open-mouthed expression of shock.

"That's a great idea," Sean says, making a note on his clipboard. "You can tell people about your performance and increase donations."

"I can actually do this on my own," I say, words finally making their way out of my mouth. "I don't need any help."

I keep my eyes on Sean as he looks up at me and shakes his head. "No, it will be better if Hank comes with you. I think he'll be much more effective at garnering funds since he's a celebrity and you aren't."

Offended, I look to the rest of the board for backup.

Lydia shrugs. "He has a point," she admits.

I suppress an eye roll. I guess the fact that I've known these people my entire life isn't enough to get them to donate . . . now they need a celebrity?

"Fine," I mutter.

Sean bangs his gavel. "Meeting adjourned!" he calls.

I bolt out of my chair and up the stairs, bursting into the parking lot with a gasp as if I'm surfacing from deep underwater. I run to my car, unlock the door, and slide into the driver's seat before slamming the door shut.

I jump as my passenger door swings open.

"Hey!" Honey shouts, jumping in. "How the hell did you get here so fast?"

I put my hands on my temples. "I can't get away from him, Honey. Hank volunteered to go door to door with me. That's weird. Doesn't he know I'm avoiding him?"

She shrugs. "I guess not. You do keep running into him."

"He's everywhere I look. In every conversation I have. On every soda errand I run. Standing shirtless in front of the Ohio Inn, like some sort of sexy, sweaty vision from my past. It's like the universe is purposely putting Hank in my path." I crane my neck around to look in the back seat. "Is he here right now?"

Honey tilts her head. "I'm not sure you can blame this on the universe. This is a very small town . . . you run into me all the time, and that doesn't mean it's some sort of grand universal plan."

I sigh. "Yes, but seeing you doesn't dredge up painful memories."

She places a hand on her heart. "Aw, you know how to flatter a girl."

"Shut up. You know what I mean."

"Okay, I know I'm joking about this, but seriously, are you okay? Because if going door to door with Hank is too much for you, I will gladly go back in there and give Sean a piece of my mind." She waits patiently for me to say something.

I sigh again. "Seeing him just brings up a lot of bad memories, of all the things I didn't do and all the things that went wrong. Of all the ways he's succeeding beyond his wildest dreams and all the ways I screwed everything up. We said we were going to take over the world, and he did it. I stayed here."

Honey laughs. "You stayed here and took over a thriving business. Maybe that wasn't your original dream, but you're killing it."

"Easy for you to say. You're doing the exact thing you've wanted to do since we were in elementary school."

"Not *exactly*. I'm not married to one of the Hanson brothers," she points out.

"There's still time."

She smiles. "Unfortunately, I'm now in love with my husband, and my feelings for Taylor and his glorious mane are but a distant memory. Sometimes things change when you grow up, you know. That's not always a bad thing."

I nod and exhale. "Yeah, I know."

"C'mere." Honey leans in and attempts to wrap me in a hug, which is hard with the console in between us. "You're a badass, successful businesswoman who smells like manure sometimes."

"Could've left out the last part."

"Honesty is part of our friendship. You can be around Hank, you know. You won't spontaneously combust. Sure, he has some accomplishments under his belt, but you're no slouch."

I smile. "Thanks, Honey. You're a good friend."

"I know." She smiles back. "Now I have to get home, or I'm

going to miss bath time. For the kids, not me. Although maybe that's a good idea for me and Brian after bedtime."

I wrinkle my nose. "Don't flaunt your water-based sex life. I'm lonely and depressed."

She laughs. "See you later, babe."

I wave as she hops out of the car and shuts the door. When I turn the key, the radio turns on, and the DJ tells me that they're about to throw it way back and play a golden oldie.

It's Shania Twain's "You're Still the One."

I groan and rest my head on the steering wheel.

CHAPTER TEN

Fifteen years ago

EVENTUALLY, HANK LEFT for college, leaving me tearfully waving on the front porch as he drove off with his truck packed full of everything he owned. He called me every night, even when I could hear people in his dorm room. Sometimes he'd call me on his flip phone when he was walking down the street or on his way to class. I knew these gestures were supposed to be sweet, but they filled me with ugly, unwanted jealousy. I wanted to be there with *him*, but I also just wanted to be *there*. I wanted to be walking down unfamiliar streets, seeing unfamiliar faces. I wanted the new, the exciting, the other. And every time I talked to him, I remembered that I had the old, the usual, the familiar.

And the *guilt*. Hank spent so much time talking to me that he could've spent doing other things. Practicing. Meeting new people. Actually pursuing his dreams instead of having his dorm room phone glued to his ear while everyone around him had a good time. He would talk about visiting me when I knew he had more important things to do. Hank was special. He didn't deserve to have some deadweight back home dragging him down.

But I knew he'd be coming back home for the fair. The Baileyville Street Fair was kind of our town's version of homecoming—everyone came back for the fried Oreos (an underappreciated delicacy) and corn dogs, the Ferris wheel that was constructed right in the middle of town, the crowning of Miss Baileyville, and the pumpkin contest, which somehow managed to grow bigger and more impressive each year.

But the main reason to come back for the fair was that it was a place to see and be seen. By going to the fair, you were basically a Hollywood actress who knowingly picked a paparazzi-heavy spot to ensure she'd be photographed while looking great. Everyone would be crammed onto that shutdown street, trying to maneuver their way over the taped-down cords with a stroller, and it was your duty as a small-town citizen to go out and be happy to see them. Or at least convincingly fake it and then tell all your friends who you ran into later.

So while Hank might have just left, of course he was coming back for the fair. Pretty much everyone was—Brian and I were still around, and Honey was coming back like she did every weekend, but almost all the kids who went away to school were making special trips back for this, even though it was right after school started. That was the power of the Baileyville Street Fair—who cared if it was your first or second weekend in college? The fair waited for no one.

Our short phone conversations were nothing compared to seeing him in person. I needed the hit of his soft scent, his warm arms, his Hankness. I'd been feeling off since he left . . . since *everyone* left, really. I felt so disconnected from the classmates I'd grown up with. I liked Brian, but there was a limited amount of time you could spend hanging out with your best friend's boyfriend before things got weird. And other than that, it was basically me, the elderly people of Baileyville, and a few stragglers I'd never been close to.

My loneliness felt like a tangible mass in my body, like it was curling its tentacles around my organs and leeching out my hope. It was hard to block out the constant loop that played in my head: *You're a loser. You're left behind. Everyone else has big dreams, but not you. You don't have anything. You're alone.* I knew those things weren't true, but I couldn't stop thinking them, and soon they'd crowded out every other thought in my brain.

Being around Hank would help, I knew. Hank always did. Even in our very first awkward moments together, I'd never felt anything less than myself with him, and I couldn't wait for him to be back.

My parents' house was only one block away from Main Street, which meant that we could hear the noise of the fair from our front porch—the rides, the thrilled shrieks of kids, the music from the carousel. Hank wasn't supposed to get in for a few hours, so I took my time getting ready in my room. I didn't typically expend a ton of effort on my appearance—what was the point, I figured, when I always ended up looking like me? But I wanted to look pretty for Hank, so I put on a simple floral top and jeans, feeling like a small-town girl in a movie.

I was swiping on mascara when my phone buzzed. I almost stuck myself in the eye with the mascara wand when I saw that it was Hank.

"Hello?" I answered quickly.

"Hey," he said, his low voice sending a quick jolt to my heart the way it always did. "Have you looked on your porch lately?"

"Why?" I asked suspiciously, the phone to my ear as I went down the stairs.

"Look out the front door," he urged me, a smile in his voice.

Through the lace curtains that covered the window in the door, I could see a figure standing on the porch. I swung open the door and there was Hank, leaning against the post, wearing a white T-shirt and his worn-out jeans and looking at me like I was a sunrise or a love song or a hot apple fritter from Betty's Diner.

"Hank!" I shouted as he flipped his phone shut and I dropped mine on the porch. I launched myself into his arms, and he easily held me up, spinning me around as I kissed him.

"Whoa," he said, laughing into my mouth. "I could get used to this kind of greeting."

"I didn't expect you for a couple hours!" I said, wrapping my arms around his neck. "I only have mascara on one eye."

He leaned his head back, studying my face. "Even with your shockingly uneven makeup, you're still the most beautiful girl I've ever seen."

"I've never heard anything more romantic in my life," I said. "You know, my parents are over at the inn right now."

"Actually," Hank said, carrying me into the house, "you're giving me some competition for the most romantic words ever spoken."

"YOU SURE YOU don't mind meeting up with everyone?" Hank asked later as I locked the door behind us.

"Of course I don't mind," I said, skipping down the steps. Truthfully, I would've been happier walking around with only Hank, but I was fine with seeing everyone else. I'd do anything as long as I was holding his hand.

"Cool," he said, his fingers squeezing mine. Walking down

the sidewalk with him, smiling as the smell of hot oil and French fries beckoned us closer to Main Street, I finally felt like myself again. I took a deep breath in, appreciating it.

"Everything okay?" Hank asked.

I nodded, fully relaxed for the first time in weeks. "Better than okay," I said.

We'd agreed to meet up with everyone by the gazebo, so after we grabbed an order of piping hot fries and doused them in vinegar, we walked on over.

Honey and Brian were already there, and she gave us a two-handed wave when she saw us. She wrapped me in a hug as if we hadn't seen each other last weekend and talked on the phone two days ago. "I missed you," she groaned.

"I missed you, too," I said, pulling back and admiring her OSU T-shirt. "Nice look. Very collegiate."

She rolled her eyes. "Natasha messaged me and was like, 'Let's all wear our college gear for the fair!'"

I glanced at Brian, who shrugged at me, seemingly unbothered. I didn't think BCC even had merchandise, other than a water bottle and a key chain they gave us at orientation (which was mostly a presentation in a lecture hall about parking permits, not a full weekend extravaganza like everyone else's). Natasha Stevenson and I had never been super close, mostly because Honey and I always thought she was a little pretentious, but it still stung that apparently everyone else got the message to wear their college shirts.

Brian didn't care, so I tried to act like I didn't, either. "Oh, cool," I said as casually as possible, glancing at Hank. "Where's yours? No Berklee pride?"

He rubbed the back of his neck. "I have a hoodie in the truck. In case it gets cold."

Honey peppered Hank with questions about college life until Natasha showed up, wearing a fitted Oberlin T-shirt and looking, somehow, different. She'd only been in a more northern part of Ohio for two weeks, and yet she had the air of someone who'd spent a year abroad.

As the fair got more crowded and the air filled with the smell of fried vegetables, fried apples, fried meat, and fried everything, more of our friends floated into the group; each person met with a chorus of cheers and a flurry of hugs. Even Shelby wandered over and gave me a nod as she focused on whatever delicacy she was eating.

I was half listening to Burger tell a story about a "sick" beer luge when Hank leaned over and said, "Hey." Even after all the time we'd been together, the sound of his voice was still like a warm sweater on a cold day. "I'm gonna go grab a lemonade. You want one?"

"No, I think I'll share yours but then drink all of it," I told him, smiling.

He grinned. "Yeah, I'll get you one. Be right back."

The group kept talking, Honey telling a story about a girl in her dorm who got foot fungus from not wearing flip-flops in the dorm showers.

"I thought that was an urban legend," I said.

Honey shook her head. "Foot fungus is no urban legend, unfortunately. She showed all of us the damage, and let me tell you, it was pretty disgusting."

"Oh shit," Natasha said, and at first I thought she was admonishing Honey for talking too much about foot fungus. But she continued, "Greg's over there. I don't want him to see me."

Greg Boyle, a classmate who went away to Miami University,

walked past us, clearly avoiding looking in Natasha's direction. I'd forgotten all about their big breakup right after graduation.

"He's gone," Honey said, watching as Greg disappeared behind a gyro stand. "And I don't think you have anything to worry about with Greg, anyway. He's too nice to be a jerk to you."

Natasha sighed, slumping her shoulders in relief. "I know. That's why it was so hard to break up with him. He's a great guy! But, like, who wants to go to college with a boyfriend at home, you know?"

She started to laugh, then stopped, pointing at Honey and Brian. "Oh, wait, I didn't mean you guys. Obviously you guys are different!"

Honey looked completely unoffended. Of course, she'd never even considered breaking up with Brian for a second, and Brian didn't look like he was worried about being left behind. They looked like two people completely secure in their love for each other, not even caring about Natasha running her mouth.

But I noticed that no one mentioned Hank and me. No one even remembered that I was there now that Hank was in the apparently never-ending lemonade line, which gave me plenty of time to wonder if this was how he felt about me. Did he feel stuck, attempting to have a social life at college with a girlfriend back home? Was I some kind of burden to him?

I stepped back from the group, craning my neck to see if I could find Hank. Just groups of teenagers, little kids jumping off the picnic tables, and old people eating funnel cakes. If he would only come back, I'd feel better.

"You think she ever gets tired of the sound of her own voice?"

I jumped, then saw Shelby standing right next to me, picking at a grease-soaked paper container full of fried Oreos.

"Who?" I asked. "Natasha?"

"She's like, 'Oh, let's all wear our college shirts,' and 'OMG, did you know my dining hall has sushi?' and 'College guys are sooo much hotter than the guys here in Baileyville.'" Shelby rolled her eyes.

I pointed to Shelby's tank top. "I see you're not wearing college gear, either."

Shelby shook her head. "We don't have T-shirts at cosmetology school. I guess I could make one out of puffy paint on a T-shirt. Maybe it would say, 'Please let me do your eyebrows, Natasha, they look like shit.'"

I laughed, then sobered up. "Her eyebrows look fine."

She looked at me, her (perfect) eyebrows raised. "Lying to people doesn't do them any favors. I could stand here and tell you that your black eyeliner looks good, but it's much kinder to let you know that you'd look less washed out in a dark brown."

I paused. "Uh, thanks, I guess?"

"You're welcome." She held out a fried Oreo. "Want one? I literally think I'm gonna puke on the sidewalk if I eat all of them. There's, like, a ton of oil in these."

"Well, you're really selling them, so okay." I grabbed one and put it in my mouth. "This is amazing," I attempted to say with my mouth full.

"I know. And Natasha's eyebrows *are* bad," Shelby said, studying Natasha with her eyes narrowed. "She's overplucking. All the Oberlin shirts in the world aren't gonna hide that."

I chewed my Oreo and Shelby continued muttering, "Over there acting like she spent the summer in Greece. Give me a break. She's still in Ohio."

"That's exactly what I said." I turned to Shelby, and we both smiled at each other. It felt a bit like declaring a truce.

"Hey. What'd I miss?" Hank slid a lemonade into my hand before he put an arm around me.

"Not much," I said, turning to smile at him. But then I noticed what he was wearing—his Berklee hoodie. He was slightly out of breath, probably because he had to run back to his truck to get it. My heart sank a little bit. Now it was only me, Brian, and Shelby without college gear, the three of us who'd been left behind. But Brian seemed happy to be with Honey, and Shelby was content to point out perceived beauty flaws.

I wasn't happy or content with this, though. I felt awkward around Hank for the first time as everyone shared stories about their dining halls or their weird roommates or the gross showers in their dorms. I could imagine them all walking around on their quads (quads were a thing you had in college, right? We certainly didn't have one at BCC . . . we had a few buildings and some side-walks), carrying textbooks and discussing, I don't know, Foucault or something. Never mind that I was also taking an Intro to Phi-losophy course as an elective, and I could probably discuss Fou-cault, too. Their imaginary Foucault discussions seemed . . . more intelligent. More collegiate.

"Hey," I whispered in Hank's ear. "I'm actually not feeling well. I think that fried Oreo kinda upset my stomach."

"I can't believe the fried Oreo betrayed you," Hank joked as he rubbed his hand across my back. "You wanna head home?"

"Um, yeah, but you don't need to come. I just want to go to sleep, so can we catch up tomorrow?"

Hank's brow furrowed. "No, I'll come with you. We can watch TV or something. I'd way rather be with you than here with ev-eryone else."

But then a big burst of laughter went through the group. Honey was doubled over with the giggles, Natasha clapped her hands, and Burger's face was red from laughing so hard. Hank glanced over at them, and I saw the disappointment that he'd missed the joke flash over his face.

"No, seriously, I'm really tired. You stay here, okay?"

"Okay," Hank said cautiously. "If you're sure."

"I'm sure," I said with a resolute nod.

He leaned forward and kissed me, like we weren't in a crowd of our friends.

"Keep it in your pants, Tillman!" Burger shouted, and everyone laughed.

"I'm gonna head out," I said, giving everyone a weak wave. Honey looked at me with concern, but I tried to give her a convincing smile. "See everyone later!"

As I started walking back to my parents' place, Shelby fell into step alongside me. "It's annoying, right?" she asked.

"What is?" I asked.

She shrugged. "Being around everyone else when we're here. Seeing the same things. Seeing the same people."

I was so surprised to hear someone else say it aloud that I almost stopped walking. "You feel like that, too?"

She rolled her eyes again. Shelby was *very* good at rolling her eyes. "Just because I look better than anyone else in this town doesn't mean I don't have feelings."

I shook my head in disbelief. "Your confidence is amazing."

"Well, I don't feel very confident when I'm around those jerks," she said. "Sorry. I know one of them is your boyfriend. But I don't need my nose rubbed in the fact that I made different choices than them, you know?"

"Yeah," I said. Because I did know, even if I didn't make a choice so much as have a choice forced on me.

We'd made it to my house, so I pointed toward the porch. "You wanna come in?"

She shook her head. "Nah. I've got an early morning tomorrow at Betty's. I'm only working there until I get my license, and then I can officially be a stylist over at Hair Affair," she said firmly, and once again, I was struck by how sure of herself she was.

"Don't let them make you feel bad," I said. "You have dreams, too, and you know what you want. Even if you don't have a T-shirt."

She smiled back at me. "Thanks, Sandy. We should hang out sometime. Since we're both around, and all. Might as well, right?"

"Might as well," I said, then gave her a wave as she walked off toward her parents' place a few streets over.

I shut the door and barely made it upstairs before I started crying. I flung myself on my bed, the pillow muffling my sobs. Here I was on the same twin bed I'd had my whole life with the same floral comforter I got when I was eight years old and we redecorated my room. Even though I was all alone, I was embarrassed to be crying about this. The fact that I didn't go away to some big fancy college? Boo-hoo. Lots of people didn't.

But that didn't change the fact that I didn't want to be here.

Downstairs, someone knocked on the door, and then it squeaked open. I sat up and quickly wiped my eyes with my hands as if that would fix whatever mess of mascara and eyeliner was going on.

"Hello?" called Honey's voice, and I relaxed.

"I'm up here!" I said, then listened to the old wooden stairs creak under her feet.

"Hey," she said, and then, "What's wrong?" as soon as she saw my tearstained face. I hadn't even turned on my bedside lamp, and I knew I looked pathetic sitting in the dim fall early-evening light in my little kid room as the sounds of the fair swirled outside.

"Nothing," I said.

She sat down beside me. "It's a good thing you don't want to become an actress, because that was an extremely unconvincing performance."

She looked at me with a total lack of judgment, like she always did. Honey was my best friend. I could tell her anything . . . and so I did.

"I felt like garbage tonight with everyone wearing their college clothes and talking about their dorms and their dining halls and their classes," I said. "I don't have a dorm because this is where I sleep. The same place I've slept my whole life. My dining hall is my kitchen, and our grocery store doesn't even have hummus, let alone sushi. And, yeah, I'm taking classes but they're here. In Baileyville. Not somewhere far away and exciting and full of new people."

She put an arm around me and I started to cry again. "And I don't even have a T-shirt!"

"I'm sorry my dumb story about foot fungus made you feel bad," she said, putting her head on my shoulder. "And I'm sorry we were talking about college so much. That sucked of us."

"Normally I would've loved a story about foot fungus. You know that."

"And I didn't even think about the shirts, but you know what? I'm not wearing this shirt again. In fact, I'm burning it." She pulled the OSU shirt over her head and threw it across the room, leaving her sitting there in a hot pink bra.

"Honey." I started laughing. "You're going to have to put your shirt back on eventually. Like to walk back to your car."

"Let them arrest me for public indecency. I don't care," she said, nose in the air.

Eventually, she did put on one of my old T-shirts, and we

watched some reality show about an aging former rock star who was attempting to date various women while they all drove across the country on a tour bus. It was a nice distraction, especially because Honey made jokes like, "I think he's wearing more eye makeup than any of the contestants," and "Do you think he even has hair under that bandana?" and for at least a little bit, I forgot about what had happened at the fair.

But when she left and I was all alone, Natasha's words played in my head. Did Hank want to go to college with a girlfriend back at home? Was I only holding him down?

It was not something I wanted to think about, but suddenly, it was *all* I could think about.

Chapter Eleven

Present day

I WISH I could go back and tell high school Sandy, the one who quietly told her gym teacher she had "feminine problems" so she could sit in the bleachers and read a book instead of suffering through volleyball, that one day she would not only voluntarily commit to physical activity, but she would love it. I attend a yoga class in the basement of the Unitarian church; I go on hikes; I wake up early to run on a regular basis. And if I don't, my mind feels foggy, my bones creak, and my back hurts. Growing up really does mess with your body *and* your mind.

Luckily, Toby loves to run even more than I do. He isn't a fan of distances, but that's okay, because neither am I. Sure, we won't be signing up for a marathon anytime soon, but an easy two miles suits us just fine.

Lord knows I need to clear my mind this morning after yesterday's board meeting and the revelation that Hank Tillman will be sticking around, so I lace up my shoes and we hit the Baileyville Bike Trail. The trail, which is built on the bed of a railroad that existed long ago, starts in town and snakes along the river, down the highway, and out into the country. It's peaceful and never all that crowded.

Which is why it seems like another smack in the face from fate when, as I run across the renovated bridge that crosses the river, I see Hank Tillman rounding the corner in front of me, emerging from the shade of the trees lining the trail.

"Holy shit," I mutter under my breath as he gets closer, and I stop running. This is my breaking point. This time, I'm not going to run away from him (which is too bad since I have the proper footwear, and I'm not holding a case of soda I could drop on myself). If this is fight or flight, I'm all fight, baby, like the angry goose down at the park who flaps its wings to make children get away from its turf. I'm that goose now, and I'm pissed that Hank Tillman keeps showing up.

At least he's wearing a shirt this time.

"Are you stalking me?" I shout.

He slows down in front of me and pulls his AirPods out of his ears. "What?"

He looks good. Damn. He's sweaty, but not in a gross way—in a Hank way, like he's glistening. Like he's on the cover of some movie about cowboys, and all he needs is the hat.

"Are you stalking me?" I repeat. "Because I can't seem to get away from you."

Toby, apparently not picking up the vibe I'm sending out, jumps up on Hank's shoulders and licks his face. Hank doesn't flinch. He pats Toby on the back as he says, "Sorry, I didn't know the bike trail was your private property."

"It's not only the bike trail—Toby, get down—it's the fair board meeting. My parents' inn. And now the bike trail and—*Toby, seriously, get down!* Why are you always around?" I shout.

I cross my arms, frustrated that Toby is fraternizing with the man we're supposed to be avoiding. Toby ignores me and licks Hank's cheek again.

He eases Toby's paws off his shoulders, and Toby sits at his feet as if Hank has a T-bone steak in his pocket. "This town doesn't belong to you, you know."

My jaw drops. I don't know what I expected Hank to do—say, *You know what? You're right. I'll pack my things and leave you alone now instead of tormenting you with my frequently shirtless presence, thus haunting your erotic daydreams when you're zoning out at work.*

Not that I've been doing that or anything.

"I know that," I huff.

"My dad asked me to help your parents with the gutters," he explains, scratching Toby's ears. "I figured it was okay for me to make sure your dad didn't break his other foot."

I rub the toe of my sneaker against the pavement. "I suppose that's true."

"And Sean begged me to perform. What was I supposed to do, say no? You know how charismatic he can be."

I involuntarily snort a laugh, then risk a glance at Hank. He's looking at me with that infuriating half smile, and I shake my head.

"Why are you here?" I ask.

"On the bike trail?" Hank raises his eyebrows.

"No, but also yes, please answer that. Are you into exercise now?" I ask, gesturing vaguely at him as if his shorts and T-shirt encompass the general idea of physical fitness.

He squints. "I guess. I could ask you the same thing."

"Oh, yeah," I say, attempting to be casual. I hop into a quick lunge. "I'm extremely healthy now."

Hank nods, crossing his arms and studying me. "I can see that. Great form."

"Make sure you don't let your knee go past your toes," I say. "Little lunge tip for you."

"I'll remember that," he says. "Next time I'm lunging."

I need to stop rambling about lunges, so I repeat my question from before. "Seriously, why are you in town?"

"Henry and I are visiting my parents," he says without hesitation. "He hasn't seen enough of them in the past five years, and we had some free time, so I figured we'd come here. I didn't plan on sticking around long, but then Sean asked me to perform and, well . . . I guess we're staying through the fair."

I nod slowly. I don't ask him where his wife is right now because, in all honesty, I don't really want to know. Even remembering that Hank has a wife, that he married another woman after I let him go, is enough to send a sharp pang of regret through my heart.

You did this, I remind myself. *You pushed Hank away and he moved on and you have no right to be mad at him about it.*

He rubs the back of his neck, the thing he's always done when he's nervous—which wasn't often, since Hank was the steadiest person I knew. He didn't get angry or yell, making him an infuriating person to argue with.

"I can go, if you want," he finally says. "I don't have to perform at the fair. I know our history is . . . complicated . . . and I'm not here to make your life harder."

I sigh. What am I supposed to say to this? *Yes, Hank, please cut your visit with your family short for my benefit. Oh, could the Baileyville Street Fair use the funds your performance would generate? Big whoop, I'm busy throwing a tantrum like I'm a toddler who dropped her sprinkle cone down at the Dairy Belle.*

This is classic Hank—sacrificing himself and his own needs to make other people happy. I didn't let him do this back when we broke up, and I can't let him do it now.

"I'm sorry," I say, and from the look on his face, both of us are surprised at my apology. "You should stay here. I'm being ridiculous."

"Are you saying," Hank asks thoughtfully, "that this town *is* big enough for the both of us?"

I try to resist a smile, but a treacherous one sneaks onto my face. "Yeah. I guess. If you want to be corny as hell about it."

"Wow, I'm a stalker *and* corny? You're not holding anything back," Hank says.

Toby whines and Hank pets him again.

I cross my arms, trying my best to remain tough.

"How about we declare a truce?" Hank asks, keeping his eyes on mine even as he scratches Toby's ears.

"A truce?" I repeat. "How does that work?"

"It means we work together on the fair . . ."

"And avoid each other the rest of the time," I fill in.

Hank pauses, thinking. "Yeah, sure. If that's what you want."

I think back to it all, watching our whole relationship spool through my mind quickly like a movie. Green grass, blue skies, starlit nights, feet in the river, warm breeze. Everything that happened before it spectacularly crashed and burned.

I give him one firm nod. "Yep. That's what I want."

"Okay," Hank says. "We should be able to handle being professional while we're working on the fair. After all, we're old now."

"Speak for yourself," I say. "Could an elderly person lunge like me?"

He smiles. "Of course not."

We stare at each other for a moment, the only sounds coming from the rush of the river beside us and the jingle of Toby's collar.

He holds out a hand and I stare at it like it's a pointed gun.

"Shake on it," he says.

I take his hand and immediately regret it—if seeing Hank wrecked me, touching him is another level entirely. I've spent years attempting to bury my memories of Hank, attempting to pretend that they don't matter. I've tried to move on, tried to date other guys, pretended to be easy-breezy when Hank's name comes up, like, *Oh, my old boyfriend? I barely even think of him.*

But none of it has worked. Seeing Hank, touching him like this, makes it all comes back to me like it happened yesterday. Like we were just in his truck watching the stars together.

"Passing on the left!" A cyclist in full gear speeds past us, and I drop Hank's hand as I jump.

"Okay." I attempt to discreetly rub my now sweaty hand on my leggings. "So we're good?"

Hank nods. "We're good. See you tomorrow morning."

I frown.

"We're going door to door," he says, his eyes still the most beautiful things I've ever seen. "Remember?"

"Of course," I say quickly. "Donations. Door to door. Tomorrow morning. Got it."

Apparently, I can't speak in full sentences anymore. Hank smiles at me and puts his AirPods back in. "See you around," he says before running off.

It's like my sneakers are stuck in place on the bike trail, because I can't move or do anything but watch Hank run away from me. Toby lets out a small, sad whine, and I pat him on the head.

"Me too, bud," I say. "Me too."

Chapter Twelve

Fifteen years ago

AFTER THE FAIR ended and kids went back to college, pretending that everything was fine got harder and harder. I didn't know when I'd make it out of there, and with each passing day, it seemed less likely that I ever would. When I figured things out, when I was worthy of him, then it would make sense for us to be together. But until then . . . I couldn't do it. Hank deserved better.

I wrote out a script, and I told him on the phone. He needed to focus on school, and I was so busy with my classes and working at the inn. Long distance was too hard. We should see other people. Name a breakup cliché, I used it.

"Sandy, this is ridiculous," he said, his voice breaking. "This isn't worth losing you over. Nothing is. I'm moving back."

I panicked. That was exactly what I didn't want—Hank throwing away his future for me. So I said the only thing that I knew would make him stay gone.

"I don't love you anymore," I said. "Not the way I used to. We've grown apart, Hank, and I can't do this."

He was silent, and eventually, I hung up. I collapsed onto my bed and sobbed. I cried so hard that I thought I'd float away—I couldn't believe I'd thrown away the best thing I'd ever had. The *only* thing I had.

But I still knew it was the only decision I could make, because I couldn't help Hank succeed. I could only hold him back.

I USED WHAT I learned in my marketing classes to help out at the Ohio Inn. I made the website functional, I redesigned the brochures, and I contributed some of my artwork for the dining room. In fact, that was about all the painting I was doing. Between school and work and the fact that painting made me remember exactly how much of a failure I was, I didn't have much time for it.

Life wasn't a book with a series of mistakes and miscommunications that led to a happily ever after—it was real life, where everything didn't happen for a reason. I wasn't a Jane Austen heroine. I was Sandy Macintosh, resident of Baileyville, and I was staying here.

I don't like to think about what happened after that, about the dark places my brain went and the depression I encountered. I stopped getting out of bed and started skipping classes. I'd thought Hank and I would be stargazing in a whole new part of the country; instead, I was spending my time memorizing the swirled plaster pattern on my bedroom ceiling. I left my room only for meals, sitting silently through dinner as worry radiated off my parents, and they asked gentle questions like, "So do you think you'll feel up to going to class tomorrow?" They didn't know what to do because I'd never caused a problem before—they were used to me being the self-motivated overachiever I'd been in high school, the one who never needed a reminder to do her homework, the one who independently worked her way through a self-made reading list so as to be better prepared for standardized tests. I was used to her, too—I missed her, but I worried that version of Sandy was gone forever. Maybe she'd crammed herself into Hank's truck along with all his belongings and sped off toward Boston, never to be seen again.

Eventually I hit rock bottom, which involved Honey finding me in my room, unshowered for a week, my hair forming a nest worthy of a medium-sized rodent and my clothes stained with Hot Pocket filling. Seeing the worry on my best friend's face—not to mention finally realizing how much I was upsetting my parents—helped me realize this was my one life. I wasn't going to waste any more time wishing it could be different. And also, there are only so many Hot Pockets one woman can eat before she realizes she has to make a change.

I started working at the greenhouse because Honey reminded me that being outside was good for me, but I still made time to help out at the inn—filling up my time was the objective. Idle hands are the devil's workshop, and an idle mind is a depressed girl's playground. Better to keep things as busy as possible—if I didn't have time to think, then I could pretend I was happy.

And after a while, I was. Kind of. Well, satisfied anyway. Honey and Brian got married while she was still in school, and they started having kids right away. I knew they could use my help, so I babysat whenever I could.

There were always other people in Baileyville who needed me.

The Street Fair Board, of course. The library needed volunteers to deliver books to homebound residents, like old Mr. Anderson, who could no longer walk to the library himself and somehow managed to request several new books about World War II every week. There was always a bake sale that needed cookies or someone to run the booth or someone to call and coordinate donations. There was no shortage of things I could do, activities that could fill up my time and make me stop thinking about Hank. So I did them.

I didn't put my paints away entirely. Shortly after I broke up with Hank, I decided to paint that magnificent moment when he first took me up to the barn. Him on the ground, the sun shining down on us, the grass so gloriously green in the early spring. I painted it and then I put it away. It had happened, and it had been wonderful, but now it was over. Like those big, silly dreams I had. Some people, like Honey, like my mom, like Hank, could follow their dreams and get exactly what they wanted. But that didn't happen for everyone, and it was foolish to pretend that it did. Some of us needed to get better dreams.

I kept painting, but only on the smallest canvases. Little four-by-six rectangles that I smeared with colors—tiny Baileyville sunsets, the river at sunrise, the trees out by the reservoir. My dreams stayed small now, like they were supposed to. Contained.

A few years after Hank had left town, I drove up to the old barn one night. I don't know why—I guess I felt like torturing myself. But when I got up there, the barn was gone. At first I thought I was in the wrong place, but then I got out of my car and walked around—I could see where it had been, a faint outline in the grass. It had been falling apart back when Hank and I had kissed there, his arms around me as we stood on that dirt floor—

either it finally collapsed or the Tillmans tore it down. Mr. Tillman, handyman that he was, probably used the barn wood to make something else.

I knew it was only a barn, but it felt like a symbol of our relationship. Once upon a time, beautiful things happened there, but then it all fell apart, leaving only emptiness where it used to stand.

CHAPTER THIRTEEN

Present day

"DID WE SERIOUSLY call this many people last year?" Honey asks, her phone in one hand and her pen poised over a piece of paper. We're sitting at the island in her sun-filled kitchen this afternoon calling our list of potential bakers for the fair's cake auction.

One of the best things about my house is that it's only three houses away from Honey's. As kids, when Honey lived way out in the country and I lived in town and we had to beg our parents to drive us to each other's homes, we used to dream about living right beside each other. "Close enough that, if one of us wanted a cookie, we could open our kitchen windows and hand one over," Honey used to say.

That's not exactly what happened, but it would still only take me about thirty seconds to walk a cookie over, so I'm counting this one in the "dreams I actually accomplished" category.

I take a bite of the snickerdoodles I made, because we really do bring each other cookies as often as possible. "Remember how it took us all day, and we swore we wouldn't volunteer for cake auction duty again this year?"

Honey stares at the list thoughtfully. "Wow, I totally erased that memory. This is like childbirth—every time I told myself I would never go through that again, but the next thing I knew, I was there on that hospital bed begging them for an epidural."

"I really hope today won't be *that* much like childbirth," I say with a grimace.

"Well, it's a lot less messy, that's for sure," Honey mutters as Brian walks into the kitchen with their toddler, Maddie, on his hip.

"Rosie and Charlie are fighting over a game of Mouse Trap gone awry," he says calmly, opening the fridge.

"Has anyone drawn blood?" Honey asks, not taking her eyes off her list.

"Nah," Brian says.

"I wanna cookie!" Maddie shouts.

"And I want to not deal with a sugar rush, so we're gonna have to agree to disagree on that one," Brian says, toasting a sippy cup of milk at me before walking into the other room.

I feel it again—that pang of longing. Not for Brian—he and Honey have been together since junior high, and he's like a brother/unpaid handyman to me. But much like with Marcia and her wife, I'm longing for that feeling of having a person. One other human being you know you can turn to, no matter what. Someone to be a team with you against the world, or against the tiny people in your home who're attempting to start a riot because of Mouse Trap.

Honey had Rosie, her first kid, in her last year of vet school. Vet school isn't exactly known for being a super-chill environment in which to raise a child, but she and Brian got through the stress by leaning on Honey's parents (and me). Once Honey graduated and started working at Baileyville Veterinary Clinic, Brian quit his job, which he'd never liked all that much anyway, to be a stay-at-home dad. And as she had Charlie and Maddie and eventually took over the clinic, he blossomed. It turned out he was not only great at being a stay-at-home parent, but he loved it.

It all made me a little bit jealous. The stability and the loyalty, being able to count on someone else. Knowing that another person had seen and loved you through every awkward stage—braces, acne, teenage growth spurts—and stayed there. It gave me an ache somewhere inside.

"I'm not even gonna bother calling Missy Jordan," Honey said, crossing her name off the list. "Last year, she brought an ice cream cake, like she didn't know the cake auction takes place at noon outdoors. And then she had the nerve to be all, 'Well, everyone loves ice cream cake!' Yeah, I *do* love an ice cream cake, but not when it's a puddle, Missy. Be serious."

I laugh. "Do you need a break? This attitude isn't becoming of a Baileyville Street Fair Board member."

Honey sighs. "I'm sorry, I'm still annoyed because this morning at the clinic, someone tried to convince me that a raccoon had impregnated their cat, no matter how many times I told them that was impossible. I gotta shake it off. This is for the cakes."

"You mean the kids."

"The cakes and the fine children of the Baileyville High School Marching Band," Honey said. "Someday my own children will be there, playing whatever instrument is lightest and cheapest, and they'll be glad I spent so much time raising money to buy them new uniforms."

"I'm sure they'll be extremely grateful for band uniforms and their mother's sacrifices," I say. "The two things children are most known for appreciating."

"Well, *I* don't appreciate your sarcasm," Honey says, then her eyes brighten. "Ooh, I remembered we have something way more exciting to talk about than the cake auction! Aren't you and Hank going door to door tomorrow? What are you gonna wear? Do you have anything that says, 'I'm a sophisticated, sexy, grown woman who's totally killing it, and I don't even *care* that you're married'?"

I try to grab her list. "Why don't you let me call Missy Jordan? I'll explain the melting point of ice cream to her. We'll have a little laugh. It'll be fun."

"Boo," Honey says. "How am I supposed to live vicariously through you if you won't even share any details? I've already read all the Amish romance novels at the library, Sandy. I need drama."

I sigh. "I ran into Hank on the bike trail this morning."

Honey gasps. "He really is everywhere! What did you do?"

I lean over the counter. "I asked him if he was stalking me and then felt bad for being mean."

She nods. "That sounds like you."

"Actually," I say, sitting up straight. "We declared a truce."

Honey raises her eyebrows.

"We're going to work together like two responsible adults who care about the community, and we aren't going to let our past get in the way of a great fair season," I say, folding my hands on the counter.

"That's . . . very mature," Honey says.

"And it wasn't even as bad being around him as I thought it would be," I continue. "He didn't rub my nose in the fact that I ruined our whole relationship, and he never tried to make me feel bad for abandoning my dreams while he followed his."

Honey frowns and walks around the counter to me. Since I'm sitting on a stool at her island and she's standing, we're almost eye to eye for once. "Is this what you think? That you ruined your relationship?"

I swallow. "Well, yeah. That's kind of exactly what happened."

Honey smiles gently. "You were a kid, Sandy. You both were. Maybe it's time you let yourself off the hook—you were doing the best you could. And please stop talking about my best friend like she's a huge failure, okay?"

I smile, even as I can feel tears threatening to spill out of my eyes.

"You might not have the exact life you envisioned when you were a kid, but maybe we shouldn't all choose our life paths when we're seventeen."

I frown. "Isn't that what you did? Went into the job you'd always wanted and married your high school sweetheart? You're living your dream."

"Hey, babe?" Brian yells from the living room. "Where's the new pack of Clorox Wipes? There's poop on the wall."

"In the bathroom," Honey yells, then gives me a wry smile. "I'm sorry, what were you saying about my dream life?"

"Why is there poop on the wall?" I whisper, unable to say the words any louder.

Honey shrugs. "At this point, I'm only surprised there isn't poop in *more* places. This is my life. I'm surrounded by excrement."

I wrinkle my nose in disgust.

"Hey," Honey says. "Maybe you and Hank can be friends. You know, now that you're a mature adult and everything."

I think about it for a minute. I can't imagine that will ever happen, that I'll ever be able to be around Hank without picturing the way my life could've been, without remembering that he has a family now and I have an empty home.

"Yeah," I say lightly. "Maybe."

Honey knows I don't mean it—we've always been able to communicate without speaking, so there's no point in lying to her. But she lets me get away with it, and I'm grateful. Instead, she gives me a sympathetic head tilt and wraps me up in a hug.

"You deserve to be happy," she says into my ear. "You know that, right?"

I nod. "I know that."

But deep inside, the part of me that's convinced I did the only right thing by letting Hank go isn't so sure. Sometimes stories end with kisses and weddings and flowers, but sometimes they end with one person alone and lonely. Maybe we all *deserve* happiness, but deserving something doesn't mean we get it.

After all, I tried to take control of my own happiness once, and things didn't exactly go the way I'd planned.

Chapter Fourteen

Eight years ago

I PICKED AT my plate of cold chicken and congealed cream sauce, half listening to the groomsman next to me talk about his job at a bank. I nodded and interjected a few "Oh, wow, that sounds really hard" comments as he complained about his work and didn't ask a single question about mine.

But it was fine. I wasn't here to hang out with Derek the groomsman, after all. I was here in Chicago for my cousin Katie's wedding. This was years after my breakup with Hank, and I'd grown up. I wasn't that aimless, hopeless high school girl anymore . . . now I was an adult who owned a greenhouse and worked for herself.

The ceremony had been lovely, and I even sort of liked my bridesmaid dress. As bridesmaid dresses go, it bore a passing resemblance to a regular old dress—no poofy sleeves, no puffy skirt, and a nice, flattering purple color.

The wedding DJ's voice boomed over the crowd, cutting off Derek, who'd been monologuing for about fifteen minutes. "And now, I'd like to welcome to the dance floor for the first time . . . Mr. and Mrs. Shannon!"

The lights dimmed, the music started, and the crowd issued a collective "aw" when they realized what song was playing: "You're Still the One" by Shania Twain.

I froze. *What are the chances?* I asked myself silently. *What are the chances that Katie would pick this almost twenty-year-old song?*

"Damn, they went for a classic," Derek said. "You know this song?"

I shot him a look. "Of course I know this song. Everyone knows this song."

He shrugged.

I felt something well up inside me. I missed Hank. I already knew I did, of course—every time I went on some pointless date, every time I painted my tiny paintings by myself, every time I got stuck talking to a guy like Derek who didn't care about anything but himself—but I never allowed myself to think about it. But now the words were in my mind, flashing lights I couldn't ignore. *I missed Hank.*

I pulled out my phone under the table and searched for his name. All of a sudden, I had to see him, had to remember his face—the same face I'd spent years trying to block out.

Derek craned his neck, attempting to look at the phone in my lap. "What are you doing?"

If I counted the question about whether I recognized the Shania song, this was the second thing Derek had asked me tonight. I appreciated the attempt, but that didn't mean I wanted to talk to him about it. "Nothing. Don't worry about it."

"Hey," Derek said, and I looked up from my phone to find him staring at me with more intensity than he had all night.

"Yeah?" I asked.

He gestured toward the door where we'd entered the ballroom. "I passed a supply closet out there when we were on our way in. You wanna, you know . . ."

He wiggled his eyebrows for a moment as I stared at him.

"Do I wanna *what*?" I asked slowly.

He sighed as if he was explaining something obvious. "Would you like to go hook up in the supply closet?"

When my jaw dropped and I didn't say anything, he helpfully added, "With me."

"Oh, my God," I muttered, standing up and grabbing the decorative shawl Katie had given the bridesmaids to wear with our dresses. Weddings must've made up about ninety percent of the shawl industry.

"Is that a no?" Derek called as I walked away, rolling my eyes.

Shania Twain's voice faded out as "Love Shack" started playing, and people jumped up from their tables to make their way to the dance floor.

I found a quiet corner and clicked on one of Hank's pictures. He was holding a guitar, sitting at a microphone, a flannel shirt rolled up to show off his forearms. He smiled at something or someone out of frame, one of those smiles I used to see so often and never took for granted.

I missed that smile. I missed *him*.

I clicked on his website and gasped when I saw his tour dates. He was in Chicago. *Tonight.* Playing a small concert venue that was also a bar.

This had to be a sign. Shania Twain, me missing him, us being in the same city—surely this *had* to mean something. I'd already screwed things up for us once by breaking up with him and forcing him away—I wasn't going to let another chance pass me by.

I didn't deserve Hank back then, back when I didn't know

what I was doing. But now, I was grown up and worthy of him. If the universe was sending me a sign via my cousin Katie's first dance, I was going to listen this time.

I jostled my way through the crowd of revelers bang, banging on the door and found Derek.

"Oh, hey," he said, looking away from another bridesmaid he was talking to. "You change your mind? Because I found someone else, but she can wait. You can wait, right?" he asked the other woman, who looked at him with disgust.

"No, Derek, gross." I rolled my eyes. "No one wants to hook up with you in the supply closet. Can you tell Katie I had to run out for a minute? I'll be back."

Derek thought for a moment. "I can say I'll tell her that, but if I'm being honest, I'm probably gonna get distracted and forget."

I leaned over to the other bridesmaid, who I'd only interacted with a little bit. "Can you tell Katie I'm going somewhere for a little bit?"

She nodded, shooting Derek one last suspicious look before walking away. I turned on my heels and ran as fast as I could toward the parking lot.

THE CAB DROPPED me off right in front of the bar, and I took a deep breath of the cool night air and car exhaust before I walked in. It had been years since I'd seen Hank's face, and now I was about to see him following his dream. The one I'd been afraid I'd get in the way of all those years ago.

The inside of the venue was noisy, and the doorman definitely gave my outfit a once-over (okay, so maybe the bridesmaid dress didn't really look like a normal dress, and maybe my elaborate updo wasn't the hairstyle of choice for most people there), but once I was inside, I was part of the crowd. I felt comfort in blending in, in being "some lady" instead of "Sandy, formerly of Hank-and-Sandy fame."

I heard his voice before I saw him. I was still pushing my way through the bar area and couldn't quite see the stage around the two tall men in front of me (because no matter how tall you are, there will always be someone taller standing in front of you at a show), but I'd know that voice anywhere. Sandpaper and honey, calloused fingers and smooth wrists. All of it as familiar to me as the Baileyville landscape. All of it, the rolling hills and the summer green and the golden light, was right there in Hank's voice.

The song ended, and once people stopped clapping, Hank started talking. If his singing voice brought me back to Baileyville, his speaking voice was like a quick nostalgia shot to the heart. I tried to stay upright—the last thing I wanted was to faint in this random bar all by myself.

"Thanks so much for coming out tonight," Hank said, eyes on his guitar. "I've got one last song, and it's a new one. Something from the next album. It's called 'Never Enough.'"

He looked up and into the crowd, and although I knew it couldn't be true—the lights on him were bright and there were so many people here—I could swear his eyes snagged on me, just for a second.

He looked back down, and his fingers began to move on the guitar. It was beautiful, like it always was. I couldn't catch all the lyrics in the noise of the bar, but a few poked through the crowd and pierced my heart.

I wanted this to work, babe, before everything went black.
Love should set you free, it should never hold you back.

I'd been unconsciously swaying to the song like everyone else, but at those words, I stopped. They sounded pretty if you weren't listening too close, but once you thought about them, they were devastating. Was it me he was singing about? It had to be. Someone holding you back? Trying to make something work? I'd avoided listening to the lyrical content of Hank's songs too closely for fear of seeing myself, but now I was confronted with the truth—Hank was singing a song about me, and it wasn't entirely flattering.

He hadn't been secretly pining for me these past few years. He'd been glad I let him go, because I was only holding him back, just like I'd thought.

I turned and pushed my way to the bar. I'd head back to the wedding reception, but what was the harm in a drink first?

I found an open barstool and ordered a whiskey. My shoulders slumped as I entertained myself by half watching the sports coverage that was on the television, where Doris Burke was talking to LeBron James. Doris Burke and LeBron James—two people who certainly hadn't stayed depressed and stagnant. Maybe I had to accept that there were people in the world like Doris, LeBron, and Hank who followed their dreams and did big things. And then there were people like Sandy Macintosh, who stayed behind. There were more of us, of course, but I'd never know their names, just like they'd never know mine, because none of us ever did anything to make our names known. We'd never be on television, never be in magazines, never be household names. When we died, no one would ever even know we existed.

I was going to cry into this whiskey at some random bar, I realized. It sounded like a song Hank would write.

"Sandy?"

I wiped a tear off my face and looked over my shoulder, then almost fell off my barstool. "Hank?"

He was there. Standing directly behind me and then sitting down on the stool beside me. It all felt like some particularly cruel dream, the kind I'd wake up from sad and angry, but it was real.

"I thought I saw you," he said, his voice half excitement and half confusion. "But I thought, *There's no way Sandy would be here in Chicago at one of my shows.*"

He really needed to stop saying my name. "Here I am!" I said brightly.

"What are you doing here? I mean, why are you—" He shook his head.

I forced myself to smile. "No, I get it. This is weird. I'm actually in town for my cousin Katie's wedding. Hence . . ." I gestured to the dress and the hair.

Hank grinned. "I thought you had a slightly different style than I remembered."

"Don't worry, back in Baileyville, I've kept up my all-jeans lifestyle. I haven't started wearing shiny dresses and elaborate up-dos for my outings to Tillman's."

He laughed and I groaned. "I actually thought this would be an okay thing to wear. I should've known I would look ridiculous."

Hank stopped laughing and looked at his lap. "You don't look ridiculous. You never look ridiculous."

I needed to change the subject, quickly. "You want a drink?"

He shook his head. "Nah. What are you . . . ?" He gestured toward my glass and then feigned shock. "I'm sorry, I didn't realize you'd upgraded from the Natty Light we used to sneak out of the market."

Now it was my turn to laugh. "We never should've done that. Your dad would've been so pissed if he caught us."

Hank thought about it for a moment. "Yeah, he probably would've. But he would've gotten over it. I mean, he got over me not wanting to run the store."

"Eventually," I said.

"It took a minute." He acknowledged with a nod. "I think he realized I would've been terrible at owning a store. As you know, numbers aren't really my thing. Or sales. Or money, in general."

"Seems like you're doing fine now, moneywise," I said. "I saw you on TV."

He laughed. "This may surprise you, but a few television appearances actually don't guarantee wealth."

I placed my hand on my heart. "I'm sorry, are you telling me you don't live in a mansion with gold-plated toilets?"

He winced. "I had to settle for bronze."

"That's it." I stood up, grabbed my purse. "I can't stay here and associate with a man who owns toilets plated in an inferior metal."

Laughing, he lightly grabbed my arm. "Sit back down."

It might have been the whiskey on an almost empty stomach (I should've eaten more of that lukewarm wedding chicken), but I didn't think that was what made me wobble. It was Hank—his touch, his hand on my arm. I missed my barstool and fell onto him, almost sitting on his lap as my arms pressed up against his chest. The smooth, worn-out flannel could have been one he wore back in high school. His other hand held me in place so I didn't slide to the floor.

My mind exploded with summer evenings and wide starry skies that seemed like they'd never end. Warm breezes that blew my hair in my face. We were in a bar, the clink of glasses and twang of something playing and the shouts of people, but in my head, we were up on that hill, the highest point in Baileyville, looking down at our futures laid out in front of us.

Hank didn't take his eyes off mine, and I realized, with a grateful sigh, that we could still speak to each other with a glance. In the dim light, his eyes were somehow bluer than ever, and I could hear what they were saying over the bar noise, loud and clear: *We belong together.*

"Hank," I said, so close that he could hear my whisper. "I miss you."

He exhaled shakily. "I miss you too, Sandy. I wish we didn't leave things so bad."

I nodded, pressing my lips together. "That was a mistake. That was *my* mistake."

He started to shake his head and opened his mouth, but I didn't let him finish. I leaned forward, pressing my lips into his. His kiss was familiar but exciting, like coming home and traveling the world all at the same time. I could've lived in that moment, in that bar with Hank Tillman, kissing him like my life depended on it.

But he wasn't kissing me back.

He gently pushed me up until I was sitting on my own barstool again. I blinked a few times, shocked.

"Sandy," he said. "I need to tell you something. I should've told you already, but we were talking, and . . ."

He rubbed his hand through his short hair, not meeting my eyes.

"What is it, Hank?" I asked. "Whatever it is, it's okay. Whatever it is, I won't be mad."

He had to know we could overcome anything together. If we'd found our way to a bar in Chicago after years apart, if fate brought us back together, then we were meant to be. We were Hank and Sandy. Everyone knew that.

"Hey, baby!"

A woman squirmed her way through the crowd and latched onto Hank, giving him a big kiss on his cheek and slinging her arm around his shoulder. "You were amazing up there. Everyone said so."

"Uh, thanks," he said, eyes darting toward me.

She looked at me and smiled wide, her shoulder-length blond hair shimmering under the neon bar lights. "Well, hey. I'm Julia, Hank's wife."

She held out a hand for me to shake, and I stared at it for a moment. Then I forced myself into action and grabbed her hand. "Nice to meet you. I'm Sandy."

Her eyes widened. "Sandy! You mean Baileyville Sandy?"

Baileyville Sandy. I wasn't sure why this stung so badly—maybe it was the insinuation that there were so many other Sandys in Hank's life that I needed to be identified by my location.

But more likely, it was that, once again, I was stuck back there. Even when I was in another state, I couldn't leave it behind. It didn't matter what I did. Hank was going places, *had* gone places, had gotten married—but I would always be Baileyville Sandy. There was no sense in trying to fight that.

"Certainly am!" I said with a smile that I hoped hid the grief flowing through my body. I glanced down at Hank's hand, at the plain, thin band on his ring finger. I should've noticed it. I imagined a ceremony, Julia slipping it on his finger, the two of them promising their lives to each other and smiling. I wanted to cry or vomit or die, or maybe all three.

"It's so great to meet you finally," Julia said. "We don't get back to visit Hank's family that often, but next time we do, we should all get together! His parents are always like, 'Please bring my son home!' but you know Hank. Can't get him to do anything he doesn't want to do. Thought we just about broke his mom's heart when we eloped instead of having some big ol' wedding."

I nodded and smiled. Of course. I knew Hank.

I couldn't sit there anymore, couldn't hear this stranger who knew Hank better than I did talk about his mom. I couldn't hear one single other word about their wedding, about their life together.

"I'm sorry," I interrupted her. "But I actually have some place I need to be, so—"

As I stood up, she looked at me with understanding. "Did you come from a wedding?"

Okay, so the bridesmaid dress definitely wasn't fooling anyone. I was in a bar wearing a bridesmaid dress, and I'd humiliated myself by kissing a married man.

"Yeah, and that's what I need to get back to. The wedding reception. You know, bridesmaid duties and all that. What if there's an important bustle-related problem I need to fix?" I was rambling. I grabbed my purse and turned.

"Sandy," I heard Hank say. "Can I walk you out?"

"Nope!" I turned back to look at him once more and instantly regretted it. Those blue eyes, the ones I thought I knew how to read. Obviously I didn't know what they were saying anymore.

That was for Julia to know now.

"It was nice to meet you," I said to her with a smile, then turned and left as fast as I could.

On the sidewalk, I gulped in air, finally letting myself cry and praying that Hank didn't follow me out, even though I knew he wouldn't. When I was his, he would've followed me anywhere, always making sure I was okay. But now he had a new girl, a new forever, a new person to look out for, and he would never leave her alone in there while he chased after someone else.

This was the end, I realized. The end of Sandy and Hank. I made a mistake by letting him go, and now I was facing the consequences. Or maybe it wasn't really a mistake—maybe, all along, it was a sacrifice I had to make. Would he have been here playing music if we'd stayed together? Julia clearly helped him be the person he was meant to be.

I was just Baileyville Sandy, and I always would be.

Chapter Fifteen

Present day

ONE OF MY favorite things about gardening is that it's all-consuming. My mind can finally stop racing as I focus on the tactile sensation of my hands sinking into the cool dirt, planting seeds, or yanking weeds out by their roots. I've always loved the daydreaming part of painting, and gardening allows me the same escape. Gardening is an act of hope, full of mundane tasks that are necessary to lead to a flower-filled fantasy. Weeding isn't terrifically exciting, but if I don't do it, chaos ensues.

So here I am, in the far-too-short old cutoffs I only wear for yard work at home, crouching in front of the flower beds in front of my porch. It's early in the morning, before the sun begins to beat down and make the work miserable. Marcia's handling the greenhouse by herself this morning until I head over later, although I'm always on call in case there's a mad rush of people looking for lawn gnomes.

Even though I'm at home, this is work, too. When you own a

greenhouse, people expect your own landscaping to be impeccable, and my lawn is my best source of marketing.

And as a bonus, it's freaking gorgeous. My California Giants
zinnias tower over everything else, each bloom a splash of orange,
red, or pink against the backdrop of my pale yellow house. Terra-
cotta pots of varying sizes hold impatiens, begonias, and a smaller
version of my beloved zinnias that I chose entirely because of their
name—Raspberry Lemonade. I'm not saying I got into the gardening business because of the creative flower variety names, but
I'm not *not* saying that.

My hair is up in a ponytail so I don't have to keep brushing it
out of my face, but I can feel that I have dirt smudged across my
cheeks anyway—even after all these years, I've never learned how
to avoid getting dirty. I'm not wearing anything on my face except
for superstrong sunscreen (a necessity in this line of work), and I
have on a threadbare scoop-neck T-shirt with a big Country Colors logo front and center. This is my happy place—in the dirt,
forgetting what I look like, drowning out all my thoughts with
work. I sing along to the Kacey Musgraves song that's stuck in my
head from an album we play all the time at the greenhouse. Vo-
cally, I'm more "contestant they show on the first episode of
American Idol to illustrate how many bad vocalists try out" than
Kacey Musgraves, but that's one of the many fantastic things
about flowers. They don't complain about your singing voice.

Toby lies on the porch, his head resting between his paws. I
stand back to admire the scene for a moment, still singing quietly
to myself. My little yellow bungalow, the peaked porch roof lined
in white and the brick chimney jutting up on the side. The painted
gray wooden steps. The white chairs on the porch, each with floral pillows, and the wicker table where Honey and I place our

glasses of (occasionally spiked) lemonade on hot nights. The zinnias stand tall and proud, swaying slightly with each small breeze that comes along, waiting for me to put them into a bouquet. *I made this*, I remind myself. I bought this house, I grew these flowers, I painted these steps. I can't take credit for Toby's perfection, but everything else is all me.

I created this home to be my oasis, and most of the time, it is—but sometimes when I look at it in the right light, it hits me that it's just a mirage. Those white chairs on the porch would be a perfect spot to sit with a partner in the evening, but most of the time, it's Toby and me. Those butcher-block counters are beautiful, but I'm usually cooking simple meals for one after getting home late from work. No matter how much colorful paint or how many beautiful flowers I have, there's still the *want*. I want someone else here. A husband. A child. My own family.

Toby stands up, tail wagging, and I turn to see whoever has him excited—probably our mail delivery lady, Heather, who carries a stash of Milk-Bone biscuits in her pockets and has won the coveted position of Toby's favorite person on Earth. But as I turn, the smile on my face morphs into a look of surprise.

"Hank?" I ask.

He walks up the sidewalk, hands shoved in his jeans pockets like he's a model for casual menswear. Toby trots down the stairs, his tongue lolling, and jumps on Hank.

"Toby, down. What are you doing here?" I ask.

"We're going door to door today, remember?" he asks, then stands back, crosses his arms, and takes in my house. "It's beautiful. The garden. The house. Your singing."

I can feel myself blushing. I know I'm not a great singer by anyone's standards, but especially not by a person who makes their living singing. And *definitely* not by someone who's probably met the real Kacey Musgraves, not this third-rate pretender with a nasal voice and a dirty old T-shirt.

"Thanks," I say.

"Zinnias, right?" he asks, gesturing toward the flowers and kneeling to pet Toby, who finally listened to my command and sat down.

I nod. "Yep. My favorites."

"Why?" he asks, and I meet his eyes.

"Well," I say, thinking about it as I turn to study the flowers. "They're so cheerful. Uncomplicated. Like sunshine personified. They're bold and dramatic, but anyone can grow them. They're unpretentious. Looking at a zinnia is like looking at a smile from your favorite person, you know?"

I look at him and see him smiling back. *Oh.*

"What's your favorite flower?" I ask, sure he won't have an answer. Or if he does, it will be something everyone likes. A rose. A daisy. Beautiful flowers, sure, but the kinds you can buy in a sterile grocery store cooler any time of the year.

"Echinacea," he says, surprising me.

"Echinacea?" I repeat with a little laugh. "What?"

He shrugs and looks a bit sheepish as if he knows this wasn't what I was expecting. "They remind me of home. Of here. Your mom grew them in your front yard in high school, remember? I used to walk right past 'em whenever I went up the front steps."

A shot of memory straight to my heart. Opening the front door to see Hank standing there, the purple echinacea swaying behind him in the dusk, cicadas buzzing, his old red truck parked on the street and waiting for me.

"They're still there," I say. "Echinacea is a perennial. It comes back every year."

"Yeah?" Hank asks. "That's kinda nice."

He's right—in a world full of terrifying uncertainty, perennials give you something to count on. The tulips and daffodils will poke through the soil every spring. The roses will bloom every summer (well, as long as you treat them right). And the echinacea will be there in my parents' front yard, like clockwork.

"It is," I say, wiping my hands on my shorts. It's then that I realize how tiny my shorts are—I would never wear these anywhere but my front yard, and I didn't imagine Hank would show up here this morning.

"I didn't expect you so early," I say. "Don't musicians sleep in? You know, after rock-and-rolling all night?"

"I play country, not rock and roll. Kiss can't tell me what to do." He reaches his arms up in a big stretch, his thin white T-shirt riding up. I resolutely do not look at his stomach. That's forbidden territory.

"In high school, you always slept in," I remind him.

"But now I like to watch the sunrise," he says, and I'm so distracted by the hair on his lower stomach that I almost don't hear him.

"What?" I ask when I realize what he's said.

"The sunrise," he says matter-of-factly. "Have you heard of it? It's when that big glowing orb comes up."

I furrow my brow. "Yeah, that sounds familiar. But you . . . you really wake up and watch the sunrise?"

He nods. Toby, having been ignored for one second, starts to whine, so Hank crouches down to pet him. "Yep. I started doing it a few years ago when I was on the road. One night, I hadn't gone to sleep at all, and the next thing I knew, it was morning. And all of a sudden, it hit me how beautiful it is and how it's there every day, but we ignore it. We're all too busy with our lives and our mornings—"

"And our big important nationwide tours opening for Jason Isbell," I interrupt.

"That was a different tour, but yes, our big important nationwide tours," Hank continues, scratching Toby's ears. Toby's in such bliss I think he'd go home with Hank if I let him. "Something about it made me feel, I don't know, it made me think that if I was missing all this beauty every day, what else am I missing? I'm supposed to be a writer, someone who observes the beauty in the small things other people don't see, and here I am ignoring this large, ostentatious, beautiful, natural phenomenon every damn day of my life."

This time, I don't interrupt with a joke. I'm too struck by his words and by how natural he looks with Toby. How much he looks like a man who should have a dog.

"So you watch the sun come up *every day*?" I ask, skeptical.

"Every day. Even once when I had food poisoning from a gas station hot dog, I still got up and hobbled outside in the morning to see the sunrise before I puked on my feet."

I frown. "Why were you eating a gas station hot dog?"

Hank looks at me, still scratching Toby's ears. "Life on the road isn't an appropriate thing to talk about in front of a lady and an innocent dog. Strange things happen, Sandy. You find yourself in front of those rotating hot dogs at a gas station and make decisions you're not proud of."

I can't help but laugh. I'd forgotten—or at least tried to forget—how easy it always was to talk to Hank. How easy everything was with him. No one else could be silly with me like this except for Honey, and I'd missed it.

"I'm a whole new Hank Tillman now," he says, and the words make my heart hurt. I never wanted a whole new Hank Tillman; I thought the old one was pretty perfect. But I can't deny that this version of Hank seems . . . different. Not that the past fifteen years have beaten him down, but it's clear that there's a weight on him that wasn't there before.

"So," he says, standing up. "You ready to go?"

I laugh. "Everyone will still be in bed! And they'll be way less likely to give us money if they're half asleep and angry when they answer the door."

"Good point," Hank says. "So we have time for donuts first. You ready?"

"I don't . . . we don't . . . what . . ." I stammer, trying to think of a reason why I can't go get donuts with Hank right now. But I can't come up with anything, and I'm not even sure I want to.

I glance down at my outfit—although *outfit* seems to be a generous term for what I have on. He stares at me expectantly, hands in his pockets.

It's silly to try to avoid Hank when that's clearly not possible, I think. *I might as well go get donuts.*

"Let me run inside and change," I say.

I CHANGE INTO a navy blue sundress covered in tiny white flowers, purely because I need to get dressed quickly and not because I'm trying to look pretty for Hank. I comb my messy hair and swipe on some lipstick. And some mascara. Oh, and I brush my teeth, but that's only because I care deeply about oral hygiene.

Toby isn't happy that Hank and I are leaving him behind, but he settles into his spot on my orange sofa. "I'll be back soon," I remind him, giving him a pat on the head. He gives me a look that I imagine means, *Girl, be careful.*

"I'm being careful," I mutter, then remember I'm talking to my dog and Hank Tillman is waiting for me outside.

Outside, Hank leans up against his truck, arms crossed. In his T-shirt and faded jeans, he could almost be High School Hank . . . you know, if not for the few wrinkles on his forehead and the sturdier muscles on his arms and the way his eyes look heavier, somehow.

Speaking of those eyes . . . I forgot how it felt to have them on me, and I watch as Hank's eyes travel quickly up and down my body. He coughs and stands up straight, then opens the truck door. I find it charming that it still has a dent in the exact same spot and still sounds like a goose when it creaks open.

"Thank you, sir," I say as I climb in and sit down, smoothing my skirt on my lap.

He shuts the door, and we're face-to-face through the open window. "My pleasure, ma'am."

He walks around the front of the truck, and I attempt to reckon with the fact that Hank used the word "pleasure." *Compose yourself, woman*, I remind myself. *Hank is married.*

And then he gets in and starts the truck, and the sound of Wham! singing "Everything She Wants" fills the cab.

"You still have this?" I screech.

I'd completely forgotten about the music in Hank's truck. The truck was ancient even when we were in high school, and instead of a CD player like I had in my *very* cool Dodge Neon, he only had a tape deck and a few cassette tapes to play on it. We'd comb through the selection at garage sales, only accepting the best of the best. After all, the glove compartment only had so much room, and we couldn't waste it on inferior tapes.

George Michael's voice blares through the truck as I remember finding this one at Mrs. Watson's yard sale after flipping through the box of tapes in her driveway, the hot sun beating down on my neck. I held it up to Hank, triumphant, certain that the brooding faces and voluminous manes of George Michael and Andrew Ridgeley would get his approval. And then this album, full of certified bangers and released before we were even born, became part of the truck's rotation.

"You'll find," he says, pulling into the street as George Michael sings about someone having his baby, "that I haven't altered the tape selection in any way. Same great tunes as always. Speaking of things that never change, are the donuts at Betty's as good as they used to be?"

I feign shock. "You dare question the greatness of Betty's? Of course they're good. In fact, they even added in a second fritter flavor. Blueberry. Oh, and now they have Cronuts."

Hank takes his eyes off the road for a moment to shoot me a skeptical look.

"What?" I ask. "Surprised we have Cronuts in Baileyville? A mere ten years after the trend swept the nation, Betty's put them on the menu."

Hank shakes his head. "So many changes around here. I don't know if I can keep up."

"I don't mean to alarm you, but we also got a Panera out by the interstate," I whisper. "The whole town lost their minds for that broccoli cheese soup."

Hank puts one hand over his heart. "Jesus, Sandy, you can't shock a man like that when he's driving. I might run us off the road."

"Barb O'Dell almost got kicked out because she threw a tantrum one day when they ran out of bread bowls."

Hank laughs, wiping his eyes. "Wow. I have missed a lot while I've been gone."

You don't even know, I think to myself.

After years of avoiding even thinking about Hank, I'm surprised by how *not* awkward this is. We talk about other things that have changed in town until we pull into the Betty's parking lot.

"Hold tight," Hank says. "Be right back with provisions."

I watch him walk into Betty's and hold the door open for the Hillenbrands, two of the many, many elderly people in town who get breakfast here every single day. Some might say it's a lack of options, but I think maybe it speaks to a comforting level of devotion. Doing the same thing every day because that's what you've always done. Finding the beauty in what you see over and over.

Also, it's worth noting that the donuts really are amazing.

Even though I'm surprised by how normal it feels to talk to Hank, I have to admit that it's strange as hell to be in this truck again, and not only because it's defying all laws of mechanics by still being functional. Mostly it's disconcerting to be sitting in the spot I occupied for so long, to be back in the passenger seat next to Hank . . . and also so close to the spot where we first had sex. It feels like the truck bed is looming behind me, waiting to tap me on the shoulder and be like, "Remember me? The place where you lost your virginity to the love of your life?"

George Michael plaintively wails about how he'll never dance again. "Sing it, George," I mutter as Betty's door opens and Hank walks out, hoisting a white donut bag in the air as if he captured something in a heist. I give him a thumbs-up, laughing in spite of myself.

"Okay, so," Hank says as he opens the door and slides in. I grab the bag out of his hand as he places two paper cups full of coffee in the cup holders. "Betty's has new bags."

"'New' is a relative term," I say. "I think they've had these for a few years."

"Well, forgive me for not knowing that," Hank says, reaching into the bag as I hold it open. The current bags have an illustration of a bright pink sprinkled donut and the words *You Deserve a Donut.* "I like this one because I do deserve a donut. Got you a maple long john, by the way."

I grimace. "They're not my favorite anymore."

Hank looks genuinely shocked. "What? You want me to go back in and—"

"I'm kidding," I say, taking my donut. "These are still my favorite."

"You're such a loser," Hank mutters, taking a bite of his blueberry fritter.

"Oh, I'm a *loser*?" I ask with my mouth full. "Ouch, someone call the burn squad."

Hank snorts and almost chokes. "Did you ask for the *burn squad*?"

"I think we're regressing to teenagers," I say, taking a sip of my coffee and letting out a groan of pleasure. "This coffee is always the best."

"I've never had any coffee that tastes like this," Hank says, taking a drink. "And I've tried a lot of coffee."

It's a reminder that Hank hasn't been here drinking Betty's coffee several times a week like I have. "I'm surprised you aren't partial to oat milk lattes these days."

Hank looks at me with a grin. "Can you imagine what Rhonda would do if I went in there and asked for oat milk? She'd tell me to get my ass outta there."

Betty Johnson, the namesake of Betty's diner, has long since passed, but her granddaughter Rhonda runs the place now and she doesn't suffer fools or special orders. At Betty's, you get what you get and you don't throw a fit. Maybe you think you don't like tomatoes, but Rhonda's here to tell you that, at least for today, you're gonna try.

I shake my head. "This town's an unfortunate place to live for the lactose intolerant."

"Not a problem if you drink it black," Hank says.

"Hear, hear," I say, and we toast our paper cups. I try not to look at him as I do so, but I can feel his eyes on me.

"It's bad luck to toast someone without looking them in the eye," he says quietly.

I stare at his blue-sky summer eyes a little too long, and I wonder what he sees when he looks back at me. Teenage Sandy shining through? Current Sandy with some slight (very slight, thank you) wrinkles and a few extra sunspots?

I take a long drink and look around the parking lot. "So how does it feel to be back?" I ask.

"Like I never left," Hank says, looking out his own window.

And as I take a sip of my coffee and mentally trace his profile, the one that's tattooed on my brain, I wonder what would have happened if he never had.

Chapter Sixteen

O KAY, LET'S DO this," Hank says, shaking out his arms and
then doing a quad stretch.

I eye him skeptically. "I don't think you need to warm up for
door knocking."

"I want to be prepared," he tells me. "You never know what
you're gonna find on the other side of a door."

I nod. "That's true. You don't know when you're going to encounter a murderer."

Hank narrows his eyes. "Is that the first place your mind went?
You think a murderer is going to answer the door?"

I shrug. "Who knows what dark secrets the citizens of Baileyville are hiding. Anyway, let's go."

We walk up the steps of our first house, where Cindy Har-
mon, the wife of Hank's old football coach, answers the door and
is so happy to see him that she donates two hundred dollars and
gives us a Tupperware container full of molasses cookies. At old
Mr. Anderson's house, we get ensnared in a half-hour conversa-

tion about the state of the Buckeyes and their chances for a championship win this year. And when we reach Edith's place, where she insists we come in for iced tea and muffins, she doesn't let us leave without giving Hank a hug.

By the end of the day, we've made five thousand dollars with the promise of more to come.

"Wow," I exhale as we sit on my porch after we've tallied up our total. "Sean wasn't kidding. We made way more than I did last year. I guess people really do love you."

Hank cracks his knuckles. "So you're glad I came along today?"

I count the pile of money in my hands before putting it in the lockbox Sean gave us. Despite my apprehension about Hank being around, this wasn't as torturous as I'd expected. I was usually so busy laughing that I didn't even have time to hate myself for all the mistakes I made with him when we were kids. Maybe that's progress.

But if I really want to make progress, I have to ask the question I've been avoiding, the one lurking in my mind every time I see Hank.

"You know what?" I give him a smile. "I am. Can I ask you something?"

"As long as it's not about when my next album's gonna come out," he says with a grin. "Heard that one enough today."

"Where's your wife?"

He looks at me in confusion. "I don't have a wife."

"Okay, well, you do," I remind him. "I know because I met her."

"I have an *ex*-wife," Hank clarifies.

My brain sends a message to my heart: *calm down*. I keep my mouth zipped shut, afraid of what might come out.

"That's right," he says, continuing since apparently I can't speak anymore. "I sit in front of you a divorced man. A total failure at marriage."

"I don't think you're a failure," I say quietly. "A lot of people get divorced."

He shrugs. "That doesn't mean I ever thought it would happen to me. Everyone in my family gets married and stays married. The same as yours."

I nod slowly. "So what happened?"

When Hank doesn't respond, I bite my lip and try not to cover my face in my hands. "God, I'm sorry. It's none of my business. I'm being nosy and—"

Hank shakes his head. "No, it's okay. It's just . . . not something I talk about with a lot of people."

As I wait for him to continue, I realize I'm holding my breath.

Hank sighs, keeping his eyes on the street. "I'm pretty used to deciding what I want and not giving up until I get it. As you may remember, I'm kinda stubborn."

"Determined," I say with a small smile.

"Whatever you call it, it didn't work in marriage. With my job, hard work pays off. Not giving up even when other people think it's a lost cause is an asset. But it turns out marriage isn't like that. You can't make someone want to be with you if they don't want to, no matter how hard you believe in it."

I nod as if I know what he's talking about from my limited dating experience. Discussing relationships with Hank feels like pressing on a bruise, but I can't make myself change the subject.

"You know that old cliché 'We grew apart'?" he continues. "It was like that, except that we started apart. There was no point in time when Julia and I were ever growing together—it's like we were always two seedlings pointed in different directions, and I tried my best to grow with her, but she had her own ideas."

"Gardening metaphor," I say with a nod. "Nice."

He chuckles. "Knew you'd appreciate that. She was much more

interested in a certain kind of . . . lifestyle, let's call it, than she was with being married. You can do all kinds of things when you're on the road, and she wanted to do most of them. I didn't. I wanted us to be a family, and she wanted to be by herself. So she is."

I frown. "So she left you behind? You and Henry?"

"She visits sometimes," Hank says. "She calls. But our life . . . it wasn't for her."

"I'm sorry," I say, and it comes out as a whisper.

"Don't be," he says, meeting my eyes. "Henry and I do pretty well on our own. We're a team, you know? My parents come to see us when they can, and we're planning on being back here more. And when we're on the road, he's got a whole team of people who look after him—not related to us but like a family."

I swallow. Of course Hank not being married doesn't change anything. He's still Hank, still gone, still on the road. And now he has a very visible, very human reminder of the fact that his life went on without me. He might not have a wife anymore, but he has a child and a job that will keep taking him away from here.

And me? Well, I built my whole life here. My business, my friends, my community—it's all Baileyville. I'm Baileyville Sandy, and I always will be.

Hank and I *were* growing together once, like two tree trunks that had intertwined. But eventually, we grew apart. And no matter what's going on with Hank's relationship, no matter how well we get along, I need to remember that.

Hank looks out at the street, watching a car drive by slowly, a golden retriever's head hanging out the window. "When Julia left, I guess I remembered what actually matters. What actually stays. And I want Henry to know my parents and my sister and his cousins better. Life on the road is fun sometimes, but that's not enough stability for a kid. He needs at least one thing that's permanent."

I give him a tiny smile. "He has you."

He smiles back. "We have each other."

"So, am I ever gonna get to meet this mysterious Henry who's always with your parents?" I ask him.

When Hank pauses, I immediately regret opening my mouth. It would make complete sense if Hank didn't want to introduce his child to the woman who broke his heart a million years ago. Given his history with Julia, maybe he's reluctant to introduce Henry to *any* women. I can't say I'd blame him.

"He's not *usually* with my parents," Hank says with his crooked smile. "But every time I've seen you, yes, they have been babysitting. Henry doesn't usually want to accompany me on my runs."

"Or your gutter-cleaning excursions," I add.

He nods. "But maybe we should've brought him along today. People might've donated even more if there were a cute kid giving them puppy dog eyes."

"Well, it's good to teach your kid to use what the good Lord gave him to solicit funds. That's what I always say."

Hank gives me an eye roll. "To answer your question . . . yeah. You'll meet Henry, and I think you guys will get along. He's quite the artist too, although so far, he's mostly working with crayons, not paint."

We look at each other for a moment without saying anything. This is what I dreamed of when I bought this house—sitting here on the porch with someone who gets me. The breeze blows softly, wafting the scent of the flowers toward us, and for a moment, all I want is to stay right here forever—to ask Hank if *he* can stay right here forever.

Then he slaps his hands on his thighs, the Midwestern way of saying, *This conversation is over*, and stands up. "I should probably go relieve my parents of babysitting duty. Also, I promised Henry a sprinkle cone from the Dairy Belle."

"Thanks for the help," I say, and once again, we're staring at each other, him standing here on my porch and me sitting on my wicker chair. I don't know what to do here. Simply brushing against him in the market was enough to almost make me combust; I can't imagine what a hug would do.

Instead, I wave awkwardly as he walks down the stairs. "Okay, bye!" I say, then watch him walk to his truck and drive away.

I let out a heavy sigh. I did it—I survived a morning with Hank Tillman, and I don't even feel like crying. It turns out the trip down memory lane wasn't half as bad as I expected. *Is this growing up?* I wonder. Maybe now that we're adults, we can be mature about everything that happened when we were kids. For a moment today, when we were in Edith's kitchen and she was basically force-feeding muffins to Hank as he mouthed, *Help me*, I felt like I did back in school, like it was us against the world. Or, more accurately, like it was us laughing at the world, like we were the only two people who understood the joke.

After all these years, I'd forgotten that feeling even existed, and I'd missed it.

If only I could feel it with someone other than Hank.

CHAPTER SEVENTEEN

OHIO'S STATE SLOGAN is "Find It Here," and Mama Macintosh really took that philosophy to heart with the Ohio Inn. The tables and chairs in the dining room are all made by local craftsmen, as are the white rocking chairs on the porch. The music that plays in the dining room is an all-Ohioan playlist (put together by yours truly). You'd be surprised how many famous musicians are from the Buckeye State.

And if I never put any Hank Tillman on the playlist . . . well, you can forgive me.

My mom had to go visit a new maple syrup supplier, so she asked me to take over the hostess table at the front door for a few hours. Maybe this should feel like a time suck, but it's one of my favorite tasks at the inn. I love greeting everyone who walks through the door with a big smile. We get the out-of-towners who are staying in our rooms, in which case it's fun to answer their questions about hiking or skiing or local Amish stores. (Out-of-towners always find the Amish community fascinating.) I can direct them to the wall of pamphlets advertising the various sights of Baileyville and the surrounding areas, and I always feel like I've missed my calling as a member of the Baileyville Regional Tourism Board (which doesn't exist, but maybe I should start it).

But it's even more fun when the locals come in to eat in the dining room. Not to brag, but we have the best weekend brunch buffet in town, and that's not just because we have the only brunch buffet in town. There are scones, muffins, bacon, maple chicken apple sausage links, some really amazing chocolate chip pancakes, and the star of the show, Scott's home fries.

I've changed out of my Country Colors "uniform" into a floral blouse and a black skirt. We don't have all that many tables, and while we stay busy and do just fine financially, it's not like there's an overwhelming influx of customers. People aren't rude to me because we all know each other here, and anyway, they can always go to Betty's if they don't want to wait.

I'm humming along to my all-Ohio playlist when the front door opens. I plaster on my customer service smile and say, "Good morning! Welcome to the Ohio Inn!" before I see who's walking in.

It's Hank's whole family—his parents, his sister, her husband, and their kids. And Hank. And a small child who looks a lot like Hank.

"Oh, hi, everyone!" I say, coming out from behind the hostess booth to give Mr. and Mrs. Tillman a hug. Even after Hank and I broke up, they still treated me like family (which, to be fair, might be how they treat everyone in town). Mr. Tillman still slipped me free candy bars if he saw me at the store, and Mrs. Tillman always told me she loved my hair and asked if I just got it cut even though I've been wearing it in the exact same style (long, boring) since puberty.

"Sandy!" Hank's sister, Melodie, squeals and hugs me as if we haven't seen in each other in years, even though we run into each other around town all the time—always keeping our small talk on neutral topics like her kids or the weather, never her brother, of course. "I didn't know you'd be working here!"

"I fill in sometimes. You know what it's like with a family biz," I say, hugging her back.

She rolls her eyes. "Ugh. Yes. Dad wishes I would still work at the store."

He shrugs. "We could use the help, and it's honest work."

She points to her children. "Dad, I have a job. It's called keeping these two from having a sword fight with the silverware during this meal."

"Don't give them any ideas," her husband, Tom, says.

"Hey, Hank," I say, then wave to the small boy holding his hand. "And hi to you, too."

"Hello," the boy says in a quiet but perfectly polite voice.

"This is Henry," Hank says, looking down at his son with an expression of obvious adoration that shoots through my heart and my reproductive organs. His son.

"Hi, Henry," I say. "How are you?"

Henry sticks a finger in his mouth, and Hank nudges him. "Henry, be polite."

"Good," Henry says. "My belly hurts. I'm hungry."

"Well," I say with a smile. "In that case, you've come to the right place. Follow me!"

I grab a stack of menus and lead their family to our biggest table, keeping my shoulders back and my head held high. Today, I'll be playing the role of Hostess Sandy, a woman who is simply doing her job and not thinking for even one second about the past or her childhood love.

"Here you go!" I say when we reach the table. I give them enough menus for the adults. "I'll get you some crayons and kids' menus, okay? Edith will be out to take your drinks orders in a sec!"

I smile widely at each of them, then head back to the kitchen, getting faster with each step until I'm almost running. I burst into the kitchen entirely too fast, nearly knocking Edith over.

"Holy mackerel!" she shouts, stepping back from the door.

I'd be surprised if Edith has ever said an honest-to-God curse word in her entire life—all I've ever heard from her is a seemingly endless stream of colorful curse word substitutes. She's relentlessly positive, which cancels out her almost brutal honesty—with her permanent glowing smile, you don't even notice when she says your new haircut looks bad. (Maybe her upbeat attitude is the secret to her long marriage with her cowboy.)

Edith is, simply put, a complex woman, and right now she's looking at me as if she's afraid I might burst into flames.

"What's wrong, sweetie?" she asks, reaching into the pocket of her apron and pulling out a tissue.

That's when I realize I'm crying—big, gulping, disgusting sobs, the kind of crying I haven't done since that night I found out Hank was married. Thank God I'm back in the kitchen, where no one can see me—well, except for Scott, who's staring at me as he peels potatoes in the corner.

I give him a wave. "Hey, Scott. How's it going?"

He raises his knife in greeting.

I blow my nose and look at Edith. "I'm okay. I just need a moment."

She rubs my arm comfortingly. "Take all the time you need. I'm in no hurry."

"Well, our first guests of the day are here. Which is the problem, actually. I've been trying to pretend I'm over Hank or that I *can* get over him, and then I saw his son, and it made me realize . . . that could've been our son. I mean, Henry himself couldn't have literally been our son, since he has DNA from another person, but we could've had a son. I could've been sitting there with Hank and his family and our child. I could've had that, Edith." I blow my nose again.

"It's okay," Edith says softly. "I know it doesn't seem like it could possibly be okay right now, but it will be. You've barely graduated from high school—you have your whole life ahead of you."

"Edith!" I wail. "I'm thirty-three!"

"Oh." She sucks in a breath. "Okay, then. I guess I see what you're saying."

I look at Scott, but he only continues his peeling.

"You may not be a spring chicken, but you've got a few years left in you. Not many wrinkles, your own teeth, an ass that won't quit." She smiles. "Any man would be lucky to have you."

"Thank you, Edith," I say. "From me and my original set of teeth. You'd better get out there. There are some children who might riot if they don't get cups of juice soon."

She smiles at me and heads out, the door swinging shut behind her.

I sigh, then rub my eyes with the tissue. I'll head upstairs to the bathroom in the Paul Newman room, which is currently unoccupied and features a fancy vanity with movie-star-worthy lighting, to check my makeup. And then I remember, again, that Scott is here, still silently peeling.

"Sorry you had to witness my meltdown," I say, sniffling. "I promise I'm usually a lot more put together than that."

He looks at me and puts down his knife. He stares at me for so long that I start to wonder if he's forgotten what I've said or if he's planning to tell me something profound, something that will change my life.

Finally, he opens his mouth. "Love's a bitch," he says with a resolute nod.

I shake my head. "Ain't it the truth, Scott," I say. "Ain't it the truth."

Chapter Eighteen

"S O," MARCIA SAYS at the greenhouse the next day. "Word on the street is that Hank Tillman's back in town for a while."

I turn to her, my eyes narrowed. "What street, Marcia? Main Street? Are you hanging out by the gazebo, waiting for someone to walk by with gossip?"

Marcia shrugs. "Shelby told me when I was at Hair Affair yesterday."

I should've remembered that news travels at the speed of light around here, especially if Shelby's involved. The only thing she loves more than doing highlights is talking about people in town. The last time I was in there, she said the words "but you didn't hear it from me" approximately five times, right before telling me that my split ends were a tragedy. I would've hated her if she wasn't right.

"You guys been hanging out?" she asks, leaning on the counter.

I use an X-Acto knife to slice open a box full of adorable planters that look like little animals. You really can't overestimate the selling power of extremely cute gardening supplies. "We've been working together on fair stuff. Why?"

I'm not looking at her, but I can practically hear her eyes widen. "No reason. Just, you know . . . wondered."

I turn around, still in my crouched position. "Marcia. Nothing is happening between me and Hank. We dated about a million years ago, and we're grown adults now. He has a kid and an ex-wife, and I have a whole life here that doesn't involve following a musician around the country. We're only hanging out because we both care deeply about this community and because the traitors who live here donate *way* more money for a famous person than they do for me."

Marcia puts her hands in the air, feigning innocence. "Okay, wow, that's a defense I never asked for, but sure. My bad. Why would I ever assume you could be interested in a hot single dad with a successful music career? Ew."

I roll my eyes. "Everyone in this town is way too invested in my love life. Is it so hard to understand that a single woman can actually be happy? Like, maybe I enjoy my life and my house and my job. Maybe I'm not some pathetic lonely lady who drowns her sorrow in ice cream every night."

I realize I already opened the box and have been slashing at it with the X-Acto knife. I let out a long exhale.

"Hey." Marcia comes out from behind the counter. "I was kidding. You know you're my hero, right?"

I frown. "I didn't know that. Please elaborate."

"You get shit done," Marcia says, crouching down beside me and grabbing some of the planters out of the box. "You're involved in everything around the town. You own a kick-ass business that's basically my dream job. You're very good at Hula-Hooping, which I know because of the time you got drunk at my Fourth of July party and insisted on showing everyone."

I think about it. "You make some compelling points. And honestly I wasn't even that drunk . . . I really like to show off my Hula-Hoop skills, even while sober."

Marcia leans forward. "And please don't act like it's pathetic to eat ice cream every night. That's called living the dream."

I nod. "I know."

Marcia stands up, placing the planters on the shelf. "Hank is a great guy, though. I don't know if you even know about this, but after I came out in high school, Josiah Portman cornered me at the drinking fountain and told me I was going to hell."

I gasp. "He did? I forgot about him. What happened to that little twerp?"

"Well, Hank was behind me in line, and he threatened to wipe the hall with Josiah's ass. So I can only assume that Josiah entered the witness protection program shortly thereafter as a means of protecting his life."

I laugh. "Hank never told me about that."

Marcia shrugs. "I kinda get the idea that stuff like that is everyday Hank Tillman behavior."

I bite my lip. "Yeah. You're probably right."

"Anyway, not my business," Marcia says, walking back behind the counter. "If you don't wanna bump uglies with the town's most famous resident, that's your business."

I frown. "I'm flexing my power as the owner-slash-manager and making a rule that we're no longer allowed to use the phrase 'bump uglies' on account of it's super gross."

Marcia throws her hands in the air. "If you're gonna keep judging my poetic language, you're gonna need to make an actual list. You got so mad last week when I claimed I was 'busting my balls.'"

"Again," I say with a sigh. "Gross. Also inaccurate."

"It's not my fault I'm an artist with the English language,"

Marcia says. "And anyway, you're only mad that I referred to Hank's penis as ugly."

"Oh, look, another banned phrase: 'Hank's penis.'"

"And you know I find all penises unattractive, as a rule." She pauses to think. "I don't know, I guess the one on Michelangelo's *David* is fine, but only because it's, like, art or whatever."

I groan. "I'm gonna report us both to HR."

"Too bad we don't have an HR department."

"Damn my lack of planning," I say as a black SUV pulls into the parking lot. We keep the front of the store wide open when the weather is nice, so we both watch the SUV park, wondering who could be inside—the thing about living in a small town is that we basically recognize every vehicle and its corresponding driver, and this Land Rover is unfamiliar to both of us.

The door opens, and none other than Hank Tillman himself steps out.

"That's not your truck!" I yell, then immediately feel heat rush to my cheeks. *That's not your truck? Great line, Sandy.*

Hank waves at us and heads around to the back seat of the SUV.

"Smooth one," Marcia mutters.

"Shut up," I mutter back as Henry bounds out of the back seat.

"No room for a booster seat in the truck," Hank says, walking toward us as he holds Henry's hand.

Marcia tilts her head, then comes out from behind the counter. "C'mere, you. You're getting a hug."

She gives Hank a big backslapping embrace.

"How are you?" he asks, his voice muffled in her shoulder.

She steps back. "Very upset, actually, that you refused to be the musical entertainment at my wedding."

Hank smiles. "Sorry about that. I don't get back here too often, with work and all."

"I can't help it that you wrote one of the most romantic songs ever recorded, and I wanted it to be the first dance with my wife." Marcia sighs. "'When the World Melts Away.' Ugh. Even thinking about it makes me wanna cry."

"Hey, Henry," I say, and he gives me a small smile with his lips pressed together. "How's it going?"

"Good," he says. "I had a donut for breakfast."

I gasp, looking at Hank. "You went to Betty's and didn't bring us anything?"

Marcia lets out a breath and shakes her head. "That's low, man."

"I assumed you went there on your own this morning," Hank says, raising his eyebrows.

"Of course I did, but it's the principle of the thing," I say. "Henry, you shouldn't be punished for your father's misdeeds. Do you want a pack of Skittles?"

"So now you're punishing *me* by giving him more sugar on top of the donut. Got it," Hank says as I walk over to the counter and grab the Skittles from our candy display. Yes, we may sell plants, but it's my firm belief that every store needs to sell candy, as well.

"Thank you," Henry says, taking the Skittles, tearing the pack open, and immediately dumping some into his mouth.

"This doesn't bode well for me," Hank says, watching him.

"So what's up?" I ask. "Did you come in here to brag about your donuts?"

"Sean texted me and asked us if we could go out to Pearl Stanley's place to pick up her doll collection," Hank says. "She wants to enter them in the doll show, but she can't drive them into town herself."

I nod. This tracks. There are so many elderly people in Baileyville that sometimes it seems like fifty percent of the adult population isn't legally permitted to get behind the wheel of a car.

"I thought we could head over there now if you're free, but I can see you're busy working," Hank says.

"So busy," Marcia says flatly, gesturing around the empty store. "The customers, they're pouring in. 'Please, have mercy on us, you've depleted our stash of garden trowels!' I shout, and still they come, an unrelenting stream—"

"Okay, that's enough." I cut her off. "But yeah, I'm working, so . . ."

"Aw, you two kids go have fun," Marcia says. "I think I can handle it right now."

I widen my eyes at her and she simply looks back at me, a smile on her face. I didn't exactly plan today's outfit—cutoff overalls, like I'm a toddler—with Hank Tillman in mind. And beyond my frumpy clothes, I'm not sure it's a good idea to spend more time in close quarters with him—not if I want to protect my fragile heart, that is.

"Let's start with why you're calling us 'kids' when you're a year younger than us," I say.

"Because spiritually I feel like your mom sometimes," Marcia says. "Go on! Shoo! Git!"

"Okay, since Marcia's very convincingly reminding me that she can handle the store, I'll go with you guys," I say with a wry smile.

"Nah," Hank says. "Henry's getting dropped off at my parents'. He doesn't want to go on an errand with us."

"Henry?" I ask. "Is this true? I gave you Skittles, and that doesn't make you want to hang out with me?"

"I want to go to Grandma and Grandpa's," Henry says, his mouth full of brightly colored Skittle mush. "Grandpa lets me play the iPad as much as I want."

"As long as he's spending quality time with a screen," Hank says. "That's what really matters."

He looks up at me, and the second his eyes catch mine, I really do feel the world melt away, just like his song.

He nods toward his SUV, smiling. "Let's go."

WE DROP HENRY off at the Tillman's impeccably maintained blue farmhouse, where the shrubs under the windows look exactly the same as they did when Hank and I were kids. After Mr. Tillman comes out to talk and remind me to make sure my dad stays off ladders, we leave the SUV there and hop into Hank's truck.

"I wonder why Sean only texted you and not me," I say after I replace the cassette tape with Ace of Base's "The Sign." "Maybe it's because I respond to everything he says with a reaction GIF he doesn't understand."

"Why was this the tape you chose?" Hank asks.

I gesture toward the tape player. "I'm sorry, do you think there's a better option than Swedish dance pop from the mid-'90s?"

"Well, yeah," Hank says. "There usually is."

"Then replace this tape player, dude," I say, leaning forward to turn it up.

"I will never do that, because this truck is a relic and a miracle."

I study his right hand on the wheel, those strong, tanned fingers. "It *is* a miracle. How is it still running?"

He turns to me and smiles, and my heart does a little gymnastics flip. "Through the grace of God."

"God's first priority being the care and maintenance of really old trucks," I say, looking away.

"Naturally."

Now we're fully out in the country, driving on winding roads that snake back and forth through the trees and over hills. The truck bumps over gravel as we pass acres of cornfields shining golden in the sun.

"Where does Pearl live?"

"Out on McKinley Road. Out in the boonies."

"We're almost into dirt-road territory," I say. "Are you sure this is a quest from Sean? Maybe you're driving me to my murder spot. After all, murderers are usually the people you know the best."

"Your 'murder spot'?" Hank asks, brow creased.

"Yes. The spot where my eventual murder will happen."

He barks out a laugh. "Sandy! What the hell are you doing that you're so convinced you're gonna be murdered? Is there a mob hit on you or something?"

I shrug. "Death comes for us all eventually."

"But usually in a more quotidian way."

"Damn," I say. "Quotidian. Still practicing your SAT flash cards."

"Ha," he says. "Real funny."

We drive in silence for a moment, the sun poking through the trees as we drive down a shady section of the road. "You know, I found out in college that I have dyslexia," he says.

I turn toward him. "What?"

He nods. "Yep. Turns out I wasn't just a little punk who didn't wanna read Jane Austen in high school."

"Hank," I say gently. "I can't believe you were dealing with that for so long, and I didn't even know."

"I didn't know, either," he says. "But when I was having trouble in college, one of my instructors recommended getting tested and, well, that was me."

"Wow," I say. "Do you take back all those uncharitable things you said about Jane Austen now?"

"I don't know. I remember thinking pretty fondly of ol' Jane after you read the book to me," he says quietly.

The word *Danger* flashes in my brain, bright red and alarming. I need to change the tone of this conversation.

"Would you like me to read you another one?" I ask lightly. "Maybe *Sense and Sensibility*?"

Hank laughs. "You know, being on the tour bus gives me a good amount of free time, and I actually read one on my own recently. *Persuasion*."

"The best one," I say quietly, thinking about the story of two people who get a second chance at love. The heroine, Anne, was in love with Captain Wentworth when they were both young—but then she was persuaded (hence the title) not to marry him. They end up meeting and falling in love again years later . . . and that, of course, has no relevance to me in this situation. None at all. I wonder why Hank chose *that* one, of all the books.

Hank puts on his turn signal, despite the fact that there's no one behind us, as we turn into a long gravel driveway. Pearl's old two-story white farmhouse looms ahead of us, enshrouded by maple trees. To the right of the house is a white barn. It's run-down, but only slightly, giving it the air of a building that was once well taken care of but has recently fallen into disrepair.

As Pearl opens the front door and hobbles onto the stairs, I see why things are falling apart—I knew she was old, but I didn't realize quite *how* old. She must be at least ninety. She has the hunched posture and gnarled limbs of a person with years of living under her belt.

As soon as the truck is in park, Hank opens his door and bounds toward her, saying, "Pearl, don't try those steps, okay?"

My heart nearly breaks thinking of this sweet old woman all the way out here by herself. I open my door and follow Hank to the steps.

"About time you got here," Pearl snarls. "Took you long enough."

Stunned, I stammer, "Sorry, that was . . . uh, that was my fault. I was working."

Pearl frowns, squinting at me over her glasses. "There's your problem. You shouldn't be working. You should be home, taking care of your family."

I use all the restraint I have to give Hank a subtle, wide-eyed glance. He looks back at me, his mouth twisted in a way that lets me know he's trying not to laugh.

"We hear you have some dolls," Hank says.

Pearl cups a hand over her ear. "You need to speak up. No mumbling. I hate it when people mumble."

"Dolls," Hank says as loudly as he can. "Can we take them?"

Pearl gestures toward the barn with her cane. "They're in there, in the box marked 'dolls.'"

Hank gives her a small wave and a smile as we start to walk toward the barn.

"For God's sake, be careful!" she shouts after us. "They're worth a lot of money."

"Doesn't it feel so good to volunteer?" I ask Hank, keeping my voice low even though Pearl certainly can't hear us.

Hank places a hand on his chest. "Consider my heart warmed. Nothing does it for me like an elderly woman shouting at me and assuming I'm going to drop a doll."

We step into the barn and are immediately plunged into darkness. There are windows in here, but they must be covered up because it's almost pitch-black. Before my eyes can try to adjust, Hank whips out his phone and turns on the flashlight. The light glides over the barn, and my heart sinks when I see how many overflowing boxes are stacked in front of us.

"How are we ever going to find a box of dolls in—sweet mother of God!" I shout, jumping and grabbing Hank's shoulder as the light catches on the blank, glassy stare of a doll poking out of a box. Honestly, it's a miracle I don't launch myself right into his arms.

"It's okay," Hank says calmly, as if we're facing a wild animal instead of (what is presumably) an unpossessed doll.

He steps forward slowly, and I realize I'm still hanging on to him like he's going to save my life. Maybe he will. That doll looks like it's out for blood.

"See? It's just a doll," Hank says, reaching out for it. He picks it up and, with a sudden movement, shoves it in my face.

"Aaaah!" I screech, falling backward onto the dirt floor.

"What are you two doing out there?" Pearl yells from the porch. "There'd better not be any hanky-panky going on in my barn!"

"As if anyone could get up to any hanky-panky with those eyes watching," I say, standing up and dusting off my butt. "I can't believe you scared me like that. This doll is haunted, right?"

"This one?" Hank asks, holding the doll up and studying it. It's wearing what looks like a torn Victorian dress, its hair appears to have been styled by a lawn mower, and its face is covered in dirt. "Really? You don't think she's kinda cute?"

I smack him on the arm.

"I don't know, I like her vibe," he says, putting her back in the box and pulling out another doll. This one is, surprisingly, even worse than the first one, because it's completely naked and missing one eye.

"We're going to die here, aren't we?" I say, shaking my head. "We're going to die in Pearl's barn because these haunted dolls are going to kill us."

"We're not going to die here," Hank says with a smirk, putting the doll back. "The dolls are going to put a curse on us, and we'll die later."

"Reassuring," I say. "Can we please get out of here?"

Then Hank turns to look at me, the smirk fading from his face, and all of a sudden, I forget that we're in the barn of an elderly woman who apparently hated our guts on sight, in the presence of dolls that may or may not be haunted and waiting for an excuse to curse us. I forget about all of it because Hank is so close to me that I can feel the warmth radiating from his chest. I can smell him, and even after all these years, he still smells like wood shavings and pine needles and home. In the little bit of light coming through the barn door, I can see the way he's looking at me, and it doesn't seem so different from the way he used to look at me back when I was his girl. Forever.

"Are you ever coming back, or should I assume you moved into my barn?" Pearl hollers, jolting me out of my thoughts. "Do I need to call the police?"

"Nope," I yell, taking a quick step away from Hank. "We're coming out!"

"I can't hear you!" Pearl yells back, and Hank and I look at each other and laugh.

"You'd better grab that box of dolls," I tell him. "Pearl's getting mad."

"*Getting* mad?" Hank asks. "I'm starting to think I don't want these dolls in my truck. I don't trust them."

"You think this face would ever hurt you?" I ask, picking up the naked doll on top and then immediately tossing it back in the box. "Sorry, I thought I could handle it, but I still can't."

Hank hoists up the box and gestures with his chin for me to go ahead. As I walk out into the sunlight, I give myself a little imperceptible shake. We say goodbye to Pearl, who frowns in response, and load up the box in the truck. *That was a close call*, I think. I was standing far too close to Hank in there and thinking things that were way too amorous, but who could blame me? I was under the influence of the haunted dolls. Maybe that's the curse they put on me—being doomed to replay memories of my high school love for the rest of my life. As long as I keep my distance from Hank from now on, it should be okay.

"Do you have to be back at work, or can we go somewhere else?" Hank asks.

"Let's go somewhere else," I say immediately.

So much for keeping my distance. I blame the dolls.

CHAPTER NINETEEN

HANK'S TRUCK SNAKES through the back roads of Baileyville until I barely even know where we are anymore. That is, until he turns onto the familiar driveway and we make our way up the hill.

"The highest point in Baileyville," I say. I remember, a little guiltily, the last time I was here when I was technically trespassing. I wince, imagining how it's going to feel to see the site of our first kiss gone, again. Like time erased it, like maybe it never even happened.

But as we emerge from the trees and the top of the hill comes into view, what I notice first isn't the barn's absence, although that spot is still empty. It's the log cabin directly in front of us.

"What the hell?" I ask eloquently.

Hank parks in front of the cabin and gets out of the truck. I'm so shocked that I can't get out of my seat until Hank walks around to my side and opens my door.

"I wasn't waiting for you to be chivalrous," I say. "I'm confused. That wasn't there before, was it?"

Hank laughs. "Fifteen years ago? No. But barns can disappear in fifteen years. Houses can show up. Lots of things can change."

You've got that right, I think to myself. Laugh lines show up on faces. Hearts break and mend and break all over again. Fifteen years is time enough for any number of changes.

"Who lives here?" I ask, finally stepping out of the truck.

"Me," Hank says, walking away from the cabin.

I follow him. "Sorry to repeat myself, but what the hell? You don't live here. You live in Nashville."

"Are you a human embodiment of my Wikipedia page?" Hank asks, amused, looking over his shoulder at me. He stops walking and turns around. "I do live in Nashville. For now. But I thought maybe I'd start coming back to Baileyville more often, and it would be nice to have my own place here. My family owns this land, and we weren't doing anything with it."

I nod, trying to speak past the lump in my throat. Why would Hank plan on coming back here more often? For the express purpose of torturing me? I was doing just fine pretending to forget him, but it's a whole lot harder to pretend someone doesn't exist when they're standing right in front of you, wearing a thin gray T-shirt that clings to their chest and low-slung jeans that are faded and ripped in all the right places.

"Plus," Hank says. "You can't beat the view."

I stand beside him as we both look out over the Baileyville valley. "The best place to watch the sunset," I say quietly.

"The ideal reading spot," Hank says, crossing his arms.

The wind ruffles my hair as I gaze over the town, at the couple of square miles where I've lived my entire life.

"Too bad we didn't bring a book," I say.

We stand there in silence for a moment, looking at how the sun touches every part of the valley. Even though talking to Hank was always fun, this was nice, too. The way we didn't have to talk all the time. The way he never felt like he had to fill empty space with unimportant words. It gave me time to think, and it made whatever he did say seem all the more significant.

"You wanna see the house?" he asks, turning to face me.

My breath catches in my throat. It's one thing to be out here in the open with Hank—the fresh air gives my feelings space to dissipate and float off into the sky. But in an enclosed environment? His home? It feels too emotionally fraught, too dangerous. In short, it feels like a really foolish thing to do.

"Yes," I say. "I'd love to see the house."

Chapter Twenty

For starters, there's a porch. I'm a sucker for a front porch, and this one has a wooden railing and a swing that's slowly blowing in the breeze. The house is new, but somehow it looks lived in, comfortable, and ever so slightly worn out. I can't help myself; I imagine what this could look like if I got my hands on it. Flowers in front, of course. A little stone walkway. Toby sitting right here.

I shake my head.

Hank opens the door and leads me inside, where the first thing I see is a massive stone fireplace that takes up most of the far wall. It's not lit now, given that it's already sweltering, but it still adds an air of coziness. The living space and kitchen take up the front room, and I can see a small hallway by the fireplace that presumably leads to bedrooms. On the other side of the fireplace, a wooden staircase leads to a loft. A guitar leans against a deep blue armchair—Hank's guitar, I realize. The old one, from high school.

I look away from it quickly, only to notice what must be the best part of the entire cabin: the windows.

"Holy mackerel," I whisper, accidentally quoting Edith. Almost the entire wall is windows, looking out from the top of the hill at the valley. The wide expanse of blue sky and the rolling green treetops makes me feel like we're in a tree house, almost like we're swaying in the breeze.

"The view was the primary motivation behind building here," Hank says. "Although that's probably pretty obvious."

I cross my arms as Hank walks across the room and stands beside me. "It looks so pretty from up here. Baileyville, I mean."

"Yeah," Hank says. "Turns out it's not such a bad place after all."

I turn my head slightly and our eyes meet. He's got to stop looking at me like that, because my brain is swimming in impure thoughts, and I'm afraid they're showing on my face. I never should've agreed to being inside with him.

"Fireplace is nice," I say loudly and awkwardly.

Hank raises an eyebrow, but goes along with it. "Yeah, you remember Dusty Smith from high school?"

"Impossible to forget someone named Dusty," I say, fixing my eyes on the fireplace as if it's the most interesting thing I've ever seen. Anything to avoid looking at what Hank's arms are doing through the thin fabric of that T-shirt. "Also, he still lives here, so I see him all the time."

"Then you know he and his family have that stonework business. They designed this, put it all up before I ever saw it."

"What about the rest of this?" I ask, walking through the room. I run my hand over the back of the smooth leather couch— usually I hate using food words to describe nonfood items (describing a person as "delicious," gross), but the only way to describe this leather is "buttery." I admire the floating shelves that look like they're made out of reclaimed wood. "You didn't do this, right?"

"I'm excited to do some work on it myself, but most of the actual construction was done before I got back," Hank says. "My dad sourced it all through his buddies. You know how he always knows a guy who can do anything."

I grin, looking at him over my shoulder. "Yeah, that sounds like Mr. Tillman."

"There are two small bedrooms and a bathroom back there," he says, then points upstairs. "And that's where I sleep, in the loft."

I turn around to face him, leaning against his kitchen counter. "I assumed you were staying with your parents."

Hank nods. "My mom would love to have me stay there. But she tends to forget that I'm a grown man now, not a football-playing teenager who needs multiple servings of lasagna every night."

"Ah, yes," I say. "I get now why you couldn't stay there. Who could possibly handle the lasagna onslaught?"

He laughs. "You know what I mean, though, right? You needed your own space."

I think back to what it was like to be staying in my old bedroom during college. How it felt to come back to that same unchanged space every day, to feel like nothing in my life was different. To feel like my role in my parents' life hadn't changed and never would.

I nod. "Yeah."

We look at each other for a moment. "This is really nice, Hank. It's really . . ." I search for the right word. "Sturdy."

He narrows his eyes. "Sturdy? Yeah, I don't live in a home made out of tinfoil, if that's what you mean."

I frown. "I mean . . . this is *real*. This isn't a place to crash. This is a home."

Hank takes a step toward me. "Are you asking me if I'm planning to stay here?"

I swallow. I don't know what I want his answer to be. The biggest part of me wants him to leave and never come back so I can stop feeling like this, so I can go back to how it was before I ran into him in the market. Comfortable. Secure. Content.

But there's a part of me that wants to hear him say he'll be here all the time. A part of me that wants him to surprise me at work or at my house every day and take me on an adventure, a part of me that needs to see his smile. And that part of me is growing with every second, with every step he takes toward me.

I bite my lower lip.

Hank keeps walking toward me, green and blue behind him in the windows. I wish I could paint this, or this *feeling*, the beauty and the uncertainty of it.

He stands in front of me, then puts one hand on the counter beside my hip, almost touching me. He leans there, his eyes level with mine. Hank and I are almost the exact same height, and I forgot what it's like to look directly into someone's eyes like this. It's never been like this with any other man—I'm always looking up or down, never quite on even footing. But Hank and I are on the exact same level. We always have been.

"I plan on being around a lot more," Hank says, answering the question I can't find the words to ask. "I've been avoiding Baileyville all these years because . . . well, because of you."

I close my eyes, taking a deep breath and willing myself not to cry. I sort of assumed we'd never talk about this, that we'd brush it under one of the cabin's rustic Western-print rugs. Part of me wants to tell him to shut up, wants to curse him for bringing this up. How I ruined us, how I ruined everything. How I messed up my own life, until I fixed it. How I let him go and lost him, how he married someone else. How we've had entirely separate lives this entire time because of me, because I pushed him away.

"I'm sorry," I whisper, pinching my eyes shut hard.

"Hey." I open my eyes to see him looking at me with concern. He reaches his hand out and brushes a tear off my face with his thumb. "Sandy. I'm not asking for an apology. We were kids, and we both made mistakes."

I try to laugh, but it comes out sad and rueful. "You didn't do anything wrong. You never have."

"Oh, believe me," he says with a grin. "I've made plenty of mistakes in my life. In case you forgot, I'm divorced. And sure, maybe that mess of a marriage was the best thing that ever happened to me because I got Henry out of it, and I would've gone through way worse if it meant I'd get to spend my life taking care of him. But I still wish there'd been some other way for us to get there, you know? Some way that didn't make me feel like such a failure, like I wasted years trying to change someone who didn't want to be changed."

I huff out a little laugh. "You're not a failure. At least you've *been* married, you know? At least you tried. I dated my way through Baileyville, and no one . . . they're not . . ."

I trail off, afraid to say what I'm thinking.

Hank places his other hand on the counter, surrounding me with him. There's nowhere else to look, no way to avoid this. Hank Tillman is all around me.

"Are you saying," he asks slowly, "that you've never met anybody else like me?"

I look into his eyes, mere inches from mine. "There's no one else like you."

He smiles with one side of his mouth. "Maybe that's a good thing."

I press my lips together. "I can promise you, it's not."

I study the freckles across his nose, the tiny scar on his eyebrow from when he fell off the seesaw when he was a kid. He's the same as always, with a few key differences. There's something else in his face now that wasn't written there fifteen years ago, something that has nothing to do with his skin or his features. He's a man now, not the boy I knew back then. He's grown up—we both have. But he's still Hank, still the person I knew, still the familiar face I come back to in my dreams.

"You look the same, you know," I say.

"You don't," he says, lifting one of his hands to touch my bottom lip. I want to protest, but there are no words in my mind right now, just random bursts of punctuation. My entire body is an exclamation point.

"You look so much better," he says, moving his hand to cup my cheek. "I've met a lot of people on the road, but I haven't met anyone else like you, Sandy. I can't talk to anyone the way I talk to you."

I nod, not trusting myself with words right now.

"You were my best friend, you know," he says. "You were my best friend, and then I . . . and then I lost you."

It isn't a conscious decision to kiss Hank, to reach my arms out and pull him into me. It just happens, like it's supposed to. This time, unlike at that bar in Chicago, he kisses me back, hard and deep. We let our bodies say everything we've been afraid to say with words, and it feels like we're apologizing for years of regret and longing and loneliness.

My heartbeat thumps out a rhythm that sounds a lot like, *I love you*. And I know that it's true, that I loved Hank then and I love him now. No one else will ever kiss me like I'm theirs; no one will ever feel like him in my arms. He runs a hand up under the hem of my shirt, and I can't help the undignified noises that come out of my mouth.

"Hank," I gasp, and then I start to cry.

Hank stops kissing me, takes his hand out from under my shirt. I feel cold without his hands on me, and I want to ask him to put them back, but I know that's the wrong decision.

"Sandy," he says gently. "What's going on?"

"We can't do this," I say, crying even harder. This isn't a dainty trickle of feminine tears—this is a full-on snot-filled sob.

"Okay," he says, smoothing my hair. "Why not?"

I try to compose myself, but it's difficult to explain what's happening when I'm not even sure I understand myself.

Hank walks over to the table by the couch, grabs a box of tissues, and brings it to me.

"Thanks," I say, taking a handful.

"Talk to me, Macintosh," he says lightly, and that makes me actually laugh.

He leans up against the counter beside me, and it's easier that I don't have to look at his beautiful face while I say this. "You were my best friend, too, you know. No offense to Honey, who's also my best friend."

"Hopefully not in the *exact* same way," Hank says.

"A few key differences. But you were . . . you were my everything, Hank. I planned my whole life around you. And when everything fell apart, I didn't have *anything*." I sniffle. "Things got bad when you went off to college. Almost everyone left. Honey came back on the weekends, but even then, she wanted to spend time with her boyfriend. I guess I could've spent my weekdays hanging out with Brian, but what would we talk about? How much we loved Honey? I felt left behind and . . . I didn't handle it well."

"I would've been there for you, if you'd let me," Hank says, and I can hear the frustration in his voice.

"Exactly. That was the problem. After you came home for the fair, and I had to be around you and everyone else who knew what they wanted out of their lives, you and Natasha Stevenson in your college hoodies, I knew I couldn't do it anymore. All I wanted was you, but I knew that if you came back, it would ruin everything for you."

"It wouldn't have—"

"It would have. You would've stayed here to make me happy, and you wouldn't have stayed in school."

His silence lets me know I'm right.

"So I told you I didn't want you around anymore, and that was a lie," I continue. "Obviously. But I didn't know what else I *did* want. I stopped painting because it only made me think about how I wasn't in art school. I stopped doing anything, really. For a while I went to my classes, but I wasn't doing particularly well in them because I guess you need to actually read textbooks and do your homework. And then I stopped . . . ugh."

I cringe, embarrassed to go on, but Hank squeezes my arm to encourage me.

"I stopped leaving my room. I stopped getting out of bed. I failed my classes, and I only ate frozen food that I scavenged out of the freezer while my parents were at work, except for the dinners my mom convinced me to come downstairs for, when I would sit there and pick at my food as they looked at me like I was this strange, sullen monster who'd replaced their golden straight-A child. I slept as much as I could because I just wanted to be unconscious. I would've done anything to avoid thinking about what a loser I was and how I'd ruined my entire life."

"You've never been a loser," Hank says.

I tilt my head to the side. "Loser's in the eye of the beholder. Anyway, one weekend, Honey and I had plans, and she walked into my room to find me smelly and horrible. You know how much Honey loves to take charge . . ."

Hank smiles. "Do I ever."

"So she and my parents basically staged an intervention, and they figured out a plan to get me back on track. I was so far gone, Hank." I shake my head. "Like, I didn't give a shit about anything, but when I saw how worried they were about me, I knew I had to do something. My *dad* cried when he saw how broken I was, which might be the only time I've ever seen him cry over anything other than a Buckeyes' loss. It was awful, and so I told myself I'd do whatever I had to do to make them stop worrying, even if I personally barely cared about getting up every morning. I started going to class again. I got a job at Country Colors because Honey swore being outside in the sunshine would be good for me."

I sigh, smiling a little bit at the memory. "And the annoying thing was . . . she was right. Eventually, I wasn't doing all of it, the classes and the working and the 'having a functional life,' for them. Eventually, I wasn't pretending anymore. I was actually building my own life, and liking what I'd built. I didn't feel like some left-behind loser anymore . . . now I had something of my own. I'm a part of this town."

Hank meets my eyes. "Yeah, you are. Everyone here loves you."

"Once I had my life together, once I owned the greenhouse and had a house, I thought . . . I don't know, I guess I thought maybe things might work out for us, and then Chicago happened."

"I'm sorry—" Hank starts, but I hold up a hand to stop him.

"We really, really don't have to talk about it. It was embarrassing, but also it made me remember all those awful feelings I had after high school. And I couldn't do that again. I *can't* do that again. What we had was special, but it's over. We've both had entire lives since then. And you'll be gone again soon, back on the road or back into the recording studio or whatever it is that your job requires . . . the point is, even if you're here sometimes, you won't be here all the time, and I will be. I'll always be here. And I just . . . I can't be here missing you."

I take a deep breath and give him a firm look. "I think we should be friends."

"Friends?" Hank asks. "An interesting proposition."

"We were always friends, Hank," I say quietly. "We were always friends first."

Hank exhales and I focus on his hands. "What you're saying . . . it makes a lot of sense, Sandy. I mean, as I've mentioned, I just got divorced."

"Yeah, you talk about it, like, all the time," I say, and he shoves my shoulder.

"I can't really do anything intense right now, either," he says. "But I'm here now, and we can't not see each other . . ."

"I think we've proven that," I agree.

"So . . . friends," he says, then holds out a hand.

"I'm supposed to shake your hand?" I ask with a laugh.

"What else do friends do?" Hank asks. "A chest bump?"

"I draw the line at chest bumps," I say.

"Okay, how about a hug?" Hank asks. "The kind of normal hug you'd give any friend."

"Right," I say, and we awkwardly lean in toward each other, our arms bumping as we find the right placement. But once I'm hugging him, it isn't awkward. Our bodies fit together perfectly, and my head finds its home on his shoulder. This simple hug feels extremely dangerous.

I pat his back. "Good hug, friend."

He pulls back. "Thanks, friend. Means a lot coming from you."

"So." I point toward the door. "I guess I'm gonna get going, and someone needs to drop off those dolls at the community center. But, uh, you picked me up, so . . ."

"You wanna stay?" Hank asks.

"What?"

"You wanna . . . I don't know, eat something? Watch a movie? Friends do that, right?"

I nod slowly. "I do that exact thing with Honey all the time."

So Hank and I make tacos together, the both of us in his small kitchen, laughing each time we bump into each other. We have beers and eat and watch some action movie, one where two giant monsters are fighting each other and destroying a city in the process. It makes us laugh and roll our eyes and shout things at the screen, and it really does feel like it used to, for a moment. Sure, Hank is sitting in the armchair and I'm on that soft leather couch, but other than that, it's like old times.

And when the movie's over, Hank drives me home, bugs splattering against the windshield as we cruise down the winding back roads. *This is perfect*, I think to myself. Maybe I even feel a little smug, thinking about how we're two grown adults who are perfectly capable of maintaining a normal friendship. I look at Hank and he looks back at me, smiling before turning his gaze to the road again. See? Normal.

When Hank drops me off, I give him a thanks and a wave, and close the truck door with a squawk. I make my way up my stone walkway, turning around once I get to my front steps, glowing with the solar lights lining my flower beds. I give Hank another wave and pause with my hand in the air as I see the look on his face. He's staring right at me, waiting until I get in the house safely, and I'm pulled back to every time he did this when we were kids. Back when I was his girl, forever.

I hop up the stairs and unlock the door as quickly as I can, then slip inside without looking behind me again. I lean against the door, pressing my eyes shut.

Toby runs in from the other room, and as I crouch down to let him give me sweet doggy kisses, I hear Hank's truck sputter away.

"Tobes," I say, "this might be a little harder than I thought."

Chapter Twenty-One

"DID YOU TRIM your own bangs again?"

Shelby meets my eyes in the mirror, her eyebrows raised. Under the black cape covering my torso, I shrug my shoulders. "It was an emergency."

She snorts. "No, what I have to deal with now is an emergency. Good Lord, Sandy."

"Shelby," I say with a smile, pleading to her vanity. "Please fix my mess of hair. No one makes me look good like you do. You're the master."

"Well." She smiles as she paints on the highlight cream and folds foil around chunks of my hair. "This is true. It's not all that hard, though. You're pretty smoking."

I attempt to turn around and give her a confused look, but she smacks my shoulder. "Stay still. And don't make that horrible face or I'll retract my comment. You *are* hot, if you let yourself be."

"I'm almost always covered in dirt," I remind her.

"Maybe some guys like that," she says breezily, moving the

brush like she's painting a work of art. "I mean, sure, you could stand to show some more boob and maybe consider a bit of lipstick once in a while."

"I don't have any boobs," I say honestly. "And dirt and hair and plants get stuck in lipstick."

"Get one with a matte finish," she says, sounding bored as if we've covered this before . . . and, in her defense, maybe we have. "I'll give you one on your way out. My charitable contribution to society."

I place my hand over my heart. "Thank you."

She smacks my shoulder again. "And you do too have boobs. Maybe you weren't blessed with these." She points toward her chest without taking her eyes off my hair. "But we've all gotta work with what we've got. For example, I was cursed with short legs, and that's why I always wear heels. Not all of us have supermodel bodies like you."

I frown. Maybe this was why she used to be so mean to me. "This might sound weird, but were you like . . . jealous of me in high school?"

She stops painting and meets my eyes in the mirror again. "Um, seriously? Yes. Duh."

"What?" I screech, and she shushes me.

"People come in here to relax, Sandy, not hear your primal wails. Of course I was jealous of you! I was short and dating Brandon Zelansky . . ."

I wrinkle my nose. "He was gross. Why were you with him?"

"A question I've asked myself a million times. But there you were, all tall and beautiful and dating Hank Tillman, every girl's dream. Brandon's idea of chivalry was paying for my Burger King order and then groping me in his car while he had onion ring breath. Everyone knew Hank Tillman was, like, the nicest boy in school, and you had him wrapped around your little finger."

I start to slide down in my chair in shame, and Shelby sighs. "Sandy. For the last time, you need to sit still. I can't work under these conditions. You're like a toddler!"

"Sorry," I say, sitting up straight.

"So what's the deal with Hank, anyway?" she asks, wrapping foil around another piece of my hair.

"What do you mean?" I watch her in the mirror, trying my best to sit still.

"He's not married anymore, right?"

I pause, open my mouth, and shut it again.

"Wait," she says. "Are you two . . . a thing?"

"We're . . . we're friends," I sputter out. "Just friends. Friends only. Friends."

She narrows her eyes at me. "Okay. Well, in that case, you think it's okay if I ask him out?"

"You and Hank?" The words come out like a whisper.

"I won't do it if it will be weird for you," she says. "But you know as well as I do that there are no single men in this town."

She lowers her voice. "I need *male companionship*, Sandy. And if you're not taking advantage of Hank's return, then someone ought to, right?"

I nod slowly. The thing is, Shelby's right. I don't own Hank, and it's not like I have any right to tell two consenting adults they shouldn't go on a date. Or hook up. Or . . . whatever. I don't want to think about it.

"Sure," I chirp. "Why not? Hank's a great guy."

"He is," Shelby says firmly, lifting up the tray with her highlight supplies. "Okay, I'm gonna go wash all this stuff. You hang out here, and I'll be back to check on you in half an hour. You need anything?"

I lift up the copy of *People* magazine I have under the cape. "I've got a lot of catching up to do with the *Sister Wives* family."

She shakes her head, exasperated. "I feel like that guy shouldn't have married so many women if he didn't want to deal with drama. Like, have one wife. Or no wives. But more than one? You're asking for trouble."

"I couldn't agree more," I say.

She starts to walk away, then leans back toward me. "You know Brandon used to drive around with an empty Gatorade bottle in his car so he could spit his chew into it?"

I grimace. "Seriously, Shelby. Why did you date him?"

She starts to walk away. "All I'm saying is, the standard for men here is, like, basement level. If I meet a good one, I'm gonna go for him."

I frown at myself in the mirror. This is perhaps the worst time to be alone with my thoughts—I look about as ridiculous as I possibly could, with pieces of foil protruding from my head at odd angles and my body ensconced in what looks like a garbage bag. And it's either stare at myself or be confronted with the mental image of Shelby and Hank on a date. It's hard to imagine which one I'd rather think about.

I sigh and open the magazine in my hands. At least I have the *Sister Wives* to distract me.

Chapter Twenty-Two

About once a month, I babysit so Honey and Brian can have a date night. I'm Aunt Sandy to the kids, and as an only child without nieces and nephews of my own, I love it. I've held all of them when they were merely hours old, and I was even present for Charlie's birth because he came early when Brian was out of town. We might not be related by blood, but they're my family.

Honey and Brian drove to Cleveland to have dinner and see the ballet tonight, so the kids are spending the night here. As usual, I might be even more excited about the idea of a slumber party than the kids are, at least when it comes to snacks. We have chips, taquitos, pizza rolls, M&M's, and there's cookie dough in the fridge waiting to be baked. I'm not necessarily saying I'm buying their affection with all the food they rarely get, but I'm not *not* saying that.

"Aunt Sandy!" Maddie yells from the living room as I grab a baking sheet. "Charlie ate all the potato chips!"

"That's fine," I yell back. "We have more. You guys ready for cookies?"

Their shouts let me know they are, and I smile to myself. *See? I'm good at this kid thing. I'd make a great mom. Sure, my kids wouldn't know what vegetables are, and they'd probably get scurvy, but at least they'd be happy.*

We're in the middle of a double feature, having watched *Shaun the Sheep* and moving onto *Shaun the Sheep: Farmageddon*. The kids are curled up on my sofa under some blankets, I can see the sun beginning to set through the back door, and I truly couldn't be happier.

I decide to bake the cookies as the movie starts, but Toby whines right when I start to scoop cookie dough onto the baking sheet. "Hey, Rosie?" I ask. "Can you let Toby out? My hands are dirty."

"Yeah." She walks into the kitchen and opens the door to the fenced-in backyard, letting Toby run outside to do his business. She leaves the door open as she asks, "You need any help?"

"You are so polite," I say. "Your parents are really raising you well. Actually, could you take this bowl of chips in to your sister and brother? I hear Charlie ate all the other ones."

She rolls her eyes. "He always does," she says conspiratorially.

Just then, we hear Toby yelp outside, and then he barrels into the room, feet scrabbling on the floor. But he isn't alone.

"What was that?" I ask, dropping my cookie scoop into the bowl.

We hear a shriek from the living room. "It's a squirrel!" Maddie yells.

"A squirrel?" Rosie asks, eyes wide. She looks at me. "Are they supposed to be inside?"

I start washing my hands. "Uh, no. I can confidently say they aren't."

We walk into the living room and see Toby standing guard by the sofa, his nose stuffed underneath it.

"Well," I say, "we have a good idea where the squirrel is."

Maddie and Charlie screech from where they're standing on the sofa. "Is it UNDER HERE?" Charlie asks. "UNDER MY FEET?"

"The squirrel won't hurt you," I say. "Probably."

"Mom says wild animals can carry rabies," Rosie says matter-of-factly. "That's why we're not allowed to touch the racoon that eats our garbage."

"I don't want wabies!" Charlie cries.

"Okay, okay." I step to the sofa and grab a child in each arm, then carry them into the kitchen and sit them on the counter. "Now you're up so high, the squirrel can't reach you."

Rosie rolls her eyes. "Everyone knows squirrels can climb. They live in trees."

"I don't want the squirrel to climb up here and bite me," Charlie sobs.

"Not helpful," I tell Rosie quietly.

She frowns. "What am I supposed to do? Not tell the truth about squirrels?"

"You are so much like your mother," I mutter. And that makes me realize who I would normally call if I were in this position, not that I've ever had a squirrel under my sofa before. Typically, any animal-related questions go to Honey. Like the time I found an injured baby bunny in my backyard or the time Toby ate an entire bag of Blow Pops meant for trick-or-treaters—wrappers, sticks, and all. (He was fine because his stomach is made of steel.)

But Honey is, of course, in Cleveland right now, which is the entire reason her kids are here in the first place. The last thing I want to do is bother her on date night.

I mentally run through the list of people I could call while attempting to comfort the kids. My parents? They're working; plus, they don't know anything about wildlife. Marcia has a well-documented fear of rodents, which I know because she loses her ever-loving shit on the many, many occasions we see mice way out in the country.

But Hank, however . . . well, Hank always knows what to do in any situation. Maybe that extends to squirrel emergencies.

"Hold on, everyone," I say with as much authority as I can muster. "I'm calling in reinforcement."

"What's 're-forz-men'?" wails Charlie as I pull out my phone and call Hank. "Is it gonna bite me, too?"

"No one is biting anyone tonight!" I shout as Hank picks up the phone.

"Good to know," he says. "Thanks for the update."

"Shit. I mean, dammit. I mean . . . oh wow, don't tell your mom and dad about any of this, kids. There's a *squirrel* in the house, Hank. I have Honey and Brian's kids here and a squirrel ran in and it's under the sofa and I don't know how I'm gonna get it out."

I take a deep breath and Toby barks.

"Okay," Hank says slowly.

"Have you ever . . . trapped a squirrel?" I ask, grasping helplessly for the words. "Am I supposed to trap it? I don't even know!"

"I don't wanna get wabies!" Charlie shouts directly into the phone.

"Hold on," Hank says calmly. "I'll be there as soon as I can. No one's gonna get wabies on my watch."

And then he hangs up.

"It's like he's a cowboy or something," I mutter, sliding my phone back into my pocket.

"We should probably move the food off the coffee table," Rosie points out. "The squirrel might crawl out to eat it."

I point at her. "Good idea, Rosie. Let's hope he stays under the couch until Hank gets here."

She helps me pick up the trays and bowls of food as her brother and sister sit on the counter, sniffling. "You said a lot of bad words, but I won't tell Mom," she whispers.

I stifle a laugh. "Thank you."

Toby growls, reminding us about our uninvited guest.

After a few tense minutes and plenty of tears, there's a knock on the door.

"We're in the kitchen!" I shout, afraid to leave the kids to get the door.

Hank slowly opens the door and walks in, keeping Henry behind him with one arm as if guarding him from attack. As Toby scrambles up from his guard post and rushes to cover Hank and Henry in sloppy dog kisses, the squirrel grabs his chance and bolts out from under the sofa.

"There it is!" I screech louder than the kids' screams.

The squirrel, presumably freaked out by all the screaming and barking, runs under the armchair. Toby growls and sniffs around it, as if he's going to do anything. Henry puts his hands over his ears and runs to the kitchen, where he joins the kids on the counter.

"Help is here," Hank says cockily over the cacophony, and I roll my eyes. "Have you closed the doors to all the other rooms?"

"No. Was I supposed to?"

"Okay." Hank gets to work closing all the doors downstairs and dragging my sofa to block off the staircase. "So what we're gonna do is open all the windows and take out the screens."

"Why?" I ask as Maddie shouts, "That's gonna let in MORE squirrels!"

Hank stops opening one of the windows and turns to look each of us in the eyes. "Do you trust me? Charlie? Maddie? Rosie? Henry? Sandy?"

We all nod.

"Good. Because I'm gonna get this squirrel out of here before it bites anyone." He lifts out the screen, then moves on to the next window, then opens the front and back door. He grabs one of the blankets from the sofa and hands it to me.

"What am I supposed to do with this?" I ask.

He grabs another blanket. "Kids, I need each of you to get a big metal pot and a spoon. Can you do that?"

I frown at him in confusion and help them find pots and spoons.

"Okay," he says, leaning down to talk to the kids. "Go stand behind the chair and on the count of three, I want you to bang your spoons on your pots. Make as much noise as you can."

Fear forgotten, the kids run toward the chair. Turns out the chance to make a lot of noise trumps being scared of a squirrel bite.

"What about me?" I ask, holding up my blanket.

"When the kids make noise, it will hopefully scare the squirrel out. You and I will flap these blankets to direct the squirrel away from the kids and toward the window or door. Make sense?"

"I feel like I'm bullfighting with a squirrel," I say. "But I'll try it. It's not like I have any better ideas."

"All right," Hank calls as we stand in front of the kids, holding our blankets aloft. "On the count of three . . . one . . . two . . . THREE!"

Rosie, Charlie, Maddie, and Henry squeal with delight as they hit the pots as hard as they can, making a ruckus that I'm sure is alarming everyone in the neighborhood. The squirrel bolts out from under the chair, looking back and forth as if evaluating his options.

"Herd him out!" Hank shouts, and the two of us flap blankets to guide it toward the nearest window.

"Is it working?" I shout with my eyes closed.

"Maybe try opening your eyes!" Hank shouts back over the noise from the pans.

I open them just in time to see the squirrel dart out the window and into the night.

"We did it!" I shout as the kids cheer, still hitting those pots with their spoons. In my excitement, I jump onto Hank and give him a hug as if we've vanquished a beast far more sinister than a squirrel.

His arms wrap around me, and for a moment, I forget that maybe I shouldn't be doing this. But friends hug, right? Friends occasionally take a minute to appreciate their friend's impressively broad shoulders and toned back muscles. Friends simply can't help but notice their friend's woodsy sawdust scent, like if Home Depot was a nightclub.

Okay, maybe that's a stretch. I pull away from him and loudly tell the kids how great they did, giving them each big kisses on the forehead and pulling Henry into a hug. "Thanks for coming to help us," I tell him. "We couldn't have done it without you and your dad."

"You guys were so brave," Hank says. "That squirrel never even stood a chance."

"So now that these are no longer necessary," I say, grabbing the pots and spoons from the kids before they can cause permanent hearing loss, "how about some cookies to celebrate our victory over that rodent?"

"Yeah!" shouts Charlie, all tears forgotten as Hank slides the couch back in place. They don't need more sugar this late in the evening, but I have to keep myself busy. The kids settle in on the now squirrel-free couch as Hank goes about shutting all the windows and doors. Even though Henry only met Honey's children moments ago, they all seem completely comfortable together. Perhaps living through the Great Squirrel Incident bonded them for life.

I assume Hank and Henry will be on their way now that the furry threat is gone, but instead, Hank settles down on the armchair. I peer at him from the kitchen, but he keeps his eyes on the television.

Eventually, the cookies come out of the oven, and I pile them onto a plate before taking them into the living room.

"Scootch," I say, crowding onto the sofa amongst the kids.

"I can get up," Hank says, standing. "You can take this chair."

"Nope!" I say cheerfully. "This is great!"

"Aunt Sandy likes to be close to us," Charlie says before burping.

"That I do," I say, and Hank sits back down, smiling.

By the time the movie is over and Shaun the Sheep has gotten into more hijinks than anyone would ever dream, Honey's kids are almost completely asleep. Henry has already migrated into Hank's lap, where he's snoozing peacefully. I herd the Michaelses into bed without brushing their teeth (another perk of not being their actual parent: I don't have to worry about dental hygiene), read a story, sing a song, come back in and do a repeat performance upon Charlie's request, and then go downstairs with a sigh.

"Rough night, huh?"

I jump and almost trip down the last stair. "Damn! I forgot you were here."

"You're very jumpy," Hank says calmly, taking a sip from a glass of water. Henry is still asleep on his lap.

"I'm not used to someone being here when I come downstairs," I say, placing a hand over my quickly beating heart and heading into the kitchen.

"You telling me you don't have a parade of men coming through your living room?" he calls as I open the cupboard.

"Uh, no," I say with a laugh, grabbing a bag of microwave popcorn. I stick it in the microwave and lean on the kitchen counter, watching Hank. He's scrolling through channels with one socked foot up on the coffee table, looking impossibly comfortable in my home, like he's meant to be here.

The first kernel pops and he looks up, eager. "You're making popcorn?"

I smile. "I assume it's still your favorite."

"Still is," he says, lifting Henry as he stands. He carefully places Henry back on the armchair, arranging a pillow under his head, then stretches with a groan. I attempt to not look at his exposed stomach or the smattering of hair there or think about that noise he just made.

"Hey, Macintosh," he says. "My eyes are up here."

Blushing, I turn around and open a cabinet, loudly moving things around as if I'm looking for a bowl. "Henry's a sound sleeper, huh?"

"Oh yeah," he says, coming up behind me and standing entirely too close. "It's great. When he was a baby, I could vacuum in his nursery as he slept, and it didn't even register with him."

"Honey's kids definitely don't have that gene," I say, reaching up to grab a large stainless-steel bowl out of the cabinet. "I'd bet fifty bucks that Maddie will be down here soon asking for a 'little drink' or telling me that her stomach hurts, so she must be hungry and she needs another cookie or five."

Hank reaches out to touch the bowl, grazing my fingers. I ignore the jolt that runs from my hands up to my heart. "Let me help you with that."

The microwave beeps, and I step away from him as quickly as possible. "Popcorn's ready!"

"There'd better be some of those crunchy unpopped kernels in there for me," Hank says.

I dump the bag into the bowl, wrinkling my nose. "You're still eating those? God, we're old now, Hank. You're going to destroy your teeth."

He points to his mouth. "Not to brag, but I still have all my original teeth."

I let out a low whistle. "Well, well, well. Let me alert the ladies of Baileyville that here in my home, I have a man with a full set of teeth."

"Don't make fun," he says, following me into the living room. I assume he'll share the armchair with Henry again, but instead he sits down right beside me on the sofa. My heart leaps as the cushions sink under his weight.

He grabs the remote, and I allow myself a moment of imagining that this is our life. We just put our kids to bed, and now we're relaxing with some trashy television and popcorn. This is our house, and we're married, and we've built this whole life together.

And then I remember my reality. That I live here in a life I built all by myself. And Hank has a job, one that takes him on the road, and an ex-wife and a whole world that didn't include me for the last fifteen years. And, most importantly, a kid who's sleeping on my chair right now. A child, one with perfect eyelashes casting shadows on his slumbering face, who isn't mine and never will be.

We're nothing but trees that grew apart.

"Want a beer?" I ask brightly, standing up quickly and heading into the kitchen. "I have soda, too, if you'd rather have that."

"A Coke's good," Hank calls as I rattle around in the fridge for Cokes in glass bottles. I pop them open and head back into the living room. I hand Hank his bottle, brushing his fingers in the process. When I sit down, I cross my legs away from him, attempting to take up as little space as possible.

"Coke in a glass bottle?" Hank asks. "Fancy. Who are you, Martha Stewart?"

I laugh, taking a sip of mine. "I don't think Martha drinks Coke. But yes, I have a theory that Coke tastes best in a glass bottle. Basically, the Coke flavor order goes: glass bottle, can, fountain drink from a fast-food restaurant, individual-sized plastic bottle, and then, very last, poured into a glass from a two liter, which is an option I would only take in an emergency situation."

Hank throws his head back and laughs, but quietly so as not to wake the kids. "An emergency Coca-Cola situation?"

I smile. "They happen."

He shakes his head, then mutters, "What the hell is this?" At first I don't know what he's talking about, but then I look at the TV screen.

"*Sister Wives!*" I shout, then remember that the kids are asleep. "It's a reality show about this family with a plural marriage."

"Plural marriage," Hank states, and I realize he's never heard the term.

"It's one guy who has multiple wives," I say proudly, as if I'm acing a test. Honestly, I probably *could* ace a test on various TLC reality shows.

"*This* guy . . ." Hank says, looking at the screen and then looking back at me. "This guy has more than one wife?"

"Several," I say. "One of them left him, though it remains to be seen if she triggered a mass wife exodus."

"Huh," Hank says, looking both concerned and confused, and we watch *Sister Wives* for a moment, drinking in silence.

When the show breaks for commercial, I pretend to be interested in an ad for laundry detergent, but Hank turns toward me.

"I'm glad you called me tonight," he says.

I take a long swig of my Coke before answering him. "Yeah?"

He nods. "Rarely does a man get the chance to impress a room full of children by vanquishing a squirrel. I'm pretty sure Henry thinks I'm a hero now. Thanks for the opportunity."

I smile. "Thanks for coming over. Seriously. Maybe I could've done it myself, but not while calming them down and assuring them that the squirrel wasn't going to bite them."

"Well, wabies is a serious worry," Hank says. "Although squirrels are actually unlikely to transmit rabies."

I study him for a moment, my head tilted. "So . . . how do you know so much about squirrels?"

Hank raises his eyebrows and points to himself. "I don't look like a guy who's removed a few squirrels in his time?"

"I have no idea what such a guy would look like," I say.

"Googled it," Hank admits. "You called, I spent about two seconds looking up squirrel-removal tactics, then I headed over, said a prayer that I read accurate information, and acted confident. That's also when I found out that rabies isn't a big concern with squirrels—I heard you guys talking about getting bitten, and I wanted to know if a trip to urgent care was in the future."

I laugh. "Okay, that makes me feel so much better. I seriously thought you were, like, some sort of squirrel expert."

"What happened during our entire relationship that made you

think, 'Damn, Hank Tillman: that guy knows how to remove a squirrel'?" he asks, laughing as well.

"I don't know!" I throw up my hands. "And I wouldn't say you removed it. I'd say you . . . convincingly persuaded him to leave."

"What can I say, squirrels respect me."

"Thanks for coming over," I say quietly, looking at our feet side by side on the coffee table.

"I couldn't live with myself if a dangerous squirrel became your roommate," Hank says. "Okay, be quiet, it's back on!"

"Wow, I didn't know you were so invested in *Sister Wives* already."

Hank throws a couch pillow at my face. "Shut up! Meri is *speaking* and she is *mad*."

I laugh, tossing the pillow on the ground. See? This is actually very similar to a night I might spend with Honey. Drinks. Snacks. Bad reality television that makes us question the ethics of what we're watching. Talking back to the TV.

The difference, of course, is that I'm acutely aware of how close Hank is sitting next to me. Of his woodsy, bergamot scent, so much more adult than whatever deodorant or aftershave he was using in high school. Of the scruff on his face and the memory of how it felt on my face when we were in his cabin.

"You okay?" Hank asks.

"What?" I ask too quickly, sitting up straight.

"Your face is red," Hank says, looking concerned.

"Yeah, I should probably get to bed," I say, standing up. "These kids wake up early, you know."

"That's kids for you," Hank says. "Always all 'I wake up at 6 A.M., I can't reach the cabinets, I don't know how to drive.'"

I smile. "A shockingly accurate portrayal of a child."

"That's cool," he says, stretching again. This time, I pointedly keep my eyes on his face. "I should get home, too. You mind if I use the bathroom first, though?"

"No problem. It's right up the stairs." I gesture toward the stairs, in case he didn't understand what stairs were.

"Got it." He walks upstairs quietly, clearly trying not to wake the kids.

While he's up there, I start picking up bowls and plates and cookie crumbs on the floor. "Honestly, kind of surprised there weren't *more* rodents in here," I mutter, thinking about sweeping up before I go to bed. Henry sleeps peacefully on the armchair, and I stop for a moment to watch the gentle rise and fall of his belly as he sleeps. He looks so much like Hank, those same long eyelashes and that same freckled nose.

"Hey," Hank says, walking down the stairs. I turn to look at him and almost drop the bowls in my arms. He's holding the painting of him on the hill in front of the barn. "Is this . . . ?"

I put the bowls down. "Uh, yeah. That's . . . that's you."

"Sorry I pulled it off the wall. I'm . . . wow, Sandy, this is really good." He holds it in front of him, studying it.

"Thanks," I say, crossing my arms. While the act of painting always made me feel like disappearing, someone *looking* at one of my paintings in front of me has always made me feel like I'm naked and being judged. Now I regret hanging that painting up, even in the upstairs hallway, where I assumed no one but me would see it. I should've kept it hidden away in a closet, the way I'd planned to after I finished it, but I couldn't resist putting it where I could pass by it every day. It was slightly painful to see it, but some days I needed a reminder that I'd had something good and bold and bright once upon a time.

"This is the day we kissed for the first time," Hank says, and my jaw drops.

"How do you know that?" I ask. "How do you *remember* that?"

He shrugs. "I mean, of course I remember that day. Memorable for lots of reasons. But this painting . . . it *feels* like that day, you know?"

I press my lips together and nod. I'm not usually concerned with absolute realism in my paintings—I care more about capturing a feeling, a mood, the way a certain light or song or breeze makes me feel. And knowing that Hank sees that . . . well, it means something to me. It means everything.

"You're good at this, Sandy," he says. "Of course you are. You don't need me to tell you that."

"Thanks," I say.

"I'm serious." He looks at me. "Do you ever put your artwork in the Baileyville Street Fair Art Show? You should enter this one."

I laugh. "Hank. Remember that year that the grand prize went to a portrait of Garth Brooks?"

He nods. "It was a very realistic portrayal of Garth."

"All I'm saying is I couldn't possibly compete with true art like that."

He puts the painting down on the couch between us. "Do you still paint?"

"Sometimes. A little. Stuff for the inn."

"You mean those tiny abstract paintings in the dining room?" Hank asks.

"You noticed those?" I ask, wrinkling my nose. "No one notices those."

"They looked good," he says matter-of-factly. "But they're not this. You should be painting things that everyone notices, Sandy. Bigger things. Things you care about."

I bristle, feeling like a cat about to hiss. I don't really need Mr. Follow Your Dreams telling me to pick up a paintbrush and trust my heart or some other TJ Maxx clearance-shelf-distressed-wooden-sign wisdom. "Yeah, well." I grab the bowls again and turn away from him. "Life gets in the way sometimes, you know?"

"Sure," Hank says, frowning. "But you have talent, Sandy. You shouldn't hide it away and—"

I spin around and give him a big smile. "Thanks again for coming over. I really appreciate it."

I walk into the kitchen.

"Uh, okay," Hank says. He gently jostles Henry's shoulder. "Hey. Bub. Time to go."

Henry lets out a sleepy groan and Hank picks him up, holding him over his shoulder like he's a sack of flour.

"Bye," Hank says, drawing the word out like he's waiting to see if I have anything else to say.

My attempt to be a hard-ass and freeze Hank out completely crumbles. "Oh, here, let me get that," I say, running across the room to open the door for them. "I'm trying to be annoyed at you, and it's not working because you and Henry are so darn cute."

Hank raises his eyebrows. "So you're saying I'm cute?"

"I'm saying you and Henry as a combination are cute. And to be honest, Henry's doing most of the heavy lifting," I say. This feels suspiciously like flirting, but Henry's butt is directly beside Hank's face as I look into his eyes, and I'm not really sure this is even a situation one could flirt in. Probably this is an absolutely normal conversation between friends. I tell Honey she's cute all the time, like when she put on that hot red dress tonight that was way too low cut for the ballet, or when she wears her scrubs that have Garfield on them.

This is exactly like that. Obviously.

"But I'm still annoyed," I say, setting my face into what will have to pass for an annoyed look. "Very. Stop telling me what to do with my art."

"Point taken," Hank says, and then he looks down at the bowl where I keep my keys. "Is this made out of a record?"

"Yeah," I say. "It's a melted Billy Joel record, so I call it the Joel Bowl."

At first, I think Hank isn't going to respond, but then I realize he's silently laughing, trying not to wake up Henry as his shoulders shake.

Good one, he mouths, still laughing.

"Thanks for appreciating it," I say, fighting a smile.

"See you around, Sandy."

I wave and shut the door quietly behind them. Instead of watching him load Henry into the SUV, which might actually be too much for my heart to handle, I turn around and creep toward the painting on the sofa, as if I'm sneaking up on my past.

I cross my arms and look at it propped against a pillow. Hank's right. It is good. But it's also full of memories—not only of who's in the painting but how I used to feel when I painted. Maybe I don't want to think about who I was then or what it was like when I was purely, absurdly happy and hopeful and looking forward to my future. I need my life now to be enough—the one I've built, the one that keeps me comfortable and content and, most importantly, not riding high on emotions that will only crash and leave me stranded.

Still, though, something about what Hank said has my fingers itching to put paint on canvas. It's late, and I have to be up early tomorrow to make the chocolate chip pancakes I promised Charlie, but I can't stop myself from going upstairs and finding the paints I shoved into my closet, along with a big blank canvas that

I bought who knows when. I haven't used it because the only painting I do now is small. I spread everything out on my kitchen table before I can talk myself out of it.

I let myself work without thinking about it, the paintbrush floating over the canvas and slashing it with color. There's Hank as he looked in his cabin, in front of the window that overlooks the valley. I work quickly, swirling the blues and greens and adding in the white fluff of the clouds.

When I'm done, I grab the old painting off the couch and place it next to my new one. They look like companion pieces, almost the same view but fifteen years apart. I still love the lightness and pure adrenaline rush of the old one, but when I look at the one I just made, I feel something different. The colors are deeper, more complex. There's a more profound feeling than happiness here—a well-earned joy mixed with regret, nostalgia, and plain old time.

My heart's beating fast like I've finished a run, and I realize that this is excitement. I'm so damn *excited* about this painting. I had fun and I made something beautiful, and it was all because Hank Tillman told me to. Because even now, even after all these years, he still brings out the best part of me, the me that I wish I could be all the time.

CHAPTER TWENTY-THREE

Now THAT THE fair is only two days away, we're in serious all-hands-on-deck mode to make it happen. Something like the Baileyville Street Fair might seem effortless, but that's only because a team of people worked and sweated and argued for months to make it happen. By the time the rides are set up and the tents are assembled and the entire town smells like French fries, it will hopefully seem as if it all happened through magic, but for now, it takes another meeting of the Baileyville Street Fair Board.

"Okay, next up," Sean says, looking at his ever-present clipboard.

For a moment, I entertain a fantasy of taking that clipboard and hiding it. I wonder how he'd react.

"Sandy?" Sean asks, and I realize he asked me a question while I was daydreaming.

"Yes, Sean?" I ask politely, and Honey snorts.

"Are you still able to sort through the art show entries?"

I give him a quick salute.

"Saluting isn't strictly necessary," he says, checking something off on his clipboard. "A simple, 'Yes, Sean,' would suffice."

"Yes, Sean," I say loudly.

"You're gonna get on that man's last nerve someday," Barb says, but she looks like she's suppressing a smile.

"That's the plan," I whisper.

I'm happy to get the art show ready—it's usually one of my favorite fair tasks. We set it up in the Baileyville Public Library, the children's crayon drawings of their cats and dogs pinned up above the picture books. While the kids' art is always hilarious and adorable, I really love seeing the adult artwork. It's my job to hang everything up and make sure that the artists' names aren't visible to the judges, who make their decisions anonymously. Yes, sometimes people paint things like the aforementioned portrait of Garth Brooks, but it's often a lot more personal. Photographs of their vacations or their grandchildren. Paintings of their families or their backyards. It's a nice reminder that creativity is in all of us, and it lives everywhere, even in the smallest town and even if it's not your job.

Sean moves on to the rest of his agenda. Making sure we have people ready to set up the stage. The logistics of displaying extremely heavy vegetables. Who's going to DJ the Baileyville Street Fair Dance, also known as the most romantic night of the year.

After Shelby forces us all to pose for a group photo to post on the Baileyville Street Fair Instagram (which she's in charge of), Sean bangs his gavel and says, "Meeting adjourned."

We all stand up, and Shelby puts her arms around Honey and me. "You bitches ready for girls' night?" she asks.

"Language!" Sean calls from his chair without looking up.

"Sean, you're not my dad!" Shelby yells back. "And this meeting has already been adjourned. You have no power now!"

Sean looks up at us, speechless in horror.

"Let's get out of here," Honey mutters, pulling us toward the stairs. "Before Shelby and Sean get into a fight."

"I could take him," Shelby says lightly as we walk up the stairs.

"I don't know," I remind her as we step into the fading light of dusk. "His upper-body strength has been honed by frequently lifting that clipboard."

Honey snorts, and the three of us start walking toward the Ohio Inn. The concept of a girls' night out might be a little different in Baileyville than it is in bigger towns. Not that I would know from experience, but I assume that girls in cities have their choice of bars or restaurants, and the option of meeting new people. In Baileyville, we have the River Horse and . . . well, the Ohio Inn.

Which is why I'm having dinner and drinks on the inn's patio with Shelby and Honey tonight. The two of them agreed to help me set up the art show in the library after we eat, after assuring me that neither of them were judges. (None of us know who the judges are . . . like the illuminati, they're mysterious and secretive.)

And although I've memorized the menu here, I have to admit that it's actually quite lovely to spend an evening sitting outside, enjoying a glass of wine while not working. A wrought iron fence separates the patio from the town square, where the gazebo is lit up. The air is cooling off in the dusk, and I'm looking forward to getting a pleasant buzz from some pink wine. My feet ache from working at the greenhouse most of the day, but Marcia took care of closing tonight—she always handles a lot of the responsibilities at the greenhouse during fair season, and I'm grateful to have someone I can count on.

I'm grateful for Shelby and Honey's friendship, too, especially because I know what it's like to be lonely. I can still feel the emptiness of those first few months I spent here in Baileyville after high school, when Honey was in school and I hadn't yet figured out how to stop wallowing and make the best of the hand I'd been dealt. And now I have a life—a real one, with friends who can meet up for mushroom flatbreads and sweet wine and lots of gossip.

Although, to be fair, I'm not so sure I want to hear any gossip from Shelby right now, given that our last conversation was about how she was going to ask Hank out.

"You ladies ready for food?" Edith asks a few moments after we've ordered drinks. She pulls out a pen from behind her ear like she's a waitress in a 1970s TV show.

"The Greek salad and an order of French fries," Honey says, folding up her menu. Honey claims that this is the ideal dinner order because you get the best of both worlds: the virtue and fiber of a salad, and the fun and greasiness of the fries.

"The garlic burger," Shelby says.

"Mushroom flatbread, please," I say, and Edith grabs all our menus.

"Comin' right up, babes," she says, heading back in.

"Okay, tell us what happened with Hank," I say, deciding to rip off the metaphorical Band-Aid instead of waiting all night to see if Shelby mentions him.

"*Nothing* happened," she says, rolling her eyes. "That's why I ordered the garlic burger. Who even cares if my breath is lethal? No one in this entire town wants to make out with me."

"Wait, what are you guys talking about?" Honey asks, eyes darting between us. "Shelby and Hank? Your Hank?"

"He's not my Hank," I say. "He's not anyone's Hank. He's free agent Hank, no contracts to tie him down."

"I asked him out," Shelby explains to Honey, then cuts a glance at me. "With Sandy's blessing, of course."

I wince. "Don't call it my blessing. That makes it sound like you asked my permission to marry my daughter."

"Whatever. I asked if he wanted to go out for a drink and . . . he said no." She looks off toward the gazebo wistfully. "Bold move, honestly."

"Why did he say no?" I attempt to ask casually, but a glance from Honey lets me know that my oldest friend can read the curiosity in my voice.

Shelby sighs. "Something about how he 'wasn't really looking to date' right now. Which is fine. Hank may be great, but I could probably use a guy with a little less baggage."

"Does Hank have baggage?" Honey asks.

Shelby widens her eyes. "Uh, an entire kid's worth?"

"I don't really consider Henry baggage," I say, thinking of the way he looked all curled up on my armchair or the way his little smile, crooked like his dad's, made me feel like smiling, too.

"I don't mean it in a bad way!" Shelby defends herself. "There's nothing wrong with Henry, and Hank is obviously a really good dad. But there's no use in pretending that having a whole dang kid isn't a pretty big deal."

Honey nods. "It's good to be honest with yourself about stuff like that. Kids aren't for everyone, which I know because I have so many."

"Anyway." Shelby waves a hand in the air. "Hank was perfectly polite about it, of course. So polite I almost didn't even notice I was being rejected. And then he ended our conversation by booking hair appointments for both himself and Henry."

I smile. "That's nice," I say quietly. A sense of relief I have no right to feel washes over me. It's not my business who Hank goes out with; after all, I was the one who told him we couldn't date.

But that doesn't mean I want him to move on with one of my friends.

"It's too damn hard to date in this town," Shelby says, her shoulders slumped as she uses her tiny straw to push around the ice cubes in her glass. "There are, like, two single men and one of them is Ed. The last time I went on a date, I had to drive all the way to Cleveland. That's simply *too* far to drive for an orgasm. It's barely worth it."

"Isn't this why vibrators were invented?" I ask.

Shelby shakes her head. "The last time I went to the adult bookstore," she says, referring to the porn shop out by the interstate that advertises itself with a large sign that simply reads *ADULT*, "I ran into Mr. Hannah, our kindergarten teacher."

"He really *is* putting himself back out there," I mutter. "Good for him, I guess."

"Not good for me. I was so turned off I left without buying anything," Shelby says, wrinkling her nose in disgust. "And it's too bad, because they have some pretty cute clothes there."

"I think that's all lingerie, Shelby," Honey says.

Shelby shrugs. "Clothing is in the eye of the beholder, I always say."

"How would you know what ADULT sells?" I ask Honey. Presumably, the store has a real name, but that's what we always called it when we giggled about it in high school.

"Even old married couples like to spice things up," she says lightly.

"Ugh," Shelby says. "Stop flaunting your abundant sex life around us. If you're not gonna loan Brian out, keep it to yourself."

Honey frowns. "Well, I'm not going to loan out my husband to you weirdos, so I guess I'll stop."

"Thank you," I say, and she sticks her tongue out at me.

"I think you're going to have to order your vibrators online like everyone else," Honey tells Shelby.

"I'm sorry if I like to buy my sex toys in person. I guess I'm just old-fashioned," Shelby says as Edith shows up with a tray. "And I don't want to hear your thoughts on this subject. You have a human vibrator at home!"

"Sorry, Edith," I say in a low voice.

"Oh, don't you ladies worry," Edith says, setting our plates in front of us. "It's girls' night! I know how it gets. The wine keeps flowing and the sex talk starts."

"You wanna join us, Edith?" Shelby smiles widely. "We're talking about the serious lack of dating prospects in this town."

Edith waves a hand. "Oh, sweetie, I wouldn't know. I locked my cowboy down in high school, and I never looked back."

Shelby scowls good-naturedly, already halfway drunk. "Boo. All you happily in love jerks should've left some for the rest of us."

"Yeah," I say, holding up my glass for a toast. "Here's to leaving some for the rest of us."

"Hear, hear," Shelby says heartily, even as Honey gives me a suspicious look.

"You know," Edith says, nodding toward Keith Monahan, a guy who graduated the year ahead of us and who's currently setting up his guitar and speakers in the corner of the patio. "There's a perfectly fine, perfectly single man over there."

"Oh no," I say. "I forgot there was live music tonight."

"No offense to Keith," Shelby says, inspecting him like he's an expensive cut of beef she's considering buying, "but he's kind of obsessed with Sandy. And I can't go after *two* men who are obsessed with my friend. It's not good for my ego."

"Hank's not obsessed with me," I say quickly. "And neither is Keith! He asked me out a couple of times. Not a big deal."

Keith strums his guitar and leans forward to speak into his mic. "Good evening, Baileyville. I'd like to start out with a song about unrequited love. It's called . . . 'Mandy.'"

Shelby turns to look at me meaningfully.

"My name isn't Mandy," I say, avoiding everyone's eyes as Keith sings something about a "tall drink of water" who broke his heart.

"Well, let me know if you need anything else!" Edith says cheerfully, walking away.

"Weird that so many singer-songwriters have been in love with you," Honey says thoughtfully.

"No one's in love with me!" I say a bit too forcefully. "Hank and I are over, and I am not interested in Keith, okay?"

Honey holds up her hands. "Okay, subject dropped."

"Sorry," I say, squeezing her arm. "But maybe we can talk about something else other than my love life?"

"It's hard when someone's singing about your love life, but we can try," Honey says, trying not to smile.

I turn to Shelby. "Do you ever think about leaving?"

She frowns at me with her mouth full. "Leaving Baileyville?" she asks as if I've suggested leaving Earth and taking a little trip to Mars.

"Yeah," I say with a shrug. "Going somewhere with more than two eligible bachelors. Or other new people, or new things to do or see."

Honey raises an eyebrow, like she's wondering where I'm going with this. I look around at the patio of the inn, at the limited square footage that has contained my life for so long. It's beautiful right now in the dim light of dusk with the twinkle lights shining, but I can't ignore the feeling in my heart that maybe there's something else.

Shelby stares out into the town square along with me, thinking. "No. I mean, not recently. I used to think about it when we first graduated and everyone was off doing other things, but I don't worry about that anymore. I love it now. I like that I know everyone I see when I walk down the street. I like knowing that if I need something, there's an entire town's worth of people I could call to help me." Her gaze drifts to Keith, who's now doing a cover of "Brown Eyed Girl." "New men, though. That part's tempting. You don't mind if I ask Keith out?"

"I seriously don't mind," I say. "Please ask him out. Please convince him to write songs about someone other than me."

Shelby tilts her head and studies me. "Why are you asking? Are you thinking about leaving?"

"No," I say quickly, almost choking on my flatbread. "Absolutely not. I have a business."

"Yeah, we know," Honey says dryly. "You're Sandy 'I Have a Business' Macintosh."

"I have a house and a life, and every person I know is here," I remind them and gesture around me. "And I love this . . . spending time with you guys on the patio."

"And as we all know, patios only exist in Baileyville," Honey says, taking a swig of her beer. And then she asks, a little more quietly, "But are you happy here?"

"Of course I'm happy," I say defensively. "I have everything I've ever wanted." A little voice pops up in my head to remind me that I don't have everything I've ever wanted, that I don't have the family I always imagined would be with me in my house, but I tell that voice to shut up. That subject—the idea that I might die alone—seems a bit too heavy for the patio, so I move the conversation along to something more comfortable. "I guess I have thought about going somewhere else for a little bit. Maybe not moving, but at least traveling."

"Oooh!" Shelby's eyes widen. "You could live in a van and travel across the country, like *Nomadland*!"

"I don't want to live in a van," I say.

"Fair. And anyway, you'd have to poop in a bucket if you lived in a van." Shelby takes another sip of her drink.

"I'm not sure pooping in a bucket was the point of that movie," Honey says.

Shelby shakes her head. "All I'm saying is, if you put Frances McDormand in your movie and she poops in a bucket, it's going to make an impression. I'm not going to apologize for remembering that detail."

I gesture toward my food. "Can we talk about something else?"

"Hey, ladies."

We turn to see Ed leaning on the wrought iron fence.

"Hey, Ed," Shelby says with a smile. "You wanna join us?"

"Nah," Ed says, gesturing toward his ponytail. "I've gotta deep-condition my hair tonight."

"Of course you do," Honey murmurs.

Ed sighs, gently tugging at the hem of his shorts. "Pretty soon, it's gonna be time to retire these babies for the year. I can already feel the chill in the air. Autumn is coming."

He sounds so sad as he says it that, for a moment, I feel a little sad, too. Soon the flowers will die, the leaves will fall, and Ed will be back in pants. And even if Hank is still around, we won't have a fair to organize. None of it will be the same.

"Summer never lasts long enough," Honey says, shaking her head.

"That's the beauty of it, though," Ed says thoughtfully. "If we had it all the time, maybe we wouldn't appreciate it. If I didn't know what it was like to wear snow pants, maybe I wouldn't even care about wearing my shorts."

"That's pretty poetic, Ed," Shelby says, raising her wineglass to him. We all raise our glasses, and he smiles bashfully. And as Keith starts to play "Hotel California," I can't help but think that even if this isn't perfect, it's still awfully damn nice.

CHAPTER TWENTY-FOUR

"DID YOU SEE that giant butt monster Emma Winters drew?" Honey asks. "Definitely blue ribbon worthy."

"All the children's artwork gets a ribbon," I remind her.

"Well that one deserves two!" she says, helping me hang a photograph of a deer in the adult section.

"I had no idea we had this many artistic people in Baileyville," Shelby says, adjusting the paintings to make room for a family portrait.

"I did," I say, because I help with this part of the fair every year. Part of it is that I genuinely enjoy seeing what people submit—the beautiful, the not so beautiful, the sublimely weird (the aforementioned Garth Brooks portrait). But it's also a reminder for me that creativity exists everywhere. The vast majority of the entrants don't create art for a living, but that doesn't mean they can't paint or draw or photograph something. It doesn't mean they're immune to seeing beauty and capturing it on paper or canvas or film.

It's also a reminder to me of what *community* means—the kind of community we have here in Baileyville. There isn't an art show if people don't take a chance and share the thing they created. There isn't a baked goods competition if people don't take the time to make cakes, cookies, and pies. There isn't a needlework show if people don't accept the vulnerability that's necessary to enter something they spent hours upon hours making and offer it up to the judges.

The entire fair wouldn't exist if we didn't all believe in it and give it our best. And that's kind of a metaphor for Baileyville itself.

I stand back and stare at the adult paintings. I didn't enter anything this year—I haven't since high school. But maybe it's time I changed that. After all, I'm part of this community, too.

"I'll be right back," I tell Honey and Shelby. "I've gotta run home and grab something."

And I do run—down the two alleyways it takes to get to my house, my cheap, dirty slip-on sneakers slapping against the pavement as I jog through the darkness to my house. Once inside, I go right upstairs and grab the painting I did of Hank so long ago, the one that captured the hopefulness and optimism of that perfect day.

And then, on impulse, I grab the one I painted the other night when Hank left—the one of him surrounded by the light coming through the window, the darker colors somehow giving it a depth that the original painting didn't have. Part of me feels foolish putting this in the fair—I'm not an artist anymore, after all, and who am I to force everyone to look at something I made? Maybe people will stand in front of it and mutter about how it isn't very good.

But this is what I like about Baileyville, right? The way everyone contributes. And if I want everyone else to do their part, maybe I have to do the same thing. Maybe I have to be vulnerable enough to put the best of me on display.

I tuck one painting under each arm and head back to the library, where Honey dramatically lets her mouth fall open when she sees me.

"You're entering something? Finally? After years of me asking you to?" she asks.

"Don't make a big deal out of it or I might take them back home," I say, filling out my information on the entry tags. They stay folded up through judging to preserve anonymity, and afterward they get unfolded so everyone in town can see who made what.

"Damn," Shelby says, looking at them over my shoulder. "These are good, Sandy."

"That's because she's incredibly talented," Honey murmurs, staring at the paintings. "I've seen this one, but is the other one new?"

I nod. "Yeah. I made it the other night."

I can practically see the gears whirring in Honey's mind—yes, my paintings are slightly abstract, but it doesn't take a psychic to know that this is obviously Hank. It just takes someone who's known me my whole life and can read my mind with one look.

I attach the tags, and Honey and Shelby each grab a painting and hang them up. I stand back and look at them there among all the other works from Baileyville residents.

They look good. They look like they belong.

Honey and Shelby step back, one of them on each side of me. I put my arms around them. "Thanks for helping," I say as we take it all in. "It looks great."

"It really does," Honey says. "You're gonna win best in show."

I roll my eyes as I smile. "It's not really about winning, you know. I think the prize is five dollars."

"The prize for blue ribbons is five dollars," Shelby says, breaking free of my embrace and grabbing her purse. "The grand prize is a twenty-five-dollar gift card to Hair Affair. Which I know because I'm the one who donated it."

"Please don't make a joke about how I could use the services," I say.

She stares at me, her eyes running over my face as if she's mentally calculating how she could improve my appearance. "I wouldn't joke about something like this. It would be my honor to help you."

I groan.

Honey laughs as the three of us head out the front door, which I lock up—I already promised the librarian I'd give the key back to her tomorrow.

"Just, like, a pedicure, please! Your feet are crying out for one!" she says as she walks toward her car.

"How do you even see my feet?" I ask her. "I'm wearing closed-toe shoes!"

"You wore flip-flops a few weeks ago, and I noticed!" she shouts. "See you girls later!"

"Maybe we'll go in for a joint mani-pedi session when you win," Honey says, bumping against my shoulder as Shelby drives past us, country music blasting out her open window.

"I'm not going to win," I say. "Didn't you see that someone took a picture of that big American flag that flies over the gas station out by the exit? That's gonna get the patriotism vote."

"It *is* a really big flag," Honey admits. "Hard to compete with that."

"Exactly," I say. "Thanks for helping me tonight."

"What are friends for?"

"Well, presumably for a lot of things other than hanging up a town's artwork in an after-hours library."

We reach my house, and Honey stops me on the sidewalk. "Hey, you know we'll always be friends, right? No matter what?"

I frown. "Yes?"

"Our friendship isn't based on you living a few doors down from me or us being able to see each other at a moment's notice. We'd still be friends even if you lived in Sweden."

"That's nice to know," I say slowly. "Although I have no plans currently to move to Sweden."

"Anywhere far away!" she says, waving her hands in the air.

"What's this about?" I ask, crossing my arms. "Are you trying to kick me out of town?"

Honey sighs. "No. But I wonder sometimes . . . are you happy here?"

Alarm bells start ringing in my head, the alarm bells that let me know someone has seen through what I thought was a perfect facade.

Because I am happy. Or content, at least. Most of the time, anyway. But those other times . . .

"Yes," I tell her firmly. "I love living here. You know that."

"I know you love lots of things about it," she says, choosing her words carefully. "But I also know that Baileyville isn't perfect. You don't have to pretend that you're living in a TV show about a charming small town. Yeah, sometimes it feels like we're surrounded by a quirky cast of characters and we literally know someone named Hotpants Ed, but let me tell you, I know what it's like to push against the limits of this place. Brian and I thought long and hard about whether we wanted to raise our girls here."

I nod. "I know."

"And I'm glad we decided to keep living here, because this is my town, too. I know you love it, but that doesn't mean you have to stay here forever if you don't want to." She pauses. "*Do* you want to?"

I bite my lip. If I can't tell my best friend in the whole world, then who can I tell? Speaking the words out loud almost feels like a betrayal of myself, like admitting that everything isn't perfect will ruin the parts that are.

But I can't help it. Here, under the flickering streetlight outside my house, I allow myself to think and say the words I've been avoiding, the ones that have been sitting heavy on my heart ever since Hank came back.

"Maybe sometimes . . . I do wonder what else could be out there," I say in a rush. "And that doesn't mean I don't love you guys or that I'm not grateful to be here with my parents and my friends and my job. But sometimes I start thinking . . . did I miss out by staying here? Did I make the wrong decision all those years ago? Did I get stuck on one path and never step off of it because I was too scared everything would come crashing down? I mean, you saw what happened the last time my plans got messed up. I fell into a Hot Pocket–fueled depression and started failing my classes."

Honey nods. "Yeah, I was there," she says softly.

"You were there and you fixed it," I remind her. "If it wasn't for you, I might've ruined my whole life."

She shakes her head. "No. You would've fixed things yourself, eventually. But I'm bossy and annoying and can't stand to see you unhappy. Which is why I'm saying something now."

I frown, feeling a bit hurt. "Do I *seem* unhappy?"

"Well." Honey pauses. "Not unhappy, necessarily. But you seem like you're . . . not done yet. Like you're waiting for your real life to begin."

I press my lips together.

"But the thing is, Sandy . . ." Honey leans closer to me, speaking quietly even though we're the only two people here on the street. "Your real life is happening right now. I don't want you to miss out on *amazing* because you're comfortable with *good enough*."

I swallow. "I'm not . . . this isn't *good enough*. This is my life and I love it. But maybe you and I can really take one of those vacations we always talk about. Go to Palm Springs and drink cocktails by a pool. That would be fun, right?"

"That would be fun," Honey says, but she looks at me like I've completely missed the point of what she's saying. "I'm gonna head home and make sure bedtime went okay. The kids watched *Frozen* last week, and now Maddie keeps waking up in the middle of the night, afraid she's going to develop ice powers and accidentally kill our entire family."

"Wow," I say, glad for the change in subject. "Kids are so creative."

"Creative and weird," Honey says, and then she leans forward and wraps me in a hug. "Love you. I hope I didn't make you feel bad tonight."

"You never could," I say. I know Honey only wants the best for me. She might be wrong, but that doesn't mean she isn't trying.

"See you tomorrow," she says with a wave, heading down the sidewalk.

I walk up my front steps and wait there on the porch for a moment, listening to Honey's front door open and close. The rest of the street is completely silent, aside from the crickets. I watch the fireflies flash in the darkness, the Morse code of their lights sending me a message I can't, for the life of me, figure out.

CHAPTER TWENTY-FIVE

AFTER MONTHS OF planning, it seems unreal that the first day of the Baileyville Street Fair could finally be upon us, but it is. Festivities begin at noon, and I wake up full of anticipation. When I was a kid, the fair was a combination of Christmas and my birthday and summer vacation all rolled into one sugar-filled, deep-fried event. And while I might be too big for the Dragon Coaster these days, that excitement lingers on, making me feel like a kid again.

The difference between being a kid and an adult, of course, is that adults have to do the planning, but at this point, most of my work is done. Each fair event is now in the hands of whatever capable person or organization is running it, so all I have to do is enjoy it all (and stay on call in case there are "critical cake auction supply problems," which sounds like a ridiculous combination of words but is something Sean actually said to Honey and me).

Since it's so early, there's nothing happening at the fair when I get up for work, but I throw on my cutoffs and a tank top and make the short walk over to Main Street to partake in one of my favorite traditions. Ever since I can remember, I've loved seeing the fair all set up before the people arrive. Before the food stands are serving anything, before the carnival games are operating, before the rides are blaring music, before the empty cups collect in the gutter, before the town square is full of auctioneers or square dancers. Walking down the middle of the street in the quiet morning, it feels like the fair is a red carpet rolled out just for me. It might seem strange to say about something that involves multiple corn dog stands, but it feels a bit like magic.

I run into Sean darting down the street with his clipboard in hand. "Sandy," he says, nodding. "The art show looks great."

"Thanks," I say. "You know, *everything* looks great. You did a good job."

He stops and looks at me. "Thank you," he says, sounding genuinely touched, and I realize that maybe we (or I) spend a bit too much time gently making fun of his clipboard and his seriousness, and not enough time thanking him for this massive undertaking. After all, I basically show up to the meetings, throw out a few ideas, and volunteer to do a little bit of the planning. He's the one in charge of making sure that everything works, and that can't be easy.

He leans closer to me, and I think that he's going to say something meaningful, but instead he says, "Make sure you check out the pumpkins. They're bigger than ever this year."

"With a recommendation like that, how could I miss them? See you later, Sean." I wave and keep on walking, taking in the last early-morning moments of silence before things get loud.

The only people here are the ones setting up since nothing is open yet, but I see my dad and Mr. Tillman outside of the inn. Being on Main Street, it has a front-row seat to the festivities and is so close to the carousel that eating on the patio during the fair is kind of like being inside a music box.

"Hey, fellas," I say, sidling up to them. "Mr. Tillman, you keeping my dad off of ladders and out of trouble?"

Mr. Tillman smiles at me, the same smile I can see on Hank and Henry. "I'm doing the best I can. And you know I keep telling you, you can call me Willy. You're not a kid anymore!"

"I will do no such thing," I say pleasantly. "Dad, please tell me the truth. Are you going to attempt anything dangerous today?"

"I'm weeding!" my dad says from where he's crouched in the flower bed. "I can't injure myself down here!"

I give Mr. Tillman a skeptical look. "Well, if there's a way, I know you'll figure it out."

"Sandy!"

I turn toward the little voice calling my name and see Henry running toward me.

"Hi, Henry!" I say with a smile. He's wearing a shirt with a fire truck on it and sneakers that look like dinosaurs.

Mr. Tillman crosses his arms. "Grandpa doesn't matter anymore?"

"I saw you this morning," Henry says simply.

Melodie catches up to us, her two kids in tow. "Hi, Sandy!" she says, leaning in for a hug. "Henry's been talking nonstop about all the excitement at your house with the squirrel."

"Oh yeah?" I ask, shooting him a grin. "It was a pretty big night!"

"Indoor squirrels tend to bring the excitement," she says, and I don't ask her how she knows. "Hank seemed like he had a pretty good time, too." She keeps her eyes on me for a while, as if waiting to see how I respond.

"Well, we couldn't have done it without him," I say. "Turns out that man knows how to remove a squirrel like nobody's business."

This all feels so normal, like I'm part of their family, although I can't shake the feeling that Melodie wishes she could cross-examine me about the state of my relationship with Hank.

She glances at Henry, who's talking to Mr. Tillman and my dad. "We're so glad you're around now instead of Julia," she says quickly. "I hope that woman gets her shit together for Henry's sake, but they're both so much happier with you."

"Oh!" I say, shocked. "Hank and I aren't . . . we're not . . ."

"Okay, come on, sweetie," Melodie says, ignoring me and rounding up all three kids. "Mama needs to get coffee, and if you're good, you'll get some of Lydia's cake pops. See you all later!"

"Bye, Sandy!" Henry says.

"See ya, Bud!" I call after him as he runs away, the promise of morning cake pops making him forget all about me. I watch Melodie walk away, wondering what she's talking about and feeling a pang in my heart for Henry.

WORK TODAY IS mostly visiting with out-of-towners who are back for the fair and want to chat, and the day goes by quickly. Before I know it, it's closing time, and Marcia and I are locking up.

"Will I see you at the concert tonight?" I ask her. It's kind of a given that everyone in town is going to the fair, especially on the first night.

"I'll be the one with the cheese on a stick," she says, walking to her car.

"That doesn't really narrow it down!" I call after her, sliding into my car.

It's golden hour, the time of day when the country looks absolutely sublime as the setting sun lights everything on fire. Honey calls this "graduation picture o'clock" because of how often we see kids setting up by the river or the apple orchard to get the best light for their pictures, but I can't be too cynical about it. Sure, it's a little bit of a cliché, but all those graduation photographers know what they're doing—it's beautiful.

I'm struck with the urge to go back home and grab my paints (apparently the painting after Hank left the other night awakened something in me), but I promised Honey I'd meet her by the livestock tent, so I drive home, park my car in my driveway, and walk over.

The livestock tents are way down at the end of the fair, where farmers can more easily load and unload their animals. It also, I can't help but notice, keeps the poop smell contained far away from the food.

"Why did we agree to meet here?" I call as soon as I see Honey standing with Brian and the kids. I hold my nose dramatically.

Honey gestures toward the pigs she's standing beside. "Does it smell? At this point, I don't even notice. You'd be horrified by the smells I encounter on a daily basis."

I hold up my hands. "No need for further explanation." Sometimes Honey forgets that not all of us are accustomed to hearing detailed explanations about animal maladies.

"Fine," she says breezily. "I'll save the story about the cow birth for someone who can appreciate it."

Brian shoots me a look. "Thank you."

"Dad!" Maddie shouts. "I want an apple dumpty!"

Honey leans over to me and whispers, "She calls apple dumplings 'apple dumpties,' and I'll murder the first person who corrects her."

"Noted," I say. "As far as I'm concerned, 'apple dumpty' is the legal name."

"I'm gonna take these hooligans," Brian says, already being pulled away by three tiny people, "and leave you ladies to it."

"Ta-ta!" I call after him, waving dramatically.

Honey links her arm in mine. "Why are you so weird?"

I shrug. "I thought my weirdness was one of my most endearing qualities."

"No," Honey says. "Your most endearing quality is the way you get me a discount on flowers."

"Aw," I say. "And my favorite thing about you is the way you give me a discount on Toby's heartworm medication! I love our needs-based friendship."

"Oooh, speaking of friends . . . did you hear that Natasha is back in town for the fair and the reunion?"

I roll my eyes. "Please. I'm a sophisticated adult woman now. I no longer have time for petty high school grudges, and I barely even remember how she used to rub my nose in the fact that she went to Oberlin and correctly predicted the demise of my high school relationship."

"Yeah, I can tell you're super over it," Honey says as we dodge a double stroller. "Seriously, people need to not bring strollers to the fair. Take it from me, attempting to navigate through this crowd is a losing battle. Anyway, I have no idea what Natasha's doing these days. I can't even see her Instagram! I'm like, 'Excuse me, who are you with your private account? Don't flatter yourself.'"

"I'm sure she'll tell us all about her life in excruciating detail," I say lightly, waving at a former teacher as we pass her. "I forget—who's performing tonight?"

"Sandy," Honey says in a mock scold as we get in line for fried apple rings. "Were you not paying attention when Sean went over the fair schedule at our last meeting? I'm disappointed in your lack of fair pride."

"I know Hank's playing tomorrow night."

"You *would* know that," Honey says, and I smack her with the hand that isn't linked with her arm. "Tonight's an array of Baileyville talent. Ed's doing his magic show."

"Fun!" I say as Shelby walks up to us, a paper container of fried Oreos in her hands.

"Why are you eating those again?" I ask. "Don't they make you sick?"

She sighs. "Yes, but fried Oreos are like a bad relationship. I can't stay away, even though they make me feel terrible."

"Speaking of which," Honey says, turning around with her apple rings in hand, "I'm pretty sure I saw Brandon Zelansky over by the Gravitron. He had on a Bud Light T-shirt and cargo shorts."

Shelby wrinkles her nose as she thinks about her ex. "Gross."

"My thoughts exactly," Honey says. "Sandy, you getting something to eat before we head over to the stage?"

"Nah," I say. "I figure I'll subsist on your leftovers when you inevitably fall into a grease coma."

"Not a bad plan," Honey says, leading us toward the stage. There's already a sizable crowd gathered on the lawn and on the temporary bleachers. We take our places standing near the stage.

"Hey!" Marcia says, joining us along with her wife, Aimee. Both of them, as promised, have cheese on a stick in hand. "Is everyone ready for a mind freak?"

I wince. "I really wish Ed would stop saying that. He's not exactly Criss Angel."

"He does have the leather pants, though," Honey points out, taking a bite of apple rings.

"I'd rather not be reminded," I say.

"Leather pants won't let you forget," Honey says, smiling.

We say hello to practically everyone we've ever met, because the fair is the social event of the late summer. It's the time when it feels like all of Baileyville comes together to celebrate what makes our town great—the resourcefulness and the creativity and the strength and, of course, the extremely large pumpkins.

"Ugh, there he is," Shelby says, casting a withering glance toward her right. We all turn to see Brandon, resplendent in his Bud Light T-shirt and farmer's tan, holding the hand of a woman I've never seen before.

"Who's that?" Marcia asks.

"Brandon," Shelby says with an eye roll. "We dated in high school, much to my eternal embarrassment."

"Him?" Marcia asks, tilting her head as if she's a golden retriever trying to understand something.

"That's everyone's reaction," I say, leaning toward Marcia. "We don't get why Shelby stooped to spend her time with him."

"Huh," Marcia says, studying him. "I've never seen such a nondescript man in my life. Truly, I see his features, and then they instantly leave my mind. His face is nothing but a smooth rock in my memory."

"Wow," Honey says, almost choking on an apple ring. "Marcia. That's, like, the most cutting insult I've ever heard."

Marcia shrugs. "I call 'em like I see 'em."

"Does it feel weird for you?" I ask Shelby. "Seeing him with another woman?"

Shelby sighs. "I know I'm always talking about how desperate I am for a man's touch, but I'm not *that* desperate. I know what that man's touch feels like, and unless he's improved his technique in the past fifteen years, it mainly involves boob honks."

"Well," I say, "let's hope, for that woman's sake, that he's graduated to any touch that doesn't include the word 'honk.'"

"Amen," Shelby says, toasting us with a fried Oreo. "But also, I don't want dating advice from any of you. You're don't know what it's like out there because you're married. Well, not you, Sandy, but we all know you're lying to yourself about your feelings for Hank."

Everyone else nods in agreement as my mouth drops open. "I don't have a thing for Hank," I start, but I'm interrupted by the sound of a very familiar, very Hank-like voice.

"Y'all talking about me again?"

I turn around to see Hank, infuriatingly sexy half smile on his face and his hand holding Henry's. "Oh . . . hey," I say slowly.

"So are we all ready to have our minds blown by the power of magic?" he asks, turning to face the stage.

"Absolutely," I say, resolutely not looking at the girls, who are probably exchanging meaningful looks right now. "I'm hoping Ed doesn't accidentally set his suit on fire again."

"Did that happen last year?" Hank asks.

"Oh yeah," Marcia says. "We had to call the squad and everything, but it was fine. Turns out Ed is great at stop, drop, and roll, and then it became sort of a magic show *and* fire safety demonstration."

Hank nods. "A combination that isn't used enough in the magic world."

"That's what I always say," I agree. "Sure, magic is great, but let me see a demonstration of the proper way to use a fire extinguisher."

"Dad," Henry asks. "Is someone setting something on fire?"

"No, Bud," Hank says. "Ed's gonna be extra careful this year."

We smile at each other, and for a minute, it's like no one else is around, like we aren't even standing on a lawn and waiting to see a magic show that might go horribly wrong.

"Hey," Hank says. "Did you check out the doll show results?"

I shake my head. "I'm too afraid. I made it out alive last time I had to be near those dolls, but I'm not so sure I'd get that lucky again. The one with the missing eye is out for blood. I can tell."

"Well, despite your feelings toward them, Pearl won a ribbon: Most Unique Collection."

I gasp. "Pearl did it! Our girl won!"

Hank shrugs. "I think they created that category to avoid making Pearl angry and invoking the wrath of her dolls."

"Whatever," I say. "You can't deny they were unique."

"Dad." Henry tugs on Hank's arm, apparently uninterested in our doll talk. "I'm bored. I wanna go ride the roller coaster."

"In a minute, Bud," Hank says, picking Henry up even though he has to weigh about forty-five pounds. To me, Hank says, "This is the first year he's tall enough to ride the Dragon Coaster."

"Oh, exciting!" I say, sharing a smile with Henry. The Dragon Coaster is a kid-sized roller coaster that goes over minor bumps extremely slowly, but the kids who ride it always scream as if they're on the Millennium Force at Cedar Point.

"Wait," I say. "Aren't you scared of roller coasters?"

"No," Hank says quickly.

"You are!" My eyes widen as I remember. "Henry, did you know in high school we took a class trip up to Cedar Point, and your dad refused to even get on any roller coasters?"

Henry looks at his dad. "Really?"

"I got on one roller coaster," Hank says, crossing his arms.

"Yeah, you got on the Gemini. One of the old wooden ones that doesn't go upside down. And the entire time we were going up that first hill, I thought you were going to pass out. He looked *green*, Henry."

Henry's eyes light up. Even at five, he knows there's nothing better than being able to make fun of your parent.

"It was bumpy," Hank grumbles. "I wasn't scared, I was uncomfortable."

"He was terrified," I tell Henry.

"Okay, listen," Hank says, a smile breaking through his annoyed expression. "You're right. I don't like roller coasters. I only got on the Gemini because I wanted you to think I was cool."

My heart attempts to fly out of my chest when he looks at me. I can still remember holding his hand on that roller coaster, telling him the entire time that it would be all right, even though he was squeezing my fingers so tightly that I was afraid he'd break them.

"Well." I clear my throat. "Who's gonna take Henry on the Dragon Coaster?"

"The Dragon Coaster goes about five miles an hour," Hank says. "I think I could handle it, and anyway, kids are allowed to go on it by themselves."

"I don't wanna go on it alone!" Henry cries, suddenly panicked. "I want you!"

Hank hesitates for a moment, enough for me to tell that even though there's absolutely nothing to be afraid of on the Dragon Coaster, he still really doesn't want to ride it.

"I'll take you!" I say, then turn to Hank. "I mean, if that's okay with you."

Hank shakes his head. "You're not going on the Dragon Coaster."

"Actually, I've been looking forward to the fair all year precisely because of the Dragon Coaster," I say. "I can't wait to feel the slight breeze in my hair as I go down that ten-foot hill. It looks exhilarating."

Hank eyes me skeptically.

"Come on." I hold my hand out to Henry, then point to the coaster, which is just to the left of the square. "We'll be riding the dragon. You stay here and let me know what new tricks Ed pulls off."

"You sure?" Hank asks me quietly, but Henry is already tugging me away. Even if I did change my mind, I wouldn't want to hurt his feelings.

"Yep!" I say, walking past the girls, all of whom look at me with eyebrows raised.

"I've got a date with the Dragon Coaster," I say confidently.

Chapter Twenty-Six

WHILE ADULTS ARE technically allowed on the Dragon Coaster, the seats certainly aren't made with a grown woman's hips in mind. I cram myself into the seat, worried that I might not be able to get out. Maybe I'm doomed to live the rest of my life going up and down these gently rolling hills, being carted around on the back of a flatbed truck as I visit various fairs in Ohio.

I fasten our seat belt and pull down the bars that go over our laps. "You ready for this?" I ask Henry.

"Yes," he says, practically vibrating with excitement.

"Keep your hands inside the coaster," shouts a bearded man as he yanks on our lap bar to make sure it's fastened. We're in the very first car—the head of the dragon, the most coveted spot, I assume—and I turn to look behind me. The ride is full . . . of children. There are no other grown-ups forcing their bodies to fit into these tiny seats, and given that I'm already taller than most adult women, I slouch down as much as I can.

But then I look over at Henry and see the giant smile on his face. I only looked that happy as a kid when there was the promise of an ice cream sundae. I sit up taller—I can do this for him.

"Enjoy the ride!" the ride operator shouts, and we start moving.

"Yeahhhhh!" Henry suddenly shouts so loudly that I jump, so I decide to echo his enthusiasm. It's not hard—the entire coaster is full of small children who are screaming at the top of their lungs despite the fact that we're going, at best, ten miles an hour.

As we climb the first "hill" (more like a mound, but I'm not judging), Henry reaches over and grabs my hand. A quick glance at his face shows his apprehension, and I'm reminded of being on that ride with Hank all those years ago.

What if what if what if, my traitorous brain asks again. *What if everything was different, and you and Hank were still together? What if you were a family? What if he was standing right beside the ride, watching his wife and child ride it together?*

My heart lurches, and not because of the roller coaster, which starts its gradual descent. Henry's apprehension turns into pure glee as we go down the hill. I scream along with him, laughing at the absurdity of it.

That's when I see Hank standing beyond the small metal fence that surrounds the Dragon Coaster, leaning up against a tree and watching us. There's a smile on his face, but he's not laughing at how ridiculous I look or the fact that I've been screaming my head off as if I'm going faster than a typical riding lawn mower. This is a smile I can't decipher.

"Hey, there's your dad!" I shout to Henry, and we both wave.

"Dad, I'm going so fast!" Henry shouts, and I laugh as I meet Hank's eyes.

After a couple more loops around, the ride is over. As we slow to a stop, Henry looks at me. "That was . . . epic," he says.

"Definitely," I say, lifting our lap bar and unbuckling our seat belt. I manage to somehow dislodge my body from the seat, and I grab Henry's little hand to help him out. He feels so small next to me, and I'm stuck with the sudden realization that I want to be in his life, the same way I'm in Honey's kids' lives.

We carefully walk down the wobbly metal steps, and as soon as our feet hit pavement, he begs, "Can we do it again? Please?"

I'm about to tell him maybe later when someone ask-shrieks, "Sandy?"

I look up, and my eyes widen when I see Natasha standing right in front of me.

"Oh!" I say, startled. "Hi!"

"I can't believe it's you!" she shouts, pulling me in for a hug. It's not altogether unbelievable that it's me, given that I live here and the entire town is at the fair, but I don't correct her.

"I can't believe it's *you!*" I say, which feels slightly more accurate. But as she squeezes my shoulders, something keeps us apart — her hugely pregnant midsection, which is currently crammed in between the both of us.

"You're . . . um . . . uh . . ." I stammer, remembering after I start my sentence that it's not a great idea to comment on someone's pregnancy unless they're in active labor or their water breaks on your feet.

She laughs, cradling her belly. "Pregnant! Yeah! Jason and I are so excited."

I nod and smile, as if I know who Jason is. "Aw, Jason!"

"Yeah. Can't wait to be a hashtag-boymom!" she says. "I grew up with brothers, so I was like, 'Help, what if I have a girl and I don't know what to do?' but as soon as we saw that ultrasound, I was like, 'Thank God,' because I *love* boys' imaginations and toys, you know? Trucks and tractors and dinosaurs . . ."

I nod eagerly. "Right. Monsters . . . superheroes . . . the color blue . . . outdated gender norms . . ."

She tilts her head at me and scrunches up her nose. "Oh my God, I forgot about how random you are. It's like, what's even going on in there?" She actually leans forward and pokes my forehead.

"I couldn't possibly tell you," I say honestly.

"But what am I even saying? You know what I'm talking about." She gestures to Henry, who's been patiently holding my hand this whole time. He stares back at Natasha as if she's an alien.

"Oh, Henry's not mine," I say. "I just took him on the Dragon Coaster."

"Hey, Natasha." Hank steps up on Henry's other side.

"Dad!" Henry says. "It was so cool. Did you see how fast we went?"

"I did!" Hank says as Henry grabs his hand, and then it's the three of us standing here in a hand-holding line, looking for all the world like a family.

You know, if you didn't know us.

"Hank!" Natasha squeals. "*Please* take a selfie with me. My girlfriends are going to flip when they see this. They never believe that we were tight back in high school."

"Why wouldn't they believe that you were tight?" I murmur quietly enough so only Hank can hear me as Natasha pulls out her phone.

"Watch your mouth," he says quietly, but I can hear the laugh in his voice.

Natasha squeezes in next to Hank and smiles, then inspects the photo. "Gonna need a filter, but that's a good one," she says, tucking her phone back in her purse. "Will we see you guys at the reunion? Jason and I will be there."

"Yep!" Hank says.

"It'll be good to have the gang all back together," she says. "Okay, well, I've gotta go meet someone, but I'll see you both later!"

"Tell Jason I said hi," Hank says as we wave and turn around.

"You know Jason?" I whisper.

Hank snorts. "No. I have no idea who Jason is."

"Ugh, this is why people love you," I say, rolling my eyes. "You're so personable. If only they knew it was all fake!"

"People love me, huh?" Hank asks, looking at me, and I realize we're still walking with Henry in between us, holding our hands.

"Don't flatter yourself," I say, gently easing my hand out of Henry's. He doesn't notice, now that he's got his dad. "Hey, did you know Natasha's about to become a hashtag-boymom?"

"Was that a hashtag-boyfetus in there?" he asks, gesturing behind himself as if pointing to Natasha's belly.

"Where have you guys been?" Honey yells as we get close to them. "You missed the entire magic show! Ed's rabbit broke loose and started nibbling on the zucchini. Barb is gonna be *pissed*."

"We ran into Natasha," I say, raising my eyebrows.

"Hashtag-boymom," Marcia says, nodding. When we all stare at her, she asks, "What? I follow her on Instagram. I see all her updates."

"She accepted your follow?" Honey shouts. "What the heck?"

Marcia sips her lemonade. "She and Jason are renovating their kitchen. It's putting a lot of stress on their marriage, but they're staying strong."

"Wow," I say dryly. "I can't believe you're missing these scintillating updates."

"What's the kitchen look like?" Honey asks eagerly, leaning toward Marcia. "I need details."

Marcia winces and shakes her head. "You don't wanna know. It's only gonna make you feel bad."

"Details," Honey demands.

"Custom-made marble countertops," Marcia says. "And they put in a window above their sink so Natasha can, and I quote, 'watch the sunset while washing the dishes from yet another delicious home-cooked meal that nourished my family.'"

"Ugh," Honey groans.

"Honey!" I grab her shoulder. "If you want to feel inadequate while looking at someone else's home, then turn on *Property Brothers* and watch Drew and Jonathan demo a Canadian couple's town house."

She sighs. "All I want is a Property Brother to demolish my kitchen."

"I know," I say gently.

"Is that literal or some kind of sexual metaphor?" Shelby asks.

"Ew," I say. "Also, there's a kid here."

"He's not paying attention," Shelby says. "I gave him the rest of my fried Oreos."

"Thank you!" Henry calls through his full mouth.

"This is why I don't use social media," Hank says. "All it does is make people miserable."

"You have an Instagram profile," I remind him.

"Wow, yeah, weird that you know that," he says, giving me one of those infuriating smiles.

"Damn it," I mutter. "I'll have you know that I also rarely use social media."

Shelby rolls her eyes. "Don't be one of those people who brags about, like, digital detoxing. Some of us need a place to post our thirst traps."

Honey pulls her phone out of her pocket and opens Instagram. "This is a good picture of you, and I didn't even know you had a belly button ring. Whoa, I think you have more likes than there are people in Baileyville."

"That's the great thing about social media," Shelby says, leaning over to appreciate her own picture. "Admiration isn't limited by geography."

"Truer words," I say to Hank.

"Hello, citizens of Baileyville."

We turn to the stage, where Sean is standing at the microphone, squinting as he looks out into the crowd.

"Woo!" shouts Honey. "Go, Sean!"

"Thank you," he says. "Please save your applause. I'm here to announce the next act."

"Love a man who gets to the point," Honey says, leaning over to me. "No idea why you guys didn't work out."

"You dated Sean?" Hank asks.

"No," I say. "Well, yes. Sort of. It was one date and it wasn't exactly a match. Let's just say he didn't appreciate the full Sandy Macintosh experience."

Hank smirks. "His loss," he says, bumping his shoulder against mine. I feel a light bulb switch on in my chest.

"Please welcome to the stage Baileyville's own Keith Monahan, singing a song inspired by . . ." Sean looks at his notes. "The most beautiful woman in Baileyville."

"Oh no," I say quietly as my entire group, except Shelby, turns to look at me. She keeps her eyes on the stage as Keith walks out.

"I'd like to dedicate this song to someone who made me believe that love is real," he says, looking right at us.

"What's the deal with this guy?" Hank whispers in my ear.

"Oh, you'll see," I say, trying to ignore the feeling of Hank's breath on my neck.

But as Keith starts playing, the chords sound unfamiliar. I don't know what this song is, but it's definitely not "Mandy."

"Did he write *another* song about you?" Honey asks, eyes wide.

Before he starts singing, Keith announces, "This song is called . . . 'Shelby.'"

As he starts singing about a beautiful woman who works at a hair salon, all of us turn to look at Shelby, our mouths hanging open.

"I'm sorry, what's happening?" Hank asks.

"Dad," Henry whines. "I don't like this song. Can we go on the Dragon Coaster again?"

"Shelby!" Honey hisses. "Explain this!"

Shelby turns around to look at us, a smile on her face. "It turns out Keith is a nice guy. And, you'll notice, he's one of the many likes on my most recent selfie."

"But . . . how?" I ask, shaking my head. "We were just talking about him last night."

"You move fast, woman," Marcia says.

"Okay, first off, you and your wife got married after five months of dating, so you're one to talk," Shelby says, and Marcia and Aimee shrug, looking pleased. "And secondly . . . I saw an opportunity and I grabbed it. Right after we left the library last night, I did some investigative work . . ."

"She means social media stalking," I tell Hank.

"And I figured out that he was down at the River Horse, so I went there and . . . well, the rest is musical history," she says, smiling smugly.

"Wow," I say. "Honestly, I'm impressed. And relieved. I was getting kind of tired of hearing the same song about me."

"Keith is actually pretty great," Shelby says, focusing on the stage again and locking eyes with him.

"What's this about him writing a song about Sandy?" Hank asks the rest of us.

"Oh, no big deal, but Keith was obsessed with our girl Sandy for a decent amount of time. Sandy, you know I love you, but it's weird how many guys write songs about you," Honey says.

"Have other men written songs about you?" Hank asks, a small smile playing on his lips.

"I wouldn't know," I say primly. "I only listen to the jams of one George Michael."

Keith strums his final chord, and Shelby runs up to the stage. He leans down and gives her a kiss while the rest of us whoop.

"I love this development," Marcia says.

"Me too," I say, genuinely happy for Shelby. Keith might be a little bit obsessive, but he clearly loves to adore someone, and Shelby has long been ready to be adored.

Keith starts playing another song while Shelby remains right by the stage. Eventually Honey wanders off to find her family, and Marcia and Aimee decide to go check out the needlepoint exhibit, leaving me with Hank and Henry.

"Well," I say, "I should probably head out. It's getting dark and . . ."

"Do you have somewhere you need to be?" Hank asks.

"No," I answer honestly before I can think of a lie. I mentally kick myself.

"Why don't you hang out with us? Henry's kinda flagging, so I'm not sure how much longer we'll stick around tonight, but we were gonna go check out his artwork in the art show."

"Henry!" I say. "It's so cool that you entered something!"

Henry nods, looking proud. "Do you think it won a ribbon?"

"I'm sure it did," I say as Hank winks at me. The tiny gesture sends a shock wave through my nervous system, which I attempt to calm down by listening to Keith sing what might be a second song about Shelby.

"Come with us!" Henry says, and it's literally impossible for me to say no to him, so I walk beside Hank as we make our way to the library.

"Have you looked at the pumpkins yet?" I ask as we walk past the vegetable display.

Hank stops, looking at the blue ribbon winner, leaning up against a table. "Dang," he says. "That's one big pumpkin."

"Some might call it . . . the Pumpking," I say.

Hank lets out a low whistle. "Wow. Cannot imagine why Sean didn't appreciate you."

"Thank you," I say. "I guess I'm an acquired taste."

"Did you make puns the whole date?" Hank asks as we keep walking away from Main Street and toward the library. The sounds of the rides and the people recede behind us. "Or did you also attempt to make obscure pop culture references that he didn't get?"

"Oh, I for sure did that too," I say. "He didn't know what *Sister Wives* was, either."

"How long has that show been on?" Hank asks.

"Since time immemorial. What's your favorite show, Henry?"

"*Wild Kratts*," Henry says. "It's how I learn about animals. Did you know a panda eats over twenty pounds of bamboo a day?"

"I did not," I say.

"And did you know that vampire bats drink blood?"

"I did know that, but I try not to think about it," I say.

"Why?" Henry asks, his little brow furrowed.

"I . . . don't really like bats," I say.

"Why?"

"He'll keep doing this all night," Hank says.

"Because they scare me," I say. "I think they're weird."

"They're not weird," Henry says. "They're awesome."

"Agree to disagree, I guess."

"What?" Henry asks, and Hank laughs.

We reach the library, but the lights are off inside.

"Oh, shoot," Hank says, looking at the hours printed on the glass door. "I forgot they're closed."

"But I wanted to see my picture!" Henry whines.

"We'll come check it out first thing tomorrow morning," Hank promises, but then I remember something.

I dig through my purse and pull out the keys. "Ta-da!"

As I start to unlock the door, Hank slowly asks me, "Why are you carrying the keys to the library in your purse?"

"I was supposed to give them back to Miriam after we set everything up yesterday," I say. "But I forgot."

"Don't they have, I don't know, a security system here? Shouldn't you have to punch in a code?" Hank asks, following me into the darkened library and looking around as if a security officer is going to leap out from behind the new-releases shelf.

"This is Baileyville," I remind him. "I'm surprised the library even locked their doors at all. People here don't believe in security systems."

"Half the people in town have a bumper sticker about how their security system is a Smith and Wesson," Hank says wryly.

"Well, I'm gonna take my chances that Miriam the librarian isn't packing," I say as I find the light switch and flick it on.

"Wow," Hank says. "I just put it together that she's a librarian named Miriam. It's like her parents predicted this job."

"She really had no other choice," I say as Henry runs toward the children's art section, scanning the wall for his drawing.

"There it is!" he shouts. "It has a ribbon! A blue ribbon!"

"I knew it!" Hank says, the jubilation so obvious in his voice that it almost breaks my heart. There's no question that Henry is his entire world, and I can't say I'm surprised to know that Hank is a good dad. I always knew he would be.

"Double high fives," Henry says, holding up both palms for Hank to smack. Then he holds out his hands to me, and I do the same.

"Congratulations!" I tell him.

"Thanks," he says modestly. "It's a drawing of a red panda fighting a hawk. I guess the judges must've thought it was cool."

"Wow," I say, inspecting it. It's surprisingly detailed and violent. "I didn't know red pandas could hold swords."

"This is make believe," Henry reminds me. "Animals can't hold swords in real life."

"Very good point," I say, turning around to give Hank a conspiratorial smile. But he's not behind us anymore—now, he's on the other side of the room standing in front of the adult paintings.

"Uh-oh," I mutter.

"Why'd you say 'uh-oh'?" Henry asks loudly, and Hank turns around to see my frozen, guilty expression.

"It's the painting," he says as I walk across the room toward him, leaving Henry to admire his drawing. "The one of me. From high school."

"Yeah," I say, coming to a stop beside him. I cross my arms and look at it. "I decided, what the hell? Why not enter it? I mean, everyone else is brave enough to share what they've been working on."

"It won a ribbon," Hank says, pointing to the red ribbon hanging off the side of the painting.

"I didn't notice that," I admit. I hadn't even remembered I was eligible for a prize . . . it seemed beside the point when I entered.

But that reminds me to look for my other painting, and Hank notices my eyes scanning the wall.

There it is, right where the girls and I hung it up last night. And hanging beside it? The giant purple "Best in Show" ribbon.

"Holy moly," I whisper. I reach out and run my fingers along the edges of the ribbon, feel the smoothness of it on my hand. "I won."

For a second, I forget Hank is there, but then I look at him. He's silent, taking in the picture with his arms crossed. He doesn't turn toward me even though he must know I'm staring at him. It gives me a rare moment to study his face without being interrupted. Those lines I know so well. The freckles that pop up after a summer spent under the sun. The seashell curve of his ear. The way his lips part slightly when he's thinking.

"This is at the cabin," he says, breaking the silence.

"Yeah," I say. "How can you tell?"

He reaches out, as if he's about to touch the painting, but pulls his hand back. "It feels like it."

My heart might beat out of my chest. All I ever want is to put what I'm feeling into the paint and hope that someone else might see it too, and knowing that Hank can feel it . . . well, I can't think of anything better.

"You're painting again," he says, looking at me, his eyes bright.

"Sort of," I say. "I painted this, and that's it so far. I did it right after you left on the night of the Squirrel Incident."

Hank laughs, rubbing the back of his neck. "I was worried you thought I was kind of a jerk."

"Why?" I ask, confused. "The squirrel probably didn't have kind things to say about you when he got back to his family, but I was grateful you helped me."

"No," he says. "I mean about painting. I was kind of . . . pushy about it. We haven't seen each other in years, and here I am, telling you how you oughta spend your time. Like I'm mansplaining your own life to you."

I nod. "That's what they always call you. Ol' Mansplainin' Hank."

"I'm sorry," he says. "But I know how much music has always meant to me and how upset I'd be if there was ever a time I didn't have it. And I know how much painting meant to you . . ." He trails off.

"I'm sorry I got weird about it," I say. "All you did was ask me if I was still painting, and anyway, you were right. Basically the second I got out my canvas and my paints and my brushes, I felt more like myself."

Hank cups a hand over his ear. "What was that? Did you say I was right?"

I laugh and reach out to pull his hand down. "You're always right, okay?"

Hank looks at me, but he isn't laughing. Instead, there's an expression on his face I can't quite read, and as I try to figure it out, I realize that I'm still holding his hand. I'm holding his hand, and we're standing so close to each other in a library after hours. A couple of months ago, this isn't a place I would've thought I'd be. But I'm not unhappy about it. Hank's presence in my life seemed like an intrusion, like an unwelcome blast from the past, but now that he's here . . . I'm glad.

"I . . ." I start.

"You . . ." Hank starts.

"I have to pee!" Henry shouts, running up to us and grabbing Hank's hand.

I quickly drop his other hand.

"Buddy," Hank says. "What have we talked about? We don't

need to yell every time we have to go to the bathroom. Regular voices are fine."

"'We'?" I ask, nervously smoothing my hair. I'm not sure exactly what Hank and I were about to say to each other, but I'm both relieved and disappointed that we were interrupted. "Is that a problem you also have?"

"Don't judge me," Hank says, picking up Henry.

"Come on," I say, walking toward the door. "You're welcome to use my bathroom. I may have broken into the library after hours, but I draw the line at clandestinely using their restrooms."

"A woman with standards," Hank says, following me. "Refreshing."

I take one last glance at my painting and its ribbon before following Hank and Henry out the door.

CHAPTER TWENTY-SEVEN

MARCIA HAS THE day off on Friday, which she definitely deserves after covering for me during most of fair-prep season. She already told me she plans to hit up the cake auction, where Ed is playing auctioneer (one of his many talents, apparently), and we can only hope no one brought an ice cream cake. Honey is on call for any cake emergencies as I easily handle the small number of people who trickle into the greenhouse looking for stone statues for their gardens or birdhouses for their front porches.

And yet it's not enough to keep my mind off tonight. Because as the workday ends and I lock up, my body trembles with both anticipation and nerves when I remember where I'm going: to see Hank perform.

I've done a lot of things with Hank since he's been back. I've visited his home, encountered haunted dolls, made some not-bad tacos, vanquished a squirrel, and even kissed him up against his kitchen counter. But one thing I haven't done? Seen him pick up a guitar. Listened to him play the notes of one of his songs. Heard his voice, so familiar, sing words I'm not sure I'm ready to hear.

The last time I watched Hank perform was the night I met Julia and ended up in tears. While I don't think tonight will be quite as dramatic, I'm afraid it won't be as easy to watch as Keith's ode to Shelby.

As I open my car door, my phone buzzes with a text.

It's Honey.

> Babe, you ready to watch your ex-boyfriend
> sing love songs, or do you want to skip town
> and flee to Sweden?

I smile, and before I can text back, my phone buzzes again.

> I only ask because I'll need to let my
> partners know I'm taking time off work. Also
> gotta find my passport. And learn Swedish.

That's a lot to handle on short notice, I text back. *Starting to think it might make more sense to watch Hank's performance tonight. It doesn't require a passport.*

Or learning Swedish, she texts back immediately. *Probably, anyway. I don't know what kind of music Hank is into these days. Well okay, if you insist, we'll go tonight. Good talk.*

I shake my head and drop my phone back into the bag as I slide into the driver's seat. I'd better get home, get cleaned up, and head over to the fair. I'll need a few corn dogs to get through this evening.

I CHECK MYSELF out in the mirror, pursing my possibly too-red lips. I finally decided to throw Shelby a bone and put on lipstick, but now I'm concerned I look like a clown, or like I'm trying too hard. I'm not sure which is worse.

It's not only Hank's performance that I'm worried about. Friday of fair week is always the night of the big Baileyville Street Fair Dance. It's a place of romance, intrigue, and, surprisingly, almost as much groping as the high school dances I tried to avoid. It's not something I usually go to, given that I don't have anyone's shoulder to rest my head on when Elvis's "Can't Help Falling in Love" comes on. There's something particularly humiliating about being a single adult at a dance and watching every couple you know gazing dreamily into each other's eyes.

But I told Honey I wanted to go tonight, for some ridiculous reason. It's not like Hank will be there, or like I even want him to be. I don't know what I want.

What I *do* know is that I spent way too long picking out my outfit tonight before going with a red gingham dress that I was hoping would say, "vintage Americana," but might be saying, "repurposed tablecloth from an abandoned picnic."

"What do you think, Toby?" I ask, but he doesn't even lift his head off the ground.

"Guess I'm on my own here," I mutter, trying to adjust my hair and then giving up. I'm going to see Hank tonight, and I'm dressed as a combination clown/tablecloth, and it's going to have to be good enough.

I FIND HONEY in the crowd gathered in front of the stage. The Beach Boys' "Don't Worry Baby" plays over the speakers, and she claps when she sees me.

"Do a spin!" she orders, twirling her finger around.

I roll my eyes but obey her, spinning around once.

She whistles. "You look hot. Doesn't she look hot, Brian?"

"I'm not going to say your best friend looks hot." Brian shakes his head.

Honey scoffs. "I mean, like, objectively."

"Objectively, I would not like to have this conversation," he says, crossing his arms. "This feels like a trap."

"That's okay, Brian," I say with a smile. "But tell me one thing: do I look like a tablecloth?"

He squints at me.

"Is it giving 'picnic'?" I ask, gesturing toward myself.

"I don't know what that means," he says.

Honey and I look at each other and shake our heads. "Men," she says. "Can't live with 'em, can't get 'em to admit your best friend looks hot."

"You wore lipstick!"

I turn to see Shelby staring at me, mouth open.

"I never thought I'd see the day!" she says. "And it looks amazing. I knew that was your shade of red."

"Shelby, are you . . . crying?" I ask as she dabs at her eye with the back of her hand.

"I'm surprised, that's all. You know that feeling when you've been hoping and trying for so long, but you think you'll never succeed? And then here you are. Finally, with lips that aren't translucent. I feel like a proud mom."

"Okay," I mutter. "I think that's enough."

The lawn in front of the stage has filled up with Baileyville residents. People are eager to see Hank because there aren't a lot of former Baileyville residents who get even slightly famous. In fact, when Morgan Shyer moved to New York City, it was such a big deal that the *Baileyville Star* interviewed her about what it was like to ride the subway, and the article ended up on the front page.

The fact that Hank Tillman was universally beloved even before he left town and became the personification of the newspaper headline "Hometown Boy Makes Good" means that everyone here feels a sense of pride and ownership over his success. It's not that people in Baileyville aren't successful or that they don't have big dreams or that they don't ever move away, but they don't move away *often*, certainly not to another state, and their dreams aren't usually creative. Sure, people do creative things, but those are hobbies. The kids who star in the spring musical belt out their songs and receive their accolades, but then they go to school for something practical. Something that leads to a job.

So it makes sense that people were skeptical when Hank made it clear that he was serious about being a musician. Of course, they bought the album he recorded all by himself senior year, which was a real novelty back in the early 2000s, when you couldn't just put your songs up on Spotify. His dad even let him sell copies at Tillman's, which made it feel more legit than the burned CD with cover art drawn by me that it really was. But it was like Hank said about football: he was a big fish in a small pond, and most people from Baileyville never expected him to move to a bigger pond. They tempered their skepticism and told his parents, "He'll make a great music teacher someday! Hank's always been good with kids!"

But when he started succeeding—you know, when he started obtaining outward markers of success that people could easily understand, like being in *Entertainment Weekly* or having an album you could buy in the Walmart out by the interstate—that's when things changed. That's when the skepticism turned into pride, and all of a sudden, everyone had always known that Hank Tillman was special. Everyone had always known he'd do big things.

And me? Well, I'm the one who *actually* always knew he was

special, the one who saw his wildest dreams coming true years before they really did. And I still let him get away, like a fish that slipped through my fingers and swam off, never to return.

Except that he did return, and he's here right now about to come out onstage. I see him standing off to the side as Sean announces him, and I hear words like "pride of Baileyville," but I can't focus because Hank is looking right at me, his eyes on me in the crowd, and nothing has changed. It turns out that seeing Hank Tillman onstage is still enough to make my knees buckle and my heart beat so hard I worry the people around me can hear it.

"You can't hear my heart beat, can you?" I ask Honey.

She frowns. "No. And take it from me, a medical professional, that's a good thing."

"Here," Brian says, handing me a corn dog with a photoworthy squiggle of mustard on its golden brown exterior.

"Thank you," I say as Hank walks out.

"I told him to go get you one," Honey says, taking a bite of her own corn dog.

"This is why you're my best friend," I say, touched.

"You guys are really sad," Shelby says, but I shush her as Hank starts playing.

I recognize these chords, and judging by the sigh that goes through most of the crowd, so does everyone else. This is Hank's big song, the one that gets played at weddings and was once even performed by a contestant on *The Voice*.

I wish I didn't know the words to this song, one that Hank almost certainly wrote for Julia, but unfortunately, the lyrics are tattooed on my brain. I know them as well as I know the constellation of freckles on Hank's forearms. It's about how much he loves the woman he's singing about and how their love will go on forever, like the sky. I hate that it makes me think of all those days and nights we spent looking at the sky in the back of his truck and dreaming about our futures. Hearing it hurts, like someone's squeezing my chest and making it hard to breathe, but as Hank starts to sing, I can't deny how beautiful it sounds. This is why people love his music so much—the words are simple, never flowery or poetic, but his gravelly, sandpaper-sweet voice goes down like good bourbon.

When the world melts away and it's you and me together,
then the sky won't ever end, and it'll be like this forever.

He sings and I press my eyes shut tight.

"You have to admit," Honey whispers, "it's a beautiful song."

"I would never pretend it wasn't," I tell her.

"Also, you have mustard on your dress," she points out.

I look down and sigh. If I didn't look like a picnic before, my mustard-smeared dress definitely looks like one now.

"Great," I mutter as Hank strums the last notes of his song and blessedly moves on to the next one.

"Thank you," he says as people clap and cheer. "I can't tell you how much it means to me to be back here performing for you all. I've been lucky enough to be on a lot of stages, but I think the stage at the Baileyville Street Fair is the best one."

Now people *really* cheer, because if there's one belief that everyone in Baileyville shares, it's that Baileyville is the best place you could possibly live.

"I've been working on my next album while I've been here, and it turns out that Baileyville inspires me more than any other place. So here's a new song. It's called 'Just Another Love Song,' and it's about someone really special to me."

I know that my heart can't actually beat out of my chest, but suddenly it feels like it might be making a break for it. Hank has been writing songs since he's been here. Since we've been spending time together.

Lots of people are special to him, I remind myself. It would be egocentric to assume that this song is about me.

I've met other women and loved them, it's true,
but no other woman has ever been you.
And when I get home at the end of the day,
there's one person I want and just one thing to say.

I exhale heavily, as if I'm in the middle of a run.

I wanna tell you that I love you and I want you for forever,
but my words come out all wrong.
So I'll do the only thing I can though it'll never be enough . . .
I'll write you just another love song.

Honey turns to look at me, eyebrows raised. "Uhhh . . . have you heard this song before?"

I shake my head, my eyes on Hank.

"It's about . . ." she starts.

"It's probably about Julia," I say firmly. "Probably he's writing about old relationships as inspiration. You know, like Taylor Swift does."

Honey's mouth twists. "Yeah, but he said it's about someone special to him."

"Maybe it's about Ed," I suggest. "Ed is special to all of us."

"When he mentions an impressive ponytail and a dedication to short shorts, then I'll agree with you," Honey says.

Brian leans over. "Yeah, I think Honey's right on this one. This song is about you."

Honey high-fives him while giving me a smug look.

"Kinda nice that we both have attractive men writing songs for us," Shelby says. "I do prefer the song Keith wrote for me. No offense. It has my name in the title to avoid confusion like this."

"See, that's what Hank should've done," Honey says, pointing to the stage with her half-eaten corn dog. "If he had only called the song 'Sandy,' we wouldn't have to have this conversation."

"You guys!" I roll my eyes. "I can't even hear the words to this song."

Shelby gives me a dismissive wave. "Whatever, he'll play it for you later. Keith plays me all the songs he writes for me."

We all turn to look at her. "How many songs has he written for you in the course of two days?"

She sips her lemonade. "I don't know, like ten? Don't get jealous because your boyfriend doesn't write as quickly."

"He's not my boyfriend and this song isn't about me and, oh look, it's over," I say with relief as Hank starts talking.

"I want to play another song that's special to me, but this isn't one of mine. This is a cover of what I think we can all agree is a modern country classic."

I don't recognize it at first, but when he starts singing, I know what it is: "She Thinks My Tractor's Sexy." Hank Tillman is onstage in front of my very eyes, he may have just performed a song he wrote about me (but I'm not making any assumptions), and now he's playing the song we listened to right before we had sex for the first time.

As I'm piecing all of these thoughts together in my head like they're a hard-to-solve math problem, Hank meets my eyes. I shake my head and smile, fake-exasperated, and give him a little wave.

He winks back at me. *Winks.* It's all I can do not to melt into a puddle right here on the lawn, leaving behind a dress that could double as a picnic blanket.

Shelby waves her hands in the air, swaying back and forth. "Haven't heard this banger in *years.*"

"Why is he playing this song?" Honey asks. "I mean, sure, the audience loves it. But it's like twenty years old."

"I never told you," I say, shimmying my shoulders without taking my eyes off Hank. "This is the song we listened to right before we slept together for the first time."

She doesn't say anything, so I look at her and see that her jaw has dropped to somewhere in the vicinity of her knees. "You little freak!" she says, slapping me on the arm. "A song about tractors? God, you are weird."

Then we start singing along, just like everyone else in the crowd. Kenny Chesney's paramour from twenty years ago isn't the only one who finds tractors sexy—apparently all of us do, because this song is bringing the house down.

And right before he strums the final note on his guitar, Hank looks out into the crowd and meets my eye again. He smiles that crooked smile, and I know it—I'm a goner. I haven't, not even for one second of the last fifteen years, ever stopped loving Hank Tillman, and I never will. No matter what happens, no matter how much I lie to myself, that man has my whole heart and he always will.

CHAPTER TWENTY-EIGHT

URING THE FIRST day of the fair, the fire station is full of
tables displaying the baked goods, jams, jellies, pickles, and
floral arrangements the people of Baileyville have entered. But
after the judging and the ribbon awarding, everyone picks up
their entries on Friday afternoon, meaning that the fire station is
now free of pickled eggs and ready for one thing: red-hot dance
moves. After Hank ends his concert to thunderous applause and a
standing ovation, Honey, Brian, and I head to the fire station,
ready to take in the ambience of the most romantic night in Baileyville.

"Damn," Honey says as we walk down the sidewalk, stepping
over the cords of the cheese-on-a-stick truck and the lemonade
truck, the siren song of "Hot in Herre" beckoning us closer. "All
the hits of at least fifteen years ago!"

"Maybe we'll take it further back and play 'Macarena,'" I say.
"I memorized those dance moves instead of the multiplication tables. I need that knowledge to be useful."

Honey looks at me skeptically. "Those dance moves can't possibly take up that much space in your brain."

"I'm very bad at math and I need an excuse. Let me have this," I say as smoke starts billowing out of the fire station.

"Is there a fire in the fire station?" Brian asks.

"Someone call Alanis Morissette and tell her to add another verse to 'Ironic,'" I say. "And no. That's obviously a fog machine."

Honey elbows Brian. "Obviously. Ms. Fog Machine Expert over here."

I sigh heavily. "I'm gonna go home. You two can grope each other on the dance floor and pretend it's high school, but I don't want to be your third wheel again."

"We didn't grope each other on the dance floor in high school!" Brian says.

I look at both of them.

". . . that much," Honey adds. "I'm sorry, but high school was a very horny time for me, and my mother was extremely strict. Dances were all we had."

I hold up a hand. "Again, I don't want to know."

"She loves it," Honey mutters to Brian, who shrugs. At this point, he's used to us talking about their sex life.

I stop in front of the open fire station garage doors, the fog obscuring my view. It's clearing out, maybe because someone realized smoke in a fire station sends an alarming message. People mill around outside, laughing and talking in the relatively cool night air, the sounds of the carousel behind us.

I am, I suddenly realize, scared to go in.

Which is ridiculous because I'm an adult woman, and I don't actually have to stand along the wall while Honey and Brian dance. I could go home to the house I own. Or, at the very least, I bet Ed would dance with me.

But I know a part of me is wishing and hoping and praying that Hank will be here, especially after the moment we shared during his performance. There's no real reason he'd decide to come to the dance—I don't think he knows we'll be here. I'm not even sure why we showed up; I guess to see if Ed suffers another dance-related injury.

I look up to see the moon shining bright and full in the sky. Does a full moon portend something ominous or something amazing? Or does full moon symbolism mainly pertain to horror movies about werewolves? I wish I knew.

"What does a full moon mean?" I ask Honey, who's deep in conversation with Brian, presumably about how their sex life has evolved since they were teenagers.

I expect her to say something about werewolves, but instead she turns to me and says, "It symbolizes adulthood, maturity, even pregnancy."

I pause. "What?"

"Think of the moon cycle as the life cycle," Honey says, getting animated the way she does whenever she talks about the things she loves, like goats. "The new moon is a baby, just being born. The waxing crescent moon is youth. The full moon is adulthood, and the waning moon is basically an elderly person. The full moon also has an intensely feminine energy."

"What the hell is feminine energy?" I ask, raising my eyebrows. "Does the energy, like, watch a lot of Marilyn Monroe films? Also, how do you know this?"

Honey sighs. "Sometimes I can't sleep, and I don't want to wake my family up, so I sit there in bed googling things like 'what does the moon cycle mean' and 'why isn't Pizza Hut as good as it used to be' and 'Mary-Kate Olsen 2007' because it makes me feel safe to see pictures of her in big scarves carrying a Starbucks cup."

"Well, as long as you're doing something productive with your insomnia," I say, patting her on the arm. "If you want, I can find a bunch of scarves and some sunglasses, and you can walk down the street with a steak on a stick and pretend it's a latte."

"You're sweet," she says, "but it's too hot for scarves."

"Hey!"

We turn to see Shelby and Keith behind us, a huge smile on her face and their hands entwined.

"Wow, Shelby," I say. "You look great."

Somehow, in the time since we saw her at the concert, she's changed into a silver dress with a plunging neckline, and her hair is in its signature long, glossy waves. Between the moon's glow and the lights from the steak-on-a-stick truck, she's sparkling, and about ninety-five percent more glamorous than anyone else at the fair.

"Thanks!" she says. "I really do, don't I?"

I glance at Keith, but he isn't looking at me. Instead, his eyes are glued to Shelby. She gives us a fluttery wave as they walk past us and into the dance.

"Come on," Honey says, grabbing my and Brian's hands and pulling us into the fire station. "Let's go spike the punch."

Inside, it's loud and crowded, and a *lot* of people are making out. Apparently, the entire town decided that this is the place for romance. I turn around to commiserate with Honey about how weird it is that the checkout guy from the grocery store is possibly giving his wife a hickey, only to see that she and Brian are already dancing and staring deeply into each other's eyes. Ethel and her cowboy are swaying slowly, and Burger is both dancing with and talking animatedly to a girl I vaguely recognize from our class—I can only assume he's sharing his fart-joke material with her.

"Oh, for Pete's sake," I mutter, trying to make my way through the crowd. I walk past my parents, and even the woman who carried me in her body for nine months doesn't notice my presence because she's under the influence of the fire station's mysteriously romantic vibe. Everywhere I look, I'm surrounded by couples dancing to "How Deep Is Your Love." Everyone in this room must have love that is extremely deep. My love, however, is "call Lady Gaga and Bradley Cooper" levels of shallow.

I make my way to the wall and lean up against the cool cinder blocks. I'm thirty-three and standing alone at the edge of a dance—it's hard to imagine how much more pathetic it could get.

"What's a girl like you doing in a place like this?"

The sound of his voice brings a smile to my traitorous lips. "You use that line on all the girls?"

"You got me," Hank says, grinning. "Just used it on Ethel, and she informed me that I can't compare to her cowboy."

"Or his butt. If the bumper sticker's to be believed, it drives her nuts."

Hank peers into the crowd. "You know, I can see why. It's a great butt."

"It has to be to inspire a bumper sticker." I stand up straighter. "What are you doing here?"

Hank nods toward the street. "My parents are taking Henry for an ill-advised late-night cotton candy, but it's fine because he's spending the night with them tonight."

"So his sugar rush is their problem."

"Exactly," Hank says with a smile as the ancient but still rock-solid Usher song "Yeah!" starts playing. We hear Burger shout, "Oh hell yes, this is my jam!" and I can't help laughing.

"But none of that explains why you came in here," I say.

"Didn't you know I never could ignore a fog machine?" he asks.

"Ah, yes. Your most defining personality trait. Your love of fog machines. Well, the fog is gone now, so no excuse."

He leans against the wall with one hand, his body forming an acute angle around me. I might actually perish.

"If we're being honest, I saw you walk in here, so I came in, too. It took me a minute to find you. I think I almost ended up in a threesome with Natasha and Jason."

I laugh, clapping my hand over my mouth even as my heart leaps. "That's horrific."

A cheer erupts from the dance floor, and we turn to see a circle forming around Ed, who is, true to his nickname, wearing his hot pants.

Hank lets out a low whistle. "Who knew he had those moves?"

"That's why he wears the shorts," I say, leaning toward Hank so he can hear me over the music. "Flexibility."

Hank nods. "Maybe it's my jeans that are holding me back."

"That's what your stage show needs," I say. "More dancing. Yes, the people love your heartfelt songs, but what they really want is to see those hips move."

"I think I ought to be less worried about my next album and more worried about learning some dance moves from Ed," Hank says as we watch Ed attempt what looks like it's supposed to be break dancing.

"Speaking of the album," I say, turning to him. "How's it going?"

"I've actually written several new songs while I've been home," he says, both of us leaning against the cool stone wall. "The cabin is a great place to write, and I've had some inspiration."

"That's good," I say as the crowd lets out a groan.

"I'm okay!" Ed shouts over the music, holding on to his thigh. "Think I pulled my groin, but I'm gonna walk it off!"

"Is this the inspiration?" I ask.

"Yes." Hank nods. "My next song is 'The Night Hotpants Ed Pulled His Groin at the Fire Station Dance.'"

A slow song starts to play and Hank holds out his hand. "Care to dance?"

There is no way to say no without being rude, and also, I don't want to say no, so I take his hand and let him lead me to the center of the dance floor.

I put my arms around his neck, and he places his hands on my hips—a familiar position for us. Although we skipped homecoming, we went to prom, so we have experience doing this shuffle in a circle as a slow jam plays.

I gasp when I realize what song is playing. "Neon Moon" by Brooks & Dunn.

"You like this song?" Hank asks, smiling.

"Who doesn't?" I ask. "But also, have you seen the moon tonight? It *is* a neon moon."

"So you're saying Sean picked some appropriate songs?"

Surprised, I laugh. "I'm sorry, Sean is the DJ? I thought he hated music."

Hank shakes his head. "No one hates music."

"He listened to NPR in the car when we were on our *one* date!" I protest. "And maybe I should've been offended, but I was mostly surprised that he could get a radio signal in his car down here, so we listened to *All Things Considered* instead of talking. I can't believe he's not only the DJ, but he played 'Hot in Herre' *in the fire station*. Sean made a *joke* with his playlist!"

Hank laughs and pulls me closer to him. "Okay, you know what? I don't want to hear another word about you being on a date with Sean, no matter how much it sucked."

"Good," I say. "I don't like thinking about it."

Call it muscle memory or being under the influence of Mr. Brooks and Mr. Dunn themselves, but I put my head on Hank's shoulder. I know this is slightly dangerous territory, but I can't help myself, and Hank doesn't complain.

"Is it weird to be back in a town where people voluntarily gather in a fire station on a Friday night to dance?" I ask him.

I can't see his face, but I can feel his smile. "I don't think it's weird. I think it's pretty nice."

"Yeah," I say, looking at the rest of the couples here swaying to the music. Honey and Brian. Shelby and Keith. Marcia and Aimee. "It is. There are a lot of things about Baileyville that seem weird but are actually pretty nice."

"I know we used to spend all our time complaining about this place and trying to get out," Hank says into my ear, "but now that I'm back—and now that I'm grown up—it feels different. I wish I could stay here all the time, you know?"

"But you can't," I remind him. "A big part of your job involves not staying here all the time."

"True," Hank says. "I'll have to go back out on tour eventually. But I'm still hoping to spend more time here. Maybe a lot more time here."

I swallow.

"It's good for Henry to be with his family, you know?"

"Right," I say. "It's good for Henry."

We dance in silence for another moment, and then I say, "You played 'She Thinks My Tractor's Sexy' tonight."

Hank laughs, low and rumbly against my ear. "I did."

"And you played a new song," I say, growing bolder. "Is that something you wrote since you've been here?"

"Yep," Hank says, and we keep dancing. I close my eyes. Is it so much to ask to stay here forever? Not in the fire station, necessarily (that would be inconvenient if there was actually a fire), but in this moment, with my eyes closed and Hank holding me and not thinking about the future or the past?

"I have a confession to make," Hank says into my ear.

My brain plays an alarm sound. "Yes?"

"I wrote 'Just Another Love Song' about you," he says.

The alarm sounds louder, so I mentally switch it off. Of course a part of me hoped that he'd written the song about me, but I was never going to say anything about it. I planned to keep thinking about it for the rest of my natural life and never find out if it was really about some other woman. "You did?"

"I did. A lot of my songs are about you, you know."

I lift my head so I can see his face. As always, I'm looking right into his eyes, not craning my neck up. There's never any effort with Hank—it's like I've always been able to see right into him. "Which ones?" I ask. "The one you sang at the bar that night in Chicago?"

Hank chuckles. "No. Definitely not that one. I wrote that one right after Julia and I got married, when I could already tell it wasn't working out because she'd rather go out all night with other guys, and it messed me up. I could barely work. Why would you think that one was about you?"

I shake my head. "I . . . I assumed. It sounded like it was about somebody who ruined your life, and I always thought about you out there performing, wishing you'd never met me. Some stupid girl back in your hometown who broke your heart."

Hank smiles a little sadly. "You did break my heart, a long time ago. But you've never ruined anything. I've always been glad I got to spend any time with you at all. Even when we weren't together, I was glad I'd met you."

I smile, afraid I might start to cry.

"All the good ones are about you," he admits. "Like 'When the World Melts Away.'"

I stop moving, unable to even concentrate on slightly picking up my feet. "What?"

He nods slowly, his face only a few inches from mine. "Couldn't you tell? Those are our memories, Sandy. It's your song."

"But . . . but everyone thinks that's your best song," I say.

He shrugs. "Maybe it is. Maybe you're my best memory."

"Hank," I whisper. "I don't think this is a good idea. This whole conversation. Friends don't say things like this to one another."

"I need to tell you something else," Hank says. "I don't want to be your friend."

I pull back a little to get a better look at his face. "You don't?"

He tightens his grip on my hips. "I want to be your everything."

Suddenly, my determination to be just friends with Hank Tillman seems pretty damn stupid. As does my worry that he'll be back on the road soon or that he has a whole life and a family without me or that I'll only get my heart broken in the end. That's a problem for Future Sandy to worry about, not Current Sandy.

"Do you want to get out of here?" I ask as Justin Bieber starts singing about peaches.

Out of the corner of my eye, I can see Edith's husband using his cowboy butt to do what could generously be described as twerking, but I can't focus on that right now. Not when Hank is right in front of me and looking at me like that.

"Absolutely," Hank says, holding my hand and pulling me through the crowd.

We walk past Honey, who mouths, *What's going on?* with wide eyes as she points to our hands.

I give her a look that I hope communicates, *We'll talk about it later*, and then Hank and I are bursting into the cooler air outside the fire station. While I love everything about the crowd at the fair, right now I need all these people eating nachos to clear out of our way.

We walk across Main Street but then start running, away from the sounds of the rides and the carnival games. I'd ask where we're going, but I think we both know. In the alley, Hank stops.

"What?" I ask. Surely he hasn't changed his mind.

"I need to do something," he says before pushing me up against the brick wall of the dentist's office and kissing me. This is nothing like the kiss at his cabin, nothing like any kiss we've ever had. We couldn't have kissed like this when we were kids—this is the kiss of two adults who've lived entire lives. Two adults who know what it means to love someone and what it means to lose them.

"Okay," Hank says, pulling back. He shakes his head.

"Why are you stopping?" I ask.

He looks at me. "Because we're in an alley in a town where we both know every resident. And also because I really don't think Dr. Mark wants us doing this up against his dental practice."

I place a hand on the brick wall. "Don't put words in Dr. Mark's mouth."

I hate to admit it, though—I can see his point. The full moon is so bright that it's seemingly shining a spotlight on us making out in an alley.

"Let's go somewhere else."

"My place," I say, grabbing his hand. And then we take off running like we really are still kids. The difference, though, is that we no longer have to make out in his truck. Now I have a whole damn house that we can do whatever we want in because I'm a grown woman and I make my own decisions, even ones that might hurt me later.

"You're way too slow," Hank says, stopping and hoisting me onto his back.

"Hank!" I screech. "There's no way this is going to be faster!"

But then he starts running, and I'm laughing so hard tears come out of my eyes, and I can't help thinking that this might be the happiest I've been in years. Maybe I'm only truly happy when I'm with Hank.

When we reach my front porch, I fumble with my keys, then we burst through the door. The second it shuts, our hands are all over each other. His mouth is on my neck, and I'm unbuttoning his flannel and pulling his T-shirt over his head.

"Wait," I say, panting. "Where is Henry?"

"With my parents, remember? Spending the night there," Hank says, working at the zipper on my dress.

"Oh, okay."

He stops, a smile on his face. "Did you seriously think I was gonna forget about my own kid?"

"Don't make fun of me right now," I say, kissing him again. I could kiss Hank all night. All month. For the rest of my life, I'd never get tired of it. He's like a book I want to read again and again, one where I discover new things each time I turn the page.

"I've been wanting to do this for so long," Hank says, his lips grazing my neck.

"How long?" I ask, running my hands along his bare chest, which is now broad and strong. He's like a well-built house, one that could withstand any sort of weather.

"I wanted to kiss you right there in the soda aisle at Tillman's," he says, moving his lips to my mouth. "But I had a feeling you wouldn't be into it."

"I was an idiot," I say, kissing him back. "We should've made out in the soda aisle."

"Noted," Hank says, and then he does something I didn't expect: he picks me up.

"Were you this strong at seventeen?" I ask, marveling.

"I've become better at a lot of things since I was seventeen," he says. "You ready to head upstairs?"

I nod, suddenly unable to form words, and he carries me to my room.

Chapter Twenty-Nine

C AN I JUST say"—I put my feet on Hank's lap as we sit on the sofa—"that doing this as adults is a lot more enjoyable than when we were teenagers?"

He narrows his eyes. "Do you mean to tell me that you don't want to have sex in the truck and then attempt to sneak back into your parents' house?"

I smile. Hank and I are eating ice cream straight out of the pint, and I put a spoonful in my mouth. "I'm not trying to diss the truck. A lot of good memories in that truck."

"That's right," Hank says, reaching over and grabbing a spoonful. "Have some respect."

"But I don't really feel comfortable sitting in the truck in just a T-shirt and underwear," I point out.

"Not the truck's fault," Hank says. "And I'm of the opinion that you should spend more time in just a T-shirt and underwear."

I kick him lightly and he grabs my foot, tickling it.

"Aah!" I screech. "I don't react well to tickling! You know that! You're gonna get kicked in the face! I'm gonna drop the ice cream!"

Hank puts my foot down. "I'll stop, but only because I know how vicious you can get when tickled."

I take another bite of ice cream and think about all the time I spent worrying about getting into trouble in high school. I spent so much time studying, but before I met Hank, I don't know that I spent any time *feeling* anything. And it's starting to seem like all these years without him have become another holding pattern, another way to keep myself from stepping out of line, taking a risk, or getting hurt.

"I was so into following the rules when I was in high school," I say wistfully. "You know, not doing anything wrong. Not getting caught. Getting good grades. And what did it matter, anyway? Sometimes I wish I could go back and tell high school Sandy to— I don't know . . . loosen up. Risk something."

Hank thinks for a moment, the spoon dangling out of his mouth in a way that somehow looks both goofy and sexy. "Hang on," he says, standing up with the spoon still in his mouth. "I've got an idea."

I frown. "Does it involve putting pants on?"

"Temporarily," he says from the kitchen, where he puts the ice cream back in the freezer.

"Then I don't support this idea. In fact, I'm going to lead a protest. A pantsless protest. I won't be leaving this couch—"

Hank runs back into the room, leaps over the back of the couch, and pins me down with an arm on either side of my head. "You wanna go break some rules?" he asks in a low voice.

And right then, when I'm surrounded by Hank Tillman—his

face in front of mine, his arms on either side of me, his breath hot in my face—I know I'd say yes to anything he asked.

"YOU'RE KIDDING ME," I say.

"Nope," Hank says. "Not even a little."

Charles Lake, named after Charles Bailey, who founded the town approximately one million years ago, is one of the most popular spots for Baileyville families to have their summer cookouts, for high school students to clandestinely party at night, and right now, it's where Hank Tillman is attempting to convince me that skinny-dipping is a good idea.

"Did you do this in school? Before you met me?" I ask incredulously. Of course I'd heard that stuff like this went on, but I was always busy with my books and my paints, and Honey was so interested in studying and Brian that it wasn't like she'd ever suggest we do anything like this. And even if I'd *wanted* to plunge my naked body into dirty lake water, I would've been way too scared of getting in trouble. This definitely seems like the kind of thing you're not allowed to do, even if there isn't a sign that explicitly prohibits it.

Hank stares out at the lake. "I'd rather not talk about my past."

I smack him on the arm. "I can't believe I never knew this about you."

Hank shrugs. "You know what they say . . . what happens at the lake stays at the lake, especially because no one had cell phone cameras back then."

"The good old days."

We both look out at the lake, at the full moon shining bright and clear across the rippling water, its reflection beaming back up at us as brightly as the real thing. Pine trees line the lake, making it feel like we're hidden away, cozy even in the openness.

"What if someone sees us?" I ask, looking away from the moon.

Hank looks back at me, his face glowing in the light. He looks like an angel, if angels were agents of skinny-dipping. He gestures around us. "Who's gonna see us, Sandy?"

I take one step toward the lake and hear the kerplunk of a frog jumping in. "The amphibian life of Charles Lake, for starters."

"The frogs have seen worse," Hank says, and then he does something that renders me temporarily speechless: he pulls his T-shirt over his head. I've seen Hank Tillman in various states of undress many times throughout my life, including as recently as an hour ago, but something about seeing him shirtless in the moonlight to a soundtrack of crickets, the heat hanging heavy in the air even this late at night, moves me in ways that I never thought possible.

"Hey," he says softly, reaching out to stroke my face. I think he's about to say something meaningful or romantic, but then he says, "Get in the water instead of enjoying the show, you perv."

"I am not a perv," I protest.

"You've got kind of a history of ogling me," he says, raising his eyebrows as he undoes his belt buckle. That *clink-clink* noise jogs my memory, and I'm like a dog who hears the sound of food hitting its bowl. I'd follow Hank into molten lava if it meant being close to him.

"All right, fine," I say. "But I'm not getting in if you're looking."

Hank stares at me, shaking his head. "Sandy. Do you remember what we were doing an hour ago?"

"Still." I feel my cheeks get hot in the darkness. "Get in. And turn around."

He sighs good-naturedly, taking off his boxers and then running into the water with a yelp. He dives under and surfaces a second later. "It's colder than I expected!" he shouts back at me.

"Keep it down!" I whisper-yell. "And turn around!"

He dutifully faces the moon and I quickly yank off my clothes, tossing them behind me as I run into the water. Logically, I know that it's around eighty degrees even at this time of night and that the water can't be that cold, but I still stifle a scream as I dunk my head under.

"Holy moly," I say with a gasp. I'm about to complain about the surprising frigidity, but my words dry up when I see how Hank is looking at me, his eyes both ravenous and awestruck. He's looking at me like I'm one of the apple fritters in the glass case at Betty's.

"You are," he says, swimming closer to me, "the most"—he pushes me up against a log that juts out into the lake—"beautiful"—he presses himself against me, my body sandwiched between him and the log—"woman I've ever seen." He leans his forehead against mine.

"You looked when I got in, didn't you?" I ask quietly, the words traveling the few inches between my lips and his ear.

"Sandy," he says, and I watch that crooked smile appear. "I'm an honest man. But I have my limits."

And then he presses his mouth to mine, devouring me with one hungry kiss after another. His strong arms grip the log and hold me in place, my feet kicking underneath us. A memory comes to me: swimming in the pond at Honey's house in our matching heart-print one-pieces and how we'd wear glittery polish on our toenails. The fish thought the shiny nail polish was a lure, and they'd nibble lightly on our toes, making us shriek in delight.

Since Hank's hands are busy holding us up against the log, there's not much we can do here—and anyway, as much as I want to, I might draw the line at sex in the lake, which seems like a bacterial horror story waiting to happen. Still, though, I put my hands on Hank's impressively muscled back and pull him closer to me. He can't ever get close enough. After all those years apart, I don't want to let him go.

A shout pierces the darkness and we both stop. It's followed by a high-pitched shriek.

"The murderer," I say, panting. "It's happening."

Hank loops an arm around me and pulls me out of the water.

"What are we doing?" I hiss. "Are we hiding? I don't want the murderer to see us! We're like sitting ducks over here. Naked sitting ducks!"

Back on dry land, Hank grabs his clothes. "It's kids, Sandy. Teenagers here to party."

"Oh, shit," I say, stumbling over my feet as I attempt to pull on my shorts. Hank trips pulling his pants on, and both of us laugh as we run through the woods, half clothed, yanking our shirts over our heads, taking the back way to his truck. The kids' voices grow closer, but we're out of their eyesight now and at least partially covered.

We both jump into the truck as if we've robbed a bank and this is our getaway vehicle, but once inside, we lean back against the seats.

"I can't believe this," I say, putting my hands over my face as I try to catch my breath. "We're adults, and we ran through the woods to avoid getting caught skinny-dipping by teens."

Hank snorts. "You know, we should've stayed there. Can you imagine how freaked out they would've been?"

We both laugh, the adrenaline of the moment catching up with us. We're parked well off the main road, mostly hidden by the low-hanging boughs of pine trees. Even still, the moon finds its way through the branches and into the truck, illuminating Hank's face. I think for a moment about painting him, but I know I could never capture this moment. Hell, Michelangelo couldn't do this justice. He'd be like, "Yeah, I handled the ceiling of the Sistine Chapel, but Hank Tillman's face? Hard pass."

"When do you have to be home?" I ask, then wince. "Sorry to sound like we're still kids."

Hank smiles. "Late tomorrow morning. Henry likes to stay as long as possible, and he and my dad have pancake-eating contests."

I lean my head back on the worn-out upholstery of the seat. "That's really sweet."

"Maybe not when you're dealing with a kid who ate fifteen pancakes for breakfast," he says. "But yeah. It's . . . nice. Nice that he can be around them."

He doesn't make any move to start the truck and drive back home, so I take the chance to ask him something I've been curious about.

"So . . ." I choose my words carefully. "Henry's mom really isn't in the picture at all?"

Hank sighs, looking out the windshield into the darkness, but he doesn't avoid the subject. That's one of the things I've always liked best about Hank—he never tries to avoid talking about the uncomfortable things, and he's never shut me out.

"She'll show up every once in a while, but always on her schedule. And she never sticks around. It's a lot for a little kid to handle, you know?"

I nod even though I can't possibly know—I grew up with two parents who loved me, who came to every single elementary school concert, who were so present that sometimes I wished they could back off for a minute.

"He likes you," Hank says lightly, gripping the steering wheel with one hand as if we're about to take off. I shiver a bit in my now wet T-shirt, and Hank immediately reaches under his seat and pulls out a flannel shirt.

"Oh yeah?" I ask in a barely audible voice, taking it from him and putting it on. It's soft and worn, and I'd think it had been in the truck since high school if I didn't know how much broader Hank's shoulders had become since then. It feels like being wrapped up in a blanket, and it smells like him—warm and woodsy. I turn to face him, leaning against the seat, my arms wrapped around myself in my too-long sleeves. "Well, I like him, too. He's a pretty cool dude."

"I think we both know where he gets that from," Hank says, pointing to himself as I roll my eyes. "But seriously, thanks for taking him on the Dragon Coaster the other day."

"Of course! I mean, did I almost get stuck in the seat? Yes. But it would've been a small price to pay to see those beautiful views from fifteen feet off the ground."

Hank laughs. "It was . . . uh, it was nice seeing you two together." He glances out the window, looking uncomfortable for the first time I can remember.

"What do you mean?" I ask.

His eyes flash to mine again, and he doesn't say anything for a moment. Finally he opens his mouth and says, "You thought it would be us, right? I'm not the only one?"

Now it's my turn to look away. There are fireflies blinking outside, and it hits me that this is late in the summer to see them—I don't know that I've ever seen them this late. It's like

Hank Tillman brought them along, like this wondrous display of bioluminescence is another gift from him.

I force myself to look back at him, unable to form words.

"Don't get me wrong, Henry is my favorite person in the whole world," Hank says. "He's perfect exactly the way he is, and I love him more than anything. But when we were kids . . . I always thought it would be us, Sandy. Us together. A house and kids. A family."

He watches my face, but I still can't say anything. I nod again, and one treacherous tear slides down my face. I wipe it off with the sleeve of Hank's shirt.

"Hey," Hank says, reaching across the seat and pulling me to him. He puts his forehead against mine, the same way he did in the lake. Reassuring me. Claiming me. Filling my field of vision. "You don't need to do that."

"I messed it up," I whisper. "I could've had everything I wanted, but I messed it up. I didn't go away to college and I didn't keep you."

Hank puts his hands on my face. "You didn't mess anything up. You broke my heart, sure, but you were right. If we'd stayed together, I probably would have come back."

I nod quickly, trying my best to stop crying.

"It's not like I *needed* to go to college to pursue music," he continues. "But I needed that time to be somewhere else. I wanted to get away from here, but I never wanted to get away from you."

"I never wanted to be away from you, either," I say softly.

"And, God, Sandy, of course I wish we spent the last fifteen years together. It kills me that we missed out on all that time. But who knows where we'd be if we didn't have all those years to figure ourselves out. The only thing we can do is be here right now. In Baileyville. By the lake. In this truck. In this moment."

He kisses my forehead. "Hank," I say quietly. "You being back . . . I don't even know what I think anymore."

He leans back and takes a look at my face. "What do you mean?"

"I thought I was happy before. My life didn't turn out the way I thought it would when I was a kid, but whose does? I thought I had a pretty good life and that if I kept a smile pasted on my face, I wouldn't have to think about the parts that didn't make me happy. That if I kept busy enough, I wouldn't have time to think about what I was missing. But then you showed up."

Hank stays quiet.

"Can I ask you something?" I whisper.

"Anything," he says, his voice rough.

"Why are you driving this old truck? I know you have a very nice SUV. I can't imagine why, whenever you're not with Henry, you're driving this old rumbly thing with the broken tape player."

Hank smiles then, a small one that's half happy, half sad. "Because of you."

"What?"

Our windows are partially rolled down, and as I wait for Hank to say something else, the chirp of crickets fills the truck like surround sound.

"I fixed it because you always liked it. Because it reminds me of you," he says quietly, his hand on the back of my neck.

I nod, my eyes on his lips. "I think that whole time that I didn't know what I was missing . . . I was missing you. I think I'm only happy when you're with me."

Hank leans forward again and kisses me hard, his mouth smashing into mine. "I'm here now," he says. "I'm here now."

CHAPTER THIRTY

"S O HOW WAS the rest of the dance?" I ask Honey the next
morning over zebra lattes at Lydia's cafe.

She takes a bite of her blueberry streusel muffin. "Fine. I think
Brian lost his voice singing along to 'Friends in Low Places' at the
end of the night."

"The man loves that song," I say.

Honey shakes her head. "Yes, but we didn't come here to talk
about the nostalgic hits of our childhood."

"Why *did* we come here?" I ask. Honey had texted me at six in
the morning, which isn't an unusual time for either of us to be up,
what with her kids and my job. But I'm not heading over to the
greenhouse until later, and so I got her text—*Meet me at Lydia's at 8*
(with no punctuation or explanation)—while I was in bed with
Hank's still-sleeping body wrapped around mine.

Hank took Toby on a quick walk around the block (and caught
the sunrise while he was at it) while I showered and got dressed,

and then I gave him a goodbye kiss that threatened to turn into a goodbye something else. We were only saved by the fact that we were on the porch.

But I made it here to the café, and now Honey is being deliberately mysterious.

"Hank spent the night last night," she says.

I frown. "How did you know that?"

She holds up a hand, ticking off the reasons on her fingers. "One, I saw you two leave the dance together, and you had your 'I'm absolutely going to get laid tonight' face on."

I almost choke on my muffin. "Excuse me? What face would that be? And when have you ever seen it in the past?"

"It's not exactly hard to translate. Two, Hank's truck was parked in front of your house. Three, I saw him walking Toby around the block this morning while I was having my first breakfast."

"First breakfast?"

"Charlie's been up since five. I got hungry and couldn't wait until eight. Don't change the subject."

"Okay, fine, Detective. You got me. Hank spent the night at my place."

Honey's demeanor changes from that of a hardened private investigator to my enthusiastic best friend. "Yay!" she says, clapping. "Finally! The sexual tension between you two was so thick I could cut it with a scalpel."

"It was not," I say, attempting to hide my smile, but it stubbornly peeks out. Like a sunrise, I can't stop it. "We also had sex in his truck after we went skinny-dipping."

Honey gasps and leans forward. "You dirty girl. So? How was it?"

"How was what? The surprisingly cold waters of Charles Lake?"

I ask innocently, picking off a chunk of muffin and putting it in my mouth.

"The. Sex," Honey says, rolling her eyes. "Was it good? Was it better than when you were teenagers? Was it worth waiting fifteen years?"

I pause, chewing, as if I have to think about it. "Yes, yes, and yes."

She squeals. "Ugh, I knew it. I've seen Hank's forearms. They scream, 'I know what to do with a woman.'"

I frown. "Forearms can say that?"

Honey looks off into the distance, like she's picturing a particularly good forearm. "Forearms can say a lot of things. Especially when there's a rolled-up flannel on them."

"Hank does wear a lot of flannel," I admit.

"Don't I know it," Honey says with what almost sounds like a growl.

"Hey." I ball up a napkin and throw it at her, jolting her out of her forearm reverie. "You've got a husband. Don't go lusting after Hank."

Lydia stops by our table, coffeepot in hand. "You ladies want a refill?"

"Yes, please," I say as Honey dramatically gets out of her chair and picks up my napkin.

"I apologize on behalf of this overgrown child," she tells Lydia. "She's over here throwing napkins at me like she never learned any manners."

"Sorry," I tell Lydia, who winks at me.

"I heard Hank spent the night," she almost sings.

"What?" I look at Honey, frantic. "Did you tell her?"

Honey scoffs. "I didn't have to tell her! Again, his truck was parked in front of your house!"

"You're not exactly discreet," Lydia adds, topping off Honey's cup. "Also Ed saw you two kissing on your porch when he was out on his morning stroll."

"Ugh," I say, hiding my face with my hands. "Is the whole town talking about this?"

Lydia shrugs. "I'd say half the town. The other half is talking about how Ed tried to do the splits at the dance last night. I'm surprised he could even go on his morning stroll, to be honest."

Honey's eyes light up with glee. "I forgot to tell you! After you left, 'Shout' by the Isley Brothers came on, and Ed decided to really go for broke when things were getting 'a little bit louder now.' He couldn't get out of the splits, and the squad had to come."

I groan. "Why does every story in this town end with 'and then the squad had to come'?"

"Because people are always acting foolish and injuring themselves," Honey says, taking a sip of her coffee. "And everyone knows the fire station dance makes people do strange things."

"I hear that," Lydia says, toasting her with the coffeepot. "Or maybe it was the full moon."

"I'm not sure the moon cycle can be blamed for Ed's overconfidence in his splits abilities," I say.

"Whatever you say," Lydia says lightly, walking away to refill someone else's coffee.

Honey sighs, both hands holding her mug. "Sorry for objectifying your man's forearms, by the way. You're right. I have my own quite satisfactory man at home."

I wrinkle my nose. "I'm gonna tell Brian you referred to him as 'satisfactory.' And Hank's not my man."

Honey raises her eyebrows at me over her cup. "Oh, he's not?"

"He's not," I say firmly. "We don't own each other. He's not my possession."

"Sure," Honey says, putting her mug down on the table. "But you're going to go with him, right?"

"Go with him where?"

She looks at me as if I'm one of her kids and I told her I didn't need a bath even though my face is covered in chocolate. "With him. On the road. You know, for his job as a big-deal, super-famous musician?"

"I wouldn't say he's super famous," I mutter. "And I don't know! He's planning on sticking around for a while, and we haven't talked about it!"

She makes a noise that's between a grunt and a snort to express her disbelief. "So you slept with your baggage-filled ex-boyfriend without discussing your future plans?"

"He doesn't have baggage," I protest. "A child is not baggage."

Honey holds up a hand. "Whoa, there. You don't have to tell me! I'm well aware that you love Henry, which is part of my point. I meant that Hank, in general, has a lot of baggage for you. Fifteen years' worth."

"It's fine," I say, crossing my arms. "You don't need to worry about it."

"Oh, I wouldn't say I'm super worried," Honey says with a sigh. "Just, you know, concerned. As your best friend and the person who's always there for you no matter what."

I bite my lip. "You mean the person who had to wipe me off the floor when I fell into a Hank-related hole after high school?"

She furrows her brow. "No. That's not what I meant."

"I won't be a burden to you if this all crashes and burns," I say briskly.

"Hey!" She reaches out and grabs my hand. "All I meant is that . . . you know you can always tell me anything, right? You know I'll always love you?"

"Of course," I say, my voice softening.

"And if you did want to head off into the sunset with Hank . . . it wouldn't be the worst thing," she says. "You know, Brian and I have been eyeing your house for a while."

My jaw drops. "And here I thought you cared about my well-being! This was all opportunism!"

"You have a better backyard!" Honey says. "And our house doesn't have a porch."

"You have a much better kitchen," I point out.

"I don't need a nice kitchen to make boxed mac and cheese for my picky children," Honey says. "And anyway, I'm not actually saying this because I want you to move away and sell your house to me, although if you could do that, I'd appreciate it."

I raise an eyebrow, waiting for her to go on.

"I want you to be happy. That's all," she says, squeezing my hand.

I squeeze hers back. "I know. And I am."

And for the first time in a long time, I actually mean it.

CHAPTER THIRTY-ONE

SOCIAL MEDIA HAS more or less eliminated the need for high school reunions. Now that it's easy to find someone's job on LinkedIn, pictures of their children on Facebook, or extremely flattering and filtered selfies on Instagram, we don't really need to catch up via awkward conversations while wearing name tags.

But the thing about Baileyville is that people here love to get together, catch up, and, well . . . reunite.

"I truly cannot believe I've been roped into going to this," I grumble to Honey as we pregame (aka enjoy half a glass of white wine, because we're old now) on my porch. "This is the last night of the fair, and I'm giving up another night of fried food so we can see the people we see every day! What's the point?"

"You can go get a corn dog after the reunion, and we don't see *all* these people every day," Honey reminds me. "Natasha's here."

"You should ask her why she won't accept your follow request on Instagram," I say.

"You're not following Natasha?" Brian asks.

"And you are?" Honey asks with such betrayal in her voice that you'd think Brian announced he was having an affair.

"Of course!" Brian says. "She's a future hashtag-boymom."

I snort, almost spitting out my wine. Sometimes Brian reminds us that even though he keeps quiet, he still gets all our jokes.

"This is bullshit," Honey says, draining her glass. "Tonight you're gonna let me scroll through all her posts and make disapproving noises."

"Sure, babe," he says, patting her on the hand.

"Happy wife, happy life," I say, and Honey makes a gagging noise.

I hear it before I see it . . . the sound of Hank's truck sputtering down the road. He parks in front of my house, and the sight of that red truck under the trees is enough to make my heart float out of my chest.

"Look who's here!" Honey sings. "Your booooyfriend!"

"You're a child," I mutter. Unfortunately for me, the mere sight of Hank stepping out of his truck turns me back into a lovestruck high school girl.

I stand up, feeling the imprint of the wicker furniture on my thighs, my eyes on Hank, as he comes up the walkway and then the creaky wooden stairs.

"Hi. Hey," I say.

He tilts his head a little before bending down to pet Toby, who's been sitting quietly at our feet this entire time but, of course, has jumped up to greet Hank as if he's a Kong filled with peanut butter. "Hi, hey, yourself. Y'all ready to reunite?"

"Woo!" Honey shouts, cupping her hands around her mouth. "Baileyville class of mumble-mumble cough-cough."

"It doesn't seem like it's been fifteen years," Brian says. "Sometimes it feels like we graduated yesterday."

"You only say that because your wife has aged like a fine wine," Honey says, and Brian puts an arm around her. Their casual physical affection makes me shoot an uncomfortable glance at Hank. We *did* sleep together last night—a public touch wouldn't be out of place. Some hand-holding? A kiss on the cheek?

Before I can stop myself, I reach out and punch him on the arm.

Hank grabs his left biceps. "What the hell?"

"Let's go get 'em, slugger," I say, trying and failing to cover up my awkwardness around him with awkwardness in general.

"Wait!" Honey says. "Let me help you put Toby inside. I love to give him his dog treats."

We leave the guys on my porch talking about the Buckeyes' chances this year (even though Hank doesn't care much about football these days, an at least vague interest in the Buckeyes is baked into most Ohioans), and as soon as the screen door swings shut and we make our way into the kitchen, Honey smacks me on the arm.

"What was that for?" I ask, opening the container I keep on the counter full of Toby's treats. "Here, you want to give one to him?"

"That's not why I came in here! Although, yes, Toby, you're a good boy and I love you," she says, handing him his treat as he sits patiently. "I came in here to tell you to slow your roll. You punched Hank in the arm and called him 'slugger.'"

I wince. "I did, didn't I? Was that weird?"

She sighs and stares at me. "Look at you. Totally, hopelessly, pathetically in love."

"I'm not"—I realize I'm almost yelling, and I lower my voice—"in love," I whisper. "But Hank and I slept together, and now I don't know how to act around him."

Honey waves me off. "Big deal. You've slept together before."

"But not in the past fifteen years, and not in a situation where we could sit around in our underwear eating ice cream afterward. This time, we didn't have to do it quickly in a truck bed before curfew."

Honey tilts her head, thinking. "I don't know, that sounds kinda hot to me."

"I'll give you a curfew next time I babysit."

She shakes her head, focusing. "You need to be normal, okay?"

"I don't know how to be normal! This is an abnormal situation! It's not every day that Hank Tillman comes back into town and sweeps me off my feet!"

Toby whines, and I hand him another treat without thinking about it.

"You're going to give that dog pancreatitis if you don't cool it on the treats," Honey warns. "And also, you need to chill and not use any more baseball terminology to refer to Hank."

I take a deep breath. "No baseball. No punching. Got it."

"*Normal,*" Honey reminds me, leading me toward the door. "Also, are you sure you don't want to sell this place? Your living room is so much brighter than ours!"

"Stop it," I hiss, and I lock the door. "You're not taking my house."

"Is Honey talking about how she wants to live in your house again?" Brian asks, hands in his pockets.

"Does that come up a lot?" Hank asks.

"Only once every few hours," Brian says.

"Not that often," Honey says as he puts an arm around her and they walk down the stairs. "But it's a nice house, and if there ever comes a day when Sandy's no longer with us, I'd like my family to occupy it."

"No longer with you?" I ask, horrified, as Hank and I follow them down the stairs. "Are you going to kill me to get my house? You're not in my will."

She gives me a betrayed look over her shoulder. "First off, ouch. Secondly, I didn't mean in the event of your untimely death. I just meant if you, you know, were ever to leave Baileyville."

Then she starts murmuring to Brian, knowing exactly what she's done.

"You planning on leaving Baileyville?" Hank asks in a low voice as we follow them down the sidewalk.

I wave him off. "Oh, you know Honey. She just says things sometimes."

"Things about you moving away from the town you've lived in your whole life," Hank says.

"Who can even tell what will come out of her mouth," I mutter, then flash him a bright smile. "Anyway, who's excited for the reunion?"

Hank answers me by reaching out to grab my hand, and the warmth of his palm radiates up my arm and straight into the rest of my body. I can't help it; I blush. Everything about Hank turns me back into a teenager, and right now, I don't even care. I'd do anything to keep feeling this way.

Even leave Baileyville? Honey's voice asks in my head.

Maybe, I answer. Maybe it's okay to admit to myself that although I've done a pretty good job of it, although I've built an admirable life, it's never been the absolute perfect fit for me.

And maybe now it's okay to hope that I could have exactly what I've always wanted.

THE HITS OF our youth are bumping at the reunion, which is at Amvets Park on the riverbank.

"It's weird to think that these were once songs we heard on the radio and not, like, in commercials for low prices at the grocery store," Honey says as Snoop Dogg's "Drop It Like It's Hot" plays.

"Nothing gold can stay. Eventually, time and commercialization come for us all, even Snoop Dogg." I turn to Hank. "Have any of your songs ever been in commercials?"

He snorts. "No, but I would sign up for that in a second. Put my song in a commercial for a car. Washing machines. Yogurt. I don't care, that sounds like a college fund for Henry."

"Even the probiotic yogurt that makes you poop?" Honey asks, wrinkling her nose. "You want one of your ballads used for that?"

Hank nods. "Even the poop yogurt."

"What up, Baileyville High?" Burger yells, his hands in the air.

"Hey, Burger," I say as Burger gives Brian a complicated-looking high five. "Did you make this playlist?"

"I did," he says with a proud smile as Usher and Alicia Keys's "My Boo" begins to play. "You like it?"

"It's taking us right back to the mid-2000s," Honey says. "I feel like putting on my low-rise jeans, except that I've had three children, and now the thought of low-rise jeans makes me feel physically ill."

"Okay!" says Burger, taking a sip of his beer and scanning the crowd. "Oh, don't forget to grab a beer. And there's cornhole!"

"Because what would a reunion be without the heart and soul of Baileyville High: cornhole?" I ask.

"Exactly," Burger says. He frowns and, as he walks away, yells, "Hey! Stimpkin! If you can't follow proper cornhole rules, you're not allowed to compete!"

I turn to Hank, laughing. "Did you miss this?"

He squeezes my hand. "I know you're kidding, but . . . I kind of did."

"Only because you totally dominate at cornhole," I say, leaning into him.

He shrugs. "I don't wanna get too cocky, but I've been known to throw a bag full of dried corn with surprising accuracy."

"Oh, hold on." I place my other hand on my forehead. "I think I'm light-headed. All this talk of your cornhole prowess is just . . . too . . . sexy . . ."

Honey pokes my arm. "Stop it, you two. You're saying the word 'cornhole' way too much, and it's starting to sound kinda dirty."

"You GUYS!"

Natasha walks toward us, arms outstretched and mouth wide open as if we didn't see one another at the fair yesterday.

"Heyyyyy!" I say through a clenched-teeth grin.

"I'm gonna go grab us drinks," Hank whispers in my ear.

"No, don't go, you can't—" I start, but he's already leaving, giving me a wink over his shoulder. I watch him walk away, surprised that I'm still in my corporeal form and not a mere puddle on the ground from the sexual power of that wink.

". . . asked Burger if they had any nonalcoholic options because, you know." Natasha gestures toward her belly as if any of us could've missed it, "And he said, and I quote, 'Oh, yeah, dude, we have Coors Light.'"

I laugh, and then we hear the opening chords of Kelly Clarkson's "Since U Been Gone."

Honey grabs my arm, closing her eyes. "Have I died and gone to heaven?"

I turn to face her. "You must have, because an angel is singing."

Kelly starts singing, and so do we, dramatically reciting the lyrics about a man who started out as friends with Kelly Clarkson (but unfortunately, as we all know, it was all pretend).

"What are they doing?" Natasha asks, raising her eyebrows at Brian.

He points at us. "They're singing 'Since U Been Gone.' This is how they always react when this song comes on."

The fast part starts, and Honey and I jump up and down, screaming the lyrics at each other.

"How could anyone dare hurt Kelly Clarkson?" I ask, tossing my hair back and forth.

"All of her exes should be arrested!" Honey shouts back. "No one should ever mess with Kelly!"

"Okay, well, I should probably find Jason . . ." Natasha trails off, looking through the crowd. "Wait. Who is that?"

"Who?" I barely hear Brian ask as Honey and I scream-sing about how Kelly's ex had his chance and blew it.

We're doing the air guitar riff when Natasha's words come into focus. "The woman talking to Hank."

Honey either doesn't hear or doesn't have the immediate connection to Hank's name that I do, because she keeps playing air guitar as I turn around, following Natasha's gaze.

"Uh, okay, way to leave me hanging," Honey says. "What are we . . ."

She trails off as we all stare at the woman talking to Hank. She's shaking her head, pursing her lips as her shiny blond bob sways. Hank puts an arm on her shoulder and steers her away from the crowd.

"Did she go to school with us?" Natasha asks. "Because I feel like I would remember someone with such striking bone structure."

I can feel Honey start to laugh at the idea of remembering someone's "striking bone structure" when I say, "No. She didn't go to school with us. That's Julia."

Honey instinctively places a hand on my arm as Natasha gasps. "Hank's ex-wife?"

I whip my head toward her. "How do you know that?"

Natasha rolls her eyes. "It's not, like, *difficult* to keep up with what people from Baileyville are doing. There are only so many of us, and I see everyone on Instagram."

"And yet you have no time to accept my follow," Honey mutters, then shakes herself off as she remembers what we're talking about.

I look for Hank and Julia, but they're nowhere to be seen.

I barely hear Natasha chirp that she's off to find Jason, because I'm spiraling.

"I'm sure they're just talking," Honey says, her voice coming to me through a tunnel. "About Henry, probably."

"I know that," I say. And I do. There's no part of me that assumes that Hank is currently off ravaging Julia in some darkened Baileyville alley. I trust him.

But these feelings I'm having . . . that's what I don't trust. Because she's here. Julia is here, in my town, and nothing has changed. She'll always be a part of his life in some way, and I'll always be exactly what she called me: Baileyville Sandy.

"I'm fine," I say.

Brian holds out the unopened White Claw in his hand, and I take it, crack it open, and chug it.

"Ugh." I stick out my tongue. "Why did I do that?"

"I have no earthly idea," Honey says. "Let's go find you literally anything else to drink. I'm pretty sure Burger is manning the grill. You want a hot dog?"

I sigh. "I'm not in the mood to laugh at this right now, but does anyone else find it funny that a man named Burger is currently grilling?"

She pats me on the back as we walk. "See, you still have your sense of humor. I think you'll be okay."

But before we can reach the grill, Julia and her beautiful hair and striking bone structure are right in front of us. "Sandy?" she asks, then pulls me into a hug.

"Uh . . . hi?" I say as she rocks me back and forth. Julia is an expressive hugger.

"Thank God I ran into you," she says when she lets me go. "I came to see Hank, and then he wandered off, and I was like, 'Oh no, I'm at someone else's high school reunion, and I don't know a soul.' But here you are!"

"Here I am!" I say with as much cheer as I can muster. Honey elbows me and I point to her. "Oh, I'm sorry. This is my best friend, Honey. Honey, this is Julia, Hank's . . ."

"Wife," she says. "So great to meet you."

I couldn't feel more stunned if Burger ran up behind us and dumped a cooler full of White Claw on my head. *Wife?* What did she and Hank get up to in that short conversation? Did they somehow reconcile, find a minister, and get remarried while Honey and I were singing along to Kelly Clarkson?

Honey's eyes start to narrow. Honey can put up with a lot of crap when people are being mean to her—like customers at the vet's office who yell at her because they have to pay for lifesaving surgery to remove a sock from their basset hound's intestines and insist that if she *really* cared about animals, she would do it for free. But when someone is mean to the people she loves? Well, watch out, because she does not and has never tolerated that. Once she heard a little girl on the playground was being mean to Rosie, and she went to the girl's mom's house, gave her a lecture on kindness vis-à-vis lessons she'd learned from Mr. Rogers, and didn't leave until she had apologies from both of them.

I put a hand on Honey's arm as a way to tell her, *Chill out*, without using any words.

"So nice to meet you," she says with sickly sweet kindness that would only seem false if you knew her.

I need to find Hank, need to talk to him and figure out what the hell this is all about. Why is Julia introducing herself as his wife when he's told me they're divorced? Hank isn't a liar, but I need him to explain this.

My eyes scan the crowd, flitting across Brian playing cornhole with Burger and Natasha pointing to her belly as she talks to an enthralled group of our classmates. Where is he?

When I look back at Julia, she's staring at me expectantly, and I realize that I missed what she said. But from the stunned look on Honey's face, I can tell that it must've been a doozy.

"What's that?" I ask brightly.

"Oh, I was yammering on about the new tour," Julia said with a wave. "It's such a big deal for him. Opening for Chris Stapleton! And Henry practically grew up on that tour bus, so I know he'll be excited to go out with his dad."

I try to swallow, but my throat has gone as dry as a flower bed that hasn't seen rain in weeks. Suddenly, all I can taste is that horrific White Claw from earlier, and I worry that it might come back up.

"Will you excuse me?" I say politely with a smile. "I need to go vomit."

I turn away before I can see Julia's expression and stomp through the crowd, pushing my way past a group of never-gonna-grow-up country bros who are wearing backward baseball caps and shotgunning cheap beers as Lonestar's "Amazed" plays over the speakers. Screw Burger's playlist. Screw these people. Screw this town.

I'm almost out of the park and to the street when Honey catches up to me, grabbing my arm. "Sandy!" she says, panting. "I know I say this all the time, but how are you so fast?"

I wipe my eyes with the back of my hand and turn to her. "I'm going home."

She wraps an arm around my midsection. "Don't worry. Who knows what Julia was talking about? Didn't Hank tell you she wasn't exactly a reliable narrator? She could be making this all up . . . and anyway, she's obviously not his wife."

"I know," I say, sniffling as I watch my former classmates have a great time drinking and reminiscing and cornholing. I want to be happy doing those things so badly, but Julia's words won't stop tumbling around in my head.

"At least let me walk you home," she says.

I shake my head. "I'm sorry, but I really, really want to be alone right now."

She nods, clearly not trusting me. I know she and Brian will walk by my place in half an hour to make sure a light's on. "Okay, sweetie. But promise me you'll talk to Hank. Promise you won't hold this against him. He's a good guy."

I offer her a weak smile. "I know."

And I do know that. Hank is the best man I've ever met, and that's why these past couple of days, these past few weeks, have convinced me that things could be different. That I could be different.

But I screwed things up fifteen years ago, and we both moved on. I built my life here out of the wreckage, and Hank started a family. We've lived entire lives without each other, and maybe it was foolish to think that a couple weeks spent driving around town in his truck would be enough to make up for that.

I don't like this feeling, and I know that because I've had it before. This is how I felt when Hank went off to college and I stayed behind, when he was off having new experiences and I was stuck in the same old ones on repeat. And no matter how great Hank is, no matter how much I want to be with him, I know it's going to end the same way. He's going to be out on the road with his job and his family.

"I'll see you tomorrow, okay?" I assure Honey, then give her a hug and cross the street toward my place. As I walk away, Avril Lavigne's "My Happy Ending" starts playing, and I mutter, "Tell me about it, Avril."

It's never a good sign when you relate to an Avril Lavigne breakup song from the early 2000s as an adult woman.

"I'll tell Hank you're not feeling well!" Honey calls after me, and I give her a wave without turning around.

I realize, with a pang, that while I completely trust that Hank didn't have alley sex with Julia, I definitely don't know for sure what her intentions are. She clearly wants to get back together with him. And if I was a good person, if I cared at all about Henry, I would want them to. I should want Henry to have both of his parents in his life, together, as stable influences, while Hank is on tour.

Did he seriously plan to go on tour and not tell me? And did he think it was okay to tell his ex-wife first?

Hank doesn't need me now, like he didn't need me then. Just like fifteen years ago, I'm nothing but a speed bump on the way to his bright future.

CHAPTER THIRTY-TWO

I'M ON THE couch, Toby on my lap, when I hear a knock on the door.

"Should I get that?" I ask Toby, who only stares at me in response.

"Some help you are," I say as I get off the couch, displacing Toby, who sighs heavily as he stretches his long legs. I know it's Hank at the door because he texted to ask how I was and if he should come over. I told him I was fine and that he didn't need to, but he wouldn't be Hank if he didn't come over anyway.

I pull open the door to see him standing there in the porch light, moths flicking against the screen.

"I come bearing fries," he says, holding up a grease-stained paper cup. "It's the last night of the fair, and I knew you wouldn't want to wait until next year to have some of these bad boys."

"Thanks," I say, smiling in spite of myself. I step aside to let him come in.

"Maybe fries aren't the best choice if you're not feeling well," he says. "But I can't remember you ever turning down anything fried."

"Put it on my tombstone," I say, pacing across the floor. "'Sandy Macintosh: the girl loved fried food.'"

"Hey." Hank puts the fries down on the table by the door and grabs my shoulders, stopping me in my tracks. "Something's wrong."

I smile weakly. "Just tired."

"So tired that you can't stop doing laps around your house?" Hank frowns.

"I saw Julia," I say.

Hank's face goes from confusion to understanding. "Oh. Right. I forgot that you two know each other."

"Well, we've met. I wouldn't say we're well acquainted," I mutter. I don't know how Hank could forget about that night. Unfortunately, it's etched onto my brain.

Hank rubs my arms, a small smile on his lips. "You aren't . . . worried about that, are you? You know I would never . . ."

I meet his eyes. "I know you would never sleep with more than one woman at a time. Yes. Of course. That's the Hank Tillman way. Monogamous sex, no drugs, and rock and roll filtered through the lens of country music."

"An unwieldy motto, but sure."

"She called herself your *wife*, Hank," I say. I can hear the whine in my voice, and I hate it.

Hank sighs. "I don't know why she said that. Julia is not a predictable woman."

"Why was she here?" I cross my arms.

Hank rubs the back of his neck. "Well, believe it or not, she says she wants to be more of a presence in Henry's life."

I nod slowly. "That sounds . . . good."

Hank shrugs. "She seemed serious this time. She wasn't drunk, wasn't high, wasn't using her relationship with another guy as some sort of threat or bargaining chip. She seemed . . . healthy. Enough for me to be hopeful about it, at least."

"Did you tell her about me? About us?"

Hank looks me straight in my eyes. "Julia has never been in the habit of telling me about the men she's seeing. Sometimes not even when we were married. So, no, I didn't tell her about us. Honestly, it wasn't my first priority."

"Oh, were you guys too busy talking about your big tour?" I ask, eyebrows raised.

Hank sighs, looking defeated. "She told you about that, huh? It's not finalized."

I throw my hands in the air, walking away from him. "What I don't get is why you'd tell your ex—or possibly current, depending on who I believe—wife about a tour before you told me. It's *me*, Hank."

"I haven't even said yes," Hank says, catching up to me in a few steps. "I wanted to talk about it with you first. But Julia . . . she's Henry's mom. She needs to know where I am and what I'm doing because it affects our kid."

Tears sting at the corners of my eyes, and I'm embarrassed because everything Hank's saying makes sense. On paper. But in my feelings, in my confused and illogical heart? It's unbearable.

Before I can fully think about the words, they tumble out of my mouth. "Did she ask you to take her back?"

Hank grabs my shoulders and leans in, close to my face. "I'm not getting back together with her, Sandy."

"That's not what I asked," I say, my heart pounding faster. "Did she ask you to take her back?"

Hank pauses long enough for me to know the answer before he says it. "Yes."

"She wants to be a family again," I say dully. "She knows she messed up, and now she wants another chance."

"That's essentially what she said, yes. But it's not going to happen."

"Why?" I ask, leaning against the couch.

Hank scoffs. "You know why."

I cross my arms. "I want you to tell me why."

"Because I can't trust her like that again. Because as much as I want her to be a good mom, for Henry's sake, I can't let her into my life in that way. Because I don't love her anymore. Because . . . well, because of you."

I stand up, suddenly frantic. "Take me out of the picture. What would you do then?"

Hank shakes his head. "What? I'm sorry, what kind of hypothetical scenario are we playing out here?"

"Pretend you never came back here, never ran into me. Julia finds you and says she wants to get back together. She wants the three of you together on that tour bus. What would you do?"

Hank pauses. "I don't know. That's not the situation I'm in, so what use is it in imagining?"

"Maybe you should give her a chance," I say, crossing my arms.

Hank's eyes widen. "I am so confused right now. We just got back together, and you're telling me that you think I should give my ex-wife another chance?"

I look at Toby, who's lying at my feet and staring at me as if he can't believe what I'm saying, either. "We never said we were back together."

Hank laughs, but there's no humor in it. "We . . . okay, well, I didn't know we needed to write up an official contract for the terms of our relationship. You said you didn't want to get any closer because you didn't want to get your heart broken. I agreed. But then you told me to come to your place. We slept together. You held my hand in front of our friends. What was that?"

I rub my temple. "Momentary weakness. Hank, where do you think this is going? Really?"

He steps closer to me, his voice softening. "I think it's going exactly where we both want it to. You come on the road with me when I'm traveling. Explore a little. Spread those wings. And when I'm not on tour, we come back here. It's the best of both worlds. Baileyville and everything outside of it. It's what we both want."

"I never agreed to that," I tell him. "I can't leave here—I have a job, you know."

"Of course I know you have a job," he says.

"We're not in our busy season right now, but things get very busy in the spring, or when I'm installing a garden. What am I supposed to tell people? 'Sorry you need plants, but I'm in Kansas City on Hank's tour bus.' How the hell is that supposed to work?"

"You have employees," Hank says. "You think Marcia can't run the place while you're gone? Hire more people!"

"But I'm Baileyville Sandy, Hank!" I shout.

"What the hell is that supposed to mean?" he asks, his voice rough.

"It means this is where I am. This is where I belong, whether I like it or not. I stayed here and I made a life here and I can't leave it all behind, especially not when there's a woman who you *already married and had a kid with* waiting in the wings!"

"This doesn't make any sense," Hank says. "You and I are both happy when we're together. You told me you always wanted to travel, didn't you? I'm not making that up, am I?"

"People change, Hank," I say, picking at a thread on the throw hanging over the back of my sofa. "People settle down. People get boring."

"You've never been boring," Hank says. "But you're being really fucking ridiculous right now."

My jaw drops. Hank has never yelled at me or said anything even slightly rude. He's always been the perfect gentleman.

"What?" I ask.

"When you broke up with me after high school, I let you go. I didn't want to argue with you to give me another chance or convince you that we were good together. I trusted that you'd figure it out yourself someday, but you didn't, not until you found me in Chicago and I was already married."

"So you do remember that night," I say.

"Of course I do. I remember everything you've ever said or done, every dress you've ever worn, the perfume you used when we were in high school. I remember *everything*, Sandy, and the main thing I remember that night is the way I felt like you ripped my heart out of my chest when you ran out of that bar, and I had to watch you go, knowing that you finally wanted me back, but it was too late. I was with someone else, someone who wasn't right, someone who wasn't you."

I swallow.

"I came back here for *you*, Sandy. Yes, so Henry could be with his family, but also for you. To see if you were finally ready to give us another chance and to see if I could convince you that we deserved one."

"Oh, so you pretended to care about the fair so you could wear down my defenses?" I yell.

"I didn't pretend anything, and I didn't wear you down. I wanted to see if you were finally going to let yourself be happy."

"I am happy!" I shout. "I am *so* happy!"

Hank leans forward. "If you're so happy, then why are you crying? If you're so happy, then why are you pushing the only man you've ever really loved out of your life? If you're so happy, then why can't you let yourself be loved?"

I touch my face; Hank's right. I'm crying, the tears streaming freely down my face.

"I know the life I chose isn't exciting and fancy and cool enough for you," I spit out. "I know I'm not on TV and in magazines and playing tributes for Vince Gill or whatever. But this is my life and it's important to me."

"Is this really the life you chose?" Hank asks, an eyebrow raised. "Or is it the life that chose you? Because it seems to me like there was one mistake fifteen years ago, one missed opportunity, and you've let that dictate all your choices. It seems to me like you could change things anytime you want, but you don't want to. You're too comfortable being miserable."

"Okay, you know what? You don't get to waltz into town after years away and tell me how I'm living. This is my life. I built it. It's *mine*."

"Well, maybe for once in your goddamn life you should think about somebody other than yourself!" he shouts.

"That's a really mean thing to say," I say, my tears temporarily paused. "And it's not even remotely true. I was only ever thinking about you and what you wanted and what was best for you."

He shakes his head. "You should—you should've—let me decide what I wanted. You're too focused on protecting yourself from ever taking a risk, though. You're never going to be happy until you *let* yourself be happy, and you'd rather stay in your own way. You'd rather be stubborn instead of let someone else in. I'd love to wait around until you figure it out, but I have a kid now.

And Henry deserves better than getting to know another woman who's gonna be in and out of his life whenever she feels like it."

He waits, but I don't say anything. I can't.

"Fine," he says, sounding more sad than angry. "If you're ever brave enough to realize how much you love me and how happy I make you, come find me. But until then, I'm out. I can't do this anymore."

"Have fun on tour," I shout after him.

I don't watch him leave; I just hear the screen door slam as I look at Toby, who stares up at me, eyes wide with concern.

I sink down to the floor, stroking Toby's back as he licks the tears off my face. "What am I doing, Tobes?" I whisper as I cry. "Why am I so screwed up?"

Chapter Thirty-Three

W HEN I ROLL into work the next morning, Marcia is already there. She hands me a coffee cup from Betty's, eyeing me suspiciously.

"What?" I ask, taking it. "Also thank you."

"I mean this in the nicest way possible," she says gingerly. "But you look like an absolute steaming pile of horseshit. Which I actually have a clear mental picture of, because an Amish buggy was right in front of me on my drive in today, and that horse was truly a poop machine. I mean, how can one animal even do that?"

"Thank you so much," I say, taking a sip. "I love how you always build me up."

"Think of this as a compliment," she says, patting me on the arm. "I'm saying you usually *don't* look like horseshit. This is out of the ordinary for you."

"You're not making it better!" I call as she goes back into the break room.

I lean over the counter, feeling like I have a hangover even though I wasn't drinking. I have an *emotional* hangover. I can't stop thinking about last night, about Julia showing up, and what Hank and I said to each other. His words play on repeat in my mind: *You could change things anytime you want, but you don't want to. You're too comfortable being miserable.*

"I'm not miserable," I mutter to myself.

"You're doing it again," Marcia calls, walking past me with a box of jack-o'-lantern pots we plan on filling with mums. Now that the fair's over, it's time to get out our fall inventory, even though it's eighty degrees and bright green leaves still hang on all the trees.

"Doing what?"

"Muttering about Hank," she says, putting down the box with a sigh. She walks back toward the counter and gives me a stare that's a combination of concern and pity. "What happened? Did you guys break up?"

"We couldn't break up because we were never together," I say, studying my hands and avoiding her eyes.

Marcia laughs. "Whatever you say, boss."

When I look up at her, her laughter stops abruptly. "Hey. I'm sorry I laughed at you and said you look like horseshit. Do you want to talk about it?"

I shake my head.

"Okay." She hesitates for a moment. "Well, I'm gonna say this, even though you're not asking for my advice. Whatever it is . . . you can fix it. If Hank's really the one for you, you can work it out. Aimee and I have our disagreements too, but sometimes I have to put my pride on the back burner and put our relationship first."

I give her a small smile. "Thanks."

She waves at me and goes back to work. I know she's trying to help, but Marcia and Aimee got married within a year of their first date. They don't have the complicated history that Hank and I have,

290 ★ KERRY WINFREY

and what are they disagreeing about? Whether to get marble or granite countertops in their new house? It's not exactly the same.

I manage to make it through the day, despite concerned looks from most of my customers, who clearly know I'm going through something. When it's time to close up shop, all I can think about is getting back home, grabbing the Oreos I keep in the freezer for emergencies, and numbing my brain with reality television of dubious quality.

And that's exactly what I'm doing a few hours after closing when Honey busts through my front door.

I sit up straight from my slouched position on the couch. Toby raises his head off my lap. "What are you doing?"

"Get up," she says. "We're going out. You are not gonna sit and mope on the couch and avoid telling your best friend every single detail about what happened last night."

I sigh and slump down again, and Toby puts his head back on my lap. "I'm not going anywhere. I'm watching *90 Day Fiancé.*"

"No, you're not, you're . . ." Honey trails off as she becomes entranced by the screen. "Okay, no, I'm not getting sucked into this. We're going to the River Horse and getting you a drink, and you're gonna talk to me, woman."

I scowl at her, but there's no point in resisting. This is Determined Honey, and she gets what she wants, so I might as well surrender.

"Fine," I say, standing up. "I'll put on a bra, but I won't change out of these joggers."

"If you want the crotch of your pants to hover around your knees, that's your decision," she says. "Let's get going."

A few minutes later, I groan as we walk into the River Horse, which is dark, wood-paneled, and lined with neon signs advertising virtually any beer you can think of. "Why am I here, Honey?" I ask.

"To get a cheap drink and a change of scenery," Honey says, pulling me over to two empty seats at the bar. Eric Church's "Springsteen" is playing and the televisions are showing . . . some sport. I'm clearly not in the frame of mind to even identify it.

"This is very much not my scene," I grumble before I notice who's sitting on the other side of me. "Natasha?"

She lifts a glass in greeting.

"Why are you *drinking*?" I ask with quiet urgency.

She frowns. "This is a Coke, Sandy. Do you honestly think I'd be in here slamming back a cocktail?"

I almost fall off my barstool when I hear her tone—she doesn't sound like cheerful, hashtagging, "look at my perfect kitchen renovation" Natasha. She sounds like . . . a real person.

"What are you doing here?" Honey asks, leaning over.

Natasha sighs. "I needed to get away from my parents for a minute, and this was the only place I could think of to go. Every other place is closed."

I nod. This is one of the main drawbacks of living in Baileyville— if you want a late-night activity, you're pretty much stuck with the River Horse or the twenty-four-hour Applebee's out by the exit (although the Applebee's at least offers half-price mozzarella sticks at night).

I'm about to ask Natasha something neutral to make polite conversation when she drops her head on the bar. "My life is such a mess," she says, her voice muffled.

Honey and I glance at each other, eyes wide, then focus on Natasha.

"Your life isn't a mess!" I say, putting a hand awkwardly on her back. "I mean, I hear you're doing a stellar kitchen renovation . . ."

"Not that some of us would know," Honey mutters, and I elbow her.

"And you're about to have a baby. Hashtag-boymom," I say more seriously and gently than anyone has ever said that phrase.

"I'm a hashtag-colossalfailure," Natasha wails, sitting up. "And being home this weekend has only reminded me how everyone else is living their dream life and mine is nothing special. I mean, yes, I'm over the moon about this baby, and yes, my farmhouse sink and double oven are beautiful. But those aren't *me*, you know? I was supposed to have an actual career. I went to college to write the next great American novel, and what have I written?"

She looks at Honey and me with wild eyes as if she's expecting an answer that we certainly don't have.

"Nothing!" she screeches. "Nothing but idiotic Instagram captions. I'm nothing but a huge waste of potential."

"That's not true," Honey says. "What does Justin—"

"Jason," I whisper.

"What does Jason say about all this?"

"Oh." Natasha wipes her eyes. "He says I'm beautiful and wonderful and the most perfect woman he's ever met in his life."

"Of course he does," I say.

Natasha snorts, then takes a swig of Coke. "But what would he know? He exclusively reads Nicholas Sparks books. He doesn't even care about my writing."

"It sounds like he's a sensitive man," Honey says. "And I've read a Nicholas Sparks book. The one where the woman dies at the end?"

"That's all of them," I remind her.

"Right. Well, I enjoyed it until that part."

Natasha looks at us in disgust. "You guys don't have to try to make me feel better. I know you hate me. I know everyone hates me."

"That's not true!" I say.

"Not *everyone* hates you!" Honey says.

I spot Burger across the room at the jukebox and catch his attention by waving my arms. He throws his hands in the air as if he can't believe he has the good fortune to see us again after only one day.

"He's really always like this, isn't he?" Honey asks as he makes his way across the bar, stopping to talk to everyone. "Can't believe you went on a date with him."

"You went on a date with Burger?" Natasha asks. "Have you dated every man in this town?"

"I've been on one date with most of them, yes," I admit.

"What's up, lovely ladies?" Burger asks, putting an arm around Natasha. She frowns and takes his arm off her shoulder as if it's a scarf she's discarding.

"Burger," Honey says. "You don't hate Natasha, do you?"

Burger looks at her as if seeing her for the first time. "Natasha? You? Of course not. I love it when you share those little videos about your kitchen reno on Instagram."

"What the hell?" Honey shouts. "What gives, Natasha? Why does everyone follow you but me? What must I do to get you to accept my follow? Do I need to crawl on my hands and knees through broken glass?"

"Let's tone it down a little, okay?" I pat her on the knee.

Natasha shakes her head. "I'm sorry. I took one look at your Instagram profile and got jealous, so I blocked you."

Honey puts a hand on her heart. "You blocked me?"

Natasha waves a hand. "You're always posting about your perfect job and all your big accomplishments, and it makes me feel like a piece of dog poop stuck to the bottom of someone's boot."

"See, you are a good writer," I tell her. "That was an evocative description."

Honey scrunches up her face in confusion. "Really? Because my last post was about how I spent the morning with my hand inside a cow's vagina during a difficult calf delivery."

"I know," Natasha says miserably, head in her hands. "You're over there living out your dream, sticking your hand inside cows on a regular basis. And Sandy owns a business. What do I have going for me?"

"Wow, Natasha," I say, glancing at Honey in shock. "We always thought you had your life so together. The fancy kitchen, your marriage, the baby . . . it all seemed kind of obnoxiously perfect, to be honest."

"Nope." Natasha points to herself. "Other than this beautiful baby I'm growing, I'm nothing but dog poop on a shoe."

"Man," Burger says, smiling and looking at each of us. "Isn't it weird that, ultimately, we're all kinda crushing it, and yet we all feel like we're not good enough? Really reminds you that social media is a highlight reel, not real life, you know?"

I tilt my head. "Burger, that's actually pretty insightful—"

But Burger cuts me off when "Friends in Low Places" starts playing, and he shouts, "Oh shit, this is what I picked on the jukebox!"

His perceptions about social media forgotten, he starts yell-singing and walks off, raising his beer in the air.

"Everyone in this town sure does love this song," Natasha says, looking confused.

"I think it only hits right after a few drinks," Honey says, then points to Natasha's soda. "Alcoholic ones, I mean."

Natasha sighs, looking at her glass. "Did you guys really think my life was perfect?"

We nod enthusiastically.

"If we hated you, it was only out of jealousy," Honey says.

"I'll unblock you," Natasha says. "Sorry."

"You're forgiven," Honey says, smiling in a way that lets me know she's probably still a little pissed.

Natasha asks the bartender for another Coke, and as she's in conversation with him, Honey leans over and says, "Don't think I forgot why we're here. What happened with Hank?"

I shrug. "Can't we talk about the basketball game?"

Honey frowns. "Sandy, that's baseball. I know you know at least that much."

"Please don't kick me when I'm down." I sigh. "Hank came over and we had a big fight and I told him he should take Julia back and he accused me of wanting to be miserable and then he left."

I pause to take a deep breath and Honey stares at me. "Hank said that?"

"Yep. Can I get a drink?"

Honey flags down the bartender. "Two old-fashioneds, please."

I wrinkle my nose. "You know I prefer white or pink wine."

Honey shakes her head. "This is a 'strong drink' kind of night. Keep talking."

"Yeah," Marcia says, leaning an arm on my shoulder. "Spill."

I widen my eyes. "When did you get here?"

"Like a moth drawn to a flame, I was pulled here when I sensed you were talking about your personal life for once," she says, gesturing dramatically with her hands.

"Ugh." I rest my head on the bar. "Whatever. I messed everything up, again, by being me. I'm a nightmare, and Hank deserves someone better than me. And for that matter, so does Henry. Hank's probably going on tour and he wants me to go with him and I can't leave town for three months because what if it doesn't work out and I end up completely broken? Except that I already feel broken now. Hank was right when he said I'm comfortable being miserable."

I sniffle into my arms for a moment before I realize no one's saying anything. I look up to see Honey, Marcia, and even Natasha looking at me with concern in their eyes.

"Oh, sweetie, come here," Honey says, sliding off her barstool and wrapping me up in a hug. Marcia follows, and then so does Natasha.

"You're not a nightmare," Marcia says.

"You deserve to be happy," Honey says.

"You're being a total idiot by pushing Hank away," Natasha says.

"I think you should really consider going on tour with Hank," Burger says.

The girls release me from the group hug, and all of us look at Burger in confusion. "I thought you were busy with the jukebox," I say. "How much of that did you hear?"

He shrugs. "Burger hears all. So what's the deal? Why can't you go with Hank?"

"Because." I gesture around me at the bar. "I live here. Not in the River Horse . . ."

Natasha snorts. "Thank God."

"But I live in Baileyville. I'm Baileyville Sandy!"

"Why do you keep saying that?" Honey shouts, throwing her hands in the air. "That's not your legal name!"

"I have a job and a life and I can't leave everything behind for . . . for . . . some man! For a chance. For something that might not even work out," I say, my voice getting quieter the longer I keep talking.

Marcia puts a gentle hand on my arm. "You do know we're gonna be closed for the season soon, right? And I think I'm perfectly capable of handling things in your absence."

"I know you're capable," I sniff. "But what about my parents? What about Honey's kids? What about . . . what about all the people who need me?"

"I'm pretty sure I can find another babysitter for a few months,"

Honey says wryly. "Maybe even one who doesn't feed my kids nonstop sugar."

"And you know every person in this town would help your parents with the inn whenever they need anything," Marcia says.

Burger raises his hand. "I would. I mean, unless it involves going on the roof. As you know, I've been banned."

Natasha shakes her head at him, but she doesn't ask.

"But I . . . but I . . . I can't!" I finally conclude.

"Babe," Honey says, sliding an arm around me. "You're scared, aren't you?"

"What would I be scared of?" I ask, reaching behind me to grab my old-fashioned. I take a sip and grimace. "This isn't white wine."

"It's not," Honey says, taking the drink out of my hand. "You're scared of change. Of taking a chance."

"I take chances all the time!" I say. "Like, for example, I tried that old-fashioned even though I know I want wine."

Everyone keeps silent for a moment.

"Okay, fine!" I shout. "I'm scared! But Hank turned my life upside down fifteen years ago, and I'm terrified of that happening again. What if I put my life on pause for him, and it doesn't work out?"

Honey shakes her head softly. "I don't think being with Hank is putting your life on pause, though. I think it's living your life."

I exhale. "Damn."

"I've seen you two together, and I know when you're happy. You seem lighter and brighter when he's around. And you're painting again," Honey points out.

"True." I nod.

"It's time you wake up and smell the coffee, Sandy," Ed says. "You're in love with Hank."

"What's happening?" I ask. "Why is everyone in town here and weighing in on my love life?"

"Because we care about you," Marcia says.

"Because you deserve to be happy," Honey says.

"To be fair, I only came here for a break from my family," Natasha says, but when Honey elbows her, she adds, "But it's also super obvious that you and Hank are soul mates."

"Two kernels in a corn husk," Ed says.

"Okay," I say slowly. "But what am I supposed to do about this? Hank wants nothing to do with me, and I don't blame him. I was awful to him."

"Oooh!" Ed's eyes widen. "Have you considered a flash mob?"

"I don't think people do flash mobs anymore, Ed," Honey says gently. "But thank you for the contribution."

"I know!" Natasha says, perking up. "Let's organize a big grand gesture, like in a movie! Maybe not a flash mob, but . . . I don't know, can someone get married soon? Sandy can bust in during the reception and give a speech about how much she loves Hank."

"That seems rude," I say.

"Or, like, is Hank going anywhere? You can chase him to the airport," Burger offers.

"The airport is an hour away," I remind him.

He points at me. "Also, do you have a motorcycle? It would be way more romantic if you had a motorcycle."

I shake my head. "This all feels very wrong."

"That's because you don't need some ridiculous grand gesture to apologize to Hank," Honey says, exasperated. "You need to be you."

Something clicks into place inside my brain. Honey's right—I don't need some dramatic public gesture to show Hank how I feel. What I need to do is . . . well, *tell* him how I feel. I have to be honest with him instead of pushing him away when things get uncomfortable. I have to trust that we can work this out, instead of running at the first sign of difficulty.

In short, I need to talk to him.

"What time is it?" I ask. "I need to see Hank."

At that moment, the bartender cuts off the music, telling us all that it's closing time and we need to clear out.

"Probably too late to show up to his house," Marcia says.

"Especially if Henry's sleeping," Honey adds. "I love you, but I would not take you back if you woke up my sleeping child."

"Fine," I say with determination. "I waited this long to be honest about my feelings, I can wait until morning."

Everyone claps for me, and Burger sticks his fingers in his mouth and whistles. Natasha covers her ears. The bartender leans over and says, "I'm glad you're having a good time, but seriously, you have to leave."

We clear out, and after giving hugs to everyone, Honey walks me to my front door.

"Good luck tomorrow," she says. "And remember: all you have to do is be honest. You guys can figure it out from there. We'll all be waiting for you when you get back."

"I love you," I say and hug her before I go inside and shut the door. I let Toby sleep in the bed with me, even though he tends to take up all the space and cram me into a tiny corner, because I need the comfort tonight. Being honest with Hank is going to be hard—how am I supposed to be vulnerable with him, or anyone, when I've spent my life lying to myself about how I feel?

I set an alarm for the crack of dawn and try to get some sleep. I'll need to be well rested if I plan on getting the man of my dreams back tomorrow morning.

CHAPTER THIRTY-FOUR

I BOLT OUT of bed when my alarm goes off. Toby follows me around the house, his paws click-clacking against the hardwood floor. I throw on jeans and a T-shirt, too scatterbrained to pay attention to my appearance. Sure, I *should* look my best when I'm declaring my love to Hank and begging him to forgive me, but there are only so many things I can focus on right now.

I take Toby on a quick walk around the block, promising to take him on a run later to make up for it. I give him a big kiss and lock the door behind me, then get into my car in the dim grayness of early morning. Before Hank's, I have one stop to make—Betty's.

Betty's is always hopping at 6 A.M., which makes sense when you remember that their morning clientele is mostly composed of elderly people who take the saying "early to bed, early to rise" extremely literally. I grab donuts and coffee and head out to Hank's place.

My goal is to be there when the sun rises, because as Hank told me, he hasn't missed a sunrise in years. If I can see him while the sun comes up, with that backdrop of glorious, reliable beauty, maybe he'll see that I can be there for him, too. Because that's what I want—to be with Hank every day, to be something he can count on. I'm tired of being afraid, tired of ignoring my own feelings, tired of being comfortable. Hank has always been honest with me—now it's my turn to let him know how I feel.

My car climbs up the driveway and I park, then sit in the silence for a moment. At my house, there are always the sounds of the occasional car, a dog barking, the distant hum of traffic on the interstate. But out here, in the country, all I hear is the rustle of leaves and the chirp of birds.

I open my car door and step out, my feet crunching against the gravel. Hank's not on his porch, so I knock on the door gently, holding the donut bag in one hand and cradling the coffee against my body.

No answer. I knock again, a little harder. Still nothing. I turn around and realize that, while his SUV is here, the truck isn't. What if Hank is somewhere else? What if I drove out here with my stupid plan, and he isn't even around?

What if he *left* already? What if he packed up Henry and hightailed it back to his real life, the one that doesn't involve a woman who plays games with him and is too weak to handle obstacles? What if he'll never know that I can do this, that I can be strong for him, because it's too late?

I knock harder. "Please don't be gone, Hank," I half whisper, a tear rolling down my cheek. "Please come back."

"What are you doing?"

I whip around, gasping and getting my own hair stuck in my mouth. One of the coffees slides out of my hand and onto the porch, splashing onto my exposed toes in my sandals. Hank watches me skeptically.

"Oh, ouch," I say through my mouthful of hair, attempting to pull it out with my one free hand. My toes sting from the burn of Betty's coffee.

Never able to watch me suffer, even when he's mad at me, Hank steps forward and takes the donut bag and remaining coffee out of my hands. "You okay?"

"Why do I always injure myself when you're around?" I mutter.

He frowns. "Did you come here this early to blame me for your injuries?"

I shake my head. "No. I came here to talk to you but you didn't answer the door and your truck's not here so I thought you weren't around but then you were right behind me and—wait, what were you doing out here?"

He points over to where the barn used to be, to a lone folding chair. "View's better from over there."

I smile, then rein it in. "You're watching the sunrise."

He nods, looking at me expectantly. It's now or never; I have to tell Hank how I feel, let him in on what's going on in my head, or else I'm really going to lose him forever.

"I'm sorry," I say.

After a beat, Hank nods. "I know you are."

We stare at each other for a moment. We're still swathed in murky gray, but out of the corner of my eye, I can see a glimmer of orange in the valley. The sun is rising, and I'm standing in front of Hank, and I can do this. I take a deep breath.

"I was an idiot, Hank. I was scared and stupid and I pushed you away because I was terrified of what would happen if I was honest about how I felt. I've been here so long that it feels like it's who I am, like I can't leave or take a break from it because then I wouldn't be myself. I spent years making myself strong after we broke up because I couldn't stand to feel that empty and alone again, but the truth is, I was only covering up my feelings. Hiding them under work and overactivity, and lying to myself. But then you came back and . . . and I couldn't lie anymore. You make me feel like I'm alive, like I can do anything. You always have. And I spent so many years feeling like I wasn't worthy of you, like you deserved better—"

Hank opens his mouth to say something, but I hold up a hand. "Please let me get this out, because if I don't say it now, I never will."

He closes his mouth and nods, gesturing toward me like, *Go on.*

"So I spent all that time assuming I knew what was best for you and assuming that it wasn't me, but . . . I should've talked to you. I shouldn't have pushed you away, back then or now. I don't want to do that anymore. I want to be with you, to work things out together, and I'm scared of that, but I can do it. For you, I can do it. Because I love you, Hank, and—"

"Sorry, but I need to interrupt," Hank says. He drops the donut bag and coffee on the table in between two rocking chairs, then closes the space between us and grabs my arms, drawing me to him and pressing his lips into mine. I thought by now we'd run through every type of kiss, but this is an entirely new one. This is a kiss that says, *Mine.* A kiss that claims me as Hank's, a kiss that means we belong together. Hank and Sandy.

He pulls back, that crooked smile on his face. I want to look at it every day for the rest of my life. "That's all I wanted to say. Go on."

I exhale a sniffly laugh, because I've somehow been crying through my whole speech. "That's all I've got. I'm not a poet like you, Hank. I can paint a nice picture, but I can't make my words pretty."

He leans forward and kisses my forehead. "I don't know, I think what you said sounded pretty perfect."

"I'm sorry I dropped your coffee," I whisper. I close my eyes because I can't even believe this moment is real, can't believe I'm lucky enough to be here with Hank, the only love of my entire damn life.

"Who said that was my coffee?" he says in a low voice. "That one was yours."

I start to laugh when I hear a voice ask, "Dad?"

We turn to see Henry standing in the doorway, wearing Spider-Man pajamas and rubbing his eyes, his hair sticking up.

"Hey, Bud," Hank says, his arms still on my shoulders.

"What are you doing?" Henry asks skeptically. "Were you kissing?"

"A little bit," Hank says with a smile. I hide my laugh behind my hand. "Why? Does that bother you?"

Henry ignores the question. "Can I play videogames, since you're busy?"

"Yeah," Hank says and Henry runs back inside. Soon, we hear the sound of videogame music floating out to the porch.

"That's Henry giving his approval, by the way," Hank says, nodding toward the cabin.

I laugh, but it turns into tears again. "I already love him so much, you know that?"

Hank wraps his arms entirely around me, pulling my head down on his shoulder. "I'm so glad you do."

From my vantage point on Hank's shoulder, I see the sun glowing in the sky.

"The sun!" I shout, standing up straight again. "It came up!"

"It does tend to do that," Hank says with a smile.

I turn my eyes away from the sky and focus on his face. "You're looking the wrong way, you know."

He looks back at me, his gaze steady and clear. "I'm looking exactly where I want to look. C'mere."

He leads me over to the folding chair where the barn used to be, sits down, and pulls me onto his lap.

I yelp. "Hank! This chair is going to break!"

"It would be a noble death," he says, laying a kiss on my shoulder.

Both of us look toward the horizon, out over the whole town. This beautiful, imperfect town that brought us together, kept us apart, and finally pulled us back together again, this time for good.

I turn back toward Hank and lean forward so our foreheads are touching, the two of us matching up like the perfect puzzle pieces we've always been. "I'm so sorry about all the time we missed," I say.

"Don't be," Hank says. "We don't have to think about the past anymore, Sandy. We have the whole future to look forward to."

Chapter Thirty-Five

One month later

THE DAY BEFORE we're about to leave for Hank's tour, I stand in his living room as he ties a blindfold over my eyes.

"Please tell me you're not going to murder me or put me in some kind of *Fifty Shades of Grey* situation," I say. "I mean, honestly, I might prefer death. You don't have a secret sex dungeon in the cabin, do you?"

I hear him laugh. "You've spent almost every night here for the past month. Have you seen a sex dungeon?"

"Everyone has secrets," I say breezily, or as breezily as one can say anything while wearing a blindfold.

"I'll direct you where you need to go, okay?" Hank says, standing behind me and placing his hands on my shoulders. I don't tell him this, but I'd go anywhere he tells me to right now. I only need his hands and his voice guiding me, and I'm set.

"Take a step . . . keep going," Hank says as I bump into the doorframe.

"You're a terrible navigator," I tell him.

"Hold on." I hear him step in front of me. "Here are the steps. Go down . . . okay, and another one . . ."

He holds my hands and guides me down the rest of the steps and across the yard. "Seriously, what's going on?" I ask.

"All shall be revealed soon," Hank says. "And . . . we're here. Take off your blindfold."

I pull it off. We're standing right at the spot where the barn used to be, and in front of us is a red-and-white picnic blanket, complete with a picnic basket.

"Sit down," Hank says, gesturing toward the blanket.

"You got food?" I ask with excitement, opening the basket. There are sandwiches and cookies from Lydia's inside. "This is amazing."

Hank shrugs, sitting down beside me. "I thought since we're leaving tomorrow, it might be nice to have lunch over here. At the site of our first kiss."

I smile at him. "You remember, huh?"

"Sandy." His voice goes soft, and he reaches out to touch my cheek. "You know I remember."

I give his hand a squeeze, then reach back into the basket and pull out a bottle. "Oooh, champagne! I feel so fancy!"

"There's something else." Hank nods toward the basket, so I reach in again and pull out a book.

"*Pride and Prejudice*?" I say in wonder. "You kept your copy? Did you have to dig through your old bedroom to find it?"

Hank shakes his head. "Nah. I didn't leave it in my old bedroom. I kept it with me."

Our sunny afternoon gets darker as a cloud moves over the sun, and I gawk at him. "What do you mean?"

"I kept it with me. All the time. It came with me to college. My first place. The tour bus. It was always in my bag, almost like you were there with me."

"Well, now I will be," I say. "Forget this old book. Might as well throw it in the garbage. Now you'll have the real thing."

"I think I'll hold on to it anyway," he says.

I think about making a joke, about teasing him for his sentimentality as a way of avoiding my own feelings, but I'm not doing that anymore. I'm not running away when things get intense—now I'm honest, even if it's vulnerable. I'll be going on tour with Hank and Henry, and when it's over, we'll come back here to this little cabin on the hill. The three of us and Toby—a family.

"I'm glad you kept it," I say softly. "And I'm glad you did this."

"You know," Hank says, sliding closer to me. "We've had a lot of good memories right here. All the milestones in our relationship. We'll probably have to get married up here."

"Get married?" I choke out a laugh, until Hank reaches into the picnic basket and pulls out one more thing. A tiny little box.

He opens it up and a ring sparkles back at me. It's a flower—one diamond in the middle, surrounded by six diamond petals. It's delicate, not gaudy, and it's the most beautiful thing I've ever seen.

"Will you be my girl forever, Sandy?" Hank asks. "I know it's soon, and if you say yes, we can have a long engagement. As long as you want."

I shake my head, ignoring the tears that spring to my eyes. "This isn't soon. I've been in love with you since I was a kid, Hank. I spent fifteen years missing you, and I don't want to spend another day without you. I'd marry you tomorrow if I could."

He smiles that perfect, glorious smile that I'm lucky enough to see every day. "Yeah? Well, hold out your hand."

He slides the ring onto my finger, both of our hands shaking.

It looks like summer and sunshine and second chances right there on my finger. I wiggle my fingers, watching how the ring sparkles against my paint-covered hands. Not only have I been so happy to be with Hank and Henry up here in the cabin, but I've been painting, too—in the living room, right in front of that big window with a view of the whole valley.

"We're getting married," I whisper, and that's when I feel it. The first raindrop. And then the next and the next, until they aren't drops so much as a torrential downpour.

"The book!" I shout. "Protect the book with your life!"

Hank tosses it into the basket, along with the food. Our eyes meet and we both laugh—the water is dripping off his eyelashes, and I know I must look like a mess. But right now, I don't care.

"Let's get inside!" Hank says, grabbing my hand and pulling me along with him.

But this time, we can't run into the barn, and we don't have to. This time, we have a whole house of our own to shelter us, a whole life together to keep us safe from any storm. As I run toward the front porch with Hank, I'm not scared of anything the future might bring. Our story is a love song, the kind that lasts forever, and the opening notes are just starting to play.

EPILOGUE

Eleven months later

"SANDY!" HONEY SHOUTS, running down the street, narrowly avoiding a stroller and spinning around a couple of handholding teenagers. "You're here!"

I open my arms and she runs into them, and then I spin her around right by my beloved corn dog stand as if we're reunited lovers.

"Why do I feel like my presence here is unnecessary?" Hank asks with a smile on his face.

Honey pulls back and takes me in. "Let me look at you. I've forgotten what you look like."

"Honey," I say, laughing. "We've only been gone for a month."

The three of us—Hank, Henry, and I, plus Toby, of course—have been at Hank's Nashville studio so he could finish up his latest album. We'd planned on coming back around this time because Henry needs to start school in the fall, but the real reason (sorry, education) was the fair, of course.

And as we walk toward the stage, Honey's arm linked in mine, I'm happy to see that it looks exactly the same as it always has.

Which is to say, perfect. The same French fry stand on my left. The same lemonade stand to my right. The same loud carousel music and smell of oil and dough in the air.

Of course, there are a couple of things that are different, one of them being the fact that Hank and I are now married. Despite Hank's offer, I didn't want a long engagement. In fact, I wanted to get married immediately—or the day before immediately, if that was possible. After Hank, Henry, and I got back from his tour—a whirlwind of cities, a blur of nights and days that ran together—we planned a shindig in the firehouse (which, of course, can hold a large portion of the town's population as long as the fire trucks are moved). We had a table full of Betty's donuts and glass-bottle Cokes, Sean DJ'd, and Ed didn't injure himself, not even when he was attempting to moonwalk.

It was a perfect day.

But as I glance back at Hank, I have to admit that this day is giving it a run for its money. I'm here in one of my favorite places with all of my favorite people. Part of me was afraid that leaving Baileyville would make me love it less—that the shine would wear off, that I'd realize it wasn't all that special compared to any large city with more than three stoplights and a Starbucks within easy driving distance.

What happened, though, was the opposite. I loved my time away, but coming back made everything in Baileyville sparkle and glow. Our cabin was even cozier. The fritters at Betty's tasted even better. And the feeling of walking down the street to the Ohio Inn and knowing every single person I passed—well, it felt even more special. I appreciate it more, knowing what else is out there. Yes, seeing other places was pretty wonderful . . . but so is what I have right here.

I feel satisfied now, knowing the whole world is waiting for me to see it. Or rather, the whole world is waiting for *us*. Touring was exciting, but it wasn't exactly the best way to really experience traveling, since Hank was working the whole time. But that's okay with me, because I know we have time to see all the things we want to see. In fact, Hank and I are planning a belated honeymoon, but we have to do it soon because, well, we have a deadline.

When we take our places on the lawn in front of the stage, Honey leans down and speaks directly into my belly button. "Hello in there, baby boy. This is your aunt Honey speaking. I hope you appreciate the musical wonder you're about to hear."

"I'm sorry," Hank says, standing on my left and putting his arm around me. "How do you know it's a boy?"

Honey shrugs. "I have a feeling."

"Oh, well, why bother getting an ultrasound then," Hank says with a laugh.

"Henry," Honey says, looking at him. "Are you excited about the new baby?"

Henry frowns, looking at the bright yellow Transformer in his hand. "Am I gonna have to share my toys?"

"Not for a long time," Honey says. "Babies don't even know how to play with Transformers."

"Okay then," Henry says seriously. "I'm excited."

I smile, instinctively placing a hand on my belly. It's barely protruding—I'm not that far along—but I already can't wait to meet this little person when they come.

And as for Henry (who somehow seems to get taller every day), I feel like I'm doing a pretty good job of being his stepmom. I know I'm not his mom, because he already has one of those, and she's actually come back to Baileyville a couple of times over the past year to spend time with him in visits that are absolutely as special and necessary as they are awkward for me. But he's mine all the same, and I'm his. The three of us—soon to be four of us—are a family. This time next year, I'll be the one getting frustrated as I try to push a stroller through the fair crowd.

I can't wait.

"So how's my house treating you?" I ask Honey.

"Excuse me," she says in mock offense. "But *your* house is the cabin. The place where you used to live is now my house."

It didn't make sense for Hank and me to have two homes in one small town, and while I had so many good memories in my place, I was ready to build some new ones at Hank's cabin. It turned out Honey hadn't been joking about wanting to buy my place, so her family ended up moving in. We didn't even need a moving truck—all of our friends showed up, and we just moved their things down the sidewalk and into my old place.

"It's mostly coated in Goldfish cracker crumbs," she admits. "But you've gotta come over for lemonade on the porch. It's the one area of the house that isn't covered in Lego pieces and discarded Barbie clothes."

"Deal," I say.

It does feel a little weird to think about my old place, where I only ever lived by myself, covered in toys and snacks. But it feels pretty right, too.

Sean walks out onto the stage and we start to cheer.

"Go, Sean!" Honey shouts, cupping her hands around her mouth. "Baileyville Street Fair Board legend!"

Sean frowns into the crowd. "If you could please save your applause for the main act. I'm happy to introduce our own Ed Howell, performing a medley of songs."

As Sean walks offstage and Ed walks on, giving the crowd a wave, I ask Honey, "Wait, why isn't he doing magic?"

Honey rolls her eyes. "You've missed so much at the fair board meetings. Barb O'Dell is still pissed that his rabbit ate her zucchini. We were like, 'Barb, you already won a ribbon. What does it matter if it has a bite taken out of it?' But between that and the fire risk, everyone decided it was better for Ed to focus on music."

"Hey," Hank loudly whispers. "You two wanna keep it down? I can barely hear Ed's accordion."

"I don't know what I expected, but I'm impressed," Honey says, crossing her arms. "Not that I'm an accordion connoisseur, but I've certainly never heard one play Michael Jackson."

I stifle a laugh, but the thing is, Ed's actually quite good, and the crowd is loving it. Maybe he should do music instead of magic every year.

"Sandy," Henry whines. "Can I have a corn dog? I'm so hungry."

"Like I could say no to a request like that. Fair time comes but once a year! As soon as Ed's done, I'll get you one."

Henry nods, momentarily pacified, and Hank shoots me an amused glance. "He always asks you for junk food because he knows you're an easy mark."

I hold my hands up in an exaggerated shrug. "Can I help it that Henry and I both have exquisite taste? That we both want to suck the marrow out of life by eating as many corn dogs as humanly possible during the fair?"

"You're ridiculous," Hank says, giving me a quick kiss, and I smile as I lean into him, feeling perfectly happy and present. All those years Hank and I spent apart don't feel wasted. They brought us a lot of pain and sadness, but they brought us some good things, too. Henry. Our careers. The community I've fostered here. We may have built our lives on our own, but now we get to share them with each other.

I lean into Hank, wrapping my arms around his chest. "I love you," I whisper.

"Is this music putting you in an amorous mood?" Hank asks as Ed puts down his accordion and strains to pick up a tuba.

"Yeah, the sound of a lone tuba player really does it for me," I say, and I feel Hank's laugh rumble inside his chest.

"I'm bored," Henry says with a sigh. "Can someone take me on the Dragon Coaster?"

"I guess I'm gonna have to do it this time," Hank says. "Pretty sure you're not allowed on if you're pregnant."

"Next year, Henry," I promise. "You and I have a date with the Dragon Coaster."

Henry tugs on Hank's hand. "Let's go, Dad."

"Hold on, Bud," Hank says, pulling me closer. "Let's just finish this song first."

Ed is attempting to play "Funky Town" on the tuba, and all of us are frozen in place as we take it in.

"This is actually very funky," Honey says.

"You know how some people play Beethoven for their babies in the womb? This is my version of that. Soak it all in, baby. It doesn't get any funkier than this," I say.

"I would be happy to play a song for the baby, you know," Hank says.

"Do you know 'Funky Town'?" Honey asks skeptically.

"Do you even play the tuba?" I ask.

Hank sighs.

We laugh, and even with everything I have to look forward to—a honeymoon, the baby, a life spent with Hank—right now I can't think of anything more perfect than this moment, right here, standing in the middle of my town with my most treasured people. And while I never could have predicted that things would happen this way, that Hank and I would spend years figuring out how to make it work, that's okay. Because we're here now, and *now* is finally my favorite place to be.

ACKNOWLEDGMENTS

A S ALWAYS, HUGE thanks to Stephen Barbara and everyone
at InkWell. I'm forever grateful for your guidance and
advice.

Thank you to Cindy Hwang, who always knows exactly how to
make my books better. We're four books in and I still can't believe
I'm lucky enough to work with you!

I'm so grateful for the hard work of Angela Kim and the whole rest of
the Berkley team, including the publicity and marketing teams. A
huge thank-you goes out to the copyeditors who keep me from embarrassing myself too much (sorry that I make you spend so much
time looking up whether fast-food items are still on menus).

Thank you to art director Rita Frangie and cover designer and il-
lustrator Farjana Yasmin for, once again, creating an absolutely
beautiful and perfect cover.

Thank you to Dr. Catherine Stoner for being such an amazing
friend for over half our lives, for letting me ask you so many questions about veterinarians (any errors are completely my own), and for

reading this book in one day. Although *Just Another Love Song* is a light and fun book, I wanted to take this opportunity to remind readers of the mental health risks involved in the veterinary profession. According to Not One More Vet (www.nomv.org/2021/09/12/ the-veterinary-mental-health-crisis-part-1-of-2-the-root-of-the-problem), one in six veterinarians has considered suicide. Please be kind to the people who help your pets. Thank you, Catherine, for being so outspoken about veterinarian mental health!

Thank you to Lauren Rochford for being my first reader and for always somehow knowing how I should fix my terrible first drafts. You're a genius and I would be lost without you!

Thank you to Emily Adrian for telling me I'm funny. It really does keep me going.

Thank you to my hometown, Bellville, which inspired so much of Baileyville.

Thank you to booksellers and librarians for all your support. A special shout-out to my Columbus stores: the Book Loft, Prologue Bookshop, Gramercy Books, and Cover to Cover.

Thank you, thank you, thank you to my readers. It's always been my absolute dream to have people who are excited to read the weird love stories I dream up in my head, and I'm so grateful for every single one of your emails, messages, and posts. I also appreciate every book club, online or in person, that chooses my books! I wish I could go to all of your meetings.

Lastly, thank you to my family. To my parents, thank you for letting me work while you play with Harry, even if it involves finding my old Furbies in the basement (no, I'm not taking them back . . . they're yours now). Thank you to my brothers for constantly inspiring me with everything you do. I'll never be as cool as either of you. Hollis and Harry, thank you for being the best part of my life. I love you so much.

JUST ANOTHER LOVE SONG

KERRY WINFREY

Questions for Discussion

1. What career dreams did you have when you were in high school? Did you end up following those dreams or did you find something new?

2. Sandy and Hank both want to leave Baileyville and live somewhere more "exciting," but only Hank leaves. When you were younger, where did you think you would end up living?

3. If you had to decide between living in a town where you know everyone or traveling the country, which would you choose? Why?

4. Sandy's mom runs an Ohio-themed bed-and-breakfast. If you opened a B&B, what would the theme be?

5. If Hank hadn't moved away, or if Sandy had gone with him, do you think they would've stayed together? Do you think their time apart helped them become ready for a lasting relationship?

6. Sandy mostly gives up on painting because it's a painful reminder of her past, but eventually she comes back to it. Are there any interests that you gave up when you got older, and what do you think would happen if you started pursuing them again?

7. Hank says that he didn't really need to go to college to pursue music, and Sandy's career isn't directly related to her marketing degree. Although both of them thought they knew what they wanted out of life when they were teenagers, it took them a while to figure out viable careers. Do you think we put too much pressure on teenagers to figure out their whole lives before they even start college?

8. Sandy has two men who've written songs about her. If someone wrote a song about you, do you think it would be a love ballad or a brutal breakup song?

9. If you were in Sandy's position and had a chance to go on tour with Hank, what would you do?

10. What do you think the future holds for Hank and Sandy? Do you think they'll stay in Baileyville?

Photo by Alex Winfrey

Kerry Winfrey writes romantic comedies for adults and teens. She is the author of *Waiting for Tom Hanks*, *Not Like the Movies*, *Very Sincerely Yours*, and *Just Another Love Song*, as well as two young adult novels. She lives with her family in the middle of Ohio.

CONNECT ONLINE

KerryAnn
KerryWinfrey
AYearOfRomcoms.tumblr.com